I0763138

The
ALCHEMARY

Also by Rachel Vincent

The Shifters Series

Stray

Rogue

Pride

Prey

Shift

Alpha

The Wildcats Series

Lion's Share

Blind Tiger

Wild Card

The Unbound Series

Blood Bound

Shadow Bound

Oath Bound

The Menagerie Series

Menagerie

Spectacle

Fury

The Alchemary

RACHEL VINCENT

HYPERION AVENUE
LOS ANGELES NEW YORK

For information address Hyperion Avenue, 7 Hudson Square, New York, New York 10013.

First Edition, April 2026
10 9 8 7 6 5 4 3 2
FAC-004510-26166
Printed in the United States of America

Designed by Amy C. King
Illustrations by Raphael Geroni and © Adobe Stock

Library of Congress Control Number: 2025946410
ISBN 978-1-368-11590-2

The authorized representative in the EU for product safety and compliance is Disney Trading B.V., Asterweg 15S, 1031 HL, Amsterdam, The Netherlands
email: DCP.DL-EU.bookscontact@disney.com

www.HyperionAvenueBooks.com

Logo Applies to Text Stock Only

For Jennifer Lynn Barnes, who is always there

One

Light shone through my closed eyelids in a warm but intrusive red glow. I groaned softly and snuggled deeper beneath a heavy wool blanket, vexed at whoever had lit a candle in the middle of the . . .

My eyes flew open, confirming a dreadful instinct that fluttered in my gut like butterflies with razor-tipped wings.

Not candlelight. *Daylight.*

I was late. Even worse, some veiled obligation tugged at my mind like a string tied around my finger. I'd left something unfinished.

No . . . not quite. There was something I was supposed to *do*, first thing in the . . .

I bolted upright and threw back the blanket; as I stood, the stone floor cold and smooth beneath my bare feet, I realized with a sudden and near-blinding panic that I had no idea what I was late for.

Or . . . where I was.

My hands opened and closed around nothing but the cool morning air as I surveyed my surroundings, trying to make sense of a room that didn't *feel* unfamiliar, and yet . . . was.

Clarity refused to rise through the fog of slumber. My heart raced.

Focus on the facts.

The room was small. A narrow bed took up a third of the space, and the rest was occupied by worn but serviceable furnishings, including a desk cluttered with heavy books—real bound volumes—as well as individual sheets of fine parchment covered in writing. There were inkwells—one overturned and empty, the other seated squarely in its cutout and properly covered—and several quills, one neatly trimmed and clearly well-used, the others whole and still clean.

The desk chair was wooden and plain. Functional. An armchair sat in the corner opposite the bed, close enough to touch from the desk because of the narrowness of the room. It was plush, with faded green upholstery. Opposite the desk, a tall wardrobe stood half open, but my gaze refused to settle on the neat collection of mostly dark clothing hanging inside, or on the lighter-colored underclothes folded and stacked at the bottom.

As I mentally sorted through the observable facts, assembling a hypothesis about where I was and how I'd come to be there, I noted several soft voices speaking indistinguishable words through the walls. And that told me more than the furnishings had.

I was in some sort of small tenement: a single-room apartment, adjoining two others.

Though inky darkness leaked beneath the door, a brilliant line of daylight shone through the vertical seam between the shutters on the opposite wall, lighting the pillow precisely where my head had been moments before.

Iron hinges groaned as I threw open the shutters, and . . .

I stumbled backward, shocked not just by the burst of cool, salty air and dazzling sunlight, but by the *stunning* vista!

Water. Crystalline blue and endless. *Water,* to the very edge of the world, sparkling in the sun. Wind stirred it in rhythmic waves that looked gentle from my vantage, but were probably crashing against . . .

I leaned out the window for a glimpse of the ground below, but there *was* no ground. I sat on the very edge of a cliff, perched upon a drop so sheer I could see nothing below my room except for several floors of the tower I was in and a few outcroppings of the rocky ledge it stood upon. The ocean crashed against the base of the cliff with no shoreline to speak of.

My fingers curled around the wooden window frame, fear slamming against the ramparts of my mind like waves against the cliffside, and I lurched backward into the safety of the room.

A soft groan startled me, and I spun to find the lump of blankets on the far side of the narrow bed *moving.* A moment later, a man sat up and the bedclothes fell away, exposing his broad shoulders and sculpted chest, laying bare his narrow waist and just a glimpse of one pale hip.

My breath seized in my throat.

He was *beautiful.* Earnest blue eyes blinked at me beneath straight, bushy brows two shades deeper than his shaggy dark blond hair, still tousled from sleep. He smiled, a sheepish expression, as if he were unsettled to be staring at me with so much flesh exposed. Or perhaps embarrassed to still be abed, with the day already started.

I gathered from that look that he knew me. Yet I did not know him.

This was his room, surely. *That* was why I didn't recognize the furnishings or the stunning, terrifying view.

Which left several very important questions, the most important of which were *Whose bed have I woken in?* and *Why can I not remember taking to it in the first place?*

"Amber?" The man's brows dipped toward the center of his

forehead, and it was the familiarity of that expression, as much as his question, that cleared the tiniest bit of the fog shrouding my memory.

I was Amber.

Amber Fallbrook . . . of Innswood Township . . . three days' carriage ride from the eastern coast.

"Are you okay?" As the beautiful young man tossed back his blankets and rose, for a moment he seemed to wobble. His face paled and his eyes closed. One hand reached for the simple wooden headboard, sturdy musculature standing out in his arm as he regained his balance.

He looked ill. From drink? Perhaps *that* could explain my lack of memory.

Yet I did not feel sick.

My focus traveled across his well-toned chest to where a pair of short drawstring breeches hung scandalously low at his narrow hips. My gaze snapped up, heat building across my face, and that was when my thoughts on the subject of the nearly naked man sharply diverged.

I felt very strongly that I should not be staring at this objectively beautiful specimen of a man while he was clearly ill and in such a vulnerable . . . state.

And yet . . .

I'd woken in his bed. That fact carried a strong implication that I'd already seen this very sight. Experienced it. Likely, I'd studied it closely, and not in academic pursuit.

The flush in my cheeks drifted down my neck, beneath my thin night garment, as if gravity were ardently tugging at it.

The facts added up to an obvious conclusion—an *intriguingly* provocative one—and—

I blinked, and the face staring at me changed. The room disappeared.

"Amber!"

The man grins at me from across a narrow alleyway, bright sunlight bleeding from between two buildings to set his blue eyes alight. Only he isn't a man yet. He is a boy. Fourteen years old. I know that, like I know I can claim the very same number of years.

I am nearly grown, and I have better things to do than follow Wilder down an alley on the edge of town to watch him prove that he can charm the alewife into giving us a sample of her latest brew using nothing but his beguiling face and a few well-chosen words applied to his mischief like grease to the wheels of a cart. I have better things to do, yet there I stand, captivated by my friend's boyish charm and—

"Amber?"

"Wilder..." I murmured, and despite the familiarity of his name on my tongue, no further understanding blossomed. He looked familiar, and some latent memory painted him with the brushstrokes of a beloved brother, and yet he was *not* looking at me like a brother.

My body's reaction to his proximity—to his relative undress—was *not* that of a sibling.

"Are you okay?" he asked. "Have I... Have I made a hopeless mess of this?"

I had no answer for him. I had no answers for myself, and with each passing second, the weight of my own nescience seemed to push me a little further toward the cliff's edge of true terror.

"Do you want me to go?" Wilder bent over on the opposite side of the bed, and when he rose with two crumpled pieces of clothing, I understood. This was *not* his room.

It was mine.

Which meant I should have recognized my surroundings.

I indulged another look around the space, noting the candle on the bedside table, the small hand-carved wooden box, and...

From somewhere beyond the room, a bell chimed, and its heavy, repeated toll sent a familiar bolt of urgency ringing through my legs, which suddenly turned me toward the corner. I reached, with no true intent, for a garment I hadn't noticed before where it lay draped over the arm of the green chair.

Intriguing! My limbs were responding to the familiar chime with actions they were clearly accustomed to taking, even though my mind had not caught up with this routine. Though my brain refused to tell me where I was. *Who* I was, beyond my given name.

Amber.

"Who—" I stopped to clear my throat. It felt sore and scratchy. "Who are you?"

Confusion washed over Wilder's expression, leaving it blank like beach sand beneath a wave's retreat.

A sharp knock echoed from the far side of the closed door, and my head swiveled in that direction as a deep voice called from beyond the room. *"Amber?"*

Wilder flinched at the voice, scurrying to find the opening in his tunic as his other garment fell to his feet again.

"Amber? I'm coming in. We need to talk," the voice said plainly, firmly.

The door creaked open before I could formulate a response.

The man who stepped inside shared Wilder's square jaw and the shape of his nose, but his coloring was different. His skin was a shade deeper, his hair a dark chestnut with subtle caramel streaks only visible where the light shone upon it. Rich brown eyes narrowed at me, flaring almost coppery where they caught sunlight from the window. He was older than Wilder, though not by much, yet his bearing and stern expression gave the impression of authority.

His imposing height and the formidable breadth of his shoulders would have made him memorable, even without the formal black cape draped over his right shoulder.

His name would not come to me, but something twisted deep in my gut as I studied him. My free hand twitched, trying to reach for him, and heat burned at the back of my throat, as though the words that had lodged there were flames ready to be spewed at him.

His brows drew together, as if he could tell something was wrong before I'd spoken a single word. Before he'd even glanced at the man standing between the bed and the wall.

Wilder had frozen, his tunic stretched over both arms and pulled taut across his chest in preparation to be dragged over his head.

"You're not dressed," this new man said, and though I couldn't remember ever having heard his voice, I knew it the same way I would know what a ripe berry tasted like before I bit into it. As if I'd experienced the tart burst countless times before.

A new heat kindled inside me with that thought, but it sputtered at the disgruntled tightening of his jaw. At his impatient huff.

This man was displeased with me.

The dark weight of his gaze suggested that was not a recent development.

"Why aren't you dressed?" He glanced around the room, evidently looking for a way to hurry me along, and when his focus found Wilder, it cooled into a malignant glare. "Am I to assume, then, that punctuality is too much to ask of your *entire* cohort?"

Cohort?

When neither Wilder nor I answered, he continued, turning that icy gaze my way. "You are both aware, are you not, that this is a single-occupancy room?"

"Something's wrong with her, Des." The words almost exploded from Wilder, as if he were desperate to change the subject. "The rest of . . . *this* . . . it can wait."

The new man—Des—turned back to me, and the room suddenly felt too warm, despite the open window. Again the space—my room—felt somehow obliquely familiar, yet still entirely alien. Just like both men.

"Amber?" he said. "What's happened?"

I stepped back, and my calves brushed the armchair through the thin material of my gown. "I do not know you."

But that wasn't entirely true.

Desmond. He hates being called Des.

Focus on the facts.

I could not be sure whose voice was whispering in my mind—my own?—but the advice felt wise: *Let the facts lead to a conclusion.*

"I don't know who you are," I said, rephrasing my statement for accuracy, since I was fairly certain that I did, in fact, know them both. "But I cannot be certain how significant that is, because I don't know who I am either. Beyond names, anyway. Still, I don't remember our names, so much as I simply know them."

Both men blinked at me. Neither moved. I couldn't even be sure they were breathing.

"My conclusion," I said, "based on the fact that this bedchamber appears to be mine, and that you both seem to know me, is that I have lost my memory."

Wilder huffed, a mild sound of amusement that inexplicably eased my anxiety, albeit only a little.

"Well," he said, "she certainly *sounds* like the same old Amber."

Two

"You really don't remember *anything*?" Wilder dropped into the green armchair, fully dressed but for his boots.

Beyond the window, birds dove toward the glittering water far below. I inhaled the salty ocean scent, attempting to synchronize my pulse with the peaceful crash of the waves. Trying to breathe past the tension in the room.

Wilder's attention was an almost physical sensation—an uncomfortable pressure, like a hand pressed to an open wound.

Desmond's felt like a sunbeam directed through a lens. His copper-hued eyes were trained on me intently. Skeptically. The arms crossed over his broad chest emphasized the sentiment.

"Nothing recent." I sank into the wooden chair, my back to the desk.

How often had I sat in this very spot? Shouldn't the chair at least *feel* familiar if it were mine?

"I remember being a child." I closed my eyes, letting memories of the past rise through the enigma of my present. Relieved by how many there were. "I remember growing up in Innswood. We grew up together. All three of us." I opened my eyes as the rest of the memory solidified. "You're brothers," I said, turning to include Desmond.

Gregory. Their surname was suddenly . . . accessible.

Desmond nodded, but his expression was inscrutable, like an instructor administering an examination. A young but unforgiving instructor with a piercing gaze. The kind that could terrify any student.

The kind one wanted, instinctively, to please.

My focus returned to Wilder. "And *you're* my best friend. At least, you were." The fact that he'd been essentially naked in my bed suggested that, at some point, the nature of our relationship had changed.

As a youth, I'd indulged and abandoned crushes on the Gregory brothers as naturally as I'd slept and eaten. But I'd never acted on those feelings, and it seemed impossible that I could have forgotten the circumstance that had put Wilder in my bed. That warmed my face and drew my gaze to him.

Wilder's attention flicked toward his brother, then back to me with a bold frankness. "We're still . . . close."

My gaze narrowed on the flowing black garment clutched in my left hand. Then on the row of gold-trimmed charcoal-colored dresses hanging in the open wardrobe. Then on the breathtaking sight through the window—a stunning and distinctive view. "We're at the Alchemary."

Wilder's blue eyes widened. "Your memories are coming back?"

"No." I huffed. "But I'm perfectly capable of deductive reasoning. This is a university cloak, and the only kind of university I would attend is an alchemy academy. There are several of those in the kingdom of Aethermere, but I would aim for the best, as would both of you. Which means we could only be at the Alkahest Institute or the Alchemary. And I know this motto," I said, pointing at three words, skillfully embroidered in the shape of a triangle on the front left side of the black robe I held. I traced the rich gold thread with one finger.

Mind, Matter, Spirit.

"And, of course, the Alchemary was always my dream." I frowned, reconsidering. *"Our* dream."

We'd had a plan, since the day the recruiter's circuit had brought her to Innswood when we were children.

"Yes." Wilder exhaled, elbows propped on his thighs, staring at his clenched hands where they dangled between his knees. "This was our dream."

"And he . . ." My gaze narrowed on Desmond. On the distinctive, elegant collar of his asymmetrical cape. "He's a professor." Which meant he'd already graduated.

Wilder snorted as he slouched backward in the chair. "Des is just a staff researcher."

There was no such thing as *just* a staff researcher at the Alchemary. I knew that beyond a shadow of a doubt. Yet Desmond seemed completely unbothered by the insult. He only stared at me. No, he was *studying* me, as if he could intuit the cause of my amnesia just from looking. As if he were puzzling through the problem with the same systematic winnowing down and testing of possible causes and solutions that he'd used on every problem he'd faced since we were old enough to wander Innswood with the other village children.

As if no scientific mystery would *dare* confound him for long.

"Am *I* a professor?" I asked him.

Desmond's eyes widened. His skepticism waned.

Wilder laughed. "You and I are students."

I turned to him, more relieved than I would have admitted. The only thing worse than forgetting part of my alchemy education would have been forgetting *all* of it. "What level?"

"This is the first week of year three for both of us," he said. Then he sat up as footsteps hurried past my closed door in the distinctive cadence of a stairwell descent. "In fact, it's the first day."

Year three. Mastery year. The final year of studies at the Alchemary.

Trials year.

"No." It was difficult enough to believe that I had no memory of being admitted to the Alchemary. Of getting my father's blessing to attend, considering his distrust of this place.

Or had I simply attended without his blessing?

Regardless, forgetting my application, interview, and admission was one thing, but the rest of it? Two entire years of classes and research? Both the Fundamentals and Proficiency years, lost to... some strange phenomenon that had also stolen the memory of whatever Wilder and I had done last night. Not to mention everything that had led up to it.

"No." The anger on the surface of my voice masked a churning depth of fear. How could I not remember my own life? My own skills and accomplishments? My... *relationships*?

Knowing who I was meant very little if I couldn't remember becoming that person. I could not *possibly* be this close to everything I'd ever wanted, yet have no memory of how I'd gotten there. No understanding of how to move forward.

"What happened to me? Why can't I remember?" I cleared my throat and forced a bit more iron into my tone. "And... am I late for something?" Hearing the rush of steps past my door had left an itching anxiety in my hands, which wanted to start gathering up my belongings. In my legs, which wanted to rush me off to... somewhere. "For class, I suppose?"

"Yes, of course." Desmond exhaled heavily. "But you can hardly attend in this condition." He turned to Wilder. "Head straight to the Conservatory and ask for Dr. Winhoof."

I blinked at him. "Winhoof, as in—"

"The director of the Panacea Project." Wilder turned to his brother, his jaw stiff. "But I don't take instruction from you. And an issue of this magnitude should go straight to the Bluehelm."

Desmond huffed. "The Bluehelm doesn't see students without appointments, and she's not the expert in this field."

"*No one* is an expert in this field," Wilder insisted. "She should know that one of her star students has—"

"Amnesia is an *illness*," Desmond snapped. But his words echoed hollowly, with Wilder's assertion still ringing in my ears.

I was a star student. At the Alchemary. At least, I had been, before . . . whatever this was.

"Or it's an injury," Desmond continued. "Regardless, what Amber needs is not an academic administrator but an alchemical physician." He turned to me, despite Wilder's narrowed eyes, with utter confidence in his own conclusion. And I will admit, I felt a bit of the younger brother's irritation.

I was fairly certain I didn't take instruction from Desmond Gregory either. Yet I could poke no holes in his logic.

"Agreed." I lifted the garment still clutched in my fist. "Though I should dress first. Is this what I'm meant to wear?"

Desmond nodded. His jaw clenched as his gaze skimmed my nightshirt, then landed on my eyes with an inscrutable weight. He opened the door and aimed that coppery glare at his brother. *"Out."*

As the door closed behind them, I heard Desmond put an end to Wilder's whispered questions with a single guttural grunt, and I turned to the wardrobe.

I changed into a fresh cream-colored linen shift, then I plucked a gold-trimmed charcoal-gray frock from its hook. The dress was of a simple cut, with front lacings and narrow sleeves that ballooned a bit around the wrist. It was functional for a student, and the only extravagance, other than the masterful and even pigmentation of the cloth, was the distinctive gold stitching—an Alchemary signature.

The frock fit perfectly, its hem barely brushing my feet.

I held my breath as I swung the gold-trimmed black cloak over my shoulders. The material *swoosh*ed, then it settled with a familiar and comforting weight, draping over my dress and my arms to trail just past my knees.

There was no looking glass in my chamber, but in staring down at myself I could see how the rich, thick black material framed the gray dress, all of it accented in gold. The triangle of the Alchemary creed lay over my heart, just to the left of my sternum.

I slid my arms through reinforced slits in the cloak and exhaled slowly. It was odd, how familiar the gesture felt. Like waking to the sound of an echo, with no memory of its source.

My uniform felt *right.* It was of an orderly shape and pleasing appearance, the dress cinched neatly at my waist, beneath the voluminous richness of the distinctive cape. Wearing it felt... momentous.

Had it felt this way the first time?

My heart ached for the bare cupboard of my memory. For the experiences I'd lost.

I can get them back.

I will *get them back.*

Determined, I set about plaiting my hair, and though I had no memory of how I typically wore it, my hands began the job as if out of habit. Quickly, efficiently, they combed my long, dark hair and braided a thick length along the curve of first one temple, then the next, trailing down and back, picking up more strands along the way, so that the braids held hair away from my face and could be tied together at the back of my head.

The result felt neat and fetching.

When I opened the door, only Desmond was waiting for me.

I stepped out of my room expecting a torchlit hallway. Instead, I found myself on a broad landing set into a spiral-shaped stone staircase that curved both upward and downward from where Desmond stood. Behind him, the expected torch was mounted to the wall, flickering with a warm golden glow.

Despite the daylight shining into my room through the open shutters, this spiral stairwell was a nest of shadows that trembled with each flicker of the torch, ebbing and flowing without ever truly receding from places the light couldn't touch.

Mine was the only room that opened onto the landing, but when I looked to the right, down the stairs, I saw an identical torchlit landing and an identical door, which rose in height to the middle of my own.

I frowned for the moment it took me to understand. "The rooms are offset. They climb the tower just like the stairs do."

"They're each offset by half, vertically, following the curve of the tower staircase," Desmond confirmed. "One dormitory room on every landing, half of those with a stunning view of the ocean. But the towers are only for Mastery-year students."

"How many of us are there?"

"Twelve, to start," he said. "Six women in this tower, and six men in the tower on the other side of the Dormitory. The wings that connect the towers house the Fundamentals-year students on the first floor, and the Proficiency-year students on the second floor."

"Fascinating." I stared up the staircase at what I could see of the landing above mine. "But more whimsical than efficient. What floor am I on? Er . . . what half floor?"

"Yours is the fifth room up. That one is the highest in the tower," he added, pointing at the upper landing.

Which meant the footsteps that had passed my door belonged to whoever occupied that room. Though I could have sworn I'd heard more than one set of feet . . .

"Are you ready?" Desmond asked.

I nodded and followed him down the dark, quiet spiral staircase, counting the four doors below mine as we went.

On the ground floor, the stairs deposited us into a round stone-tiled foyer. To my left, a gracefully pointed gothic archway opened into a long corridor lined with closed doors, which could only be the Fundamentals-year dormitory rooms. Torches were mounted on the wall between them, flickering with that same warm reddish-yellow light.

A second, identical archway led from the round foyer into a shorter door-lined corridor running perpendicular to the first, and I surmised that the Mastery towers stood at the corners of a U-shaped building, connecting the long center wing to the shorter wings on each end.

On my right, opposite the longer corridor, stood a single richly carved door echoing the shape of the gothic arches. Desmond opened that door and led me out of the dormitory onto its broad side lawn, which sloped gently up until it dropped into nothing over the cliff. Into the ocean below.

"An island..." I murmured as a memory surfaced—not of being here, but of hearing about this place. "The Alchemary is on an island."

"Indeed."

Directly ahead, the glittering ocean stretched into infinity, and on my right, the women's residential tower rose toward the sky. At my back lay the rest of Alchemary Island: a campus—and a life—I could not remember.

I stared out at the ocean, letting the cool, salt-scented breeze lift the ends of my hair. But Desmond turned as if the view meant nothing to him and marched away from the cliff. I followed him along the short wing of the building, and when we rounded it, I discovered that as I'd guessed from inside, the Dormitory, a masterpiece of dark stone and gothic arches, was shaped like a rectangle missing one long side, with a tower shooting up from each corner. Its central wing, perched on the very edge of the cliff, was twice as long as the two side wings, and the windows were constructed of multiple panes of clear glass, joined by lead seams.

The Dormitory was extraordinary: symmetrical and grand, yet with a warm and quite solid feel, thanks to the sheer volume of stonework and the three-tiered fountain at the center of an interior courtyard that opened directly onto the rest of the campus.

It was a marvel of design and construction, and given that I'd been raised by a master stonemason, it should have been indelibly imprinted upon my memory from the moment I'd first seen it. Yet I could not remember ever laying eyes on the building before that morning.

With a sigh, I turned from the Dormitory courtyard to face a long, neatly manicured quadrangle and the rest of the campus. "Let's go," I said.

And with that, I set off down the lawn, leaving Desmond to follow.

"And you're certain you didn't hit your head?" Dr. Winhoof asked for the second time as he ran his hands over my scalp and through my hair, destroying my braids. His touch was professional and thorough, but not what one might describe as tender.

He pressed too hard again, forcing my head forward, and I turned sideways on the table, dislodging his touch. My fingers began winding strands of hair back into my braids as I glared out at the room—a cold space full of hard surfaces, stocked with aggressively sharp and pointy medical . . . tools.

This place and its equipment felt entirely unfamiliar and disconcerting. The marble slab examination table leached ice into my bones through the thick material of my dress, and the unyielding attention of three different men—Wilder had rejoined us—made me feel like a lab specimen in a jar.

"I have not hit my head that I can recall," I said. "But, to reiterate, the problem is that I cannot recall much of anything."

"But there's no swelling?" Desmond said from one side of the table. "No obvious . . . depression?"

The only pain in my head was from the frustration of their interrogation. That, and the glare of half a dozen lanterns against the white marble walls.

"I'm *fine*!" I snapped. "I can't detect any physical ailment or injury," I clarified. "I know who I am and where I'm from, and while I don't know how old I am, precisely, I know when I was born and I'm perfectly capable of doing the math, and given that this is evidently the first day of my third year at the Alchemary—"

"You turned twenty-two three months ago," Wilder confirmed from the wooden stool across the room where he had perched after telling our instructors to expect our absences today. "Though you refused to indulge a celebration."

I frowned at him, momentarily distracted from the problem at hand. We'd always celebrated my birthday with a simple fruit-filled flat cake and, as we'd gotten older, a few sips of whatever ale or wine we could procure. "Why wouldn't I want a celebration?"

"You were busy." His gaze flicked toward Desmond, and I couldn't interpret the unspoken communication. "Studying."

"Well, this is fascinating," Dr. Winhoof declared as he stepped back from the table to better assess me, wispy strands of his straight white hair stirring with the motion. "Total loss of all recent memory, with no known injury or illness. Was there any sort of shock, perhaps? Psychological, or . . . traumatic?"

I blinked at him, unsure how I could be expected to answer.

Dr. Winhoof laughed, thin arms practically flapping at his sides, billowing his long black robe. "Why in the heavens am I asking you?" He turned to Wilder and Desmond. "Well, *did* she suffer any sort of physical, mental, or psychological shock last night?"

The Gregory brothers shared a meaningful glance, but I couldn't tell whether it indicated an unspoken question or a silent admission.

Maybe they were thinking—as I was—of the fact that Wilder and I had woken up in my bed, indecently dressed, and that Desmond had seemed wholly unprepared for that sight. Which seemed to imply either that I hadn't informed him of the nature of my relationship with his brother, or that the nature of that relationship had changed too suddenly for disclosure.

But would that have been enough to shock my mind into abandoning every memory I'd formed in adulthood?

"I can't think of anything that would account for this," Desmond finally said, arms crossed over his gray tunic. "But then, I wasn't with Amber when she lost her memory." He turned a pointed scowl upon his brother.

Wilder stared back almost defiantly. "As far as I know, she did nothing last night that she hasn't done many times before."

My face burned hotter than the lanterns positioned around the room.

Desmond shifted—a subtle realignment of his entire form, without moving an inch from where he stood—and the effect was like storm clouds rolling across the sky. A threat gathering on the horizon.

But before the storm could break, the door behind him opened, and the fraternal tension was dispelled.

A young woman stood in the threshold, holding a stylus and a wax tablet. She wore a student's uniform identical to my own, except that beneath her gold-trimmed black cape her frock was a deep blue, belted at the waist with an embroidered rust-colored fabric.

I stared in surprise for a moment. Was gray not the standard color?

The student was my age, with brown skin, a pouf of shoulder-length reddish curls, and smoky-gray irises ringed in a striking darker shade. Her gaze lingered on me for a second, brows dipping almost imperceptibly. Then she stepped back to hold the door open.

An older woman stepped into the exam room, her distinctive black robes almost shimmering in the glow from the lanterns. Her elaborate gold-embroidered collar trailed to form stiff, thick, formal lapels among copious folds of a fine material. Her dark eyes stood out against pale skin, her cheekbones sharp above gaunt shadows.

"Thank you, Cressa," she said, nodding at the student aide, who stepped inside and closed the door behind them.

"Bluehelm." Dr. Winhoof's small, mildly amused smile blossomed into a tooth-filled half-moon that took up the lower third of his face. "How wonderful of you to drop by. We have the most intriguing case, involving one of the Seminary's most accomplished pupils."

"So I've heard." The Bluehelm's voice was soft and rich, yet unquestionably commanding.

Though I could not have said whether it was from a latent memory or logical deduction, I understood that she was head of the Alchemary, in charge of the Seminary and its students as well as of the Conservatory and its researchers. Given how busy she clearly was, I could not imagine how or why my condition had drawn her attention.

"Amber Fallbrook," the Bluehelm said. "I understand you've come down with a peculiar ailment."

I nodded, unable to tell from the greeting whether or not the Bluehelm and I had met before.

Dr. Winhoof stepped in front of me to address her. "Catastrophic memory loss. No known cause, including injury, trauma, or illness. We were about to assess the scope of the loss, but I expect that to be a lengthy process."

The Bluehelm placed one hand on the doctor's shoulder and firmly directed him to the side. Training her dark-eyed gaze on me, she asked, "What is the most recent thing you remember, before you woke up this morning?"

"It's not that simple a process, I'm afraid," Dr. Winhoof interjected with an animated one-handed gesture. "We'll have to—"

"This will suffice for an initial estimate." The Bluehelm's focus held mine. "Amber?"

"I'm not certain," I admitted with a frown. "I woke up with no idea where I was or how I'd gotten there, but I wasn't *surprised* to be there. I cannot remember most of my adulthood, but neither do I feel like a child. There is no one distinct memory I can identify as the most recent I can recall. It isn't as if I went to sleep in my childhood bed, then woke up at the Alchemary. The reality is less clearly defined."

"What is it like, *precisely*?" she demanded.

Nearby, Cressa waited with her stylus poised over the wax tablet.

I closed my eyes, trying to collect my thoughts, suddenly afraid that my future at the Alchemary might be determined by what I said next.

What *was* this like?

"It's like walking around in a room after someone has blown out the candle," I said at last, opening my eyes again to find the Bluehelm waiting expectantly. "I know that if I move about, I'll find a table or a chair or a desk, because the furnishings are still there, even if I can't see them."

Her gaze narrowed on me, and vaguely, I was aware of everyone else watching in absolute silence, breath practically—perhaps literally—held.

"So, your memories are still there?" the Bluehelm said, her brows arching only slightly with the question. "Like hulking shapes in the dark?"

"I can't say for sure, obviously. But I certainly feel like knowledge has been cut off from me. Not destroyed. Just . . . *obscured* by a fog, or locked behind an iron door in my mind."

And in that moment I understood one thing for certain: If that were the case—if my memories *were* imprisoned in a cell of my mind's own construction—I *would* find the key to that door. Or, if need be, I would take a battering ram to the whole damn thing.

During the third and final year of study, colloquially known as the Mastery year, students undergo a series of four trials, intended to test their comprehension of specific alchemical principles and formulas, as well as their ability to call upon those skills in moments of mental, physical, and psychological strain. Students who pass one trial will continue their studies and prepare for the next. Students who fail will be dismissed from the Alchemary immediately, though they may take the institution's accreditation exam and earn a license to practice provincial alchemy under the Alchemary's banner.*

Students who pass all four trials may be offered a permanent position at the Alchemary, as a practicing alchemist and researcher, or as an academic instructor.

**The institution anticipates that a certain percentage of trial failures will be fatal.*

—from the *Alchemary Student Handbook*

Three

I shivered on the exam table, chilled by the smooth marble surface despite the weight of both my shift and my frock.

Across the room, Desmond stood huddled in the corner with Dr. Winhoof and the Bluehelm, discussing my future as if I couldn't hear them. As if my thoughts on the matter held no relevance.

Wilder snagged my cloak from a coatrack in the corner and draped it over my shoulders. "Chin up, Amber. It's not all bad," he whispered as he rubbed my arms through my sleeves, as if he knew they were covered in gooseflesh.

"How is losing every aspect of my adult life not 'all bad'?" I demanded in a matching whisper.

A brazen grin lit up his blue eyes, like a candle flaring behind stained glass. "You still have me, and I find you more fascinating and mysterious than ever."

I rolled my eyes at him, fighting a smile. "You're suggesting that should be my primary concern?"

"Well, it certainly is *mine.*" He boosted himself onto the table next to me and bumped my shoulder with his own. But then his gaze, too, was drawn toward the meeting in the corner of the room.

"With all due respect, madam," Desmond said, "given that Amber is suffering from what appears to be *profound* amnesia, of an unknown nature and cause, I see no way for her to safely proceed with her Mastery year."

Irritation spiked in my heartbeat, briefly blurring the edges of my vision. My hands clenched around the edge of the exam table.

Wilder shot me a sympathetic look.

"The trials are dangerous enough for students who know what they're doing," Desmond continued. "And regardless of her status at the school yesterday, *today* she can't tell the difference between precious metals and base metals. Between a solution and a suspension."

That was *not* accurate. I still had the foundational-level knowledge I'd come to the Alchemary with—what I'd learned as a child from my mother—but it would do me no good to argue with his assertion.

The past half hour had been spent in examination of my memories, and to my surprise, the Bluehelm had stayed for the entire exam, her aide taking distressingly few notes, because there was little, evidently, that was noteworthy.

I remembered nothing after my eighteenth year, but part of that year, too, was spotty. There was no clean line dividing the "before amnesia" and "after amnesia" portions of my memory, but Dr. Winhoof had determined, through exhaustive questioning, that I remembered nothing of my time at the Alchemary. Nothing of the skills I'd gained or the projects I'd worked on.

Despite his hyperbolic stance, Desmond was correct: I was not ready for the Mastery-year trials.

And yet that bolt of anger—of indignation—persisted, burning in my belly like an incompatible meal. I'd wanted to be an alchemist for most of my life. I'd grown up in my mother's village apothecary shop, hearing stories of the Alchemary and the great works done there—done *here*—by the most accomplished scientists in the world. Amnesia had not erased my drive to become an alchemist. And the knowledge that I'd been *almost there* before *whatever* had happened—the knowledge that I'd worked, and studied, and sacrificed, and learned, all for *nothing*—had left me bitter on a level that stretched beyond present and past, and burrowed deep into my soul.

Rather than end my ambition, amnesia had left me *motivated*.

I couldn't be sure how I would have reacted to something like this if I hadn't forgotten my entire adult life, but this *felt* like a moment for fighting. Not for giving up. Not for going home with my metaphorical tail between my legs. And not just for my future as an alchemist.

For my memory.

Whatever had happened to me to drain the well of my memory, it had happened here. It was related to this place, somehow. And I could not shake the certainty that if I left, I would be abandoning my best chance of reversing the loss. Not just of my alchemical skills, but of my *life*.

"As badly as I hate to admit it," Dr. Winhoof said. "And as dearly as I would love to study this case . . . I'm afraid Desmond is correct. The trials are much too dangerous for someone with inadequate knowledge of alchemy, regardless of the reason for that inadequacy."

A strangled sound leaked from my throat, and Wilder's hand curled around mine, warming my fingers. "There's still time," he whispered.

Dr. Winhoof turned. "What was that?" he asked, but I could see from the twitch at one corner of his mouth that he'd heard perfectly well. That he concurred with whatever Wilder's point was, but he didn't want to be the one to make it in front of his superior.

Wilder cleared his throat. "I said there's still time."

"For *what*?" Desmond glared at his brother.

"For her to learn. To *re*learn. The first trial is six weeks away, and—"

"And you think she can relearn two full years of studies—not to mention all the time spent on her independent project—in a month and a half?" the older Gregory brother demanded.

Wilder glanced at me, and his smile buoyed my confidence. "I think that if anyone can, *she* can."

"Exactly how strong a student was I?" I asked, vexed that I couldn't answer my own question. That I couldn't feel pride in my accomplishments—whatever those were.

"Cressa?" The Bluehelm glanced at her aide, who pulled a string-bound book from the bag slung over one shoulder. My name was written on the cover of the slim volume.

Cressa opened the book, balancing it over the tablet she still held in one hand, and her dark brows rose as she scanned a chart filled with brief scores and notations.

"You were an *extraordinary* student," she said as she closed the book. Then her gray-eyed gaze met mine, and it was cooler than I'd expected, given the compliment. "Academically speaking, anyway."

The Bluehelm seemed unsurprised by the assessment, and I realized that though she might not have known the particulars, she must have been familiar with my accomplishments. Why else would she have come to assess one ailing student when she likely had a full agenda on the first day of the semester?

"Is it possible?" I asked. And though the decision would ultimately belong to the Bluehelm, I found myself looking at Desmond instead. "Isn't it at least *possible* that if the knowledge is still locked up in here"—I tapped on my temple—"that studying what I've already learned could just sort of . . . jar it all loose?"

And that staying here, where something had clearly gone wrong for me, could show me how to set things right again?

No one seemed willing to hazard a guess.

"Even if it doesn't," Wilder finally said, "there's always the chance that your memory will come back on its own. Right?" He turned to Dr. Winhoof, who looked completely uncertain and distinctly uncomfortable with that predicament. "It'd be a shame for her to drop out and go back to Innswood, only to recover her memory next week. She would have missed a week of classes and research. And trial prep."

Desmond made a dismissive sound. "The chances are very slim that that scenario will prove even remotely relevant."

"And yet . . . that chance exists?" The Bluehelm turned to Dr. Winhoof. "Can we say for certain that it doesn't?"

He frowned. "Cases of amnesia are very, very rare, and these are extraordinary circumstances. In most of the cases I'm familiar with, the victim's memory did eventually return. I cannot guess how quickly that might happen for Ms. Fallbrook, but I also can't say it won't happen. The truth is that it could happen tomorrow."

Desmond crossed his arms over his chest, his left side hidden by the drape of his asymmetrical cape. "And it might *never* happen."

"As I see it, we have two options," Dr. Winhoof said. "We can allow her to stay, with certain conditions and restrictions, to give her memory a chance to recover. Or we can dismiss her from the Alchemary, which would be denying her the chance to prepare for the trials even if her memory comes back." He cleared his throat. "It seems to me that less harm would be done by the former option. After all, if her memory fails to return, she can always be excluded from the trials and sent home."

His logic lit a spark inside me that was part determination and part fear. I could *not* lose this opportunity.

"I want to stay," I said. "I *should* stay. I have clearly earned my place here, and I have no doubt I'm capable of applying that drive and determination to recovering everything I've lost."

I took a deep breath and fixed my gaze on Desmond for a moment before shifting it firmly toward the Bluehelm. "Please. I want to stay."

Desmond's coppery scowl burned into me, before he, too, turned to the Bluehelm. "I must *officially* object. No student who lacks a grasp of basic alchemical theory belongs in the Mastery-year class, regardless of the—"

"Consider yourself heard," the Bluehelm interrupted. "And your objection noted. But given that you are neither a physician nor one of Ms. Fallbrook's instructors, you lack standing in this debate, and I agree with Dr. Winhoof, that she should be allowed to stay, at least for now." She glanced pointedly at Cressa, who began scribbling madly on the wax tablet as the older woman spoke. "Under the following conditions . . ."

"This is good news!" Wilder elbowed me as we headed out of the Panacea wing of the Conservatory into the atrium, a towering tribute to cold white marble and clean lines. "You get to stay!"

"For now." I felt obligated to temper his celebration with reality as his excitement echoed around the tall, hand-polished walls.

Where the Dormitory was dramatic, warm, and almost oppressive with its dark stone, windowless corridors, and soaring towers, the Conservatory was cold and clinical: a study of polished planes, right angles, and sharp corners. The only curve in the building that I could see was the spiral staircase rising from the grand, three-story atrium, and even that felt nothing like the tower staircases in the Dormitory.

These steps were wide and bright, each tread precisely level and even, unlike the stone treads of the tower staircases. Even the torches mounted on the Conservatory walls burned with a clean, crisp white light that felt almost cold, despite the heat and illumination they gave off, and could not have been produced without a lab-created fuel and treated wicks.

But the marble . . .

How, exactly, did I know the marble slabs were hand-polished to their extraordinarily reflective finish? I couldn't remember learning that, or ever having toured the Conservatory, which meant I'd probably heard about the construction of this building from my father, when I was a child.

He and my mother had shared disparate opinions about the Alchemary. Her memories of the campus were nostalgic, until the bittersweet ending of her Mastery year.

My father disapproved of alchemy entirely, but he never tired of discussing the master craftsmanship that had gone into the construction of the most prominent university in the kingdom of Aethermere—one of the most famous campuses in the world. He wasn't just *a* stonemason. He was *the* stonemason—head of the mason's guild and a high-ranking member of the Toolkeepers.

As a teenager, I'd worried that my familial affiliation—the Toolkeepers' disdain for alchemy in general and the Alchemary specifically—would keep me from being admitted. Or that he would forbid me from attending if I did get in.

And yet here I was, a star student, known to the Bluehelm by name.

Anxiety crawled along my spine as I stared at the interior of a building I found both inspiring and intimidating. The conditions the Bluehelm had set, though they were everything I'd wanted five minutes before, suddenly felt cruel and impossible. She was to receive reports every fortnight from each of my professors on my progress, to make sure my scores didn't drop below the sixty percent mark. If they did, I would not be allowed to undertake the first trial.

The Black Trial.

"Why do you look so glum?" Wilder threw his arm around my shoulders and squeezed, half guiding me past tall pillars and benches built into the wall of the atrium. Past tile-lined recesses in the walls and rectangular leaded glass windows that allowed daylight to paint the white floor with warmer streaks of color.

Something pointed pressed against my hip from beneath his cloak.

"You got exactly what you wanted!" he declared as we stepped over the Alchemary creed—*Mind, Matter, Spirit*—carved in the shape of a triangle in the center of the floor.

Yes, I had, and that didn't feel like a novel state of affairs for me. Yet I was no longer certain I could actually capitalize on the opportunity I'd demanded.

"What is poking at me?" I asked, seizing his cloak to pull it back.

Wilder's brows rose, and before he could voice the ribald jest clearly burning the end of his tongue, I thumped the dark green leather sheath hanging at his hip.

"Since when do you carry a blade?"

"Since I've developed need of one," he said. At my questioning look, he sighed. "Brigands sometimes lurk in shadows, across the bridge. You should not go into Saltstrand alone."

"Duly noted."

"We should celebrate," Wilder declared as he shoved open the heavy mahogany double doors in the center of the front wall of the atrium. "A drink. You probably don't even remember where to find one around here, so it'll be your first time. Again." His eyes sparkled as he grinned down at me, holding the left-hand door open. "*Everyone* should be lucky enough to have their first time twice!"

The innuendo sent a private little thrill to glow with promising warmth in my belly. Fresh questions bloomed like roses on the branching stems of my amnesia, and more than one of those questions felt like it was rooted squarely in the sapphire depths of his gaze.

"Or—and I know this is going to sound absurd," I warned, "we could *go to class*."

He laughed, despite my willingness to stomp all over his bacchanalian plans, and as he backed down the front steps ahead of me, he was at eye level with me for a moment. "Our next class doesn't start until after lunch, and our first class"—he pivoted to peer at the clock tower at the center of a building to the north—"is about to end."

"Oh." I followed his gaze to the clock face. I'd officially missed a class I couldn't even name. As had Wilder, on my behalf.

"If you really can't remember this place—"

"I cannot."

"—then why don't I give you a tour?"

I smiled with a glance around the quadrangle, my gaze skimming the central fountain, several elaborately carved statues, and a handful of tall shrubs trimmed into the shapes of various animals.

"I suspect I can see most of it from this very spot. That's the Dormitory." I pointed directly across the length of the quadrangle to the dark stone building on the eastern cliff. "And given that *that*"—I spun to look up at the white marble building we'd just emerged from—"is the Conservatory, then that must be the Seminary," I said with a glance at the building forming the northern side of the quadrangle on our left, which boasted the clock tower. "Where our classes are."

"Good guess," he allowed with a pout.

"Deductive reasoning," I corrected. "It's too big to be the Refectory, which means we must take our meals over there." I shifted my gaze to the building forming the right side of the quadrangle, to the south. It was a single story, easily the smallest and most humble of the main buildings.

"Yes, but what about—"

"The bridge? I can see it from here." From where we stood, the bridge connecting Alchemary Island to the mainland north of us was, in fact, easily visible, though it would have been blocked by the Seminary from nearly any other angle.

The bridge was a massive, graceful stretch of gray stone, supported by pillars built into the edge of both land masses. It spanned the strait with a single large arch that allowed boats to pass beneath. It would have been a landmark all on its own, were it not overshadowed by the various striking buildings of the Alchemary. The famous Alchemary gate stood at the end of the bridge, defining the campus's northern border in a functionally artistic display of cast-iron bars, leaves, vines, and flowers.

The bridge was also the only way onto the island, short of taking a boat all the way around the coast to the dock on the southwest side, where uncultivated woodland gradually sloped toward a rocky shoreline.

I couldn't remember ever seeing that shore, but I'd certainly heard about it as a child.

"The woods, then," Wilder said, following my gaze to the land that stretched behind both the Refectory and the Conservatory. "Or the menagerie."

"Soon," I assured him. "But for now, I have to start . . . studying. I suppose."

"Studying what? We missed class."

"Studying my *life*. I don't know what research I was working on or how I'd planned to prepare for the trials. I don't even know who I was as a person yesterday. But there's likely evidence of all of that in my room."

"You're overlooking one other very valuable source of that information. And I happen to know that he is *very* generous." Wilder threw his arms out, as if he were inviting me for an embrace, and the impulse to accept it was surprisingly strong.

I couldn't remember the nature of our relationship, but I felt very alone in my current reality, standing outside of my own memory and experience. And he seemed willing to step into that distressingly foggy place with me. Or, more accurately, to help me clear the fog.

After all, what were the chances that the man who'd woken up in my bed knew nothing useful about my life?

"You're offering to fill me in on what I've forgotten?"

"I'm offering to do *anything* you need."

I blinked up at him, choosing to ignore the subtext. "That's very kind of you," I said as a familiar feeling crawled up my back and across my shoulders. A feeling that we were no longer alone.

Just as that sensation settled in, sinking through flesh and blood into my very bones, vague movements on the edge of my vision solidified into black-cloaked human forms.

Students. Classmates. The first class of the day was over, and I could feel heads turning our way.

I aimed an acknowledging glance at several unfamiliar faces, but I found my focus straying back to Wilder. To what suddenly felt like safe territory, despite the fact that I had no more memory of him over the past two years than I had of any of these other students.

They all seemed to recognize me, but there were no friendly looks or cordial nods. No one was smiling.

The front door of the Seminary suddenly flew open, and several more students emerged, their dark cloaks flaring back in the cool autumn breeze. A young man with brown skin and a young woman with long, voluminous blond hair bounced down the front steps onto a stone pathway that meandered fancifully around the lawn with no clear aim, only to wind up beneath my very feet. They looked up, deep in conversation, and words seemed to trail away from the girl as she tossed a thick, loose braid over one shoulder and her eyes found me.

She elbowed the young man and nodded in my direction. Her sudden broad smile had the affectation of a stage masque as she marched toward Wilder and me, eschewing the circuitous path, determination practically thundering from her steps.

My veins sparked with a sharp dread I could not contextualize.

She and I were not friends. Though my memory had hidden the details, my body's reaction to her was quite clear.

"Yes." The word flew from my mouth as I grabbed Wilder's arm, to his obvious surprise. "Yes, please, come help me."

I shot the blond girl and her male friend a smile—despite my panic, I didn't want to appear rude—then I spun on my heel and half dragged Wilder across the lawn, past a couple dozen nearly identically dressed students toward the Dormitory perched on the edge of a cliff, at the other end of the quadrangle.

Four

Wilder sank into the armchair in the corner of my small room as if he'd been there a thousand times, and I found myself envious of his comfort. In *my* private space.

"Where should I start?" he asked. "Do you want to hear about the brilliant essays and heroic works of admittedly novice alchemy that earned us our spots at the Alchemary? Or do you want to know about how respected you are as an academic and how beloved I am across campus for my jovial nature and my generous distribution of the hangover cure I developed one afternoon last year?"

One of us, evidently, was having a lot of fun on campus.

"You developed a hangover cure in a class lab?" I marched past him and threw open the shutters, letting in a glorious breeze and the salty scent of the ocean. "Using ingredients intended for student projects?"

Wilder snorted. "You said it *just like that* the first time. But no. I snuck into Desmond's lab. In the Apotheosis wing of the Conservatory."

"Apotheosis?" I blinked, a little surprised to hear what discipline Desmond had chosen. "The effort to transform people into their ideal and most perfect state?" The definition came unbidden, and the voice reciting the words in my head was my mother's.

"Yes. My brother is trying to perfect the human form, both mind and body. Yet somehow, in that endeavor, he manages to seem even less human than he used to."

"Certainly less kind, anyway," I agreed, thinking of his effort to get me expelled.

Apotheosis was, in my opinion, the least interesting of the three disciplines. Had my opinion changed during my first two years at the Alchemary? Or was my academic disdain the reason Desmond was so eager to have me sent away, when Wilder, Dr. Winhoof, and even the Bluehelm had seemed willing to let me stay?

"I want to hear about all of that." I stood in the center of the small, narrow space and glanced in turn at the wardrobe, the unmade bed, and the desk piled high with papers, unsure where to begin: the personal or the academic?

"But," I added, "there are more immediately relevant bits missing from my memory. For instance . . . what classes am I taking? And what time do they begin, exactly?"

Surely there was a course list buried somewhere on my desk. . . .

Yet even as my attention narrowed on several stacks of parchment, the breeze from the open shutters sent them fluttering toward the edge. With a groan, I grabbed a wooden box from my nightstand and used it to anchor two of the stacks at once.

"All Mastery-year students take the same courses," Wilder said. "The Ethics and Advancement of Alchemy, and Advanced Alchemical Ethics and Advancement is from nine to eleven, two days a week. Theories is from two to four in the afternoon, those same two days. Which is nice, because during Fundamentals year we took five classes, and during Proficiency we took three."

Two classes for my final year. That felt doable.

"And, of course, you're a teaching assistant."

"I . . . *am*?"

Wilder nodded. "You, and everyone else currently ranked in the top half of our cohort. Which—happily—means that my services are not in demand." He frowned. "I misspoke. My various services are *quite* in demand, on many corners of campus. But I am not required to grade papers for free on behalf of a Fundamentals-year professor."

"What professor am I supposed to assist?" I asked.

"Robards. He teaches a couple of things, but I believe you're only on the hook for Introductory Theories of Alchemy."

"When does that meet?"

"Um . . ." Wilder rose and leaned over the desk, where he shuffled through the sheets of parchment and finally plucked one up. "Here it is." He scanned the text. "From one to two in the afternoon, three days a week. Starting today." He handed me the paper, and I scanned a written schedule of my classes—the very information he'd just rattled off.

"And on the other days?" Tuesdays and Thursdays were blank on the schedule, as was Friday, outside of the introductory course.

"Any time we're not in class, we're expected to be working on our independent research projects or preparing for the trials. Mastery-year students each have a dedicated lab space on the top floor of the Seminary, in the Advanced Studies lab. Most of us moved all of our stuff in last night." Wilder grinned, looking almost sheepish. "It was kind of stupid and ceremonial. But I admit, it was fun. We have access to professional-grade resources now, and to plenty of space." He leaned closer to whisper, one brow arched. "And we're largely unsupervised."

"*Most* of us moved our stuff in?" My thoughts had caught on that word like a thorn in the hem of my skirt.

"You didn't show up," he admitted.

"Why not?"

Wilder laughed, but the sound lacked true amusement. "Amber, you have never been what one might call forthcoming."

"But you're my best friend." *At the very least.* "Are you not?"

He nodded, vague frustration flickering across his expression.

"So . . . did you at least ask me?" I set the schedule on my desk, anchored beneath an empty inkpot.

"I didn't get a chance. Last night got away from us both, and I was going to inquire today why the top student in our Mastery year would skip setting up her private lab space. But then . . ." He shrugged.

"Then I woke up missing two years of my memory."

I thought about that as I began straightening the bedclothes, noting that they were not much different than the rough, unbleached sheets I'd slept on at home. The mattress was a thin but sturdy woolen fill inside rough canvas. The only real luxury was the frame itself, considering that I'd slept on a mattress on the floor until I'd left home.

Well, the frame, and the fact that every student at the Alchemary evidently had a private room.

Wilder was clearly no longer impressed by the facilities, but a space to call my own felt novel and special to me. Especially one with a vast view of the ocean.

"Is that normal?" I asked as I tugged at the wool blanket sharply, then let it settle smoothly over the bed. The motion felt practiced. "Did I often fail to show up?"

"For something school-related?" Wilder leaned back in the chair with his arms crossed over his chest, his cloak stretched taut across widely spread knees. "No. You skipped your share of *parties*, but in two years, you have never missed a class, a lab space reservation, or an academic consultation."

"Until last night." I tucked the blanket around the end of the mattress in two directions, executing a perfectly straight corner I could not remember learning.

"Until last night," he agreed.

"But you saw me later. After the lab setup. Clearly," I added, gesturing a bit awkwardly toward the freshly made bed.

"Yes. The rest of us crossed the bridge into Saltstrand for a drink afterward. One last hurrah to the end of break and the beginning of Mastery year."

"And did I show up for that?"

Of course not. I could see the answer on his face.

"Hours later, I saw you as I was making my way to my room," he said. "I was . . . a bit unsteady. You were kind enough to help me upstairs."

"To *my* room?"

He only lifted one brow, which seemed connected to the matching corner of his mouth.

We would certainly be talking about *that* in more detail later. But in less than two hours, I was meant to help a professor I couldn't remember meeting with a class I couldn't remember anything about, and despite my apprehension and need to understand as much as possible, as soon as possible, the rumbling of my stomach reminded me that I hadn't yet eaten.

There didn't appear to be so much as an apple core or crust of bread in my room.

"What was I researching?" I sank into the chair in front of the simple wooden plank forming my desk. There were so many stacks of parchment that I hardly knew where to begin. What to read first. Which was why it took me at least a minute to realize he hadn't answered.

I twisted in my chair to find Wilder watching me with an oddly pensive look, and for a second, I was surprised by the strong resemblance to his brother. Part of that was the silence. Even when we were children, Desmond had been much more likely to make me wait for his reply. To give me a chance to think of an answer myself. To almost *demand* that of me, without a word.

Wilder, though... He'd hardly had a thought that hadn't spewed forth unbidden, whether or not it was suitable for whatever company we were in.

"What is it?" I finally asked, unnerved by his silence.

"I..." He exhaled. "I suppose I thought that if anything were likely to jog your memory, it would be your research. You were... *ambitious.*"

That felt true, and yet also a bit insulting. He said *ambitious* as if I'd been reaching for stars forever out of my grasp.

I was *driven.*

Yet I could not recall what I'd been working on. In fact, the harder I tried to remember, the further the information seemed to recede into the dark vacuum of my memory. But I knew that I'd been *driven* to get there. Wherever I'd been going.

Wilder sat forward in the chair. "So... you don't remember?"

My huff sounded exasperated. "I suspect we're both going to get very weary of you asking me that. *No,*" I confirmed, looking up from the thin sheets of parchment in my hands—a fortune in paper, such as could likely only be afforded by an institute like the Alchemary. "I do not remember, and the truth is that I can make neither heads nor tails out of anything written here."

The individual words I understood. But the sum of them?

My complete incomprehension of what had clearly been my passion sent a cold shiver up my spine.

"Amber." Wilder's voice was oddly even, as if he were trying to imply neither approval nor judgment in whatever he was about to say. "You chose Transmutation as your discipline before we even started our Proficiency year. But . . . you . . . you were trying to create the Philosopher's Stone."

"I . . ." I blinked at him. Then I gave my head a firm shake. "No. Ridiculous." I spun away from him and began sorting the sheets of parchment on my desk into stacks that felt little more than random. "The Philosopher's Stone is a *myth*. An alchemist's fairy tale."

Wilder shrugged. "You always did like a good story."

"I like good *science*. And . . ." I frowned at him. "That doesn't even make any sense. The Philosopher's Stone doesn't fall under the field of Transmutation. If it *were* possible to create the stone, it would require principles from all three disciplines."

Transmutation, Apotheosis, and Panacea.

"But it *isn't* possible," I continued. "So, I was . . . what? Trying to bring a fable to life?"

"Maybe." Wilder finally stood and snatched a stack of parchment out of my hands before I could crumple it in frustration. He grinned down at me, and though his back was to the light from the window, his eyes seemed to sparkle with amusement. "Maybe it *is* impossible. And yet, it certainly isn't boring."

"Unlike Apotheosis," I muttered, thinking of stern-looking Desmond and his devastatingly uninteresting academic pursuits.

Wilder laughed. "You said that to his face, when he told us what discipline he'd chosen."

I found that thought oddly comforting; it seemed to mean that I hadn't changed, fundamentally. That I was still the same person I'd been the day before, even if I couldn't remember becoming that person.

And if I were still the same person, there was hope that my memories and skills could be recovered. That I could still accomplish the goal I'd set for myself long before I'd truly understood what life and work at the Alchemary would be like.

That I could succeed where my mother had failed.

Before I could interpret the bitter taste that thought left in my mouth, a melodic tone sounded through the room, echoing from under the door and through the open shutters.

It was the clock tower. Not the big one in the Seminary, though that was no doubt also ringing, across campus. We were hearing the smaller one built into the center of the Dormitory itself, facing the interior courtyard.

It rang again and again, until I'd counted twelve chimes.

Noon. I had one hour until class. One hour to come to as much of an understanding as possible about alchemy in general and my research specifically. The urgent, hollow feeling in my belly made all of that feel impossible.

"Wilder." I turned away from the window. "I've identified the Refectory, but . . . can I afford to eat?" I hadn't found any currency among my belongings.

His smile was very kind, and a little sad. "Yes, of course. Admission to the Alchemary includes both room and board, at no upfront cost. Though as alumni we will both be expected to contribute to the institution someday, either as staff researchers, like Desmond, or through donations."

Those donations, I knew, were not purely tokens of generosity. An Alchemary-accredited alchemist who practiced outside of the institution itself, as my mother had, would only be granted permission to fly the Alchemary's seal in exchange for those yearly donations. The seal was a great advantage, but it wasn't cheap.

"And do I just . . . show up at the Refectory?"

"Of course—you're starving," he said, frowning. "I am, too. They'll be serving the midday meal now, but . . ." Wilder's focus settled on me with an assessing weight. "Are you sure you're up to that? People will ask questions, especially considering that before this morning, you never missed a single class. Have you . . ."

He cleared his throat. "Have you decided what you want to tell people? How *much* you want to tell them?"

In fact, I hadn't even considered the issue. Nor had I considered how I would react when strangers called me by name and expected to be recognized. How terribly rude would I seem, if I couldn't name a single person standing in front of me?

"Could you possibly go eat, and bring something small back for me? Perhaps . . . pocket a roll from your plate? Or an apple?"

Wilder snorted. "Those huge gears in your brain will only turn on real food; you've told me that more than once." He stood and leaned down to kiss my forehead, a gesture that reminded me of our adolescence, even if his lips felt warmer than I remembered. Even if they lingered longer.

Even if my hand wanted to reach for his, just to feel its warmth.

"I'll tell the staff you're ill and ask them to pack you a proper meal."

Wilder peered out the window briefly and then turned toward my door. He looked relieved as he headed out on his mission, and truth be told, I envied his quest for food, whereas I could only turn back to the pile of largely incomprehensible notebooks and stacks of parchment. The only thing I truly recognized among them was my own handwriting.

As far as I could tell, *I* had written every single word of this sizable collection of theorems, axioms, theses, charts full of data, and innumerable, indecipherable alchemical formulas and notations.

It was *months'* worth of research. Maybe years.

Was this standard? Had Wilder accumulated a similar pile of original research over his course of studies? That seemed difficult to believe of the Wilder Gregory I'd grown up with. It also seemed like quite a lot for any student just starting their Mastery year, considering my classmates had *just* moved into their dedicated lab spaces.

How could I have already amassed such a body of work?

You were... ambitious. Wilder's worlds floated back to me, a newly created memory, and for a moment, I worried that I'd lose that one as well. That I might lie down for a nap and wake up missing even *more* of my life.

I shoved that fear aside. It was counterproductive, and I had no time to waste.

The logical conclusion, based on Wilder's assessment of my ambition and the evidence of it in my own handwriting, was that I'd started my Mastery-year independent research project earlier than most. *Very* early.

The Philosopher's Stone.

A skeptical huff exploded from deep in my soul. I might as well have been trying to reverse time. Or bring my mother back from the dead. Surely I hadn't worked to get into the Alchemary—to get to the top of my class—only to waste my time on a mythical object.

But the records—what little I could comprehend of them—seemed very serious. Very organized.

Driven.

I sorted the papers into separate stacks of charts, graphs, and data sets. One of known theorems and principles. One stack of theories and brainstorms, words packed densely onto every page, so that hardly a glimpse of parchment could be seen through scratchy strokes of ink, even in the margins, where my handwriting trailed vertically in addendums as meandering as the print itself.

But then I realized the pages were marked with a somewhat complicated numerical code, and I reorganized them all chronologically so I could experience my work in the order I'd done it, allowing me to learn along with Past Amber, as she hopefully explained her thoughts and theories in the order she'd come up with them. Progressing in complexity and difficulty.

As I stared at the stacks, leaning into the flickering light of the desktop lamp, my gaze landed on the small wooden chest I'd been using as a paperweight. It was no longer than my forearm. The hinged top was slightly arched, with a simple clasp on the front.

A warm tightness spread beneath my rib cage as an old memory settled into place. The chest had belonged to my mother. When I was little, she'd kept her most valuable and difficult-to-acquire alchemical components inside, in carefully corked and labeled vials and bottles. So that was what I expected to find when I opened the latch and lifted the lid.

Instead, I found only two things: a ring with a single lustrous, clear gem, and a small book of parchment bound with a soft leather cover.

The ring was a simple gold band, the stone distinctive for its size and its round shape with few, large planes.

Rose cut. The words echoed through my mind. The rose cut prized luster over glitter, though I had no idea how I knew that.

Curious, I tried the ring on, but while it was too big for my smallest finger, it was too small for the others.

It must have been my mother's. If it were a diamond, that thought would feel ridiculous. My parents had never been wealthy. But this was almost certainly lead glass, produced through an alchemical process of the sort my mother had had a particular knack for, which she would occasionally make and sell to women in our village who could not afford precious stones. I had no memory of her wearing this piece, but I'd discovered after her death that there were several things I hadn't known about her.

Holding the ring gave me a vague feeling of nostalgia. I missed her *enormously.*

The book was plain by the standards of any library volume—I knew that, though I couldn't recall having been in the Alchemary's library—still, it was quite an expensive personal possession.

My hands shook as I lifted it, noting that its pages formed a thickness equal to two of my fingers. It felt . . . important. Like that feeling I'd had earlier, that there was something I was forgetting. Something beyond the bulk of my recent memories.

I flipped carefully through the pages, expecting to find instructions or theories. I expected the book to be an alchemical text I'd borrowed from the library or from one of my professors—something I could study as I worked to catch up with my classmates and recover lost knowledge.

But the book was not what I'd expected, in several ways. First, nearly one-third of the pages were blank; it was a journal, not a textbook. And oddly, while I recognized the curves and truncations particular to my own handwriting, I could not recognize the language I'd written in.

I knew some of the letters, but others appeared foreign. Some of the symbols were just that—not letters, truly, and not numbers, but some other form of notation.

Given that I had written the contents—of that, I had no doubt—I should be able to understand it. So why . . .

A firm knock echoed against the door. I dropped the journal on my desk and leapt up to answer it, expecting to see Wilder, his arms loaded with food.

Instead, I found Desmond standing alone on the dark landing.

Throughout history, no pursuit has both confounded and enraptured any branch of academic inquiry like the effort to create the Philosopher's Stone.

Despite its name, the Stone, should it ever be produced, is no more likely to take the form of a rock or a crystal than that of a fluid or powder, and though most alchemists are reluctant to speculate about its form or appearance, they understand well what humanity stands to gain from its creation.

The Philosopher's Stone will harness the ability to transform any material into its most elevated state of existence. While it is most often sought as a means of transforming base metals into silver and gold, thus furnishing its bearer with virtually unlimited wealth, the alchemical magnum opus would also be capable of curing illness, of extending life, and potentially of purifying the human soul . . .

–from *The Unfaltering Quest for the Philosopher's Stone*,
by Betta Gifford

Five

"I hope you've come to apologize," I said, one hand on the doorjamb to block Desmond's path. Barging into my room once was one time too many.

His eyes narrowed at me, and the lantern from the landing half a floor down caught his irises, which flared red-brown in the light. "Assuredly *not.* I don't expect you to be happy about what I said to the Bluehelm, but I certainly expect you to respect my opinion."

I glared up at him. "Desmond, why on earth would I respect an opinion intended to see me exiled from the institute I've dreamed of attending since I was a child?"

He looked as frustrated as I felt. And more than a little offended. "Because it was a logical recommendation, based on an honest assessment of your capabilities." His irritation intensified, until I somehow felt both angry with him and ashamed of myself in equal measure. "We may seldom agree, but we've always been able to respectfully *disagree,*" he said, and the deep, stern quality of his voice—an oddly *personal* sort of censure—triggered an unexpected flush just beneath my skin. "We've always been able to appreciate each other as rational individuals. For the most part."

My brows rose as I stared up at him. "What, may I ask, would the lesser part look like?"

He scowled over my shoulder, scanning the room behind me. "You have been known, on occasion, to indulge a less-than-rational impulse."

Oh. *Wilder.*

"I'm alone." I pushed the door all the way open to support my claim. Not because it was any of his business, but because I was already quite weary of feeling caught between the Gregory brothers. I'd played peacemaker and tiebreaker for half of my childhood, and I had no intention of reprising that role as an adult.

"In that case, may I come in?"

"Are you prepared to apologize?"

His scowl darkened. "The Amber Fallbrook I knew as of yesterday would never have asked me to."

"I'm *not that Amber*!" Frustration spilled up from my soul like a geyser. "I don't even know who she was! I don't know who *you* are. Not *this* version of you, anyway." I glanced over his formal, asymmetrical cape, across the broad expanse of his shoulders, but then my gaze snagged on his obviously trim and powerful torso, and heat gathered in my face.

My focus snapped back up to his eyes.

He looked . . . not quite puzzled by my reaction, but certainly fascinated. As if I were a solution suspended over a flame on his laboratory station, and he was perfectly content to study my transformation.

To watch me . . . simmer.

"I cannot say what my most recent experience of you was, before this morning," I continued, desperate to drag my thoughts back on track. "Not precisely, anyway. But it would certainly be from before you left for the Alchemary, four years ago. I know you as a spindly twenty-year-old boy, still growing into his height and more than ready to stretch his wings and soar free from his little brother and the tiresome girl from across the way. Those memories feel aged, but I have no more current knowledge of . . . who you've become. And yet somehow, you're now . . ."

A *man*. Fully grown, with a man's broad, powerful proportions, and an unfamiliar glint of entitlement shining in his eyes. But I couldn't say any of that aloud.

"You're now basically a professor, at the best alchemy university in the world, and—"

"I'm an alchemist," he interrupted. "A second-year staff researcher, in the Apotheosis division."

"I know. Wilder told me you're trying to perfect the human form."

He actually smiled, just a little. "Not the physical form, specifically. And not from an aesthetic perspective. That would be purely subjective. I'm working toward a functional efficiency of physique and intellect that—" He held up a hand and shook his head, swallowing the rest of his explanation. "My work is not relevant to this situation."

It was more interesting than I'd expected, however. He wasn't trying to make people pretty. He was trying to make people *better*.

"My point is that I don't know you anymore," I insisted, forcing myself back on topic yet again. "And if you think you know me, then your hypothesis is deeply flawed. I don't know the girl I was yesterday, and you don't know the one I am today."

Desmond's eyes widened, and for a second, he seemed truly startled. As if some gear in his brain had slipped into a new and unexpected formation. As if I had changed shape, right there in front of him.

"No, I suppose I don't," he said, his voice a bit softer than before. "But what I *do* know is that if I'm discovered loitering outside your room, no amount of rational explanation will be able to silence the grinding of the Alchemary rumor mill."

I crossed my arms over the front of my cloak. "Well then. If I can't convince you I have the ability and the work ethic to thrive at the Alchemary, I suppose you'd better go."

Desmond exhaled slowly. "You should not be here, but that has nothing to do with ability or with work ethic." His voice was oddly gruff, gaze trained on me with an intensity that made me wonder if he could see straight through my eyes into memories I had no access to. "In fact, I greatly respect everything you've accomplished. That's why—"

"What have I accomplished?"

"Pardon?" His shoulders tensed, hands hidden at his spine.

"Wilder told me about the Philosopher's Stone," I admitted, and Desmond looked so startled that I wanted to stuff the words back into my mouth.

Of *course* he hadn't known what I was researching. Why *would* I have told a respected professional alchemist that I was wasting my time and the school's resources chasing after a myth instead of pursuing more practical and achievable goals?

Wait. . . .

A bonfire exploded behind my cheeks. "Wilder was joking, wasn't he? Playing a prank on the poor girl with amnesia, convincing me that I'd been researching something so *utterly* ridiculous . . ."

I glanced back at my desk. At the papers stacked there.

"And here I've been, trying to understand all this, assuming it pertains to a professional interest in the *Philosopher's Stone,* of all things!" I spun to face the window, hoping the ocean breeze would cool my face. "He'll consider amnesia a *mercy* by the time I'm done with him."

Desmond made a strange sound deep in his throat, and I turned to see his expression shifting rapidly as his thoughts seemed to kaleidoscope. Finally, he settled on sympathy. Which irked me on a bone-deep level.

"Wilder wasn't lying." His mouth quirked up for an instant. "Though I can understand why you'd draw that conclusion. My brother *was* serious once. But then he recovered."

I laughed, and Desmond looked surprised. Almost nostalgic. And I wondered if, in that moment, he was seeing the Amber he remembered from childhood.

How different was she from the girl he'd known yesterday? From the girl I was now?

Curiosity made a mockery of my willpower, and I sighed. "You may come inside, if you'll answer some questions."

Yet Desmond hesitated in the doorway, as if the price might be more than he was willing to pay. After a moment, though, he stepped over the threshold, almost formally. As if he were stepping into another world.

I retreated to put space between us, and the back of my foot collided with something on the floor. As I felt myself tipping, my arms shot out, flailing for balance. A startled sound leaked from my throat, and . . .

A hand closed over my wrist, arresting my fall.

In the time it had taken me to lose my balance, Desmond had somehow crossed the room and seized my arm.

I stared up at him, stunned by his speed and his quick thinking, and suddenly I became distinctly aware of the warm iron of his grip.

"Thank you," I said, righting myself.

He dropped my arm as if my skin had scalded him.

I glanced down to see what I had tripped over and found a leather satchel, which I'd only vaguely noticed in my original perusal of the space. "Um . . . are you familiar with my work?" I asked, nudging the satchel out of the way with my foot. "With my research project, I mean?"

"You'd have a difficult time finding someone here who is unfamiliar with the Philosopher's Stone." He glanced at the bed, then looked away quickly. His attention skirted over my desktop, as if its contents held no interest for him at all, then finally landed again on me.

"That isn't what I asked. Did my work show any promise? Was it . . . good?"

He frowned, studying my face, and I had no idea what he saw there. But then he exhaled, and his gaze . . . hardened. "You've earned your place as a student, Amber. But that doesn't mean you deserve it now."

Sparks fired through my synapses, arcing through my soul like flaming arrows of indignation. "That is *precisely* what it means."

His jaw tightened, but he did not argue.

"We don't get along, do we?" I leaned against the edge of my desk, irked that he'd grown so tall and so broad. That this Desmond didn't match the one in my memory. "Maybe we do respect each other as 'rational individuals,' but you don't like me as a person, do you?"

Something dark shifted behind his eyes.

"Do I like *you*?" I demanded.

He crossed his arms over his broad chest, and his cape fell forward with the motion, hiding the left half of his torso. But it might as well have covered his face, for all I could read of his expression. "Other than Wilder, I'm not sure you care about anyone in the world." His voice was hard, each syllable the harsh grind of a blade against a whetstone. "Except for yourself."

His arrow found its mark, and I flinched with the impact. "What happened between us?" I blinked up at him, searching his gaze for the boy I'd once known. "We were friends, back in Innswood. True, you were an arrogant bore, but—"

"*I* was arrogant?"

"But you weren't *cruel*," I finished.

"I'm not trying to have you removed from the Alchemary out of *cruelty*," he snapped.

Startled, I gripped the edge of the desk to steady myself. "You're still trying to get me expelled?" What did that mean? He was trying to get the Bluehelm to change her mind? Trying to prove I didn't belong?

"Dismissed. Not expelled," he corrected. "This isn't a penalty."

"But you're still trying to—"

"I'm doing what's *right*."

"For *whom*?" I demanded, anger sparking in my veins like a lit fuse. "If I've earned my place here, who are *you* to decide I don't deserve it?"

He exhaled, nostrils flaring. Teeth clenched. "I know you can't possibly understand what I'm about to say, if you don't remember your time here—"

"If?" I stared at him, incredulous. Bruised by his skepticism.

"—but I don't owe you an explanation."

I could only blink up at him, stunned silent, while my thoughts raced in circles.

The temerity!

"Is this about Wilder?" I asked. "It's *quite* evident that you didn't like finding him in my bed, and—"

"Enough!" Desmond growled.

"Am I not good enough for your brother, or is he not good enough for me? What, exactly, is your objection to our—"

"That is *enough*!" he snarled through clenched teeth, hands fisted at his sides. "It isn't your fault that you don't know what you're talking about, but that doesn't change the truth of the matter."

"So *tell* me what we're talking about."

For a moment, he looked thoroughly, vengefully tempted to do precisely that. But then his mouth snapped shut. I could practically see him turning the key in the vault, locking away whatever he knew of my pre-amnesia existence, because of some discord I could not remember.

Footsteps and the rustle of clothing drew my gaze to the door as it opened. Wilder stepped inside, holding a cloth-wrapped bundle tucked beneath one arm. From it emanated the scents of fresh bread, strong cheese, and some sort of roasted fowl.

An errant dark blond wave fell across his forehead. His gaze flicked from me to his brother, who towered over me now, dominating the center of my private chamber with nothing more than the space his broad form required and the words still echoing in my head.

"Well, I see Desmond has been spreading his usual good cheer." Wilder sounded positively merry, despite the obvious tension. "What have I missed?"

"Not a thing." I stared boldly up at Desmond, who held my gaze with a steely-eyed one of his own. "Your brother was just leaving."

Six

"Do I know any of them?"

I scanned the quadrangle stretched out before us: a rolling lawn accented with artistically trimmed shrubs, geometrically shaped flower beds, and meandering stone-paved walkways. Moving across the space were half a dozen young people dressed in variations of my student uniform. Most wore gray dresses or slacks, but the occasional flash of a blue belt, a green ribbon, or a rust-colored vest caught my eye as well.

Wilder tucked his arm through mine, bumping against my satchel as we headed down one of the stone paths, and the gesture felt both affectionate and bit... intentional. As if the display of affection were signaling something.

I couldn't decide how I should feel about that. We'd spent half our childhood scampering through Innswood arm in arm, but this felt different. Our relationship had clearly matured along with our bodies, and fifteen-year-old Amber would have been thrilled to see Wilder looking at me then the way he was looking at me now—as more than a playmate. Or at least, as a different *kind* of playmate.

And the truth was that amnesiac Amber was more than a little thrilled as well. Wilder was confident and charming, and his eyes sparkled a brilliant shade of blue. His attention felt like the warmth of the sun on my face.

But the cavernous pit of my memory was difficult to bridge. How had we evolved from friends into lovers? What was the catalyst for that transformation? Had he suddenly looked at me differently one morning, over tea? Had our hands brushed in the tight confines of a shared lab space?

His attention followed mine, flitting from face to face across the quadrangle, his arm warm in my grip. "They're underclassmen."

"All of them?" I asked.

He nodded. "I don't know the Fundamentals-year students yet. And I must say, they look young. But I know most of the Proficiency cohort."

"As do I, I suppose?"

He considered the question for a moment. "At a glance, certainly. But I'd be shocked if you knew many of their names. You've always been less social than I."

"Speaking of which..." I tightened my grip on Wilder's arm. "Why does Desmond hate me?"

I caught his quizzical look from the corner of my eye, but his steps did not falter. "He *does* seem a bit cross. But I'm fairly certain that's his natural state, at least since he graduated."

"He wasn't like that as a student?"

Wilder shrugged. "He was in his Mastery year when we were in Fundamentals, and he had little time or patience for us. But he does seem much grouchier since he joined the Alchemary staff. My conclusion has long been that adults have no time for fun."

I glanced up at him. "Wilder, *we're* adults."

He shook his head solemnly. "We're merely *of age*. There's a difference."

I considered his theory as we turned right onto a north pathway, headed toward the Seminary with its impressive central clock tower. "But he seemed quite specifically convinced that I don't deserve to be here. Can you shed any light on that matter?"

Wilder stopped abruptly and turned to face me. "Amber, you are the most gifted student in our cohort. Quite possibly the most gifted student in a generation. If Desmond is angry, it's because that's what they used to say about *him,* before *you* came along."

The Seminary—the academic heart of the campus—was an imposing building, both inside and out. It was three stories of brownish stone, with a spiraling turret staircase on each end, both capped in sloping, round copper roofs that had long ago oxidized into a green patina.

Inside, the first floor boasted large lecture halls, meeting rooms, and the library; the second floor held smaller classrooms, professors' offices, and conference rooms; and the third floor was taken up with various laboratory spaces and storage.

Wilder led me left from the entrance, past the central split staircase and into the western wing of the building. My heart thumped as we came to a stop outside an imposing set of doors. They were tall and arched at the top, made of heavy, formal carved panels of a dark-stained wood, standing open like the gates of hell. The buzz of voices from inside said I was among the last to arrive. And that the Fundamentals-year students were very excited to attend their first class at the Alchemary.

I'd likely felt the same way, two years before. But today, I felt... unqualified. How was I supposed to assist a professor with a class I couldn't remember taking?

"You'll be great," Wilder whispered as a girl in a black cloak brushed past us and through the open doorway.

"How do you know?"

He grinned down at me. "You're always great. It's rather annoying, actually."

I laughed.

"And anyway, the bar's not high," he added. "When we took Intro, our TA pretty much just graded papers."

"Ms. Fallbrook!"

I spun, startled, to find a middle-aged man heading down the hallway toward us from the western staircase, his long black cape billowing behind him. The professor—what else could he be?—had brown skin, prominent freckles, and tight, dark curls, shot through with streaks of gray.

"Professor Robards," I said, taking a chance when he stopped beside me, in the threshold of the classroom. "How nice to see you."

He gave me a pleasant wink. "Professors have no control over which teaching assistants are assigned to them, you know. But I made a point of mentioning your name every time I had occasion to speak to the Bluehelm's assistant."

"How very kind of you," I murmured.

His focus shifted to Wilder, and he stood a bit straighter. "Mr. Gregory. I hope you are well. *And* that you're not intending to follow Ms. Fallbrook into my class."

"Indeed, I am not." Wilder grimaced. "Once was plenty for me."

"I assure you the feeling is quite mutual," Professor Robards grumbled.

I stifled a smile, and Wilder bumped me with his arm.

The professor pulled his overstuffed satchel higher on his shoulder and gestured for me to precede him into the classroom. "After you, then?"

With one last glance at Wilder, who waggled his eyebrows encouragingly at me, I stepped into a large, bright lecture hall dominated by tall, narrow windows and dark, heavy wooden furnishings.

Silence descended, and three dozen wide-eyed faces stared down at me from several rows of tiered bench seating.

"That one's yours," Professor Robards whispered, gesturing at a small wooden desk to one side of the room, angled to face both the students and the substantial podium at the center of the front portion of the classroom. The front of the podium was carved with the Alchemary creed—*Mind, Matter, Spirit*—in the familiar triangle shape. Behind the podium, a long framed slate board was mounted on the wall, dusty from recently erased chalk markings.

I sat at the small desk and opened my satchel to retrieve a notebook and a quill, while he took up his position behind the podium.

"Good afternoon!" Professor Robards began, and his voice, with its deep timbre and cadence of gravitas, felt instantly, comfortingly familiar, even if I could not actually remember having heard it. "My name is Lionel Robards, and this semester I will be teaching you Introductory Theories of Alchemy in a class called 'Intro' by most of my students. To my left—your right—you will find our class teaching assistant, Amber Fallbrook, who is currently the top-ranked member of the Mastery-year cohort."

Top . . . ?

My face warmed. I'd been told I was *a* top student, but no one had actually mentioned my ranking.

"—should feel honored to have been admitted into the Alchemary," Professor Robards continued, and I realized I'd missed part of what he was saying. "But at the same time, you should feel the weight of expectation. Of responsibility.

"There are thirty-six of you now, at the beginning of your Fundamentals year. I want you to look around at these faces, because at the start of your Proficiency year, there will be only twenty-four. And at the beginning of your Mastery year? You." He pointed to a boy in the second row, who wore a rust-colored scarf beneath his cloak.

"Twelve, Professor Robards."

The professor nodded. "That is correct. One-third of the faces you see in this room will make it to year three. And only a handful of those will pass the trials and be invited to join the Alchemary." He glanced around the room. "Only the most gifted and hardworking among you will become my colleagues."

Benches groaned as students shifted in their seats.

I shared their discomfort.

"So! Let's begin with the basics. With the most important question: What is alchemy? Other than the most powerful and difficult to learn of the arcane studies?" Professor Robards stepped out from behind the podium, his eyes alight with passion for the topic. "There is a force in the universe that propels it toward change. Constant, unceasing change, of every sort, and in every direction. We do not know what that force is. Though we can see it at work—though we can collect and analyze data based on what we observe—we do not understand that force itself. Part of what the Alchemary seeks to do is gain that understanding. What we know so far is that nature's tendency in the face of change is toward *entropy*. Toward chaos and destruction."

Robards slowly paced before the front row as he spoke, turning frequently to eye a seemingly random student. "You can see this for yourself, everywhere you look. Living beings—plants, animals, people—die, and they decompose. Their physical matter breaks down into chaotic states, into particles too small to discern with the human eye. Though you cannot see or feel it, this planet is slowly slipping beyond the sun's influence, and the brightest minds in the world agree that someday—our children's children will be dust in their graves by then—our planet will be too far away from the sun to benefit from its life-giving light and warmth. This chaos is clear in broken bones and shattered crockery. In quiet, private discord and in raucous arguments at the emperor's court, as well as in riots among the general population. It is present in everything, at every level, visible and invisible. Sometimes it is seen, sometimes only felt.

"But that trend toward entropy is as real as the stone beneath your feet. This is because disorder and destruction are easier to accomplish than order and creation, in the same way that it is easier to let a stone roll downhill than to compel it *up* that same hill."

Professor Robards paused dramatically, and though I already knew much of what he was explaining—my mother had taught me basic alchemical theory when I was a child—I found myself hanging on his every word. "Alchemy seeks to pull that stone uphill. To guide nature away from entropy and toward order. To nudge everything it touches toward a higher state of being.

"Alchemists have the ability—the *responsibility*—to influence that natural force of change. To seek to slow and to guide it. To reverse entropy, so that life—on any of those levels, visible or invisible, physical or mental, global or personal—can progress instead of breaking itself down. Alchemy seeks to elevate life, in all its aspects, toward a greater form."

Apotheosis, Desmond's discipline, focused alchemy's goals specifically on the human mind and body. Transmutation, which I'd evidently chosen, sought to transform inorganic materials into a higher state of being. And Panacea, which was Wilder's focus, worked to heal ailments and illnesses and to ameliorate organic material of a nonhuman origin, including both plants and animals.

"How do we accomplish this, you're probably wondering?" Another dramatic pause from Robards, and this time his smile developed slowly, like a blossom opening. "Alchemy can distill that natural element of change into a physical form: into a substance called *beyn*. Once it has been distilled and purified, beyn can be added to any alchemical formula in ways devised by the scientists in residence here at the Alchemary. And what do those formulas make?"

A girl in the fourth row raised her hand.

"Yes!" Robards called on her enthusiastically, his entire arm pointed in her direction.

"Elixirs."

"Indeed! As you know if you've done your preparatory reading, *elixir* is the general term for any alchemical compound. Within that category, we have potions, decoctions, tinctures, ointments and liniments, serums and tonics, embrocations, and solutions, all of which fall into several categories of strength, called 'grades,' which require escalating levels of knowledge and skill to prepare. How many grades are there?"

Four, I thought from my desk.

"Four!" a boy in the highest row called out. "Beginner, intermediate, professional, and elite."

"That is correct," Robards said. "But next time, wait to be called on."

The rest of the class snickered.

"Various elixirs can make your food taste better and slow its decomposition. They can treat illness and temporarily change a person's disposition. Alchemy can turn base metals into bronze and silver—someday, some believe—into gold! It can reverse some of the stages of life—butterfly into cocoon?—or slow them down."

Adrenaline spiked in my veins, and my blood rushed faster. That was what I wanted. I'd *always* wanted to be one of the people making those marvels happen. Changing the world.

I wanted to harness forces of chaos and repurpose them for my own will. *That* was why I had come to the Alchemary.

"All of that takes experience, and skill, and a very specially trained thought process. But it's all possible! And you will learn that process here at the Alchemary!"

The students broke into applause, and I didn't realize I'd joined them until I stabbed myself in the palm with the point of my own quill.

Seven

After class, I joined the flow of students headed down the broad main corridor toward the foyer of the Seminary, where Wilder waited near the bottom of the wide, split central staircase. He stood with a girl around my age and a guy with rigid rust-colored cuffs affixed to his sleeves, in the style of the kingdom of Falkrest, Aethermere's seafaring neighbor to the north.

Wilder laughed at something the Falkrestor said, tossing his dark blond hair, and my heart caught in my throat as I watched him. He seemed so at ease here, among some of the sharpest young minds in the world, but that didn't surprise me. I'd always known how gifted he was.

But I got an odd feeling as I watched him, like maybe Desmond wasn't the only one who'd changed during the years my amnesia had devoured. *I* had changed, clearly. And while Wilder still seemed charming and outgoing—as welcome in any group as he'd always been—something felt different about the way he conducted himself now. Maybe it was because the stakes were higher than in our home village.

Or maybe I simply wasn't yet accustomed to seeing him here, in this place where *I* wanted to belong, among strangers who shouldn't have felt like strangers.

Maybe I wasn't accustomed to sharing him with the world.

When he turned and saw me, he smiled. He said something to

his friends, who glanced my way, then headed up the stairs with the crowd, leaving Wilder and me alone in the foyer.

"How'd it go?" he asked as I came to a stop at his side.

"It was actually kind of amazing." I mounted the first step, bringing myself to eye level with him, and my breath caught at the intimacy of the new perspective. At how immediate his gaze felt from mere inches away. "Professor Robards is very passionate about alchemy," I said, rushing ahead to disguise my sudden nerves. "And I suspect his class will be a great refresher for me. I'm really hoping it'll trigger my memories of concepts I've already learned."

"That's about all it did for you the first time," Wilder said as we began climbing the stairs. "Considering that your mother taught you most of the base-level stuff when you were a kid."

"Well, a reminder can't hurt. He's starting them with the history of signature notation. Next week, I'll have thirty-six essays to grade on the subject, and after that, they're expected to start developing their own notation styles."

"That'll make their work difficult to read for a while, until they decide exactly how long their flourishes and how tight their swirls should be."

"Oh? Is there an objective standard?"

"Not really." He grinned down at me as we reached the mid-level landing. "The length of a flourish varies by individual, and they're all unique. Though some are more noteworthy than others."

I blinked up at him as innocently as I could manage. "Would it be too bold of me to inquire about the span of *your* flourish?"

Wilder's brows arched. Then he gave a mock frown. "I blame that question on your recent memory loss." He leaned close to whisper into my ear. "Before today, you were as familiar with the impressive span of my flourish as I am with the devastatingly tight coil of your swirl."

My face flamed, but I had only myself to blame for the trajectory that led to this double entendre.

Wilder laughed again at my expression, his head thrown back, blue eyes glittering in the light of a wall-mounted torch. "You're a much saucier conversationalist today than you were yesterday."

"I suppose I'll have to take your word for that."

We passed a couple dozen students in the second-floor hallway, clustered in groups of two and three, outside of various classrooms.

"Wilder!" A girl with a blue ribbon braided through her pale hair fell into step on his other side, ignoring me entirely. "Are you free tonight? I was hoping to discuss something with you." Her gaze slid my way. "Privately."

A bolt of jealousy bristled the tiny hairs at the back of my neck, but Wilder didn't miss a step. "I'll make time. Find me in the Mastery student lab, after the evening meal," he practically whispered.

She squeezed his arm, then pivoted and returned to her friends.

"What was—"

Before I could finish my question, or decide how possessive I should be of his time and attention, a boy broke from his friend group as we passed and began walking backward in front of us, evidently unconcerned about colliding with a classmate.

"Amber, you're looking well," he said.

"Thank you. I—"

He turned to Wilder, dismissing me entirely. "How was your summer? Were you able to perfect that decoction we discussed in the spring?"

"I had limited resources at home, but I did make some progress," Wilder said, his voice lowered into that same near whisper. "Give me a week to take advantage of the lab space here and I'll have something for you."

"Good man!" the boy declared with a wide smile. Then he clapped Wilder on the shoulder and disappeared down the hall behind us.

"What was that about?" I asked.

"Later," Wilder murmured, coming to a stop in front of an open set of tall doors at the east end of the hall. "This is us."

From the room beyond, several voices were engaged in vibrant discussions, and to my utter frustration, I did not recognize a single one.

"Deep breath," Wilder whispered when I could only stare into the room full of strangers. Then he tucked his arm into mine again and subtly tugged me over the threshold into a central aisle between two rows of double-occupancy desks.

"Wilder!" A boy with squarish spectacles perched on the narrow bridge of his nose stood from a chair to my right, then wedged himself into the aisle, directly in our path. "Where were you two this morning? Keryth said she heard voices from Amber's room, then she saw you come out of the Conservatory after class. None of my business, of course, but it sounds like you both had *quite* a summer." But his eyes seemed less delighted with that prospect than his smile would otherwise indicate.

Had I? Had Wilder and I spent the summer in Innswood, with our families? Was that when we'd crossed the line from friendship into . . . my bed?

Was everyone else as surprised by that as Desmond had clearly been?

"You're right, Petyr," Wilder said. "That *is* none of your business." But then he winked, and the result was that rather than brushing off the question, he seemed to be hinting that he and I shared some scandalous secret he could not *possibly* divulge.

My face flamed, and Petyr's brows rose as Wilder led me past him, headed toward an unoccupied table halfway up on the right side.

"Petyr Lorena," he whispered. But then he offered no more intelligence on our inquisitive, bespectacled classmate, because as we took our seats, the curly-headed girl in front of Wilder turned to face us, one arm draped over the back of her chair, her stiff blue cuffs standing out against her white sleeve at a distinctive, pointed angle.

"Wilder," she said, then her green eyes focused on me. "Amber."

"Yoslyn Savva!" he greeted her, and I got the distinct impression that he'd said her full name for my benefit. "How was your summer?"

"Abysmally dull," she said. "There's nothing to do in my hometown, and my family is entirely unimpressed that I've made it to the Mastery year. My mother is making me pretend I'm apprenticing with a cousin in the country, learning to compound aromatics." She rolled those green eyes. "You're all so lucky." Her gaze flickered toward me again, then back to Wilder. "I don't suppose you have anything I could drop into their tea, do you? Something to make them more accepting of alchemy as my chosen path? At least while I'm stuck there with them?"

Wilder gave her a sympathetic smile. "That seems a bit extreme, but if you still feel that way going into the winter holiday, come see me." He paused with a glance my way. "If it makes you feel any better, not everyone in Aethermere approves of Alchemy either."

She turned to me, puzzled. "Wasn't your mother an alchemist?"

"Amber's mom was a third-year washout," a new voice said, and as my temper bloomed hot behind my sternum, I looked past Wilder to see a familiar girl settling into a chair across the aisle, a shiny green ribbon braided through her blond hair. She was the classmate who'd called out to me that morning from across the quadrangle. The one I'd fled, on instinct, though I couldn't even recall her name. "But her father," the girl continued, "is a Toolkeeper."

"Keryth," Wilder said with a scowl. "May I remind you that *you're* responsible for what spews from the geyser on the front of your face? Make better choices."

She waved off his rebuke as her gaze slid to me, her smile just a tad too wide. "Amber knows I mean no harm. *Most* of us are going to wash out this year."

Yoslyn squirmed in her seat, and Wilder looked distinctly uncomfortable, but Keryth was right. According to my mother, no more than three students from one cohort had ever been invited to join the Alchemary as staff members or instructors, and some years, none were invited at all. Because some years, no one passed all four trials.

Those who washed out in the third year could take the Alchemary's accreditation exam and practice off-campus, under the Alchemary seal, as my mother had. But clearly, none of my classmates wanted to truly contemplate failing one of the trials. Or being passed over by the institute that had trained us.

Being relegated to the second tier of alchemy: provincial practice.

"My point," Keryth continued, "is that Yoslyn's parents might disapprove of alchemy specifically, given her native land's affinity for aromatics." An incense-based rival art of alchemy. "But Toolkeepers reject *all* of the arcane studies." She turned to Yoslyn. "So if anyone understands how it feels for your family to utterly reject your life choices, it's Amber Fallbrook."

"And before the midterm exam, I expect you to have memorized all of the advanced formulas and to have come up with—and had officially approved!—a Mastery-year field of study in general as well as a specific project thesis. This can be an improvement upon an existing theory, an attempt to disprove an existing theory, or you may—the more ambitious of you—come up with an entirely new premise. Any questions?"

Half of the class scribbled anxiously on loose sheets of parchment; the sound of quills scratching felt both familiar and soothing. As did the knowledge that while they were all taking notes about how to *begin* their independent research projects, I'd been working on mine for at least a year.

As it turned out, the copious notes on my independent study were *not* standard among our cohort. I truly had been an extraordinary student, it seemed.

That knowledge would have brought me more comfort if I could remember any of the work I'd done. Any of the progress I'd made. If I could make even the slightest sense out of my own notes.

While she waited for replies, Professor Edmiston slid one hand into her tangle of dense silver curls and fluffed them at the root, a gesture that seemed more habitual than truly functional.

Her hair did *not* lack volume.

I stared at the sheets of parchment on the table in front of me. I'd taken extensive notes for two straight hours, covering a shameful amount of expensive parchment and draining half of the inkwell set into the front edge of the table, equidistant from my side of the shared surface and Wilder's.

I glanced at his notes and was unsurprised to see that he'd barely covered the front side of one sheet. But his work was not a proper bar against which to measure my own. As a child, he'd done the bare minimum expected of him in nearly every endeavor. He'd been forgiven for shoddily performed chores because of his charming smile, and he was generally gifted enough, academically, to perform at an average level with no effort whatsoever. A prospect that used to infuriate me on two levels.

First was the fact that since he never really studied, he had far more leisure time than I, and far more than was good for him, truth be told. And second, I found it scandalous how accomplished he could have been at just about anything, if he were to ever actually put forth a respectable effort.

I found it equally scandalous how little he cared about that.

Wilder had glided through life as an ardent underachiever, and I couldn't imagine that had changed in the past two years. Though he'd clearly performed well enough to stay at the Alchemary.

While Professor Edmiston answered questions and restated the hours when she would be available to students in her office, I glanced at the table to my left, where Keryth sat with that same young man from the quadrangle. The one with light brown skin and dark, slicked-back hair. I hadn't caught his name during class, and I couldn't see his work from where I sat. But Keryth had taken thorough notes, and the volume of her writing—though it was not as great as mine—set me at ease a bit, as it cast my own work as not entirely unreasonable.

As, perhaps, reasonable for a star student who had not lost her memory.

I *did* know the name of the quiet young woman seated in front of me and next to Yoslyn. Cressa, the Bluehelm's student aide, still wore the blue frock and rust-colored belt I'd noticed when she'd stepped into Dr. Winhoof's office that morning. She'd hardly glanced at me before taking her seat at the beginning of class, but Wilder had whispered to me that her surname was Baxter, and that she and I were acquaintances at best.

The impression I'd gotten, more from his tone than his words, was that neither she nor I was exactly considered sociable.

Cressa Baxter had taken consistent but sparse notes, and she clearly had no trouble keeping up with Professor Edmiston's lecture.

I, on the other hand . . .

I sighed softly as I stared at my parchment again. I'd scribbled madly, writing down nearly everything the instructor had said so I could study it later. So I could compare it to the notes on my desk and hopefully decode the advanced concepts, based on the more basic ones I'd taken notes on two years before.

Or maybe I could talk Wilder into explaining some of it to me.

I'd understood generally what Professor Edmiston was talking about. I knew all of the words, and I knew how to spell them. But my rudimentary understanding was insufficient to allow me comprehension of advanced-level theories.

I was quite simply not up to this level of alchemy.

And yet, as soon as I'd seen the symbols for salt, and copper, and sulfur, and lead, I'd recognized them. Writing them had felt familiar, and my hand had moved all on its own, forming curves and slashes on the page in a distinctive style that I recognized from a few of the symbols in my journal.

Signature notation.

Double entendre aside, my swirls really *were* tight. Learning to make them quickly had likely taken months of practice.

"Amber?" Wilder said, and when I looked up from the desk, I found him standing over me, his chair pushed back, his "notes" folded and tucked beneath his arm.

He hadn't bothered to bring a satchel.

"Are you ready?"

Professor Edmiston was gone, as were half of the students. Cressa glanced at me, tight reddish ringlets swishing around her head as she slid her own materials into her bag, and though a couple of our classmates seemed to be watching me curiously, she volunteered nothing of what she knew of my condition. Instead, she slung her bag over her shoulder, offered me a quick, lukewarm smile, and marched out of the room.

"Amber?"

Dread pooled cold and thick in my belly as I turned left to find Keryth frowning at me from across the center aisle, her blond braid draped over one shoulder. The young man stood at her other side, clearly ready to leave, and now that I could see him up close, I noticed his slight scruff of a beard and bright green eyes.

"Yes?" I slid my notes into my bag, careful not to crease the parchment.

"Are you well?" Keryth asked while I clawed at the brick wall of my memory, desperate to carve loose a chunk with her companion's name on it. "I don't think I've ever seen you so quiet in class. You didn't even correct Edmiston when she pointed to that vial of cinnabar and called it colcothar."

"You're criticizing her for not being rude to our professor?" Wilder asked, one brow lifted in her direction.

"Of course not," the young man behind her said. "But you must admit it's out of character." He turned to me. "And you skipped class this morning entirely."

"I'm fine," I said, wondering if it sounded awkward that I hadn't yet used his name. Panic had left me adrift in everyday conversation, trying to recall how often, under normal circumstances, people said each other's names. "I . . . overslept."

Judging by Keryth's shocked expression, complete with an openmouthed stare, I could not possibly have come up with a less believable excuse. "*You* overslept? By two hours?" Her hazel eyes narrowed. "It certainly wasn't a hangover. You didn't even come to—"

"Are those the trousers you wore last night?" the green-eyed boy interrupted, and I followed his gaze to the left hem of Wilder's slacks, where it brushed the top of his shoe beneath his unfastened cloak. "They're still stained from the ale you spilled at the Dusty Beaker."

Keryth's shock melted into a scandalized understanding as her gaze slid from Wilder to me. "*Overslept,* indeed? I'll trade my notes from this morning for your notes from last night," she said to me with another suggestive glance at Wilder.

She reached across the aisle as if she'd tuck her arm into mine and drag me off for some gossip.

"Sorry, Keryth." Wilder tugged me closer, subtly pulling me away from her. "We have plans for the afternoon."

"Plans." Keryth's smile made intimate assumptions. "Well, when you're done, you let me know if either of you want my notes." Then she tucked her arm into the green-eyed boy's arm instead and pulled him with her into the hall.

Leaving me alone in the classroom with Wilder.

I spun and punched him in the shoulder.

"Ow!" He frowned. "I just saved you from being interrogated by Keryth Malcom, who would have figured out within minutes that you have absolutely no memory of her."

"She's going to figure that out anyway. I'm assuming that none of the twelve students who've made it to Mastery year are complete idiots, though I am starting to wonder about you!"

"That's uncalled for. I am both blatantly brilliant and entirely underestimated, which is a rather difficult combination to maintain."

"You made salacious implications to Petyr, and now you've given Keryth the impression that you stayed the night in my room," I hissed, glaring up at him as I lifted the strap of my satchel over my head and onto my opposite shoulder. Innuendo between the two of us was one thing, but—

"I *did* stay the night in your room," he mock whispered. "And that secret was never going to keep. Keryth's room is the only one above yours. She clearly heard us talking this morning, then she saw me come out of the ladies' dormitory tower. And my room is right below Lennox's, in the gentlemen's tower, which means he probably knows I wasn't there last night. Eventually they would have put those two pieces of information together. And by 'eventually,' I mean in the next half hour. Because what they *think* we're sneaking off to do is what they're *actually* sneaking off to do. And have been doing for a year and a half."

I had to think about that for a second. "They're a couple? Keryth and . . . Lennox?" I put the names and faces together in my memory and waited for some sort of mental click to lock them in place.

It did not come.

"Keryth Malcom and Lennox Pettifog. They're what you might call on again, off again. And they've been on again since they came back from the summer break. Somewhat exuberantly, based on what leaks through the top half of my dormitory wall."

"And us?" I glanced at the doorway to make sure no one was hovering in the hallway, listening. "Are we *on*? Or was last night . . . an anomaly?"

Being with Wilder felt familiar and comfortable, and there was definitely chemistry. But the surprise from our classmates—and from Desmond—made me wonder if this shift in our relationship was recent.

His gaze held mine, but I got the distinct impression that his hesitation wasn't simply an effort to get the phrasing right. Rather, he seemed to be trying to assess whatever he saw . . . in me.

Finally he smiled, his expression taking on a playfully ribald tone. "Last night was definitely . . . anomalous. One might even call it a deviance."

"Is it a family trait of the Gregorys to refuse to answer a question directly, or is that specific to you and your brother?"

His smile faltered. "What did you ask Desmond?"

"I'm not answering your question until you answer mine. Are we *together*, Wilder?"

His sigh seemed to carry the weight of the world. He sank into Keryth's chair, and when I remained standing, he took my hand. For a moment, he only stared at my fingers, running one thumb over them.

I focused on the sensation. Of the feel of his skin against mine. Trying—*desperate*—to remember it.

"Amber, do you recall anything about last night? Anything at all? Even just an image or an impression?"

I looked up from our hands to find him watching me with his heart in his eyes, and it hurt me to answer. But I owed him the truth, if I was going to ask him for the same.

"No. I'm sorry, but I don't remember a thing, as badly as I'd like to."

The sadness echoing behind his eyes gutted me.

"Was that our first time?" I asked, still trying to draw the memories out. To trigger recollection with fact. "Are we a couple? Or was that just . . . the human version of a chemical reaction?"

Wilder laughed, and he looked as surprised by his own amusement as I was. "A chemical reaction?"

"You know . . . two reactants introduced into the same space, resulting in a change of energy or yielding a product. Or a . . . clearly defined result."

His smile grew. "Oh, there was a *result*. And I'd call it pretty clearly defined."

I pulled my hand from his and smacked his shoulder again, but I couldn't resist a smile.

"If last night was a chemical reaction, it was definitely exothermic," he continued.

My smile grew. "So . . . it was hot?"

"Exothermic as hell," he confirmed with a shameless grin. But it faded quickly. "Though . . . that doesn't matter. None of what happened between us before this morning matters, Amber. It . . . can't."

My frown came unbidden, the strength of my disappointment unexpected. “Why not?”

“It doesn’t matter because you don’t remember it. So, to you, it didn’t happen. And I can’t in good conscience go forward as if everything is the way it was yesterday, when you have no memory of how we got there. I . . .” He cleared his throat and settled his gaze firmly on mine. “Until you recover your memory, what matters is what happens going forward. There may very well be another chemical reaction, but first, we’ll have to”—he shrugged—“set up the whole experiment again. We can’t just repeat it, when you don’t understand all the ‘preparation’ that went into it in the first place.”

“When did you get so good at logic?” I demanded, finding it shockingly difficult not to pout.

Wilder laughed as he stood. “I told you. Blatantly brilliant and *entirely* underestimated.”

Each master alchemist is expected to develop a distinctive style of writing—their signature notation—both as a mental exercise, to keep the mind properly focused upon theories and formulas as they are developed, and as an identifying feature of their work. Ideally, future scholars will be able to identify at a glance the author of any original text based on the signature notation alone, and throughout history, many of the most recognizable have gone on to become iconic representations of the art.

—from *The Noble History and Enduring Art of Signature Notation*, by Cyr Brommley

Eight

"Developing your own signature notation will take a lot of practice. But in the end, your effort will be worth it."

Professor Robards roamed the lecture hall as he spoke, slowly making his way up the tiered seating and down each row, glancing in turn at each student's slate as they painstakingly formed the same symbols over and over again using lengths of chalk carefully sharpened into points. "It is important for an alchemist who plans to make a career of research to develop their own signature notation so that their discoveries—"

And their failures, I added silently, from my little desk at the front of the lecture hall.

"—can be accurately attributed to them when they're studied by future generations of students and scholars."

I tried to picture myself, two years younger, sitting on a bench halfway up the span of risers, laboring over my entry and exit strokes. Struggling to even out my interlinear spaces. Debating the balance between my ascending and descending flourishes.

Along with all of that, I would have glanced left, right, and over the shoulder of the student in front of me, desperate for some assurance that my emerging style looked sufficiently different from theirs. That my work would stand out.

I couldn't remember doing any of that, yet I must have spent hours—weeks—during my Fundamentals year developing and practicing my own style on a slate, to keep from wasting ink and parchment as I developed the flare and grace of every stroke. As I'd tailored the curves, slashes, crosses, and vertical and horizontal lines. I'd drawn the shapes over and over. I'd written and erased, and written again, until my hand formed the symbols spontaneously as soon as I'd thought them. And though I could remember none of that process, its result remained.

Lead, I thought as I stared down at the parchment on my desktop. My right hand drew a tall, narrow cross with a hook shaped like a lowercase letter *h* extending from the bottom half. And though that felt complete, my quill kept moving, extending the curve below the end of the cross and curving it under, then back up and out, to form a distinctive curlicue.

I drew the symbol for copper—a simple stick figure, with only a round head and arms, though my quill added flourishes on the ends of the horizontal cross line.

And salt, a perfect circle with a horizontal line through it, only my quill thickened the sides of the circle and the ends of the horizontal line, so that the symbol looked thinner on the top and bottom than on the sides.

So many alchemy symbols came to my mind without effort. My hands drew them in my own signature style without hesitation. And yet . . .

My focus strayed to the leather-bound journal open on my lap, hidden from view.

I knew, from some instinctive corner of my absent memory, that I'd written them. But I could not read a word of my own writing.

Movement from the risers caught my eye, and I glanced up to see that a student in the third row had raised her hand. Professor Robards was across the room, advising a boy in the first row.

The student met my gaze, and my pulse spiked. I couldn't ignore her now that she knew she'd been seen.

Varrah. I remembered her because I'd read her name aloud from the roll book, three class periods in a row. And because while her right eye was deep brown, her left was a pale green.

Heterochromia. My brain supplied the term as I slid my journal back into my satchel and rose from my seat. I climbed the first two risers to stop in the aisle beside Varrah's table, where she sat alone, though most students sat in pairs.

"Hello." I sank onto the bench next to her. "How can I help?"

She hesitated, blinking at me for one oddly weighty moment.

"I don't think I'm doing this right," she finally said, and the distinctive sound of her voice—the way it seemed to echo in two slightly different pitches—triggered my sudden understanding.

When I called the roll, Varrah always raised her hand rather than answering aloud. I'd assumed she was just shy, but that clearly wasn't the whole story.

"Oh!" I gave her a friendly smile. "You're from Eria? The unified provinces?"

She nodded warily, and I realized why she was sitting alone. "And they're all being absolute cods about it?" I said with a subtle glance around the room.

"It's okay. I'm accustomed to it," she whispered, and her voice seemed to tickle my eardrums. The feeling wasn't unpleasant, but it *was* strange.

I tried not to stare at the thin vertical scar directly over the center of her throat. It was faint enough to be undetectable from more than a couple of feet away, but now that I'd noticed it, my gaze felt drawn to it.

"Well, give them a chance," I whispered. "Sometimes it takes people a while to get used to things they're unfamiliar with. I'm not saying it *should*. I'm just saying . . . don't count them all out yet. It's still the first week."

"Were you lonely, in the beginning?" Varrah asked, and an ache blossomed deep in my chest.

I could not remember my first weeks at the Alchemary, but with two of my childhood friends also attending, I likely had not been lonely.

"My mother was," I confided in a soft voice. "She was the only member of her cohort from the kingdom of Lysëa, and she told me that she felt very out of place at first. But she came to love her time at the Alchemary. And to make many good friends." Though my father liked to ignore the truth of that in order to dwell on her departure.

"May I be so fortunate," Varrah said. Then she gestured to her slate. "I'm picturing a vertical symmetry between the symbols for tin and lead."

Listening to her took a lot of concentration. Not because I couldn't understand her, but because there was a very real risk of getting caught up in—*trapped* by—the ethereal quality of her voice itself. It was eerie and hypnotic.

"But . . . is this too thick, for the scythe?"

"Scythe?" I studied her slate. "That's actually supposed to be reminiscent of a crescent moon," I said. "As in the symbol for silver. It's built into the symbols for quicksilver, tin, and lead." Reading through the most basic of my own notes had been sufficient for me to relearn the alchemical table and the origin of the symbols. "But yes." I tilted my head, squinting at her writing. "It *does* look rather like a scythe. And I think your instinct with the style is strong. This would be much more distinctive if you could master a truly thin 'blade.' Especially as you move toward the points on each end. Let it get a little thicker in the center, maybe? To give the symbol some weight? That will require a bit more pressure in the middle of the stroke, and a slant of your wrist at the start and finish."

Her eyes lit up, and she swiped a cloth over her slate, then bent over it again with her chalk, which had been carefully sharpened to an effective, slanted point. "Like this?"

"Yes!" I smiled at her. "I think that's the beginning of a beautiful signature tin symbol! Now you just have to draw it about five thousand more times, until your hand forms the movement all on its own, quickly and smoothly. Without any pause for thought."

She considered that for a second, and I could see how intimidating the idea must have been. But then she hunched over her slate again and got to work.

"Do you mind if I ask what province you're from?" I said, watching as she painstakingly drew a long row of nearly identical tin symbols.

"I'm from Reachan," she said. "The southernmost province of Unified Eria."

"I know it!" I couldn't resist another smile. "I mean, I've never been there." That I could recall. "But when I was a kid, my father did some work on the Sakros of Echoes. He consulted on the design of the Sakros of Whispers as well, in Parlaan. He's a stonemason."

Varrah's eyes widened. "What a strange, strange association gifted to us from the cosmic chaos! It's entirely possible that I met your father on the street when I was a child!"

"You might have!" I agreed. "He loved Reachan. He came home raving about this little fried donut he used to buy from street vendors. It was evidently tossed in fine-ground sugar seasoned with a local spice, a bit like anise. My stepfather has been trying to replicate that morsel, based on nothing but my father's aging recollection of it, for the better part of a decade."

At least, he had been, last I could remember.

Varrah's gaze went distant. Nostalgic. "Kokos," she whispered, the two tones of her voice diverging distinctly on the long *O* sounds. "I love them filled with pear jam, right out of the fryer."

"My father insists they're delicious. He loved everything about your land."

He'd carried on about the architecture of Unified Eria, where all of the public buildings were designed to amplify or obscure a specific tone or to maximize a specific facet of auditory perception. And in addition to the food, he'd been fascinated by an inherited tendency of the local population to be born with some form of heterochromia. About half of the populace, he'd said.

Varrah's voice, though. That wasn't inherited.

"Do they practice much alchemy in Reachan? Or in any of the provinces?"

She made an eerily multitonal amused sound, deep in her throat, then suddenly looked embarrassed by the impulse. She shook her head. "The only arcane study permitted in most of the Unified Eria is auriculia. We call it the Craft." She frowned, considering. "That's the only *really* unifying cultural aspect of the provinces."

My father had said something similar—that their Craft was the only thing truly bonding the Eria provinces, despite the conflict between provincial dynasts.

And that Craft didn't solely involve their altered voices. The ears were modified, too, though there was no visible scarring for that procedure.

I knew better than to ask Varrah about her voice. About what the procedure had done to—or for?—her ears. Natives of the unified provinces were not permitted to divulge such information to outsiders. And even if she were allowed to speak of it, asking would be rude.

"So, how did you wind up at the Alchemary?" I asked instead.

"My cousin married a vintner from Aethermere," she said as she turned back to her scythes. "I spent my eighteenth year with her, to learn winemaking in the local tradition, and when the Alchemary recruiter came to town, testing alchemical potential, I... took the assessment." She glanced up from her slate. "I suppose I scored well, because he recorded my information and said that if I were interested, I could pursue an education at one of the greatest schools in all the world." Her gaze intensified. "Even in Unified Eria, we know of this place."

Our academy had long ago attained global renown, but according to my father, in many places, that fame was more of an infamy. Including in the unified provinces.

"And your parents allowed you to attend?"

"No." Varrah looked up at me, her gaze... haunted. "They forbade it, and when I enrolled without their blessing... I was disowned. I am no longer permitted within the borders of Reachan."

"Oh, Varrah," I whispered, fighting to breathe past a sudden sharp ache in my chest. "I'm so very sorry!"

She only shrugged. "My cousin and her husband have agreed to take me in during the winter break. She will try to broker a reconciliation with my mother, who might then work slowly on my father."

I found myself at an utter loss for words.

"Very well. That's enough practice for today," Professor Robards said, and I looked up to find him standing behind his podium. "Your signature notation essays are due on Monday, and if you find extra time over the weekend, aim for five hundred repetitions per day, per symbol, on your slates. Signature notation does not develop without *extensive* practice!"

The class groaned, and I stood back as they gathered their things and tromped down the risers, headed for the door.

"She seems to have taken to you," Professor Robards said, glancing at Varrah's empty seat once the classroom had emptied. "Well done."

I held my tongue for a moment while I gathered my things, then I faced him as I settled the strap of my satchel over my shoulder. "If I may ask . . . why do you sound surprised by that?"

"I mean no offense," he assured me. "It's only that I requested you as my teaching assistant because I knew you would be the most careful and accurate grader out of your cohort. I'm pleasantly surprised to see that you're good with the students as well."

He was giving me a compliment, and I would not be so rude as to question it. And yet . . . pleasantly surprised was *still* surprised.

Nine

"What do the colors mean?" I asked Wilder as we stared out at the quadrangle from a bench in front of the Refectory.

He reached into my folded-handkerchief pouch and plucked out a dark morsel of dried fruit. "In this state? Not much, really. I can hardly tell any difference between the cherries, the cranberries, and the currants. And the smaller prunes." He tossed the morsel into his mouth. "Cherry. Though I'd have guessed it was a currant."

"Not these colors. *Those* colors." I gestured toward the quadrangle again, where a couple dozen other students milled in groups of two or three or sat studying on benches artfully positioned on the edges of various flower beds and pathways. "If the Alchemary uniform is a gray frock and a black cloak, why do so many of them wear blue belts, green ribbons, and rust-colored . . . cuffs? And headbands? And . . . laces? I've even seen frocks in those colors."

Wilder followed my gaze. "Oh. The Alchemary *provides* a standard gray frock, for you ladies, and a gray vest for the gentlemen. But students are welcome to wear frocks and vests of the Alchemary style in any color, if they provide the clothing for themselves. As for the choice of colors . . ." He shrugged. "They're just declaring their affinities."

"Affinities? For blue, and green, and . . . brown, with a bit of red stirred in?"

He chuckled. "For various mineral resources. Mined from water, or vegetation, or from the earth itself. For instance, an alchemist with an earth affinity would use salt mined from deposits in the ground, while someone with a water affinity would prefer salt evaporated from seawater."

"How would you get salt from vegetation?"

His brows arched, giving him thoughtful expression. "Usually, that means salt of—"

"Tartar," I finished. "Which is produced as a calcination of tartar, which is a by-product of winemaking. Which involves grapes, which are, of course, a plant."

"Precisely. You are a *very* quick study, Amber."

He looked proud, and I could not resist a smile.

"Salt can also be extracted from the roots and leaves of certain plants, especially during the growth phase. But that's a huge effort, and it depends, somewhat, upon how much salt is present in the soil and in the water source. Fortunately for those of us who wear the green"—he tapped on the moss-colored leather scabbard attached to his belt—"having an affinity for one kind of mineral source doesn't mean you can't use the others. It just means you have a preference."

"And people who wear multiple colors have multiple affinities?"

"Exactly."

"Is one affinity better than the others?"

"Yes, of course!" Wilder grinned. "Botany affinity is obviously the best."

I rolled my eyes.

He laughed. "Everyone will say their own affinity is the best, naturally. But that's no more accurate than when we used to say that Innswood's alewives were the best in all of Aethermere. They said the same thing down the road in Kingswallow, and who's to say who was right? Or that *any* of us were right. At the end of the day, everyone gets drunk on their favorite ale. It's a matter of preference. But it's also a bit of... an identity. I know I have a preference in common with anyone out there wearing green. And if I run short of some ingredient, those are the people I'd turn to for help, and the ones I'd help in return. Because we prefer—and *prepare*—the same kinds of source materials."

"What about those who wear no colors? They have no affinity?" No... identity?

He shrugged. "Or they prefer *all* of the mineral sources. Which is essentially the same thing as preferring none."

"Minerals for what? As ingredients in alchemical formulas?"

Wilder nodded. "Yes, as base-level ingredients. But also as a source for beyn."

Beyn. The distillation of the natural element of change, and a key ingredient in any alchemical compound.

"We all start off in Fundamentals year using one of the basic formulas for beyn. There are several associated with each affinity, and several known as balanced formulas, which use sources from all affinities. But as we learn, we begin to... experiment. To decide what works better for us, as individual alchemists, and to customize our recipes. By the time an alchemist reaches the master level—not the Mastery year, as a student, but the true master level of alchemy—they've developed their own very specific and personal beyn formula, and they usually guard it as a secret."

"But... alchemy is about making a better world. For everyone." I twisted on the bench to face him. "Why would they deny others a better way to do that, if they have it?"

Wilder gave me a sad smile. "The ideal doesn't always line up with the reality, Amber. Not just in alchemy, but in life."

"I suppose that's true."

"Alchemists here do their work on behalf of the world at large. They're just often unwilling to disclose *how* that work gets done. Operations at the highest level have become a bit... proprietary."

I frowned out at the quadrangle, squinting against the afternoon sun. "I don't understand that."

Wilder snorted. "You certainly did last week."

I glanced sharply at him. "What does that mean?"

He sighed. "You're . . . different now. More like you were when we first got here, I guess."

I thought about that for a second, fighting a tight discomfort in my chest. "If you didn't like me before, why were you in my bed, Wilder?"

"Oh, ouch." He laid one hand over his heart and gave me a dramatic pout. "That's a bit . . . reductive."

"How so?"

"Well, first of all, I *did* like you." He took my hand, winding his fingers between mine. Stroking his thumb over my knuckles. "*Never* doubt that. Second, even if I hadn't . . ." He shrugged. "You don't have to enjoy someone's company in a conversational sense in order to enjoy it in a . . . physical sense. Some ingredients complement each other on a dinner plate. Others combust upon contact."

"Some couples are comfort food, like sautéed carrot with parsnip," I said, "while others are saltpeter, sulfur, and charcoal?"

"Precisely." He grinned, squeezing my hand. "Incidentally, I'm making note of the fact that you listed *three* ingredients in that last scenario."

I huffed at him. "Saltpeter, sulfur, and charcoal are the primary ingredients in black powder explosives, Wilder."

His right eyebrow hooked upward. "Oh, *I know*."

I tugged my hand gently from his grip, despite my reluctance to lose the warmth of his touch. "And my affinity?" There hadn't been a single scrap of color in my wardrobe. "Do I prefer none of them or all of them?"

Wilder snagged another bite of fruit from my pouch. He frowned at it for a second, clearly trying to identify the dried morsel. Then he turned that frown upon me. "Honestly, I have no idea. You were always very... circumspect. With your formulas, I mean. And your ingredients. In fact, your recipe for beyn was such a jealously guarded secret that you would only make it in private."

I blinked at him. "Was *I* a master alchemist?"

He laughed. "No. You were a student."

"Just like everyone else." My face flamed at my own presumption. At my own ego.

"You *were* a student," he said. "But not like the rest of us. That's why she let you stay."

"The Bluehelm?"

Wilder nodded. "She isn't willing to let you go, if you could *possibly* recover your memories—your skill—because of what you could contribute to this place as a researcher. Because any success you—and Des, truth be told..." He shrugged. "Any success you two bring to the Alchemary would become part of *her* legacy."

A bittersweet relief washed over me. My accomplishments should be part of my own legacy. But if the Bluehelm's personal ambition was the only thing keeping me on the Alchemary campus—giving me a chance to recover my memories—so be it.

"You're not the only one, though," Wilder said as I fished the last dried cherry from my pouch. I gave him a puzzled look. "You're not the only balanced affinity," he clarified. "At least, I assume you're balanced. I've never seen you show any preference."

"Who else?" I asked around the last sweet, tart bite of cherry.

"Cressa."

"The Bluehelm's student aide?" I pictured her tight reddish ringlets and gray-ringed eyes. "Come to think of it, she does wear all three colors."

Wilder shook out my empty handkerchief and folded it on his lap. "Some people say there isn't really any such thing as balance.

That everyone prefers one option at least a *little* more than the others, and anyone who claims otherwise is lying to themselves."

"And what do you say?"

He smiled and pulled his cloak back to reveal a subtle row of rust-colored buttons on the asymmetrical line of his vest. "I say it doesn't matter. And it's none of anyone else's concern whether I have as much earth affinity as botany affinity, or which of those I choose to wear. If at all. And the same goes for you. You like what you like."

I smiled and leaned left to bump his shoulder.

As we stood from the bench, a sudden commotion from the quadrangle drew my attention. Five black-clad men ran along the southernmost of the long cobblestone paths stretching from one end of the quadrangle to the other. They were headed east, toward where the Dormitory sat perched on a cliff, looking out over the sea. As I watched, two students scrambled, startled, from the path to let them pass.

The men ran in unison, at a pace that did not suggest any urgency. In my experience, the only people who ran were children on an errand, adults responding to an emergency, and . . .

"Soldiers?" I asked as the men moved rapidly closer. "They're . . . training?"

Wilder nodded. "The Crown stations a small number here, for emergencies. There are always two at the gate and two at the dock on the south side of the island, when a delivery is expected. A few more roam the campus, to 'keep the peace.'"

I hadn't noticed. Of course, I hadn't been to the bridge or the dock, and I'd been too busy studying and avoiding my classmates to spend much time exploring the campus.

"That seems a bit—" My mouth snapped shut as the soldiers crossed in front of us on the path, and I realized with a start that the fifth, who ran at the tail of the formation, without a partner, wasn't a soldier at all. He wore a black tunic and loose, dark trousers that were similar but not identical to the others', and his dark hair shone with caramel undertones in the sunlight.

"That's Desmond," I whispered, gripping Wilder's arm. "Why is he training with the soldiers?"

Wilder huffed. "He's picked up some strange habits in pursuit of apotheosis. But that one is beyond me."

I could only stare as the runners passed us, and I wasn't sure whether to be relieved or insulted that Desmond did not look my way. That he did not, in fact, seem to know I was there.

He ran with no visible effort, every stride long, and smooth, and strong. He was in total control of his form—of every joint and every muscle. Each movement seemed the perfect fusion of grace, coordination, and power.

Was this how he'd crossed my room in the blink of an eye, to avert my fall? Was he simply so in tune with his own physical form that it obeyed his impulses before they were quite fully formed?

Had Desmond begun his quest to perfect the human form . . . with his own?

The Avalona Emerald, the famous and distinctive eponymous ring given to the queen by her husband on their wedding day, was a fifty-facet triangle-cut stone, unique to the queen herself. Largely because on the day he commissioned the ring, Emperor Eldon officially declared the triangle cut verboten to anyone but his royal bride. Which sent the gem—much like their love—into the realm of legend.

—from *Royal Gems Throughout History*

Ten

"And she just sits there the whole time, scribbling on her parchment as if she's determined to write down every word the professor says."

Keryth's whisper carried toward me from the other side of the library shelf. I leaned closer to the bookcase, inhaling the comforting scents of leather bindings and old parchment. Disappointed that they did little to calm the unease fluttering behind my rib cage.

The student library was a low-ceilinged space at the back of the first floor of the Seminary. It held only academic journals, research logs, and textbooks: simple, sturdy volumes intended to be handled by generations of students. There were three or four copies of each, carefully handwritten by scribes kept busy—and likely wealthy—with a standing order from the Alchemary to copy and replace the aging volumes. Students had unlimited access to the books but were not allowed to remove them from the library. And we were expected to share.

Researchers, however . . .

Wilder had told me there was a research library in the Conservatory, accessible only to permanent staff of the Alchemary. That library contained one-of-a-kind texts, including many famous illuminated manuscripts, which students lacked the experience and knowledge to understand. And the permission to touch.

In some deep corner of my soul, I ached to see those texts. To read them. Even just to run my fingers over the bindings and be in the general proximity of such mind-boggling science, innovative theories, and wise words. But that would be foolish, considering that the two volumes I currently had hidden in my satchel were beginner level, at best.

The shelves in the student library were made of weathered wooden planks held together with iron plates and rivets. The shelves were open, making them accessible from either side of the shelf.

I peered over the top of one row of books and saw Keryth seated across from another student at a table. Her back was to me, but her voice and her long blond braid, threaded through with a green ribbon, were enough to confirm her identity.

“Don’t you find that more than a bit odd?” she whispered, leaning closer to the girl across the table over the text that lay open in front of her. “That she takes so many notes?”

“Oh, I don’t know.” The freckled brunette shoved a ringlet over one shoulder, and a newly formed memory supplied her name as Yoslyn Savva. The girl from Falkrest, whose parents disapproved of alchemy. “Amber has always taken lots of notes.”

My hand tightened around the strap of my satchel. I’d been more concerned with sneaking out of the Fundamentals-year shelves without being seen than with what they were saying, until I’d heard my name.

“Not like this,” Keryth insisted. “It’s like she doesn’t trust herself to remember a thing the professor says. She doesn’t ask questions anymore. And a week into class, she hasn’t shown up at the Mastery lab space even once. That is *not* like Amber Fallbrook. Last year she spent *all* her time at the lab, working on that secret project. Practically rubbing our faces in it.”

I frowned. Why would I have rubbed anyone’s face in my work?

"So, what's your theory?" Yoslyn asked. "Do you suppose she's ill? A barmaid in Saltstrand said there's a malady going around town. Some strange contagion that renders the patient catatonic and alters the—"

"Does she *look* catatonic to you?" Keryth snapped.

Yoslyn shrugged, loose light brown curls bouncing with the motion. "Perhaps she has a mild case."

"Of *catatonia*?"

My most pressing issue at the moment was neither illness nor even amnesia. It was the fact that Keryth and Yoslyn sat between me and the exit.

I swallowed a groan.

Until I managed to relearn the basics of alchemy, I would be unable to continue my research project, pass my classes, or prepare for the trials, and after days spent struggling to understand my own inscrutable notes, I'd finally decided to try the library after my afternoon snack with Wilder. The underclassmen were in class, and I'd assumed that since there were no Mastery-year courses on Friday, my peers would be ensconced in the lab space on the third floor. No one should have been around to see me perusing textbooks far below the Mastery level.

The appearance of the most gossip-prone student in our cohort was a definite wrench in my plans, but I had no more time to hide in the stacks. Spine stiff, I hiked up the strap of my satchel and marched down the aisle, letting my heeled boots clack loudly as I rounded the end of the shelf and stepped into sight.

The gossip went silent.

"Good afternoon, Amber!" Yoslyn's voice was too bright to sound natural. Her green-eyed gaze strayed toward the shelf I'd just rounded. "Are you . . . lost? In the Fundamentals-year section?"

"Just reshelving a book someone left out," I said, a bit surprised when the lie slid out easily.

"There are staff members who do that," Keryth said. "*Your* job is to study, not to clean." Her brow crinkled in an affectation of concern. "Are you well, Amber? You seem a bit . . . out of sorts."

"I'm fine. Thank you for asking. Again. I'll see you in the lab," I added as I headed for the door, silently cursing myself before the words had faded from my ears.

Appearing at the lab would do me no favors. I wasn't even sure how to properly set up my station.

Silence echoed behind me as I pushed open the left half of the double door into the hallway. I could practically feel both gazes on my back, but—

"Ow!"

"Oh!" I gasped, startled to realize the door I'd swung open had hit Cressa Baxter in the face. "I'm so sorry!"

"The *right-hand* door," she snapped, clutching her satchel and her wax tablet to her chest. "We use the *right-hand* door, so those exiting a room don't hit those entering."

"Yes, I—" Had no memory of that custom at all. Though it made perfect sense. "Again. I do apologize."

The door swung shut behind me, leaving us alone in the dark-paneled hallway.

"How are you?" she asked, her irritation seeming to fade. "I can't imagine how difficult all this must be."

"Well, it will be easier when I stop assaulting people with doors," I said.

Cressa smiled, her gray eyes crinkling almost sympathetically. "You clearly don't remember being hit with one, the second day of Fundamentals year."

"I— No," I admitted. "I remember nothing from the past two years." And somewhat less than everything from the year before that.

"Lennox came barreling out the 'in' door from the Refectory and hit you right in the forehead. You were stunned and disoriented and had to spend a night in the infirmary for observation, and I grew concerned that Wilder would beat him senseless."

I resisted the smile forming on my lips. "Well, I assure you I won't forget about the doors again."

Cressa nodded, reaching past me for the knob, and impulsively, I put one hand on the sleeve of her blue frock.

"You didn't tell anyone, did you?"

She turned from the door, her face entirely clear of confusion; she knew exactly what I was talking about. "I hear a lot of privileged information in my role as the Bluehelm's student aide, and I am not at liberty to divulge any of it." Something inscrutable passed behind her gray eyes in the candlelight flickering from the wall sconce. "Some of us take our duties and obligations seriously."

"To the Bluehelm?"

Cressa blinked. "To alchemy. To the *Alchemary*. You must remain focused on the goal, to the exclusion of all distractions, if you ever hope to achieve it." She reached for the knob again, but her attention remained on me for a moment longer. "I won't tell them," she said. "Because it isn't my place, and it isn't their business. But *you* should tell them." She pulled the door open, lowering her voice to a whisper. "They're going to figure it out soon anyway."

With that, she marched into the library and let the door swing shut behind her.

She was right, of course. My illness—or my accident, or trauma, or whatever it was . . . While my academic struggle was none of my classmates' concern, it would doubtless affect them, especially if we were paired for an assignment, or if I were invited to a study group.

Yet there seemed no good time, nor any good way, to confess to my current state of scholastic decline.

I clutched my satchel as I continued down the first-floor corridor into the foyer, careful not to let my heels clack against the broad expanse of smooth gray stone. Students were not allowed to remove texts from the library without express permission—a rule I'd been "reminded" of two days before, in a decidedly humiliating encounter with the librarian—and that I had several of them in my bag at that moment made me eager to go unnoticed.

I glanced into every lecture hall I passed and was tempted to linger outside a couple of them. To listen as the distinguished voices of professors whose courses I'd already taken explained concepts that had since become lost to the dark vault of my memory. But the fear of being caught kept me moving past sconce after burning sconce mounted on the dark paneled walls.

Relief cooled my overheated face as I pushed open the front doors and emerged onto the quadrangle, directly across from the statue of Emperor Eldon and his beloved Avalona, lovingly embracing in larger-than-life marble perfection. I'd walked past it daily for almost a week, but I hadn't taken the time to admire it up close, despite my curiosity, because the quadrangle was usually spotted with classmates I wanted to avoid. Halfway between the noon and the evening meals, however, it was largely empty. So I crossed the lawn toward the statue. An alternating series of curved benches and shrubs formed a ring around the marble emperor and his queen, outlining a bed of crushed white stone at their feet.

Eldon and Avalona were carved in extraordinary detail, his arm curving around her back, both claiming and guiding her while she stared up at him adoringly, her right hand lightly clasped in his. The famous Avalona Emerald on her finger had been stripped of its celebrated color by the marble, but not of its distinctive shape.

I stared up at the statue, stories from childhood swirling through a fog of nostalgia in my mind, until a familiar, bright male voice rang across the open space at my back.

"With funding contributed almost equally from the generosity of the Crown, alumni largesse, and profit from the Alchemary's services to local communities, we are able to take on every student fortunate enough to be admitted at no cost to the pupil."

I turned as Lennox Pettifog came to a stop in front of the Seminary, his short, dark curls fluttering slightly in the breeze, and a dozen other people stopped with him. Facing him.

He was leading a tour group.

I'd taken a tour of the campus myself once. The Gregorys had been kind enough to let me tag along, back when we were yet adolescents with ambitions of being admitted to the most prestigious alchemy institution in the world.

"As you can see, while the Alchemary is comprised of several buildings, the primary structures are the Conservatory, where our staff researchers work, developing new theories and techniques and exploring our three core disciplines." He gestured across the quadrangle as he spoke. "The Seminary, where instructors teach our student residents, the Dormitory, where our students live, and the Refectory, where we all take our meals. I'm going to take you— Oh!" Lennox turned to face a young woman who had raised her hand. "Yes, there's a question?"

"Where do the teachers—the professors—live?"

Lennox smiled brightly, his freckled cheeks bunching with the expression. "Most of the support staff have homes and family across the bridge in Saltstrand, but the resident members of our faculty—including most of the professors and researchers—are housed in separate apartments at the rear of the campus, where they have the space and privacy befitting permanent members of the Alchemary. That building is not on our tour."

In the four days since I'd woken up on campus, I had yet to see the faculty apartments, though I knew they were tucked just on the edge of the forest, beyond the south side of the quadrangle on the path toward the southern beach and its dock.

The tour continued and I turned toward the Dormitory, but before I'd made it more than a few steps, purposeful footfalls drew me from my thoughts. I looked up to find Professor Bollinger, my Ethics and Advancement of Alchemy instructor, deep in conversation with Professor Edmiston, her mass of silver curls *almost* tamed by a cobalt kerchief draped over them and tied at the base of her skull. They came from the direction of the Refectory, each holding a cloth-wrapped bundle mottled with damp spots that could have been either grease or juice leaking from their lunches.

Both of my current professors—each of whom had asked me to come see them at my earliest convenience—were headed right for me, when I'd been avoiding them for a full day.

I *was* planning to meet with them. They'd been informed of my condition, and I owed them a conversation. But I wanted to have a better grasp on the basics before being ensnared in a private discussion with two experts in the field.

I swiftly rounded the royal statue and kept myself out of sight until I heard them ascend the stairs of the Seminary, still deep in conversation. When I was sure they had disappeared into the building, I stepped out from behind the statue, clutching my satchel as I waited for my pulse to slow to its normal pace.

Unfortunately, I found myself staring into a set of deep brown eyes, irises so dark they looked like the depths of my morning cup of tea.

I recognized the young man from class—the chin stubble he'd regrown by nine in the morning was difficult to forget—and though I'd caught him looking at me several times, we had yet to exchange a single word. That I could remember, anyway.

"Amber Fallbrook," he said.

"Pryce Wishart." I was *unreasonably* pleased to have a name to throw back at him.

One bushy brow hooked steeply over a tea-brown eye, one corner of his mouth teasing upward. "Were you just concealing yourself behind Queen Avalona's marble skirt? From our *professors*?"

"I— No. Of course not. I was just . . . looking for something."

His grin widened. "And would that something happen to be your dignity?"

"No, I—" I sighed as his other brow rose to mirror the first. "Well, I suppose it might be dignity-shaped, at least."

Pryce laughed, his head thrown back to reveal two rows of perfect white teeth. "Why would *you*, of all people, be hiding from the faculty?" When I had no answer, he leaned in to mock whisper, "They know where you reside. They *will* discover you."

I blinked slowly, struggling for a reply. "I'm not hiding. I'm just . . . delaying the inevitable, I suppose. They've both asked to see me, and I don't really want to meet with them. At the moment."

Pryce only watched me, clearly waiting for more.

"I'm a little behind, academically," I finally admitted.

He rolled those dark brown eyes, skepticism on display. "How is that possible? You've gone through an entire inkwell in two class periods. You've taken more notes than Professor Edmiston even brings to class, so—" He bit the words off, gaze narrowing on me. "Unless you're not taking notes at all."

Pryce stepped back, crossing his arms over the front of his blue vest, his gaze lingering long enough to discomfit. "You're behind because you haven't paid a single bit of attention, have you? You're working on your research project in class, right there in front of the professor."

It wasn't a question. He'd drawn what must have felt like an iron-clad conclusion.

Pryce leaned closer, his boots grinding in the bed of crushed marble. "When are you going to tell us what you're working on?"

"I . . . cannot."

He scoffed. "You've been saying that for a year. But truthfully, Amber, there are no hard feelings, at least on my part. You can tell me what you're up to."

I blinked at him, and he mistook my confusion for surprise.

"Honestly." He laid one thick hand over the front of his vest, ostensibly covering his heart. "I was furious at first, obviously, but you were right. I overcame the passion of my anger. And I'd truly love to know what you're working on. And *where* you're working. Have you been allotted a private lab?"

"A private . . . ?" What in the name of mayhem was he talking about? Why would the Alchemary award private lab space to a student?

He shrugged. "Well, you're obviously not set up alongside the rest of us."

"Oh. I—" I had no answer for that, and the faint shine of envy in his eyes triggered an uncomfortable itch beneath my skin. "I swear to you that I've not been afforded any resources denied the rest of the class."

"Oh, I know. You've *earned* everything you've gotten, haven't you?" He was still smiling, but his words sliced with a blade's edge, though I couldn't quite fathom the meaning.

"I have to go." I stepped around the nearest curved bench onto the lawn, more unnerved than angry, though I felt like I *should* be angry.

I marched down a cobblestone path in a random direction, my stolen textbooks forgotten until I'd managed to collect my thoughts, several minutes into the unnecessary detour. Frustrated, I turned to find that Pryce had perched himself on the front steps of the Seminary, a book open on his lap, where he was now talking to Keryth Malcom. Both of them watching me.

I couldn't suddenly reverse my course without practically admitting that I'd had no destination in mind when I'd fled Pryce, and that I had let him fluster me to the point of a mental fog.

The only logical way to save face was to keep marching forward, as if I'd intended to head straight for . . . the Conservatory. Its smooth, hulking exterior rose before me, sunlight glaring off the gray-veined white marble.

Surely I could sneak out the back and go the long way around the quadrangle, headed east behind the Refectory, and approach the Dormitory from the southern side.

Arrogantly determined, I marched up the front steps and into the atrium of the Conservatory, my heels echoing on the smooth, slick stone. Other than a few benches built into the walls and a commemorative plaque hanging near the base of the staircase, the atrium was empty. It was brutally austere, in stark contrast to the inviting wood panels and well-worn rugs of the Seminary. Even the torches hanging at fixed intervals on the curved walls shone brightly, their flames unnaturally white.

The atrium—and presumably the entire building—felt cold and bare. Harsh and unforgiving. Unwelcoming.

Why, I could not help wondering, had I been so determined to earn a place here, when this building felt like a terribly unpleasant place to work?

Shivering more from the ambience than the temperature, I glanced around in search of some obvious path toward the back of the building, but the round front chamber offered only two possible routes forward. The broad staircase curving along the rounded left wall or a set of doors at the back of the atrium opening into the Panacea wing and the infirmary.

I would *not* go unnoticed in the infirmary.

Which left only the front door, which represented a total retreat and admission of defeat, and the stairs: a deeper commitment to my own fraud.

I exhaled as my gaze traced the staircase, rising in graceful curves past the second floor and up to the third. The atrium stretched that entire height, and . . .

I blinked, a gasp slipping from my throat into the weighty silence of the imposing space, as my gaze found the ceiling.

"Oh *my* . . ."

Eleven

In sharp contrast to the cold gray and white marble and stark lines of the Conservatory atrium, its ceiling was a graceful wonderland of curves and colors. Above the staircase, the marble bricks narrowed as they spiraled inward, forming a dramatic shape like the shell of a nautilus. Set into that spiraling marble framework were a series of brightly colored stained glass scenes, framed by thin strips of lead.

It was *stunning*. The contrast of cold white planes with boldly pigmented scenes... Of straight lines with elegant curves... It was a feast of divergent colors and textures, none of it visible from the outside or obvious from the first floor. Until one looked up.

In fact, when I'd come to and from the infirmary, the day I'd awoken with amnesia, I hadn't even glanced at the ceiling.

I turned a slow circle, my mouth agape, my satchel hanging forgotten against my right hip.

Sun shone through the panels at an angle, casting colors upon the curved staircase walls with extravagant, exaggerated proportions, as if the images had been both blurred and stretched by the slant of the light.

The sight lit a fire deep in my soul. An appreciation for beauty beyond what I could express or explain.

I recognized several of the scenes depicted. The young emperor Eldon courting his beloved Lady Avalona. Their wedding, with the officiant at the center, the royal couple facing him and the royal witnesses on the edges of the scene. Lord Calyx, the venerable father of alchemy, stood to his emperor's left, but the identity of the woman to the new queen's right had been lost to history long ago.

One panel showed the royal couple on their matching thrones. Another the presentation of their ill-fated only child. And another the tragic queen on her deathbed, mere days after her son's death.

The spiral-shaped series of images was a timeline of the legendary royal romance, brief though it had been. The choice, like that of the central statue in the quadrangle, might have seemed odd, if not for the fact that it was Emperor Eldon who had commissioned the construction of the Alchemary.

Why not dedicate such a beautiful work of art to his first marriage and fabled love?

"One of the less utilitarian uses of alchemy, to be sure," a voice said from behind me, and I whirled to find Dr. Winhoof standing in front of the wooden doors, having just emerged from the Panacea wing.

I'd been so caught up in the beauty overhead that I'd heard neither footsteps nor the squeal of hinges.

"But visitors seem to appreciate it," he continued, casting a fleeting glance upward before his gaze settled on me again.

"Uses of alchemy...?" I pondered softly. But then I understood. "The colors."

He nodded. "Leaded glass. Though that's a misnomer, at best. It took more than one hundred different alchemical compounds to create those colors, most either refined or harvested right here on the island, from the forest, from the menagerie, or in a laboratory." He made a sad little *tsk* sound. "It's beyond me that the project ever found funding, considering that it performs no function. And yet... people still stare."

"It's beautiful," I breathed, my gaze straying to the glass again. But then I dragged my attention back to him.

Dr. Winhoof studied me. "How are you feeling? Have you come for a checkup? You aren't scheduled, but I could probably—"

"Oh, no, thank you, I'm—"

A familiar name caught my eye as I scanned the plaque set into the wall beside the base of the staircase, grasping desperately for an excuse to avoid another examination.

Desmond Gregory, Tier 1 Staff Researcher
Apotheosis Division, room 208

"I'm here to see Desmond. Gregory. The researcher," I added, gesturing aimlessly at the plaque, which was in the shape of a scroll, half rolled on top and bottom. "We're old friends."

"Indeed." Something flickered behind Dr. Winhoof's professional smile, but it was gone before I could interpret it. "I believe he's on the second floor."

"Yes. Thank you," I said, though amnesia had rendered me forgetful, not illiterate.

I started up the stairs, one hand trailing the stone banister, and I didn't exhale until I heard the wooden door close again one floor below. Would Dr. Winhoof hear my steps if I went back downstairs and out the front door?

I had dozens of questions about classwork and my research, and Desmond was the person most likely to be able to help me. But he was also the least likely to be willing. And the last thing I wanted was to give him another chance to tell me I didn't belong at the Alchemary.

Still . . . maybe I could prey upon his sympathies.

No.

I needed his help, not his sympathy, and the Desmond Gregory I knew—at least the young man he'd once been—could be reasoned with. After all, we respected each other as rational individuals. Or so I'd heard.

Determined, now that I was just steps from his office, I marched down the hall, my heels echoing on yet more marble, my satchel thumping against my hip.

The entire second floor, it turned out, was the Apotheosis division. I wandered quietly past door after door, reading the names written on slates mounted to the right of each one, but Desmond's was not on any of them. Of course, the titles indicated that these lab spaces belonged to senior researchers.

Desmond was a junior researcher, just beginning his second year.

I found his name around a corner at the back of the building. It was the only one written on its framed slate, though there was space for several more. I pushed open the heavy wooden door without knocking, bracing myself to see him . . . maybe standing at a lab table, wearing goggles and a lab coat. Maybe seated behind a desk, scribbling notes in a journal.

Instead, I found only an empty outer office, connecting a small suite of workspaces. On one end, the door to a private lab stood open. It appeared, at a glance, to be fully furnished and rather spacious, but empty.

Two other doors also stood open, but those rooms were both empty and sparsely furnished, as if they were not just unoccupied for the moment but entirely vacant. Unassigned.

The last door was closed, and from beyond it, two voices rose in heated conversation. I tiptoed toward the door, drawn, somewhat shamelessly, by the intensity of the discussion.

Desmond was angry with someone.

Shocking.

"—but she wouldn't listen. She's insisted on staying. On trying either to 'jog loose' her memories, as she calls it, or to relearn alchemy entirely. And the truth is that I wouldn't put either of them past her. But it isn't safe for her here."

My jaw clenched as I pressed my ear to the door, trying to hear more clearly, even as anger burned behind my cheeks.

"This place isn't safe for anyone," the second voice said, and I gasped.

Sudden silence echoed from beyond the door, and I took a step back. Then, fueled by a burst of adrenaline, I threw the door open. Both men turned to stare at me. Desmond stood at the left side of an empty lab table, jaw firmly set. The other man ran one hand through his thick silver waves before scruffing it over a neatly trimmed darker gray beard. His brown eyes found me from the other end of the table, and his patient smile triggered a bolt of irritation deep in my gut.

"Hello, Father."

"Amber." If Desmond was surprised to see me, he recovered quickly. "Have a seat."

"I certainly will not," I snapped, my hand clenching around the strap of my satchel.

My father chuckled and pulled me into a warm hug, and it took every bit of effort I possessed to resist returning the gesture. When I only stood stiffly in his embrace, he finally let me go and stepped back to study my face.

"Perhaps you can imagine the jolt of fear a father feels when he gets an official correspondence from the institute to which he's entrusted his daughter, saying that she's ill, and he should come for her immediately. And perhaps that will cool your temper, just for a moment?"

I rolled my eyes. "You entrusted me to the Alchemary? I'll admit I cannot remember the circumstances, yet I find that difficult to believe."

My father blinked, and when he glanced at Desmond, I understood that my response was confirmation of whatever he'd been told.

"I suppose I'm recalling your departure in terms that are a bit generous to my part in everything. But I was hoping, given that we haven't seen each other in two years, that you might be in an indulgent—perhaps even a nostalgic—mood."

I could only frown at him, wrapping my arms tighter around my torso until my angry gesture probably looked like I was giving myself a hug. "I haven't been home in two years?"

"You've spent every break here at the Alchemary," Desmond confirmed, even though I had *not* been speaking to him. "Studying. Working."

"Oh!" My father turned toward the table and lifted his bag, a leather satchel he'd been carrying since I was a child. He pulled a wrapped bundle from it. "Martyn sends his love. And a currant loaf."

At the scent, my mouth betrayed me by watering.

"He remembered how you used to forget to eat while you were studying."

Desmond made a strange, soft sound at the back of his throat. "She still does that."

Not that *he* would know!

"What's going on here?" I demanded, accepting the wrapped loaf but willing to bend no more.

None of this was Martyn's fault, and if I could remember being away from him, I'd probably miss him terribly.

My father pulled a folded sheet of parchment from his bag. "I got—"

"A correspondence. So you said. But if you've come to take me home, why are you in Desmond Gregory's office instead of my Dormitory chamber?"

"We were about to go find you," Desmond said, though—again—I'd not been speaking to him.

"I'm not leaving," I insisted, my focus still glued to my father.

"As I was just telling him," Desmond said, and finally I turned on him, exasperated.

"Could you *possibly* be so kind as to quit this exchange? It does not involve you."

Desmond's brow lowered, his copper-brown eyes flashing with irritation. "We're standing in my private laboratory."

"I can remedy that." I tucked the currant loaf under my arm and snatched my father's bag from the table. "If you wouldn't mind?" I gestured at the door with his satchel.

My father turned back to Desmond. "It was good to see you again, despite the circumstances. I do hope you'll keep in touch."

"Of course. Good day, Mr. Fallbrook." Desmond took up a position behind a table holding a complicated array of beakers, burners, and piping. "Amber."

I led my father out of the room and closed the door harder than was truly necessary.

As I marched us toward the stairs, I glared at him. "Why on *earth* were you wasting your time with Desmond Gregory?"

He chuckled. "My dear, I can only answer that question by returning it to you."

Toolkeepers forgo reliance on alchemy and all other arcane arts in order to preserve the tradition of skilled labor and the merits and integrity of an honest day's work. Toolkeepers further reject the impatience and greed that drive demand for alchemical shortcuts and conveniences in favor of patience, hard work, and an enduring commitment to community at every level.

—*The Toolkeepers' Creed*

Twelve

"This place is stunning," my father admitted, staring down the length of the quadrangle. "You were right about that."

From our bench in the Dormitory courtyard, we could see most of the campus, and our view of the Alchemary was much more peaceful than my experience of it had been over the past few days. As we approached the end of the school day, students milled on the grass in the shade of shrubs shaped like animals and gathered on the steps of the Seminary, reading from their notes or chatting with friends. Professors ambled down the cobblestone walkways in pairs or walked alone but with purpose, distinct from the students even at a distance, for their brightly trimmed regalia.

"I can see why you like it here."

But how could he, when *I* couldn't even remember what I'd liked about this place, other than my studies?

"Amber." My father's hand covered mine, and I turned from the view of the quadrangle to look at him. "Are you happy here?"

"I don't know. I've told you, I can't remember anything. How can I know if I was happy?"

"Are you happy here *now*?" he clarified. "Without your memory. Because you can always come—"

"No." I sipped cooling tea from my mug and leaned back, grateful that we had the courtyard to ourselves, at least until my classmates headed toward the Dormitory to rest or study before the evening meal.

"Desmond says they don't know what happened to you. I will admit, I am concerned. I've seen firsthand this new pestilence. The Crown seems . . . troubled. They're keeping it quiet, of course, but more than one citizen of Innswood has been taken away in the dark of night, for quarantine and treatment—"

"Father—"

"—stiff as stone, skin tinted an odd flaxen hue. As if they were jaundiced. The gossip calls them aurums, and there seems no cure."

"I'm not sick. You have my word."

He nodded, silver hair gleaming in the sunlight. "Desmond agrees. He says they've found no evidence of injury or illness. Nor any indication that you did this to yourself. In the lab."

I turned to him sharply. "Is that what you think? That I'm so incompetent as an alchemist that I . . . obliterated my own memory?"

"Of course not." He turned to face me more directly, and I felt the full weight of his attention. "I don't know what kind of alchemist you are, because I haven't seen you since you left home. But I have never, since the day you were born, known you to fail at something you set out to do. And yet *something* must have happened."

"I am not immune to curiosity on that subject myself," I mumbled, frustrated to realize that several students were headed our way from the quadrangle.

"Neither is Desmond."

Exasperation burned deep in my throat. "Why are we talking about Desmond Gregory?"

"He's worried about you."

"And . . . ?" I demanded. "I assume there's more to that?" Based on a tone of voice I remembered quite well.

"And . . . he wrote to me personally, apart from the official communication from the Alchemary. His letter arrived first. He must have paid to have it expedited by direct rider, and if I'd been home when it was delivered, I'd have left before the official correspondence even arrived."

I sat silently for a moment, letting that tidbit ricochet through my thoughts. Hoping it would settle somewhere logical. "What did his letter say? Only that I'd lost my memory?"

"He didn't mention your memory." My father's voice felt still and heavy, like fog clinging to my mother's grave.

I turned to look at him again, at a loss for why Desmond would write to him without mentioning my amnesia.

"His letter was more of a note. It simply said you are in danger." My father smiled at two Proficiency-year students as they passed us on their way toward the fountain, gazes lingering on his brown leather coat, cut in the distinctive Toolkeepers' style. "And that I should take you home."

I huffed, irritation tightening my grip on my mug as I lowered my voice. "If I am in danger from anyone, it is from him and his ego. He isn't *worried* about me. He's *angry* with me."

"Why would that be?"

"I haven't the slightest clue. Perhaps we had a falling-out. Or perhaps our friendship failed to thrive in a university setting. Maybe we are academic rivals—"

"He isn't a student."

I threw one arm up in frustration and could practically feel gazes turning my way. "Then maybe our personalities are immiscible, like oil and water," I whispered. "Like molten silver and lead. Regardless, it is not Desmond Gregory's place to decide where I should be. He does not speak for the Alchemary. And he certainly doesn't speak for me."

"He only wants to help—"

"He wants me sent home."

My father sighed, watching a cluster of Fundamentals-year students as they settled onto the lawn nearby with textbooks and cloth-wrapped snacks. "Well, I cannot say I disagree with him in that regard."

"Why do you hate this place?"

He chuckled. "Do I need a reason, beyond the fact that it's stolen my daughter's life from her?"

"You hated the Alchemary long before my amnesia," I whispered, boldly meeting the stare of a boy in a rust-colored vest.

"I said nothing about your memory, Amber. I said it stole your *life*. Just like—"

"Don't," I snapped softly, pivoting back to my father. "Don't conflate me with her. I am not my mother. And it wasn't the Alchemary that stole her life."

It was the fever.

And before that, it was *him*.

"Amber, my dear," my father began, and there was an odd deliberation in his voice. As if he were, for the first time I could remember, hesitant to speak his mind.

What could possibly be the root of that development? The alchemy students eyeing my Toolkeeper father as if he were trespassing on their hallowed campus? Or some desire to repair the distance that had grown between us?

"If there are no signs of illness or injury," he continued, "and if there was no accident in the course of your research . . . there are few explanations left for what could have caused your memory loss. Nor can we be entirely sure that amnesia was the intended result of . . . whatever happened."

"Father—"

"But we *can* be certain that *something* happened. And as I'm sure you would agree, as a scientist, things do not happen spontaneously. There must have been a cause. A . . . catalyst?"

A sick feeling churned deep in my stomach. "What are you saying?"

He twisted to take my hands in a warm, iron grip, but his gaze skipped across the other forms now populating the courtyard, staring cooly at us even as they maintained their distance. "Someone has done this *to* you, my love."

"No—"

"Someone here. At *this institution,*" he whispered. "Someone has hurt you, and we don't know that the threat has passed. And you can't remember what happened. You can't remember who means you harm."

"A scientist would not assume a scenario and look for evidence to support it. They would assess the evidence *first,* then draw a logical conclusion."

My father frowned. "Is my conclusion not logical?"

"It is," I had no choice but to admit. "But it isn't the *only* logical conclusion, so it cannot be assumed. Even if someone has done this to me—and I'm not prepared to say that is the case—we don't know the intent was to hurt me. It's entirely possible that the goal was to eliminate me as competition. Or to drive me from the Alchemary. Or simply to even the odds for one of my competitors, as I'm forced to spend time recovering my memory rather than preparing for the trials and maintaining my class rank."

"But—"

"You're biased, and you're letting that bias cloud your perceptions. You're letting it lead you to conclusions that would give you what you want from this scenario." My return to Innswood. "And there are plenty of people here who want the same thing. Any one of them could have been responsible."

He leaned closer, lowering his voice even further. "Why would you want to stay here, if that's a possibility?"

"Father!" I blinked at him, stunned by how hard he was working to resist comprehension. "If someone resorted to sabotage in order to neutralize me as a competitor, I must be *fierce* competition. I must be truly gifted as an alchemist. And that makes me even more determined to stay here and face my enemies. To accomplish what I came here to achieve!"

I ignored all the students pretending not to stare at me, clearly trying to hear our argument over the flow of water from the fountain. I had eyes only for my father as I searched his gaze for some sign that what I wanted from life actually mattered.

"I understand that. But if I am right . . ." His forehead crinkled, his lips pressed thin. "If this place is as much a danger to you as it was to your mother—"

"I am *not* my mother."

"And I thank the cosmos for that every day. It would break my heart if—"

"Don't," I repeated, sharper this time. "You don't get to talk about her. You gave up that right."

"Amber. My dear." He exhaled slowly. "I didn't leave because I stopped loving her. I *never* stopped loving her. Love was not our issue."

"I know. It was just the wrong kind of love."

He nodded. "She was my best friend. We were confused for a while about the nature of our relationship, but I won't be sorry for that, even if we both got hurt, because we got *you* out of it."

"I know."

And the truth was that as angry as I was about the dissolution of their marriage, even a decade later, I would not begrudge him Martyn. And I would not deny Martyn my father.

It was not Martyn's fault that my father left us. That his love for my mother was of the wrong sort to support marriage. I wasn't so much angry *at* my father as I was angry *for* my mother.

"But that doesn't change anything," I continued. "She's mine now. Whatever is left of her. Not yours."

He nodded slowly, and I chose not to see the pain in his eyes. "If that's the way you want it."

"It isn't an issue of what I want. That's how it *is*."

We sat in silence for several minutes, sipping lukewarm tea. Picking at the currant bread on the bench between us.

Finally, he sighed. "Desmond says the trials—"

"I'll be *fine*."

"Amber—" His voice broke on the second syllable, fracturing my name into a thousand shards. A thousand pinpricks of pain. "I can't lose you, too." He lifted a cloth to his eyes and swiped brusquely at them, as if the goal were to eradicate his tear ducts, rather than simply to absorb the moisture. "I *won't*."

"No," I assured him. "You won't."

"You don't have to do it."

"Of course not." I stared straight ahead, letting the students still milling about in the courtyard blur as my unblinking eyes went dry. "If I haven't recovered my memory or relearned enough alchemy to give myself a fighting chance, I won't do it."

But it wouldn't come to that.

"Promise me."

"Father . . ."

"If you want me to leave you here—if you want me to give my word to Martyn that you are safe, and I didn't just abandon you to the wolves that devoured your mother whole—you will promise me."

"Fine. But that's the last time you are allowed to wield either my affection for Martyn or my mother's memory like a weapon."

My father nodded, smiling tenuously. "That seems a fair exchange. Your word for my . . . laying down of emotional arms."

"In that case, you have my word," I lied.

My father swiped at his eyes one last time. Then he pocketed his handkerchief and broke off another hunk of Martyn's currant bread. "Did you know that Toolkeepers laid every stone on this campus?" he said, plainly trying to change the subject to something less emotionally volatile. He'd raised his voice, more than willing to educate Alchemary students on the illustrious history of his profession. "One hundred fifty years ago, when we were all unified under one guild, but led by the—"

"Stonemasons," I finished. I'd heard the story at least a hundred times, but he never tired of telling it.

"Indeed. We have always accepted the burden of leadership."

"A selfless act, no doubt."

He chuckled. "Toolkeepers' legend has it that while the Crown commissioned the Seminary's design from its own architects, the Conservatory was designed by the royal alchemist, Lord Calyx himself."

I pictured the father of alchemy as he stood next to the emperor in the atrium's stained glass. "Really?"

"That building was his passion toward the end of his life, when his scientific pursuits proved . . . fruitless."

"They weren't *fruitless*," I snapped. "Calyx set the Alchemary down the path of its most noble pursuits; not every farmer gets to harvest the fruit of his own labors."

My father's brows rose. "It seems propaganda has proven immune to your amnesia. How much have you remembered?"

"None of it. Not a single day spent here, before this week."

"I see. . . ." He nodded slowly, and I could tell from the tight line of his jaw that he *did* see.

I'd known the history of the Alchemary since I was a child, and it wasn't from propaganda.

It was from bedtime stories.

Half an hour later, we'd spoken on topics that could be addressed and eschewed those that still could not, and though I couldn't remember the absence from my father, I felt content for the moment to have him near, despite the gulf that lay between us.

Perhaps because of it.

With a sigh, my father set his teacup on the bench and stood, clearing his throat rather formally.

"Well, Amber," he said, collecting his satchel from the ground as I stood. "I do hope you'll see fit to come visit this year. You could travel with the Gregorys, or I could send a carriage. Or I could arrange to have work nearby, around the time of your holiday, and fetch you home myself, if you wouldn't entirely detest a couple of days spent on the road with your father."

I extended my hand for him to shake. "You have my word that I will consider it."

My father's palm slid against mine, his fingers gripping my own warmly. He held my hand for a moment, looking right into my eyes. "And should this entire proposal prove little more than an old man's whimsy . . ." A grin tugged at the corner of his mouth and at what had become, since I'd last seen him, a rather spectacular silver mustache. "A simple correspondence from my daughter would not go amiss. I should dearly love to know when you've recovered your memories, and what astonishing feats this malady has hidden from you."

"Those would likely be alchemical feats," I informed him. "And you have little stomach for the practice."

"Indeed. But I have nothing in this wide world but affection and pride for my daughter. Even if her interests oppose my own."

"In that case . . ." I took a deep breath. "There is a Family Weekend coming up soon. I hear there's a festival on the first night. You would not be unwelcome, should you and Martyn choose to attend."

My father leaned in and pressed his lips to my forehead. "I will do my very best."

After he had gone, I turned to clear away our teacups, and I found his handkerchief lying on the bench, where it had fallen from his pocket.

For no reason I could understand, I picked up that handkerchief, still damp with his tears, and I stuffed it into the pocket of my frock.

Thirteen

As the sun rose on Saturday morning, five days since I'd woken up with amnesia, I finally stepped for the first time into the third-floor lab devoted to use by Mastery-year students. As I had hoped, the space was almost entirely abandoned.

Almost.

Wilder Gregory rushed from table to table like a man gone mad. Like a man possessed by the spirit of alchemy and at home in its demanding embrace.

He looked wild, and driven, and passionate. It was mesmerizing.

For some time, I only watched him, delaying the announcement of my presence, as curious about when he would notice me as I was about what, exactly, he was doing. And as I stood in the doorway, leaning against the thick wooden frame, a calm descended over me despite the early hour. Despite the constant, grinding anxiety of my own ignorance and the weight of my secret.

I felt at home here, though I could not remember ever having utilized an alchemical laboratory.

It was the sounds. The gentle bubbling of half a dozen liquids. The soft sputter of flames and the clinking of glass against glass. Each noise felt familiar and made sense, like the crackle of the fire in my childhood hearth.

It was the sights as well. Tables, and stools, and copper piping. Parchment, bound notebooks, and charcoal pencils. The furnaces, one bricked into each of three corners of the room, and a fourth towering like a castle turret toward the ceiling.

Athanor.

The name of the specialty furnace bloomed from the dark recesses of my mind, unbidden. I could not remember learning it, yet I knew it, just as I knew that it was kept burning at a constant, low temperature, in order to . . .

But then came the limit of the imageless memory: one fact liberated from the prison of my mind, while countless others remained bound in chains, behind locked doors.

Yet even with no memory of ever having done so, I suddenly felt like I could easily step into the room, slide onto a stool at an empty table, and know in exactly what order I would pull my notes from my satchel and begin setting up my supplies. I knew how I would lay out my writing utensils, arrange my pipettes, and organize my thoughts into orderly lists of tasks, testable theories, and goals.

The mental skit had the feel of a ritual I'd performed a thousand times.

Though my understanding was that each student had been assigned a single lab table, and presumably a specific, requisite number of supplies, Wilder had projects in progress at three different stations. Powdered substances sat on scales. Brightly tinted liquids bubbled in bulbous beakers suspended above flames of varying heights and colors. Two different alembics dripped distillations into vials suspended by thin iron and copper frames. Hourglasses of various sizes stood on all three tables, positioned next to specific tasks.

As I watched, Wilder spun from one table to the next, where he bent to peer into a small hourglass on its level. Then he seized a glass pipette and used it to add several drops of oil to a flame burning beneath a distinctive bulbous, flat-bottomed vial filled with a simmering scarlet fluid.

Awe filled me as I stared around the room. This was a student space, yet its supplies were of the finest quality. The glass was thinner, smoother, and clearer than I remember ever seeing in my mother's apothecary shop in Innswood. A cabinet across the back of the room held row after row of beakers and vials. Scales and burners. Alembics, retorts, and receivers. Mortars, pestles, and crucibles. And a substantial array of hourglasses in every conceivable size, their sand ranging in color across the rainbow, and presumably ranging in texture as well.

Wilder hummed as he worked, grinning faintly when a color pleased him or the level of a flame looked just right. I couldn't help but smile as well. He looked so practiced and efficient. So comfortable in the lab, doing a dozen things at once, and . . .

He turned to grab a scale sitting at the end of one of his tables, and his eyes finally found me.

"Great writhing caduceus!" he swore softly, free hand clutching at his chest. "You startled me, Amber. What the hell are you doing, haunting the lab like a ghost?"

I laughed. "If I am a ghost, then *you* are possessed." I gestured at the chaotic, if fascinating, display spread out before me.

"We are quite a pair," he agreed with a contented nod. "Come in and close the door."

I pulled the door shut behind me, sparing a moment to look through the gorgeous stained glass panel set into its center, at eye level. Blues, and reds, and greens, each brighter than the next, all of them thin, crystal clear, and stunning.

"When you said to meet you here at dawn, I assumed you'd be running late." I had never in my life known Wilder to get out of bed unprompted. In fact, both his mother and his brother used to complain that he would keep the hours of an owl, if he were allowed, and that if they forced him awake during the morning, he would drag his feet about the house like a spirit wrested from its own grave.

I saw no sign of that indolence as Wilder rushed across the room and back, grabbing supplies and mixing chemicals with hardly a glance at the notes lying scattered across all three tables, in places perilously close to open flame.

"In fact, I was late," he admitted, setting three flat-bottomed bulbous vials on the edge of a table. "But that was six hours ago. I've since more than made up for it."

"You've been here all night?"

"Of course not! I didn't start until eleven, and even then I got decidedly little real work done, because Keryth and Lennox were hunkered over their clumsy little grade-one tincture, trying to discover why it had congealed like milk left on the table overnight. I finally had to run them out of the lab myself."

"And how did you do that?"

"I 'accidentally' vented a suspension with an aroma not unlike the excrement of a cat who has consumed the aforementioned curdled milk." He laughed as he turned back to the storage cabinet for a third alembic. "They couldn't clean their supplies and flee fast enough."

"Wow," I breathed as I set my satchel on an empty stool. "You make alchemy sound so glamorous."

"It *is* glamorous." He set the alembic down and seized my waist, pulling me close so that his words brushed warm and damp against my earlobe. "It is vital, and thrilling, and *stimulating*," he whispered, and sparks trailed up and down my spine. "And even when it doesn't progress like you hoped, it's still the second-most fun one could ever have in a laboratory setting."

"*Second* most?" I pushed him back but couldn't resist a grin at the shine in his blue eyes. I took an exaggerated look about the room. "I feel the inexplicable need to scrub every surface in the room, in case you've had the *most* fun there, with some girl whose name I'm suddenly grateful to have forgotten."

Wilder laughed, one hand splayed over his heart. "Tonight, my passion has been only for alchemy. You have my word."

A little thrill of satisfaction settled into my gut, flaring into the soft warmth of a banked coal.

"Thank you," I said as he lurched toward the table on his right just as the final grains of a bright blue powder drained through the top half of a small hourglass. "For helping me. I was up half the night studying, as I have been all week, and while everything I read makes sense—it settles into place quickly and logically—the sheer volume of what I have yet to cover feels insurmountable."

"Oh, I assure you, it's . . . mountable."

"*Sur*mountable," I corrected.

Wilder only grinned as he removed a small flame from beneath a suspended flat-bottomed vial full of a murky brown liquid.

"And regarding practical application . . . well, I've managed none of that so far. There are only four weeks left until the first trial, and I haven't managed to produce a single elixir." I yawned into my own closed fist. "I don't suppose you've started any tea? The stronger the better?"

"Um . . . no." Wilder left the vial to cool while he began counting out weights onto one half of the scale he'd just set up. "But you're welcome to boil some water over that flame, if you've brought some tea leaves. If not, Yoslyn keeps a pouch of loose leaves in the cabinet under her table, and she won't notice if you pinch a few."

"What makes you think she wouldn't notice?"

He shrugged. "She's never noticed when I borrowed a pinch of her powdered cinnabar." He set the vial on the scale, having accounted for the weight of the vessel first by placing an identical empty vial on the other side; then he took note on a sheet of parchment of how far the scale dipped. "Life would be very difficult for me around here if our classmates actually kept track of their supplies. . . ."

After another moment he set his quill down and met my gaze. "Okay! I guess we should get your lab station set up."

"Yes. And in that vein, I have two questions. First, which of these is mine, and second, why do you appear to have three?"

"This one is mine." He laid one hand on the center of the three occupied tables. "That one is yours," he added with a gesture to the table on his left. "I've been borrowing it at night, considering that it's thus far been unoccupied."

"I see. And that one?" I said with a glance at the far table, where two different solutions sat cooling over extinguished open-flame burners.

"Lennox's station."

"And should I assume he's ignorant of this arrangement?"

"I think we should both assume that Lennox's ignorance knows no limits. Thus the congealed tincture."

"Even if that's accurate"—though in truth, he seemed like a perfectly competent alchemy student, based on my limited interactions with him in class—"isn't it against the rules to borrow other students' space and supplies without permission?"

Wilder gave me an odd look, coupled with a strangely soft, quiet smile. "What use have I for rules, when it is results that matter?"

"That sounds like a quotation. Are you referencing a textbook?"

"A *walking* textbook, of sorts." His smile seemed to . . . sadden. "I am quoting the great Amber Katherine Fallbrook, alchemy student extraordinaire."

"*I* said that?"

Wilder nodded. "As often as you said 'Good morning, Wilder. You're looking *particularly* virile and attractive today.' Which, in case it wasn't clear, was quite often."

I laughed. But the sound faded when I glanced across all three occupied tables. "What time do the other students usually arrive?"

"Not until after morning tea, which is served an hour later on the weekend." He glanced through the window, clearly judging the quality of the light. "We have around three hours, by my best guess. And that's perfect, because I have *just* finished with your station and am now free to show you how to clean the equipment and set everything up fresh."

"You say that as if it's part of the favor you're doing me, yet I feel as if I've been manipulated into doing your chores for you, as when we were children."

"I never manipulated you!" he declared as he began corking the open vials suspended on iron frames on my workstation. "Grab the colophony, will you? Third vial from the right, on the storage shelf."

Colophony, I thought, taking advantage of the opportunity to quiz myself on recently relearned vocabulary. *Tree resin often used for airtight sealing of glass vessels.*

"You never . . ." I scoffed as I proffered the requested vial.

"I'm afraid the facts are on my side," Wilder insisted with a cheeky grin. "Your memory is demonstrably faulty, and *my* recollection of the situation is that you *wanted* to help me with my menial obligations so I could accompany you to the pond for swimming."

An image flashed in my mind of Wilder, standing in the local pond, naked from the waist up and glistening. We'd been sixteen or so, and water—

—runs down Desmond's scowling face in a dozen rivulets, dripping from the thick length of his lashes. Dangling from his nose and the hard line of his clenched jaw.

I laugh, going up on my toes. My tongue darts out to catch the drop threatening to fall from his chin, and before I can lower myself again, his hands catch around my waist, holding me in place while his mouth crashes down over mine.

Desmond tastes like tea, and iced sweetbread, and like the cold, fresh rain pouring over us in the dark, drenching my hair and sweetening our kiss, making me shiver against the warmth of his body pressing the length of mine. . . .

I finally pull away, breathing hard, my hands clutching around damp handfuls of his cloak. Heat blossoms low in my belly, an aching hunger that food could never satisfy. But when I look up, his copper-brown eyes have brightened into a sparkling cerulean. . . .

"Amber?"

I blinked and found Wilder staring at me, a beaker evidently forgotten in his grip.

"What happened? Are you okay?"

Not even a little bit. Was that a memory? Had one slipped between the bars of its cell, or had the jailer released one poor, emaciated scrap of a recollection just to toy with me? It wasn't accurate. It couldn't be. Brown eyes don't just *become* blue.

Would it do me any good to have my memory back, if it could not be trusted?

"I'm fine," I lied. "Just tired. How are you so alert, having been up all night? I can hardly keep my eyes open."

"Try a swig of that moss-green solution, on the far table."

I followed his glance to Lennox's workstation, where I'd noticed two solutions cooling. "Why? What is it?"

"It's an elixir of concentration. It will keep you alert, as if you've had four cups of tea, while it enhances your ability to focus on the task at hand."

I stared at the vial, yet another of the distinctive flat-bottomed variety, frowning at the clear liquid. "You made this?"

"I made it, I consumed it, and I will offer it for purchase."

"To whom?"

Wilder shrugged. "Several of the staff members, when they're approaching a deadline and aren't pleased with their results.

There aren't enough hours in the day left for them, so they must steal hours from the night."

"Like you do," I murmured.

"Precisely. And I'm not the only one. Lennox has bought a few doses, over the past year."

Understanding flared like a torch, burning off a bit of my own naivety. "You run a business," I said. "In secret. And those students, from the first day of class? The ones who accosted you in the hallway? They're your customers?"

"They are *among* my customers." He watched me carefully, assessing my reaction.

"Lennox Pettifog is one of them?"

"Occasionally. I have to be careful when I offer him an elixir of concentration, though, because when he takes it, he stays in here for hours, and I can't get anything done myself."

"Because you need . . . secrecy?"

"My business requires an absence of prying eyes, yes." Wilder returned to my station, empty-handed, and began disassembling an alembic for cleaning.

"What grade are these?"

"That is difficult to say, because there are no grade scales on record for these particular, *original* formulas." He gave me a saucy wink. "Though, naturally, I'd guess based on efficacy that they're professional grade, at least."

"Of course you would." I knelt to examine his vials from eye level.

"The elixir won't hurt you. You have my word. I would never give you anything that would harm you, Amber."

His eye contact was direct and open. It hid nothing.

"I know. Thank you."

I started to politely turn down the offer anyway, leery of potential side effects and possible insomnia. But then I thought about how much I still had to learn, and how few hours I had left before the first trial.

"Thank you," I repeated as I reached for the vial.

"No!" Wilder lurched forward and snatched it before my fingers had more than brushed the warm surface of the glass. "That's *fern* green. I said to sip from the *moss* green." He tossed his head toward the other vial.

Perhaps someone with a botany affinity would have known the difference?

My heart leapt into my throat, startled by the mistake I'd almost made, even though I had no real conception of it. "Why? What is the fern green?"

Wilder looked embarrassed for one fleeting moment. Then he visibly shook off that impulse and grinned. Deliberately. Widely. As if he were trying as hard to convince himself of his amusement as he was to convince me. "This is a *special* elixir, for Professor Robards."

"My boss, Professor Robards?"

"Indeed. Perhaps you've noticed that he pulls his curls back to cover a thinning spot on his scalp?"

I had noticed, but . . . "How is that any of your business?"

"It's my business, precisely because it *is* business. He's in the market for a hair-loss remedy, though that isn't the only measure he takes to ward against age-related infirmities." Wilder waggled the vial, and its contents sloshed softly within.

I had the distinct impression I was supposed to understand the purpose of the elixir. "Is it for his joints? Do they trouble him?"

Wilder laughed, his head thrown back, eyes crinkled with true amusement. "An aching bone *is* his problem," he conceded when he'd calmed enough to speak. "But likely not whichever one you're thinking of. Professor Robards needs an elixir to allow him to perform."

I blinked at him.

"For his *wife*," Wilder added. After a further pause, he sighed. "In their *marital bed*? Because without it, no one tells *him* how distinctly virile and attractive he looks, at his age."

My brow rose as comprehension finally dawned. "You've made an elixir to help him . . . rise to the occasion?"

"Precisely. And not for the first time."

"How?" I demanded with a glance at his notes. There weren't a dozen words in total on any single page. No formulas at all. They were more like . . . reminders. Hints that only Wilder would understand. "How do you know how to make such a thing?"

"Trial and error, mostly. More error than anything, in this case. I stumbled upon the formula a year and a half ago, when I was trying for a different kind of stimulant entirely." His grin grew more heated. "Imagine my bewilderment when an attempt to solve a more innocuous social malady led, instead, to an entirely different manner of . . . affliction. Although I hesitate to characterize that particular condition as an adversity."

"You took this elixir yourself?"

"Who else am I meant to test it on?" His grin crinkled the corner of his eyes pleasantly as he leaned closer to whisper, "I will say, even when the result misses the mark a bit, I am generally quite pleased with the outcome of any endeavor in the lab. And that time was no exception." He winked. "Despite every attempt to *remedy* the situation, I missed three classes. Otherwise, I would have made *quite* the public spectacle."

I blinked at him. Then I burst into laughter, even as I flushed from head to toe at the mental image of Wilder walking around campus with a distinctive bulge in the front of his robe.

And thoughts of what his attempts to "remedy" the situation might entail.

Had I been involved?

"What was the original 'social malady'?" I asked, a grin lingering on my face.

His own smile faded at the reminder. "I . . . It doesn't matter."

"It might," I insisted, shifting uncomfortably on my feet as I tried to come up with a tactful way to explain my concern. "If this is an ailment we shared, due to . . . evidently . . . the nature of our relationship. This 'social malady.'"

For a prolonged moment, Wilder only stared at me. Then comprehension dawned behind his eyes, which brightened as he threw his head back and laughed. "No, no, Amber," he finally said while I stared at him with my arms crossed over my chest. "This was not a physical ailment. And certainly not of an intimate nature. It was an issue of the mind, though I'll admit, I find it equally embarrassing."

I shook my head, brows knit together, somehow even more confused by his explanation. "What could be as embarrassing—"

"Nothing." He turned away from me to neutralize the inside of a used vial before he began washing it. "It doesn't matter."

A tiny crack opened in my heart as I watched him, his shoulders hunched, his jaw tight. I felt bruised by the understanding that he was unwilling to trust me with . . . something.

"Presumably"—I began, as I carefully carried two vials and an alembic toward him from my half-empty workstation—"this is something I was already aware of, before."

In my pre-amnesia life, when I'd known who I was, and who he was. And who *we* were.

"Yes." He turned to take the vials from me, and his gaze held mine for a second, some unspoken pain welling behind his eyes. "But you look at me differently now. You don't remember my struggles. My failures. I find myself reluctant to disclose them and watch all of this"—he waved his free hand in a circle around my face, indicating my expression—"change."

"Wilder." I caught his arm as he tried to turn. "I want it all back. Good and bad. I want your *trust* back. Your confidence."

"Those golden eyes will be the death of me," he whispered staring straight into mine. "Very well." He sighed. "During our first year—Fundamentals year—I suffered from a particular lack of confidence. A certainty, deep down, that I did not belong at this hallowed institution."

I frowned. "Why would you ever think that? When we were children, the recruiters came to Innswood specifically to see *you.* To see shocking feats of alchemy performed by a twelve-year-old. Don't you remember? It was pure luck they even noticed Desmond and me."

His grin bloomed again softly. "I was a bit of a miscreant, wasn't I?"

"A bit?" I scoffed, and Wilder laughed.

"Well, it turns out that playing around with alchemy is fun." He gestured at the three tables still occupied with his illicit projects. "But classwork is *hard,* and for the first time in my life, it wasn't enough to just be . . . me."

The backs of my eyes stung as I watched the remembered insecurity play out behind his expression. I took his left hand and squeezed, encouraging him to go on as my thumb stroked over the long-healed scar from a chemical burn on the back of his knuckles.

"I understood how everything works in here." He gestured again at the lab tables. "But in there . . ." His arm swept downward, indicating the lower floors of the building, dedicated to classrooms. "Dates of important discoveries, the history of the Alchemary, lives of important historical figures, even the names of twenty different styles of beakers—I know how to *use* them, but does it really matter what they're called?"

Yes, of course it mattered. Without the names, how could

one ask for a specific beaker, list it in a requisition form, or pass the complete details of an experiment forward as knowledge of the craft?

"The names of techniques and various theorems? Lab reports and inventories, and detailed records of every failure? How does any of that help?"

Oh, Wilder. I squeezed his hand harder.

"I know, I know," he whispered. "I can see it on your face. You know how important all of that is, and you don't even remember learning any of it. I know it's important, too. But I'm not good at it."

"Oh, I'm sure—"

"No." He twisted his wrist slowly until my hand was cradled in his, and a shiver ran up my spine as his thumb stroked my palm. "I'm good at a lot of things. *Really* good at a couple of them." A rakish heat flared behind his eyes. "I understand that with the same open-eyed objectivity with which I swear to you that I am *not* good at the pedantic aspects of alchemy. Which are largely all that are measured around here. All that are valued. So for the first time in my life, friendships—relationships—were being formed based on a common measure of worth, and . . ." He exhaled slowly. "I was found lacking."

"You were left out." I couldn't help wondering if I'd been one of those turning away from him.

He nodded. "And that led to me losing confidence in other areas." He shrugged, and the motion tugged my hand. "But there's an elixir for everything, right? And the one place I hadn't lost confidence was the lab."

My nose crinkled as I looked up at him, suddenly aware of how close we stood. "You made a cure for . . . insecurity?"

"Not a cure. A treatment. It only works temporarily, but it *does* work."

"How so?"

Wilder shifted awkwardly on his feet, reluctance layered into his hesitation. "It dulls inhibition, allowing the more entertaining and charismatic aspects of one's personality to shine through. There's also some evidence that it draws others to you, through the bodily emission of some essence we cannot yet detect through scientific measures."

"Some secretion—a natural bodily extract or vapor—we cannot see, smell, or taste . . ." I mused, intrigued by the idea.

He smiled, clearly pleased by my interest. "Not consciously, anyway."

"Have you discovered the manner of secretion? Is it something in the saliva? The sweat? Humors exhaled from the lungs?"

"I do not know, and the truth is that my studies don't lie down that path," he said.

I swallowed a pang of disappointment. That path sounded *fascinating*.

"My point is that while I did not succeed on the first attempt to make this elixir, a use became clear for one of my more utilitarian failures, and now Professor Robards can keep *Mrs*. Robards happy. And likely some women *other* than Mrs. Robards, if we're being honest."

He leaned closer, though there was no one around to overhear, and his smile was back. "Take a good look at him when he arrives for class. You'll notice that some afternoons, directly after the lunch hour, he seems to be in *rather* a good mood. And that he may smile surreptitiously at a certain female member of the faculty."

I wasn't particularly comfortable having that kind of intimate knowledge about my favorite professor.

"And Professor Robards pays you for this . . . merchandise?" I asked.

Wilder shrugged again, and this time he looked away. "In a manner of speaking."

I watched as he sealed the vial and stored it carefully in the cabinet beneath his own workspace.

"Now. Let's clean off Lennox's station so I can help you set up yours." He grinned at me as we worked, his blue-eyed gaze setting off a host of familiar sparks deep in my belly. "I must say, Amber Fallbrook. This tutelage arrangement is *quite* a reversal of roles for us."

Fourteen

"Don't forget, your theme papers on the history of the quest for the Elixir of Life are due next week," Professor Bollinger said as he erased the large, framed black slate at the front of the small classroom. "Make sure you've had your thesis topic approved by the end of our next class. I don't want any of you repeating territory. That makes these assignments exceedingly boring to read."

A couple of students chuckled.

From my right, Wilder yawned. He'd spent another late night in the lab, and both his morning tea and his elixir of concentration were clearly wearing off. "If you write my paper for me," he leaned over to whisper, "I will do *anything* you want. Massage your feet. Serve you tea and scones in bed. I'll even undergo the Black Trial for you."

I snorted softly. It was a ridiculous offer. We'd be in the first trial—the Black Trial—at the same time, in full view of all of our classmates, our professors, and the official observers. I would be on my own, and the reminder of that, even in the form of a jest, made my arms prickle with gooseflesh.

I was not ready.

I slid my notes into my satchel and dropped my quill into the inkwell cradled in a cutout at the front of our shared table, but before I could stand, already planning to claim a corner table and a kettle of strong tea for us both at the Refectory, I heard my name.

Alarm raised the fine hairs at the base of my skull, and I looked up to find Professor Bollinger staring right at me. "Yes?"

"I need to see you for a few minutes after class." He failed to add *if you're available*, or *if you don't mind*, or even *please*.

"Of course." I slouched back into my chair, struggling to resist a scowl as Wilder stood without me. "Get us a corner table?" I whispered.

He nodded. "Black tea and a fig fritter to split. It'll be waiting. . . ."

With that and a sympathetic smile, he headed into the hall with our classmates.

As Professor Bollinger sank into an empty chair across the aisle from me, the distinctive heavy clank of the classroom door closing drew my attention. I turned to find Professor Edmiston headed toward us, her heeled shoes clacking beneath the swishing hem of her long professor's robe.

I'd been ambushed. Truthfully, though, I deserved no less, having ignored summonses from them both.

"Amber." Professor Edmiston shoved a chin-length silver ringlet back from her face. "Thank you so much for making time to meet with us."

As if I'd had any choice.

"We've been informed by the Bluehelm about your condition," she continued. "And we thought it was important to communicate with you directly about the issue, though we hadn't intended to wait until halfway through the second week of the term."

Which was my fault, though she was kind enough not to point that out.

"Our understanding is that you remember nothing of your first two years at this institution," Professor Bollinger added, small, round spectacles perched precariously near the end of his nose. "Has there been any improvement since the initial diagnosis?"

"Unfortunately and decidedly not," I said, clutching my satchel to my chest. "Since the school year has just started, I assume you have no real measure of the kind of student I am—" But my words dissolved into a bitter aftertaste as I noted the discomfort that had settled over both of their expressions. "I've been in your classes before?"

"Fundamentals year," Professor Edmiston confirmed. "For Basic Alchemical Equations. You were the quickest study I've had in my fourteen years as an instructor. Not coincidentally, you were also one of the most verbose, though always on the topic at hand."

Embarrassment flooded my cheeks, and that heat only intensified when Professor Bollinger spoke. "You were in my Accuracy in Records and Note-Taking practicum during your Fundamentals year. Among the strongest in the class," he added. "Though Keryth gave you some stiff competition."

I had no idea what to say, so I chewed my bottom lip and clutched my satchel tighter, fighting inexplicable feelings of guilt over how badly my performance this term must be disappointing them.

It was not my fault I couldn't remember what they'd taught me in terms past. That I knew of, anyway. And yet guilt over my impending failure felt like a massive weight on my shoulders, slowly pressing me into the ground. Into my own professional and academic grave.

"How are you faring so far?" Professor Edmiston pulled a silver barrette from her pocket and shoved it into her hair at her temple, to hold back the troublesome curl. "Are you keeping up, by any measure of the term?"

"I'm doing my best," I assured them. "I stay up half the night, every night, studying by candlelight, and I believe I've picked up the basic concepts extraordinarily quickly. By my own judgment, anyway. Some are difficult to master, without instruction, but most of them make sense once I've had a chance to study them. As if

I just need to be *reminded* of them, in a manner of speaking. But I owe you both the truth," I added, and Professor Bollinger's brows rose. "I am not at the level of my classmates. *Yet*."

I likely wasn't yet at the level of most Proficiency-year students either, though I could probably have given the Fundamentals-year cohort some stiff competition.

My instructors glanced at each other, and I had no way of interpreting the look they shared.

Professor Edmiston spoke first. "Amber, do you honestly believe that you will be ready for the first trial in just a few weeks?"

I opened my mouth, but the words at the back of my throat seemed to be functioning less as a means of communication than as a dam across a river, obstructing the flow.

I could not force them forward. Nor was I sure what shape they would take, if they ever broke free.

"Do you understand what the trial will entail?" Professor Bollinger asked, and I could only shake my head.

He sighed and looked at the other instructor for some tacit approval before continuing. "We are not supposed to speak about the trial in advance of it, but your classmates have at least some vague understanding of what's coming, based on rumors they've heard over the years. Rumors you can no longer remember. So I say this not to give you any advantage, but to try to restore the balance between their understanding and yours."

"And to give you a grasp of the grave threat the trials represent to anyone who is unprepared," Professor Edmiston added.

Her colleague nodded. "The Black Trial is about spiritual death, so that you can be 'reborn' during the White Trial, in the purification phase."

The goal, I understood, being the perfection of the human mind and body. Or at least, the elevation of both to a standard worthy of an enduring position at the Alchemary.

"You and your classmates will each be administered a poison. A *real* poison," he insisted, and his somber expression gave me no reason to doubt the claim. "You will then be given a chance to concoct an antidote to the poison so you may cure yourself. Obviously the goal is not just to demonstrate your skill and save your own life, but to do that in time to avoid permanent damage from the poison."

"Or death," Professor Edmiston added, somewhat unnecessarily.

"Do . . ." I cleared my throat, fingers digging into the leather of my satchel, where my nails no doubt left their imprint. "Do students ever actually die during the trial?"

Professor Bollinger nodded. "Every year."

"You need not be among them, Amber," Professor Edmiston added. "But I'm afraid that at your current skill and comprehension level, there's little chance of any other outcome."

Despite the logic in their warning, indignation pricked at my nerve endings. "You're trying to frighten me?"

She sighed. "We're trying to reason with you. You've always been a flawlessly logical pupil, and your memory may be gone, but your intelligence clearly is not. You can understand the deficit you're facing. The very slim chance of your success. Of your survival. Your fate is in your own hands, child." Her tone very nearly pled with me, independent of her words. "Pride and ego are not worth dying for."

Tears pricked at the backs of my eyes, but I blinked them back, fighting the grim conclusion that true comprehension of the Black Trial brought with it.

I could quit, or I could fail. And failure, under this particular circumstance, would come for me in the form of my own demise.

I thanked my professors for their concern and assured them I would thoroughly consider their warnings as I moved forward. But that I *would be,* at least for the moment, moving forward. Because while death might be the ultimate reward for my hubris, I could quit at any point up until the moment I was offered that poison, and quitting before I knew without a doubt that I would not survive would be pointless.

Everything I had ever wanted was to be found at, and *only* at, the Alchemary. That had always been true. Now, however, the school also represented my best and possibly only chance to recover my memory.

The instructors dismissed me with identical disappointed expressions, which seemed to follow me as I moved down the center aisle toward the door, past table after empty table, my satchel thumping against my right hip. I pulled the heavy door open and stepped into the hall, fighting tears again, now that no one could see me, and . . .

I gasped, startled to see Pryce Wishart coming out of the classroom across the hall. He smiled when he saw me, but then he went about his way without a single word or glance back.

Dread pooling hot and thickly viscous in the pit of my stomach, I peered into the room he'd just left and found only an empty classroom, with no sign of a recent class or meeting in progress.

As his steps faded in the direction of the central staircase, I could not shake the feeling that moments before I'd emerged from Professor Bollinger's classroom, Pryce's ear had been pressed against the door.

The symbol for the Philosopher's Stone is a circle inside a square, inside a triangle, inside another circle, and each shape represents several overlapping concepts, touching one another at distinct points.

The inner circle represents the feminine, the mind, infinity, the inner spirit, and the element Water. The square represents the masculine, structure, matter, and material, as well as the physical body and the element Earth. The triangle, an equilateral, represents with each of its sides the connection between mind, matter, and spirit, as well as the element Fire, which represents transformation. The triangle also represents balance and stability. The outer circle represents the macrocosm and the whole, the unification of everything within and the final elevation of a form into its greatest potential.

—from *The Unfaltering Quest for the Philosopher's Stone*,
by Betta Gifford

Fifteen

After the midday meal on Saturday, I returned to my bedchamber to find that a letter had been slid under my door. The seal—bronze-colored wax imprinted with a version of the Toolkeepers' crossed-hammer sigil—told me that it was from my father.

I'd found no such correspondence among my things, upon waking with no memory, which meant either that my father had never written to me before or that I had not kept his letters.

I settled at my desk with a tight feeling in my chest and broke the seal. That feeling expanded into a soft pressure as I scanned the familiar handwriting.

My Dearest Amber,

I am writing to you from a carriage, on my way toward the southern reaches of the kingdom, to where I have been called to supervise the construction of a new public bathhouse. Please excuse any stray marks as the result of skittish horses and an uneven road.

I have given Martyn your love, and we are both delighted by your invitation to the Alchemary's Family Weekend festivities. We shall endeavor to attend, if at all possible. While I regret the cause for my recent visit, I welcome any opportunity for your company, and it has been far too long since I last saw your face.

I have, since the day you were born, been able to measure my own worth from the weight of your gaze, and on my return journey, your honey-colored eyes haunted me, as they so often did when you were a child. I greatly regret the rift between us. And while I cannot strike past mistakes from our history, nor can I return memories I was never privy to, I can *offer you this memory from your childhood, which I have always treasured:*

When you were but five or six years of age, there came a rainy morning when you were forbidden to go out, and you were quite cross about the circumstance. To appease you, your mother gave you a scrap of parchment and a chunk of charcoal and told you to draw whatever suited your fancy. I returned for the midday meal expecting to find your parchment covered in flowers, rabbits, and perhaps a vial or two from your mother's apothecary shop.

Instead you had spent the entire morning painstakingly translating the verbiage from an old public-notice flyer into your mother's native tongue, though you hardly knew how to write a word of it. She said you'd run into the front of the shop at least a hundred times to demand instructions on how to form the letters, even as you insisted on writing them all yourself.

I knew then that nothing could stop you from whatever you set your mind to. And that you had more serious, ambitious ideas than most other children. I see that same passion and determination in you now, and though our views on the ethical use of alchemy instead of labor are quite divergent, I know that you have only good intentions. And while I believe the Alchemary should not exist as an institution, I am grateful to both the academy and to the world that you can be counted upon to measure their worth, as you have always been the measure of mine.

Love always,
Your father, Cornelius Fallbrook

Tears filled my eyes as I reread his words for the third time. I had only the faintest memory of the morning he'd recounted, but the fact that it had remained with him meant more to me than I was truly willing to admit. So I tucked his letter into my mother's small wooden chest, alongside her ring, and I turned my attention to my studies.

Hours later, I looked up to find candlelight flickering across the curved stone walls of my small bedchamber from three different angles, casting overlapping shadows. I stared at them, watching the meaningless silhouettes jitter.

My window was closed against the cold night air, but I could hear the soothing crash of waves against the cliffside below, and, given my exhaustion, the rhythmic sound threatened to lull me to sleep.

With a sigh, I forced my attention back to the sheets of parchment on the desk in front of me.

Two of my candles sat on the desk, at opposing top corners. The third cast its weaker light from the bedside table on my right. They were more than capable of illuminating my work and could not be blamed for my lack of attention. In fact, the third candle almost seemed a waste of resources, considering how often my mother and I had shared a single candle placed at the center of the table when I was a child.

For the third time in the past hour, I read through my notes from class, slowly and painstakingly, comparing the symbols and concepts to one of the Fundamentals-year texts I'd "borrowed" from the library.

Slowly—*so* slowly—I was unraveling the knot of facts and theories tangled in my mind like the various balls of yarn my mother had used for knitting most evenings. I'd never thought of her yarn as a knot before, because she'd always been able to gradually, neatly unwind it. My ball of academic yarn, however . . .

I felt like I'd plunged my metaphorical knitting needle deep into the ball and plucked out random loops, all of which were too tangled with the rest of the material to come free. To give me more than a rudimentary glimpse of how they were coiled and what they meant.

With a frustrated sigh, I closed the textbook and snatched my journal from the corner of my desk. Tonight, I could understand little more of the borrowed text than of my own encoded writing, so why not dig at that ball of yarn instead?

At least that might break up the monotony.

This time, instead of focusing on all of the writing I couldn't understand—the vast majority of what was on the pages—I focused on what few alchemical symbols I *could* recognize.

Iron. Copper. Salt. Gold. And the squared circle: the alchemical symbol for the Philosopher's Stone.

A circle inside a square, inside a triangle, inside another circle, each of them touching at various sides and points.

Curious, I opened the textbook again, searched the appendix, then flipped to the pages concerning the meaning of the symbol. The combining of water, earth, and fire, of mind, matter, and spirit. The importance of balance and stability.

I read the words over and over, tracing the shapes with my gaze, then with my finger, reciting the meaning, well aware that two weeks before, all of it had held an intimate and presumably clear meaning for me.

I understood the words. I even understood the concepts. But trying to figure out how they all fit together made me feel like I was flailing in a pit of those academic yarn balls, being poked with fifty knitting needles at once every time I tried to move.

Several polite taps echoed against the door to my chamber, then it creaked open as I turned.

Wilder smiled at me in the flickering glow of my candle, and my heart leapt at the sight of him.

"Come in!" I rose to tug him inside, his hands strong and warm in my grip, and both the dirt beneath his fingernails and the scents of earth and freshly cut vegetation told me he'd spent the afternoon behind the Refectory, in the small forest where he often harvested his own ingredients.

He glanced at the parchment spread across my desk. Voice teasing, his eyes sparking with good humor, he asked, "You do know what they say about girls who spend the entire weekend studying, don't you?"

"They survive their Mastery-year trials and go on to live long, successful lives?"

He snorted. "Precisely. I am certainly not thinking of a different and much less socially stimulating answer to my own question."

"Socially . . . stimulating?"

He shrugged, one brow arched. "I care not if you hide yourself from the entire student body, so long as you don't hide *your* student body from *me*." His hands gripped my waist, and warmth glowed low in my belly. I leaned into his form and indulged a long breath dragged in through the linen draped over his chest. His scent washed over me—fresh earth and sweetened tea—and for a moment I clung to him, my fingers tangled in his tunic, low at his waist, and in the thicker material of his cloak.

My heart thudded almost painfully. There was *something*. . . .

A memory? No, more of a feeling. An impression that defied words.

I chased after it, inhaling again, deeply. My grip on his clothing tightened, and a primal sound ground up from his throat. He buried his face in the loose braid above my ear, and I clung to him, trying to draw a mental image from this ghost of a sentiment. Trying to identify it. To define it.

At last, I let him go with a sigh. Embarrassment burned beneath my skin.

"I do apologize. That was entirely inappropriate—"

"Nonsense." He reached out and tucked a strand of loose hair behind my ear. "It was . . . What did you call it? A chemical reaction? This is us, setting up that experiment, anew."

"Exothermic as hell," I murmured.

"Indeed." His pupils flared. "Though I suppose we should close the door."

I grinned. "*Scandalous*, Mr. Gregory."

His smile widened. "One can only hope, Ms. Fallbrook."

Wilder pushed the door closed, then crossed the room with several purposeful steps and sank onto the edge of the green armchair. The change in his bearing—the almost formal way he sat and the way his gaze kept returning to the door—sat heavy on my heart.

"You're not coming tonight, are you?" I asked.

We'd made plans to study in the student lab that evening. Well, plans for *me* to study—to get caught up on lab techniques and common practices—while he furthered his illicit black-market business.

"I'm still coming," he assured me. "But I'm going to be late. I have to make a delivery across the bridge, in Saltstrand."

"What kind of delivery?"

His grin faded into a soft but unyielding look. "The kind you're better off not knowing about."

"I already know what you do in the lab after hours," I pointed out, quite reasonably, in my own opinion. And while he nodded, there was something unspoken in his smile that made me feel naive.

Perhaps I didn't know *all* of what he did in the lab after hours.

Perhaps his illicit side business could work to my advantage.

"Will you . . . Will you make an elixir for me? Will you give it a shot, at least? Or perhaps work with me to create what I need?"

Wilder's left brow arched, giving him an intrigued look that I found inexplicably alluring.

He leaned forward and took my hand. "Whatever can I do for you, Amber?" he asked as he tugged me closer.

The low pitch of his voice tugged sensitive threads deep within me. Was it possible that obvious and true interest in a woman's needs and ideas could make an already fetching man even more appealing? Was anyone at the Alchemary studying that phenomenon?

"Wilder, I *must* recover my memory. Desmond insists that I'm in danger here, and my father believes that danger comes from some specific, unknown source. From an individual. And that the threat may not have passed. I remain unconvinced by either of those theories, yet I cannot dismiss them. And even if they prove baseless . . . I need my life back. I need to remember what I've learned, and what I've accomplished, and how I've changed, and how my relationships have evolved." I squeezed his hand. "*You* seem to have a treatment for every deficit. Concentration. Confidence. Tolerance. A man's ability to . . . perform. Can you help me overcome the deficit of my memory?"

"With alchemy?" He seemed both interested in and skeptical of the possibility.

"That is generally the focus around here."

"Indeed. But . . . there is quite a bit of trial and error in my approach."

"I am aware."

"And that takes time."

"Which is unfortunate. But that time will pass regardless. I may as well be making layered use of it, don't you think?"

He nodded slowly. "But Amber, I have no one to test developing versions of your memory elixir on, other than you. No one else has your symptoms. And I'm concerned that one of the aforementioned errors in the process could make things worse. That you could become ill or injured."

I frowned, searching his gaze. "If you had someone else, you would risk injuring them in the testing phase?"

"I don't relish the thought," he admitted. "But if the alternative was to risk injuring *you*? I would not hesitate."

A complicated mixture of emotion exploded within me. An affectionate warmth, tinged with a thread of horror.

"But we don't have that option," he continued, gently squeezing my hand. "And I'm not convinced that the possibility of recovering your memory is worth the risk of an adverse result."

I pulled my hand from his grip. "I appreciate your caution. But that is my decision to make." And he showed no such caution when he tested his elixirs on himself. "Will you help me?"

Wilder scrubbed his hands over his face, blond hair falling over his fingers with the frustrated gesture. Finally he looked up at me. "Of course. But only because I'm afraid that if I don't, you'll try it on your own, despite the fact that you've recovered very little of your skill in the lab."

"How well you know me," I murmured.

He rose and laid his hand on my shoulder. "You go ahead. Set up your station and get started with the Fundamentals-year exercises. I'll be there as soon as I can."

"What if someone else comes in?"

Wilder looked amused and a little sad; yet again, his expression left me feeling naive, as if I were missing something that should have been patently obvious. "No one else will be studying, Amber. It's Saturday night. Our entire cohort will be at the Dusty Beaker within the hour."

"Have I been there?" I asked as a now-familiar discomfort anchored me to the stone floor, like weights sewn into my skirt. "At the Beaker?"

An alehouse just past the bridge in Saltstrand, I had gathered from overheard conversations. A place where students hung out on the weekends. Professors, reportedly, withdrew to a room in the back, where they could unwind out of sight of their pupils.

Wilder's smile loosened. "You were never a regular, but you've certainly been there. *Everyone's* been there." His brows dipped as he studied me. "Would you rather meet me there tonight? There's no edict declaring that you must study *every* night."

I laughed, but the sound felt bitter, even to my own ears. "Alas, I have no time to waste with ale and revelry. Though I *will* be brewing some of Yoslyn's tea tonight. And I took extra pastries from the Refectory at the noon meal, just for this occasion."

"That sounds nice," he said as he headed toward the door, and he genuinely seemed to mean it. "Try not to blow yourself up before I get there."

Sixteen

My lab station looked perfect, as far as I could tell. What I'd considered an art, when I watched Wilder do it, now seemed more of a science, and I was nothing if not eager to apply logic to any new scenario.

Within half an hour of arriving, I had, carefully following the directions, set up three different experiments, burners waiting unlit under various beakers, receiving vessels positioned beneath the open ends of condenser tubes. I'd organized pipettes by size and divided my selection between the three experiments. My parchment lay ready, alongside quills and a full inkwell.

I was standing at the back of the room, making a list of materials as I perused a selection of powdered substances of various bright and intriguing colors, stored in jars above a selection of mortars and pestles, when the shuffle of feet against the stone floor at my back made me smile.

"Took you long enough," I said without turning.

A male voice scoffed, amused. "If I didn't know any better, I'd say you understand what you're doing."

I froze.

That was not Wilder's voice.

"And yet . . . I do know better."

I turned slowly, scrambling for a response, to find Pryce Wishart standing on the other side of my lab station, his chin stubble having grown into an actual beard this late in the evening. His hands rested on the table, as if he'd just surveyed the landscape and found it unexpectedly serviceable. But he wasn't looking at the table.

His muddy tea-colored gaze was squarely focused on me.

"I'm afraid I have no idea what you mean," I finally said, hoping my tone discouraged further discussion rather than demanded an explanation.

"I do believe there are many things you genuinely don't understand at this moment." He held my gaze with a boldness that made me uncomfortable. "But *that* is not among them."

I noted the skeptical arch of his brow, the tight line of his jaw, and a smile that looked genuine. He wasn't happy, in the traditional sense. He was invigorated by the circumstance. By the effort that had clearly led him here at this specific moment.

"You were listening yesterday," I said, careful not to phrase it as a question.

His smile did not so much as flicker. "Most assuredly."

"You had no right." I took a deep breath, but there was little I could do about the gooseflesh rising on my arms, despite the warmth in the room from the athanor in one corner. "That was a private conversation."

Any hope I had of shaming him suffered a swift death when his smile twisted into a smirk. "*You* are accusing *me* of crossing an ethical line? The irony burns like splashed acid, Amber." He paused, assuming the affectation of a suddenly remembered thought. "Though I suppose it doesn't burn you at all. Because you truly can't remember what you were like."

"Whatever you think I did . . . I apologize," I said as he rounded the table toward me. My heart pounded like thunder, echoing in my ears so loudly I could hardly hear my own words. "And you said it was water beneath the bridge."

"So it is. I'm not here for revenge."

Yet he kept coming. His approach felt bellicose, his tone quarrelsome.

I moved backward, and he met me step for step until the small of my back hit the wooden surface of the supply counter, and a soft grunt of pain burst from my lips.

Pryce took another step, so close now that I could feel his breath on my face. "This feels peculiar," he said. "You look so guileless."

"What was I before?" I asked, and I hated the question the moment I heard it. I hadn't meant to ask. Not to ask *him*, anyway. The fact that he clearly understood more of who I'd been than I did made me feel raw and vulnerable.

"You were . . . *bold*," he said. "Oblivious and driven. Callous, in the name of alchemy. But there was a wild passion beneath all of that. Fueling it, I would guess. You had this burning need. Like a *glow*."

He stepped incrementally closer, until I felt myself shrinking against the countertop, clutching at the edge of it with both hands. Then he leaned forward so that his words lived against my cheek, twisting this moment with the imposition of a vile intimacy: "Is that heat still in there?"

"Step back," I demanded softly.

For a moment, he held his ground. Then, to my surprise, he complied.

I exhaled, and immediately I understood my mistake. I looked relieved, which exposed my fear. My vulnerability.

His focus narrowed on me with this new understanding. With a new measure of whatever boundary he'd been testing. "I'm here to support you, Amber. You meant it when you said you'd fallen behind, academically. I understand that now. And I can help you catch up."

"I don't need your help." I edged to the side, sliding along the polished wooden countertop, shifting my grip with each of two steps.

But then he cut me off, matching my strides easily with one of his own. "You do, though, because no one else knows how far you've fallen. How little of a threat you now represent. How easy you would be to knock off, at the first trial."

My heartbeat spiked. Did he mean I could be easily bested? Or . . .

"Are you threatening me?"

"I'm offering to keep your secret. To help you catch up." He shrugged, yet the gesture looked anything but casual. "And in return, I'll accept . . . whatever you feel you have to offer."

I tried to push past him, and anger flared behind his eyes. His hand closed around my wrist, squeezing until I gritted my teeth against the pain.

"Listen to the proposal," he whispered fiercely. "You owe me that, at least."

I glanced past his left shoulder, only to find the door closed, flickering light from the sconce across the hall shining through the leaded glass window, casting red, green, and blue shadows on the floor.

Wilder would appear any moment, but I would *not* threaten Pryce with the arrival of an ally, because at some point, I would have to stand on my own two feet. Even if they felt mired in quicksand at the moment.

"You're looking for Wilder Gregory?" Pryce scoffed, and I went cold. "He'll be a while. It's *possible* we bumped into each other on the bridge, and several of his precious vials shattered in the collision. It'll take him a while to replace them and continue his errand. If he even has sufficient inventory for that."

He knew I was waiting for Wilder, and he knew where Wilder had gone. What he'd been doing. Was he a threat to Wilder, too, with this knowledge?

A bolt of anger shot up my spine, fire raging in my gut like a chemical burner with too much fuel. I ripped my arm from his grip and shoved past him, grabbing my satchel from the edge of the counter as I darted between two empty tables.

Pryce caught up to me several feet from the exit, but he only managed to grab my bag. His sudden grip spun me around, and I backed toward the closed door, facing him now, both of us clutching a side of my satchel.

"Don't overreact." His voice was soft and steady. Low-pitched and far too calm. "Your medical condition is on record, and if you go around spewing unfounded accusations against upstanding and well-regarded men in this program, the only logical conclusion will be that your condition has progressed. That it might have been caused by ingesting an untested, unapproved elixir created by a classmate of dubious repute."

"You are a *brute*," I growled at him, fire licking the back of my throat. Hatred singeing my teeth.

"I am *recompense*," he snarled in return, his composure finally close to breaking. "You are reaping what you've already sown—it's not my fault you don't remember the original sin. Though maybe you should start looking into whose fault that is."

A fresh flare of anger swelled deep within my chest, and I jerked on my satchel as hard as I could. He lost his grip, and my arm flew up to sling the satchel over my shoulder, until my hand slammed into something hard. I heard a series of sharp cracks. Pain sliced through my knuckles.

Pryce gasped and backed away, his anger at me eclipsed by the shock of whatever I'd just done.

I spun around, my satchel swinging at my side. Blood welled from three of my knuckles and from a long cut across the back of my hand, glittering oddly in the torchlight flickering through the brightly colored leaded glass.

Through what was left of it, anyway.

Previously, the stained glass window had taken the shape of a blue beaker suspended above a flame comprised of hundreds of shards of hand-tinted glass in every possible shade of red and yellow.

Now the top of the beaker remained, its narrowed, lipped mouth intact. But the bottom half of it and most of the flame were gone. They lay spread across the floor at my feet in a thousand shards of brightly tinted glass.

"No . . ." I swore softly. I'd broken a *one-hundred-fifty-year-old* work of art—one of few parts of the Alchemary constructed by the alchemists themselves, rather than by the Toolkeepers hired to bring the designer's vision to life.

Leaded glass was an alchemical art. A *master* skill, involving an intricate knowledge of which elements could produce which shades and how to stabilize them all. And how to mold the lead frames and cut the glass shapes perfectly.

I clutched my bag and pulled the door open. Then I ran down the hall, chased by both the echo of my own footsteps and the horror of what I'd done.

Pryce's parting shot echoed down the corridor toward me: "You'll be lucky if they don't throw you out just for that."

Seventeen

My gulping breaths reverberated around me in the narrow eastern stairwell as I raced down two flights of stairs, then down the central corridor and out through the front doors. I burst into the quadrangle, gasping for air, tears burning in my eyes. I slung my satchel over my shoulder, dimly noting how cold the wind felt against the back of my injured right hand. Then I took off across the grass, with no destination in mind.

My feet moved of their own accord, my brain still mired in the shock of what I'd done as I weaved between hulking topiary sculptures that looked ominous, swathed in the moonlight, though they looked almost whimsical during the day.

I didn't realize where I was going until I found myself in the first-floor atrium of the Conservatory. *Why* did my legs keep bringing me here, all on their own?

The scroll-shaped plaque by the stairs caught my eye again, and again Desmond's name held my gaze. He would know whether I should formally apologize to Pryce and the school, offer to work off the debt, or just write to my father to come get me so I could slink off in quiet disgrace.

No.

My spine straightened, my fist clenching around the strap of my bag. I would not leave.

As scared and embarrassed as I was—as angry and flustered—that was not an option.

My head fell back, and the sight of the moon shining through the spiraling display of leaded glass overhead sent a wave of nausea through me. It was a stunning reminder of the art I'd just destroyed. Of why and how that had happened.

I swiped tears from my face with my left hand and turned toward the staircase, leaning for a moment against the wall to catch my breath, to breathe past the nausea, and when I straightened, I realized I'd left a smear of blood across one edge of the plaque bearing Desmond's name, just below the top roll of the sculpted scroll. Cursing softly, I wiped it clean with one edge of my cloak, then I took the steps two at a time, all the way to the second floor, racing through a rainbow of colors cast by moonlight shining through the glass panels in the ceiling.

I forced myself to walk down the hall like a sane person, instead of racing as if an entire pack of wolves were on my trail, and only when I stood outside of Desmond's suite—his name still appeared alone on the slate—did it occur to me that there was essentially no chance he'd be inside at this time of night. And even if he were, he was more likely to capitalize on the broken stained glass to get me removed from campus than to give me any true advice.

Dejected, I turned from the door without knocking and headed toward the stairwell, the back of my right hand pressed against my cape to keep blood from dripping on the white marble floor.

I was halfway down the hall when the squeal of hinges echoed startlingly all around me.

"Amber?" Desmond's voice washed over me, and I froze. "What's wrong?"

I turned to find him studying me from the doorway, most of which his broad form occupied. His gaze raked over my tear-damp face, and he frowned, a thunderous expression I couldn't quite interpret.

Then he stepped to the side and held the door to his suite open. "This way," he ordered.

As unreasonable as it felt, I wanted to object, more to his tone than to his offer. But considering how much trouble I was in . . .

Desmond's office was a small, neatly organized lamp-lit room attached to his private lab space. He sank into his desk chair, the only one in the room, and motioned me forward.

My feet would not move. Not even the few steps from the doorway to his desk.

With a sigh, he stood and took my left hand, calloused fingers warm in mine, and tugged me forward patiently until we stood in front of his chair. But instead of sinking into it, he gently lifted my satchel from over my head and set it on the floor, propped against his perfectly ordered bookshelf. Then he lifted me by my waist, without even a grunt of effort.

I gasped at his touch and felt my face flush, even as I grasped at the slopes of his biceps to steady myself. Before I could form thoughts coherent enough to truly question what was happening, he turned and set me on his desk.

A soft sound escaped my throat, and though I could ascribe no specific meaning to it—no intent at all; it was pure reaction—Desmond's mouth quirked into a private little smile that was gone almost before I'd seen it. That smile sent a shower of sparks to explode in my belly.

I clenched my teeth and avoided all analysis of what that might mean, other than that I was in shock and in pain, and nothing made sense at the moment.

He sank into his chair, which put him at eye level with my breasts and made me reluctant to breathe too deeply, even though he wasn't looking. "Give me your hand," he ordered softly.

"No."

I don't know why I said it. He was trying to help. But I was angry at him. And not for any of the myriad reasons that could logically have justified the emotion. Not because he wanted me gone, or because he'd written to my father without my knowledge. Not because he'd met with my father in secret, where they'd discussed my future without my participation.

Not because he was clearly trying to remove me from authority over my own life.

I was mad at him—*furious*—on a deeper level, for some reason I could not remember. Was that obscure reason also the cause of his ire at me?

"No?" He sighed again and looked straight into my eyes. The left side of his face was lit by the lamp burning on the desk, and the flicker of light and shadow only emphasized the strong, well-proportioned features he shared with Wilder—and the coloring he did not. "Why won't you give me your hand?" he demanded in a soft, impatient growl.

"Because I'm *angry* with you."

Amusement flashed across his expression, followed by what I could only describe as the briefest flicker of nostalgia. Of . . . settling in. As if he'd just entered a room he remembered fondly.

But then it was gone.

"What, may I ask, does your anger have to do with the injury you're hiding from me?"

"Not a thing," I admitted. "But you cannot possibly expect me to obey just because you've given an order. I remember nothing of my adult life before I lost my memory, yet I am *absolutely* certain that I did not obey orders just because they were given."

That amusement was back, and this time it clawed at my nerves, fraying my patience. "No," he confirmed with a sharp shake of his head. "You have never been what I would characterize as compliant." He cleared his throat and looked up at me without a hint of a smile. "May I please see your hand so I can do you the favor of assessing and treating the wound?"

I hesitated for another second. Then I held out my right hand, bloody knuckles up. "You may. And thank you."

He examined my hand without touching it at first. Then he leaned to one side and pulled a rounded leather bag into his lap. I recognized it as a laboratory aid kit, mostly used when someone sustained a burn or cut themselves on broken equipment.

"That is not from a busted beaker or pipette," he said. "The cut would be on your palm. Or a finger." His voice hardened a bit. "What have you done, Amber?"

"In my defense," I began, "I was *attempting* to resist prostituting myself under duress in exchange for help in remedial alchemy. But the result was somewhat less effective than I might have hoped, and the short end of it is that the mastery cohort lab space is now missing a *gorgeous* leaded glass window." I sighed miserably. "Half of it, anyway. Though I suspect that if it is removed for repair, what remains of the glass will crumble."

Desmond's hand stilled inside the aid bag. His gaze snapped to mine. "You were *assaulted*?"

"I suppose," I said, though I had not considered it in that light. "And in return, I inadvertently assaulted the leaded glass window."

"Wilder?" he almost growled, his pupils tightening to little more than dark pinpricks within the coppery-brown depths of his irises. "Is that why you're here?"

Confusion made me physically recoil for a moment, and the rage burning within his visage kept me trapped in that moment even longer. "*No!* Of course not. Why would you even think—"

"You were in the lab, in the middle of the night. Wilder is the only one who . . ." His words faded, evidently as my denial sank in.

Some of the fire was extinguished from his expression, but the rest smoldered there, ready to flare at any moment.

"Does everyone know about that?" I asked. "About his . . . nighttime activities?"

Desmond huffed as he pulled a clean cloth from the bag and folded it into a neat square. He took my right hand in his left and began to gently blot the blood from my wounds. "Who was it?" he asked as he worked, without looking up from my hand.

His skin was warm and rough in places, calloused in a way I would not have expected from a man who'd spent the past five years in classrooms and labs.

And . . . training with soldiers, evidently?

He looked up, and my gaze swam in his until I felt like I was drowning. "Amber?"

"It doesn't matter," I finally said.

"It most certainly does. This bully could have something to do with what happened to your memory. And he's obviously still a threat."

I shook my head. "He found out about my amnesia from eavesdropping. I practically caught him. Before that, he truly had no idea."

"That doesn't mean he isn't responsible for it. Amnesia could be an unintended consequence of something he did. Something he . . . slipped into your tea."

"I suppose that's possible." Pryce was furious with me about something, after all.

"I need a name," Desmond insisted.

I sighed. "Pryce Wishart."

His jaw clenched. "I will deal with him."

"What does that mean?"

"Are you hurt? Beyond this?" He lifted my hand, and when it caught the light from his lamp, he frowned at my wounds, as if he were just then seeing them.

"No. I'm fine."

He lifted my hand higher, and I resisted the urge to squeeze his fingers. To steal more of their warmth. "What did you take?" he asked, tilting my hand so that the light shone on it more fully.

"What do you mean?"

"Did Pryce give you something tonight? Force an elixir upon you? Did you drink or eat anything in his presence?"

"No, I—" My teeth clicked shut, and his gaze snapped up to mine.

"Amber?"

"It wasn't him. I . . . Wilder makes an elixir that can help you concentrate. Help you stay awake, and . . . Well, I've had a lot of late nights, trying to catch up with what I should know already."

He scowled, and I scrambled to change the subject.

"How did you know? You can see that in my blood?"

"There are always side effects. *Do not* take anything Wilder gives you."

"But it works."

"It's unproven." His voice hardened. "Unapproved. Untested. It's *dangerous*."

"He's helping." I pulled my hand from his grip, and I felt the loss of it like an ache deep in my bones. "And anyway, I have little choice. I have to study at night to catch up, and that's also the only time I can work in the lab without the rest of my cohort realizing I'm not at their level. Which feels like a moot point now. Pryce knows. And now that I've rejected his 'proposal,' he's going to tell them."

Desmond waved that off as if it didn't matter. "They were always going to find out. But you won't be working in that lab anymore, anyway."

"I don't have any other—"

"There." He glanced over my shoulder and through the door at his own lab. "I have more than enough space."

"Desmond, I can't work in your lab."

He arched one brow at me. "Where do you suppose you worked all of last year?"

I could only blink at him. "I couldn't possibly have—"

"Proficiency-year students don't have a dedicated lab space, because most don't start their independent research until the third year. You worked here with me for your entire second year at the Alchemary."

Alongside him. Not truly *with* him, surely.

"Why would . . . Desmond, why would you offer me lab space, if you're trying to get me kicked off campus?"

"I'm trying to have you removed in part for your own safety, and—"

"In *part*?"

"—given that goal, it would be hypocritical of me to abandon you to an unsafe work environment when I could offer you a secure space instead. Especially considering that I've made no headway with the Bluehelm. She's decided you're in no danger until the Black Trial, and she will reassess your progress at that time, assuming you continue to pass your classes." He set the bloodstained cloth on his desk, then gently lowered my hand onto my own thigh. "Of course, this incident might change her mind."

"And if it doesn't? You clearly don't enjoy my company," I said, and Desmond huffed again, but he did not argue. "Is that because we did not get along, as lab partners? Would that be an issue this time?"

"That was never our issue, Amber. We've always been able to respect each other—"

"As 'rational individuals.' So you said. What was it, then? Why don't I deserve to be here? You disapprove of my field of study? Of my work on the Philosopher's Stone?"

Desmond's gaze held mine with a weight I could not measure. With some internal conflict I could not understand, as if two discrete halves of him were at war. “I have no problem with your field of study. But I could not always condone your . . . methods.”

A strange tightness spread throughout my chest. Desmond’s disapproval felt bitter and humiliating, as if I’d disappointed a mentor or a favorite instructor.

Had he been my mentor?

How thoroughly must I have let him down, if he wanted me removed from the entire island even though I couldn’t remember my missteps?

“I don’t want to crowd you,” I finally whispered.

He gave me another look I could not interpret. “There’s plenty of space. You’ll have your own section of the lab, and your own supplies. I’ll have your proportion of the student allotment transferred here, and you’re welcome to anything of mine that you need.”

“Why?” I asked, before I could even fully work out what I meant. “Why would you do that for me, if you don’t believe I deserve to be here?”

Desmond’s focus seemed to narrow on me. To sharpen. “Because removing you from the student lab will keep you safe from Pryce Wishart.” His words, too, took on a honed edge. “And it will keep the rest of your cohort safe from *you*. Even if that means I’m forced to . . . supervise.”

Indignation blazed beneath my skin, but I swallowed it, denying him a glimpse of how deeply his words stung. “Why would they need to be protected from *me*?”

“Because the fact that the Alchemary is a danger to you is only one half of the equation. The other half—equally relevant to my efforts to have you removed—is that *you* are a danger to *the Alchemary*.”

I could not fathom how I could be a danger to the entire institution, but the fact that he clearly believed what he was saying left me too hurt and exhausted to argue further.

"Very well," I said. "I will move in tomorrow. But consider yourself warned: You may be getting more than you bargained for."

His narrow-eyed censure faded into a sad look that deepened the ache in my chest. "Alas, Amber, I know *exactly* what I'm getting into."

As I stepped down from the bottom stair tread into the Conservatory atrium, my gaze caught on the scroll-shaped plaque on the wall. Not on Desmond's name and office number this time, but on an odd smear on the top right corner, just beneath the top roll of sculpted parchment. With a sinking feeling, I realized that the blood I'd accidentally smeared there had stained the plaque itself, to which the metal nameplates were attached.

How was that possible?

I moved closer to examine the plaque, wondering if it were made of some kind of porous stone, but it was smooth, both to the eye and to the touch. This one was about the height of my forearm and the width of three of them laid side by side.

Bone.

The answer came to me with a start.

Staff alchemists were permanently appointed to the Alchemary, and not just for life. When one died, hopefully after a long tenure spent serving the institution itself as well as the field of alchemy, that alchemist's body went on to serve the cause in every way possible. That last sacrifice was considered a true honor and the sign of a scientist thoroughly dedicated to the craft.

Bones, I knew, had many uses, most of which required them to be purified, then dried and ground into a fine powder. Which could then be distilled, mixed into various solutions, or . . . used as the primary ingredient in a compound that could be baked into any shape, both functional and decorative.

Alchemists, I'd learned, could become forever a part of the Alchemary they'd served.

But *how* had I learned that?

My father.

The memory came all at once. My mother had been regaling me with tales of the wondrous academy, of colorful elixirs and suspensions with miraculous properties, and my father had interrupted to accuse the founders of "ghoulish proclivities." Of testing their arcane products on the bodies of deceased colleagues, distilling fluids from corpses donated to the institution, and sometimes using those same bodies to fertilize the soil. When my mother dismissed that as utter nonsense, he'd told us both about the bone plaques, and that he'd once seen the recipe for how they were created, in a tome of Toolkeeper secrets, which he should—admittedly—not have been revealing, even to his beloved family.

My mother had shrugged off his story as just that—legend with little basis in truth—and scolded him for telling such a gruesome tale to a child.

But his story had stuck with me. And now I was staring at evidence of its accuracy. What else could this plaque be, sculpted into such a specific shape, beyond what was possible with molten metal poured into a mold?

Wonderful. I'd ruined another priceless and irreplaceable architectural element, this one formed from the final, corporeal donation of an alchemist so dedicated to his craft that he'd wanted to live on forever as a literal part of the Alchemary.

At least this time no one would know I was responsible. And considering how disinterested most of the staff alchemists seemed to be in anything that happened outside of their laboratories, it could be weeks before any of them even noticed.

I ran one finger over the top right edge of the plaque, above the nameplates, frowning at the strange shape my bloody handprint had left. Nearly a quarter of my palm had landed on the plaque, smearing most of the corner with my blood, but it hadn't soaked in evenly. In fact, the stain seemed to have . . .

I sucked in a breath and backed away from the plaque. Then I stepped forward again, squinting. My blood had not simply been absorbed everywhere it had been smeared. Rather, it seemed to have reacted with the plaque in specific places. In faint but distinct shapes.

🜍

An upward pointing triangle mounted on a balanced cross: the alchemical symbol for sulfur.

My blood had revealed *writing* hidden in the bone.

Eighteen

I dreamed of never-ending strands of alchemical scribbles—about bone and blood—and I woke before the sun came up on Sunday, desperate to know why the plaque in the Conservatory had been secretly marked with the symbol for sulfur, and why my blood had revealed it.

Could there be other, similar symbols concealed elsewhere on campus?

Unable to sleep further, my thoughts racing like a horse with its tail ablaze, I rose and went about my morning ablutions, eagerness buzzing in my fingertips and aching in my legs like cramped muscles impatient to *move*. I felt driven.

No, I felt *pulled*. As if someone were tugging at a cord fastened around some memory, taunting me from the impenetrable recesses of my own brain.

Had I seen that symbol before? Or another like it? Why had it set my sleeping mind and my waking impulses afire? Because I'd already trodden this path, though I could no longer remember? Because it was related to the loss of my memory?

Or simply because my brain was fatigued from trying to relearn two years of concepts and skills? Of dissolution, purification, calcination, coagulation, and distillation. Of alembics, retorts, vials, flasks, crucibles, and athanors. Was it any wonder I felt pulled toward something entertaining?

According to Wilder, I'd always been more entertained by my own exploits than by any ordinary bacchanalia. . . .

I pulled my hair into an efficient but somewhat unkempt bun, slung my satchel over my shoulder, and proceeded straight to the Seminary, where I spent the last half hour before dawn exploring the building in search of any more plaques made of bone.

My probe uncovered several interesting alcoves I could not recall having seen before, as well as sundry supply closets, faculty-only spaces—both offices and a rather posh-looking lounge—and more portraits of Emperor Eldon and Queen Avalona than I could even count. The Alchemary was nothing if not grateful to its original benefactor.

But to my disappointment, I didn't find a single plaque made from the ground bones of dead alchemists. Even the large, ornate decorative plaque in the Seminary's rear courtyard, commemorating the planting of the massive Avalona Oak in memory of the dead queen, was made out of cast iron, with gilded lettering.

I already knew, by virtue of living there, that there were no bone plaques in the Dormitory, and there were no signs of any kind at the Refectory. Which meant the remainder of my search could safely be limited to the Conservatory.

The sun peeked over the lush forest behind the Refectory as I crossed the quadrangle. The island sloped gently toward the coast on the west and south sides, so gradually that the ocean was not visible in those directions.

Candlelight gleamed from the windows of the Refectory—the kitchen staff began their work quite early—but I had yet to see a single student, researcher, or faculty member out and about, which was both advantageous to my mission and unsurprising on a weekend.

Beneath the Conservatory portico, I peered at a plaque bolted to the marble front wall. It was identical to the one in the atrium:

powdered bone, compressed with other binding ingredients into a malleable shape. The commemorative statement—the year the building had been completed, along with brief verbiage about what that completion meant for the Alchemary—had been hand-etched into the surface, each line filled with delicate yet sturdy gold filigree, which stood out sharply against the soft white of the plaque itself.

Before I could think better of what could only be described as a terrible and impulsive plan, I pulled a pair of shears from my satchel and opened them. For a moment, still largely shielded from the rising sun by the massive building, I held the blade over my open palm. But I used my hands every minute of the day, and a large cut down the center of my palm would invite questions. Especially if anyone noticed a bloody smear across the front of the plaque on the Conservatory's portico.

I pushed up my left sleeve, then carefully—and somewhat hesitantly—I pressed the tip of one blade into the crook of my elbow. But I found it unaccountably difficult to actually break the skin. Cutting myself open felt counter to all instincts of self-preservation. And yet . . . I wanted answers. So I pressed harder, clenching my jaw, holding my breath until I felt the dull slice of pain and an eerie popping sensation as my skin split.

The shears were not particularly sharp.

Blood welled around the metal tip, and I made myself press harder, despite the unease squirming in my gut like a snake through a marsh puddle.

Heart thumping, terrified that someone would round the corner of a building and see me, I dipped the fingers of my right hand into the palette of my left elbow as if they were the bristles of a gruesome paintbrush.

I took a deep breath, mentally girding myself against the bevy of bizarre questions and accusations that would surely assail me if I were caught—if unaccountably losing years of my own memory weren't enough to get me committed to the closest asylum, I was fairly certain that desecrating the Conservatory with my own blood would do just that. Then I swiped my messy fingers across the top right corner of the plaque in as orderly a manner as I could devise.

While I waited for a symbol to appear, I swiftly cut a strip of material from my underdress and used it to wipe excess blood from the plaque, cleaning up my mess as best I could. I folded the cloth and pressed it into my wound, pinning it in place with my arm bent to stop the sluggish flow of blood while I stared out into the quadrangle to make sure it was still empty.

On the weekend, the morning meal wasn't served until nine, and while researchers seemed a devout and dedicated bunch who often worked weekends, I'd never seen the Conservatory windows lit up at dawn.

When I turned back to the plaque, I was elated yet somewhat surprised to see that a symbol had appeared in precisely the same position as on the one in the atrium. It was dim—a pale shadow of an image—and at a glance, since I'd wiped off the excess blood, all anyone would likely notice was a smudge on the corner of the plaque.

But I'd seen the pattern.

Quickly, I pulled my journal from my bag and scribbled the alchemical symbol—mercury—onto a blank page at the back. To the left of that, I wrote the symbol for sulfur. Then I scurried into the building, relieved to be sheltered from potential prying eyes.

I tiptoed past the marble benches built into the walls of the atrium and peered at the plaque by the stairs. My blood had almost entirely faded from view, as if the bone had absorbed it, and the symbol had disappeared along with it. If I hadn't seen it myself, I'd never have known it was there.

Which made me wonder: Had the symbols been visible before, then faded away? Or could I possibly be the first to discover them? The latter possibility sent a thrill firing through my veins.

I headed up to the third floor.

An hour later, blood had crusted in the elbow of my frock, and a staunch little weed of hope grew in one neglected corner of my soul.

I arrived at the Refectory before there was any food to be served, so I sat at a table with a pot of tea, a sheet of parchment, and a hundred questions about the symbols I'd found on nearly every bone plaque mounted on a wall of the Conservatory.

All but one of them, in fact.

It was a formula of some kind. A list of ingredients, anyway. But for what? An elixir? The invisible ink itself?

For all I knew, I'd just discovered the components that would make the Philosopher's Stone.

The very idea that I might have spent two years fruitlessly researching a list of ingredients that were literally written on the Conservatory walls made me chuckle, softly but somewhat hysterically. Fortunately, there was no one around to see me laugh alone in the dining room, at my own notes. If those ingredients could be combined to make the Philosopher's Stone, they *would* have been, and the Stone would be known to alchemy.

Its creator would be the most famous and lauded alchemist in the world.

Alas, the Philosopher's Stone was a legend, no more real than Emperor Eldon's immortal love for his doomed queen. Much less real than that, in fact. His love had spawned stories, and statues, and paintings.

The Philosopher's Stone had spawned nothing but overwrought rumors.

For whatever reason they'd been written—and hidden—the symbols were real. But what good was a list of components with no measures or instructions? Without any indication of what the mysterious formula would produce?

But perhaps, if I could find a formula that included all of—and *only*—those specific components . . .

Fortunately, Past Amber had taken copious notes on every formula she'd ever come across. So I pulled a thick stack of her notes from my satchel and started reading.

An hour later, food had been set out by the staff and sunlight slanted across my table from an uncovered window. I blinked against encroaching exhaustion. Adventure had been more than enough to keep me awake, despite my lack of sleep, but sedentary research, it turned out, was not.

Steam wafted toward my face as I poured a fresh cup of tea. The warm, fragrant mist was comforting. I took a long sip, and as I set the cup down, my free hand slid into the pocket of my cloak, my fingers curling around the smooth, cold vial hidden there.

Despite Desmond's order to abstain—or perhaps because of it—I'd brought Wilder's elixir of concentration with me.

The Refectory was usually sparsely populated in the mornings, a fact I'd learned quickly, but today, the few other students breaking their fast all seemed to be staring right at me. To my utter frustration.

None were Mastery-year students, and they all had the decency to look away when I met their gazes. But something had clearly changed since the night before.

With a sigh, I left the vial in my pocket and forced my attention back to the stack of parchment on the table.

Minutes later, familiar footsteps drew my gaze.

"*What* is going on this morning?" Wilder demanded as he sank into the chair next to mine. His tray held two bowls of porridge and two fresh pastries, and he set one of each in front of me.

"Thank you!" I shoved my notes into my satchel as if I were thrilled for an excuse to stop studying, and not at all as if I were hiding anything from him. "They weren't serving food yet when I arrived." I dropped a kiss on his smooth, freshly shaved cheek, then dug into my porridge.

His brows rose, but he didn't ask why I'd woken so early. He knew well that apprehension and study often robbed me of sleep.

"I heard your name at least four times on my way from the Dormitory," he said as he tore an edge from his scone. "And everyone in the Refectory is staring at you."

"Have you been to the lab yet today?" I asked, watching steam rise from my bowl.

"No. And I'm sorry I stood you up last night. I had an incident on the way to my delivery, and—"

"I know."

Concern creased his brow. "What am I missing?"

"Lean slightly to your left, and I'll tell you."

His frown deepened, but he leaned to the side.

With him mostly blocking me from sight, I withdrew the vial from my pocket and administered several drops of the elixir into what remained of my tea, which gave my cup a familiar, comforting scent.

At least one of his ingredients had a mildly pleasant floral taste, and I suspected he'd harvested it from the forest himself.

"What happened to your hand?" Wilder demanded, his gaze caught on my bandage.

I did not answer.

He held his position until the vial was safely secreted away again. "Very well, now—"

"One moment." I lifted the cup and drank deeply, slowly, from the cooling liquid until I'd drained it. Then I returned the cup to its saucer and smiled wearily at him. "Thank you. It's been a rather trying morning."

He gave me an odd look. "The less sleep you get, the more you look and sound like your old self."

"I cannot tell whether that's an insult or a compliment." Whether he preferred this version of me or the previous one.

"It's merely a simple observation."

Yet it felt anything but simple.

"What's happened, Amber?" His typical grin was conspicuously absent as he plucked the last bite of scone from my plate. "Why is your name on every tongue?"

I sighed. "There are two possible causes for that phenomenon, and I haven't yet gathered enough evidence to draw an accurate conclusion."

"Go on. . . ."

"Last night, though you did not meet me in the student lab, Pryce Wishart did."

"Pryce." Wilder scowled. "He—"

"Collided with you on the bridge and smashed your deliveries." I nodded, holding his gaze with a meaningful one of my own. "I am aware."

"That was bad enough, but before I could retrieve my satchel from the ground, a carriage came storming across the bridge and flattened it, shattering everything that hadn't broken. I was *inches* from being thrown over the edge myself."

A carriage had come to Alchemary Island in the middle of the night? "Whose carriage? What was the hurry?"

He shrugged. "I only caught a glimpse of the seal as I gathered my things, but it appeared to belong to the Crown. The guards didn't even stop it for an inspection."

The Crown?

But Wilder was still stuck on another point, his cheeks bright with fury. “And none of that would have happened if not for Pryce. That drunken clod. I had to walk all the way back to the Dormitory and raid my—” His frown deepened as understanding blossomed. “How did you—” Full comprehension seemed to slam into him with the force of a charging bull. “He did it on purpose.”

I nodded, and a complicated series of emotions cycled across his expression, darkening his eyes. Making his lips twitch and his teeth clench. It was like watching spring harden into a cold, harsh winter, without passing through summer or fall.

The only conclusion I could draw with utter certainty was that he had a better understanding than I did of why Pryce might do such a thing.

And yet Wilder asked me, “What did he want? What did he say?”

I glanced into my cup, wishing there was some way to procure a second pot of tea without leaving my seat. “He offered to ‘help’ me relearn the basic principles of alchemy without revealing my deficiency to the rest of our classmates. But he heavily implied that there would be a price. That I already owe him, somehow, and should be *grateful* for the offer.”

Wilder’s brows furrowed until I saw far too much of his brother in the expression. “And may I assume that you declined his ‘offer’ in some fantastically violent manner?”

“I certainly tried. However, my blow landed not upon Pryce’s face—a fact I regret more with each passing moment—but upon the leaded glass window in the door. Which shattered, and has left me watching the Refectory entrance this morning in anticipation of my own expulsion. Which will surely come in the form of a scowling Alchemary official.”

Wilder blinked. “You broke the window? The *one-hundred-fifty-year-old* stained glass?”

"Which was original to the construction of the building? Yes. And now I cannot deduce whether everyone is staring at me because they know I'm about to be expelled for the destruction of irreplaceable Alchemary property or because Pryce has told everyone that I am now a substandard student, incapable of earning a place here." I shrugged as I scraped up the last bite of porridge from the edges of my bowl. "I suppose the specifics don't really matter."

"Every bit of that matters." Wilder turned in his chair to pointedly return the stares of a handful of underclassman.

"Why does the Refectory always feel largely abandoned first thing in the morning?" I asked as I collected my empty dishes on his tray.

"You and I asked the same question during our first week here." Wilder gave me a wistful smile. "Our wealthier classmates do not break their fast until the midday meal. They're taught, it turns out, that eating first thing in the morning is a sign of gluttony, except in the case of children and manual laborers, who will require the energy. They're not eager to be associated with either category."

I lifted one brow. "That is asinine."

Wilder threw his head back and laughed. "And you said something very similar two years ago." He stood and picked up the tray. "As badly as I hate to admit it . . ." He lowered his voice. "We need to talk to Desmond. He'll know how to mitigate the damage."

My mouth opened, but no words would come out, and I could not understand my reluctance to tell Wilder that I'd already spoken to his brother.

"I . . . um. I saw him last night," I said finally as I followed him with my teacup and saucer, my satchel bumping against my hip.

Wilder's next step faltered, almost imperceptibly. "When?" He set the tray on a cart near the kitchen door and turned to take the cup and saucer from me.

"Right after it happened. He cleaned the wound." I lifted my hand to show him the bandage, beneath which my cuts had scabbed over. "And he . . . invited me to work in his lab."

"Well, that seems unnecessary."

I frowned up at him. "Wilder, I can't work in the student lab. Not with Pryce standing just feet away." I would feel him watching me. We might wind up at the supply cabinet at the same time, and I wouldn't be able to trust that that was coincidence. I couldn't possibly focus, knowing that every time he whispered to another student, he might be talking about me.

"When I'm finished with Pryce Wishart, he'll wish he'd never heard your name," Wilder said, his voice oddly deep. "He will *not* be a problem for you again."

In his eyes flashed a danger I'd never seen before, and if I were not mistaken, the hand at his waist seemed to be wrapped around the hilt of his knife.

"Wilder, I swear to every force of entropy in the universe that if you unsheathe that blade—"

"Actions have consequences, Amber." His brows dipped into a firm, grim line. "Actions against *you,* in particular."

"One can only hope," I replied. "But those consequences will *not* involve your blade."

He released the hilt, and a hard sort of joy glinted in his eyes. "Fortunately, I have far more effective and less conspicuous tools at my disposal."

I elected, for the state of my own anxiety, not to ask for any details, in hopes that whatever action Desmond was pursuing would render Wilder's solution unnecessary.

"It may be a moot point anyway. There's every chance in the world that they'll expel me when I cannot pay for the window."

"They're not going to expel you."

"You don't know—"

"I know." Wilder extended one arm toward the exit, inviting me to precede him. "If the Bluehelm wants you here despite your amnesia, she's not going to hold an accident against you."

"Well then, maybe you can come with me." I ignored the weight of several stares as I headed out of the Refectory. "Desmond has the whole laboratory suite to himself, as far as I can tell, and I'm sure he'd be happy to have you—"

"Oh, he certainly would *not*." Wilder followed me onto the quadrangle, and though he clearly had more to say on the subject, we'd gone a half dozen more steps, eschewing the stone path to walk in the grass, before he spoke again. "Desmond hosted you in his fancy private laboratory last year."

"So he says."

"But he refused to offer me the same invitation. He said that as a staff member of the Alchemary, he could not be seen to support my illicit activities. Though he was kind enough to label it as 'research,' even as he looked down his nose at me. Which left me no choice but to sneak into the student lab space in the middle of the night."

Wilder glanced at me, and I could only shrug, aware, again, of other students looking my way as they walked in groups across the quadrangle, whispering to one another.

"He has a valid point," I said, doing my best to ignore the gossip.

"Only because the research board rejected my proposal to pursue my project in an official capacity, as my Mastery-year research. This is the kind of thing that could bring in a significant profit for the Panacea Project." Wilder's eyes lit up, his voice taking on a new intensity. "What I'm doing *helps* people."

I arched one brow at him. "Like Professor Robards?"

He rolled his eyes. "That's the look the research board gave me. Yes, like Professor Robards, though I certainly didn't mention any of my clients in my proposal."

"Do you really think enabling him to cheat on his wife is helping him?"

Wilder frowned. "I *have* helped him. And it's not my place to pass judgment on his decisions. I am not privy to the way his marriage functions." He cleared his throat pointedly. "I've also helped myself—and you—focus and stay awake. And I've helped myself set aside the anxiety keeping me from becoming a real part of the community here."

That he had. Everyone knew and loved Wilder.

"All of that adds up to a worthy contribution to the Panacea Project," he declared in a fierce whisper. "I *am* bringing the human mind and body closer to perfection."

"But they didn't see it that way."

He scowled. "They called my elixirs a gimmick. They accused me of 'playing at alchemy' in a way that is scandalous and beneath the dignity of this institution. And they strongly encouraged me to realign my vision and to direct my innate talent toward a 'more respectable' branch of Panacea."

"Which would be what?"

Wilder shrugged. "As of this moment, my research is officially 'undeclared.'"

"Well, that is a travesty," I assured him with a grin. "But not surprising, given how devastatingly brilliant and underappreciated you are."

Yet I could not help noticing that despite considering Wilder's research scandalous and beneath the dignity of the Alchemary, Desmond hadn't tried to get *him* removed from campus.

Nineteen

That afternoon, as I crept silently up the Conservatory's grand spiral staircase, I couldn't help but stare at the bright images painted on the curved walls from sunlight shining through the stained glass tableaux overhead. I had no time to linger, but the images were *so* striking, and the queen's death scene in particular was astoundingly clear and detailed, despite being stretched by the angle of the sun.

Most of the staff researchers took Sunday off, but the infirmary on the first floor never closed, and it was entirely likely that Desmond worked every day of the week. But he *had* offered to let me use his lab. Obviously he intended for me to use the space for schoolwork and to prepare for the Black Trial, and I would have to claim that's why I'd come, if he was working. But I held out hope, as I snuck down the second-floor hallway, that he had taken the afternoon off.

I needed privacy, in order to work on the secret bone plaque formula.

I could never reveal my discovery—and my defacing of the Conservatory plaques—to Desmond, but my instinct to hide it from Wilder had taken me by surprise. As if Past Amber wasn't sure I should trust him.

Wilder and I had parted ways after breaking our fast, and I'd spent half the day poring over Past Amber's notes. I discovered only one formula that contained all of the components I'd found symbols for. I had no idea what the formula was for, or what it would do. Unlike the rest of my notes, that particular sheet of parchment had no heading declaring its subject, and it was undated. If it weren't in the same handwriting as the rest—*my* handwriting—I'd likely have assumed it was someone else's work.

The fact that it was clearly mine, despite lacking my usual annotation, only amplified my curiosity.

Thanks to the shattered stained glass window, I could be kicked out of the Alchemary at any moment. My dreams could already be over, along with any chance of recovering my memory. For all I knew, this little project was the academic version of a chicken flapping uselessly around the farmyard, not yet aware that it had already lost its head.

But if so, I would flap away at alchemy until they plucked my plumage and dragged me bodily through the gate, across the bridge, and off the island.

I hesitated at the door to Desmond's suite, my heart racing. Then I let myself into the foyer. The door to the lab stood ajar. The space looked empty, but there was every chance he was in the office, going over notes.

"Hello?" I called, stepping partway into the lab. "Desmond? Are you in here? Is it okay if I . . . ?"

The door to his office also stood open, but a glance inside told me the small, neat room was empty.

I exhaled, buoyed by relief even as I made a conscious effort to ignore an undercurrent of deep suspicion.

As far as I knew, Desmond Gregory had no hobbies, other than training with soldiers. What on earth could he be doing on a Sunday afternoon?

Whatever was occupying him likely wouldn't take long. That knowledge spurred me into action, and I set my satchel on the nearest lab table.

The necessary components and supplies were pretty basic. At least, I assumed they must be, since I knew what they all were. It was the specific *combination* of components that felt unusual, based on what I had thus far relearned of alchemy, and *that*, in addition to the fact that the component symbols had been literally written on the Conservatory walls, hastened me as I gathered the required equipment.

The supply closet was impeccably well organized, and I was careful to take no more than I needed, hoping such small portions would go entirely unnoticed. The only one I was unsure of was Desmond's supply of beyn.

I had yet to remaster my own beyn formula—my notes on the matter were distressingly vague—so I had no choice but to borrow a dropperful of Desmond's.

The stronger the beyn used, the more powerful the elixir would be, but I had no idea how strong his was. Or what source materials he'd used. Or how they could affect the potion. Under normal circumstances I would never use an ingredient without any understanding of what it would do to my formula. But I could practically feel the clock winding down toward Desmond's return, and I couldn't be sure I'd ever be allowed in an Alchemary lab again. Or that I would even still be a student by the end of the day. So there was no time to debate my options.

Excitement bubbled just beneath my skin as I lit burners and measured ingredients. As I checked and double-checked instructions, then squinted at the simmering fluids to assess the colors as they gradually changed from one bright hue to the next.

Finally, to my relief and unending excitement, I bent to peer into the bulbed beaker as my mystery concoction cooled within it.

The color was compelling—a pale but almost fluorescent blue that seemed to virtually glow within the vial. Though surely that was the light from the candles I'd lit.

While it cooled, I cleaned everything I'd used, careful to position the equipment exactly as I'd found it.

Then, nearly two hours after I'd begun, as late-afternoon sun shifted slowly across the floor from the laboratory window, I realized I had no idea what to do with . . . whatever I'd just made.

Was it invisible ink? To test the theory, I dipped an edge of parchment into the vial.

The color stained it but failed to fade.

Maybe it only works on bone. . . . It was not beyond the realm of possibility that this formula was specifically designed to react with the material composition of the bone plaques. Maybe that was why the formula had felt so odd, despite my lack of remembered experience.

Excited by that thought. I gathered my satchel and took the warm beaker and a small horsehair brush into the hall, where I had to remind myself to be quiet, despite the rush of blood through my veins.

Any plaque would probably do, but the one least likely to be seen by any researcher that stepped into the hall was at the back of the building, outside an unoccupied office suite. That plaque was the only one that had revealed no hidden symbol, so it seemed like the perfect place to leave one myself.

What would I want to write for some intrepid future student to find? Or future researcher, more likely, considering that few students had access to the Conservatory.

While I considered the question, I dipped a scrap of cloth into the beaker and used it to dab a bit of the warm solution on the lower left corner of the scroll-shaped plaque, to test it. To my surprise, the ink disappeared almost immediately.

I frowned at the plaque. The invisible ink Wilder and I had made as kids had taken several minutes to fade from visibility. Clearly this was a different and much more complicated formula, assuming that was what I'd actually made, but...

What if it wasn't? We'd made invisible ink as *children,* with far fewer and simpler ingredients, and no flame required. So why...?

An odd, anxious anticipation seized me as I carefully set the beaker on the floor and scratched open the scab from the cut I'd made inside my elbow. A drop of fresh blood welled up, and I smeared it on the plaque, directly over where I'd painted the formula, using my right index finger.

But the "invisible ink" did not reappear. Nor did my blood stain the plaque. Instead, it beaded up like sweat where it had been smeared over the substance, though there was no color change on the plaque itself.

Maybe this plaque was different somehow. Maybe that was why it was the only one with no symbol. Or maybe the original had been replaced at some point.

If that was the case, had I missed whatever symbol had been painted on the original plaque? Was my concoction missing an ingredient?

No. Past Amber's weird formula was the only one I'd found that used all of the other symbols. The formula felt complete. And if that were true... there had to be some other reason this plaque had revealed no symbol. Some other reason the formula disappeared instantly and didn't function like invisible ink.

Curious, I dipped the rag into the beaker again and smeared another streak boldly across the center of the plaque.

It immediately disappeared, to no effect.

Hmmm... Still holding the beaker, I pressed my right cheek against the wall next to the plaque, peering into the narrow, dark gap between the plaque and the marble wall. But I could see nothing.

An idea sparked, and I spun to grab the nearest torch from its wall mount. Carefully, I held the torch up so that it cast light into the gap, and this time, with my face pressed against the marble, I could see that the hardware that held the plaque to the wall shone oddly in the firelight, with a bluish metallic glint.

Acting purely on instinct, and the knowledge that base metals are the primary target of any transfiguration attempts in alchemy, I carefully poured the bright blue concoction behind the plaque, doing my best to hit the glinting bits of metal. Whatever they were.

Despite my care, some of the thick liquid slid down the wall. I returned the torch to its mount, and as I was wiping up the bluish drips, a strange, soft hissing sound echoed from behind the plaque.

Startled, I popped up onto my feet just as the plaque swung away from the wall, opening on concealed hinges to reveal a neat, square compartment cut into the marble behind it.

Excitement spiked my pulse, and I realized two things at once: My pale blue concoction had dissolved the small bits of metal that had held the plaque in place, and there was something *in* the hidden compartment. Something round, made of a standard metal that glinted softly—normally—in the torchlight.

I reached into the small hole, and my fingers closed around something curved and slightly warm. At first, the object resisted my effort, but then I pulled harder, and it came free with a soft click. From the inner wall of the compartment, a small metal clasp slid forward, protruding a fraction of an inch beyond the hole, and I realized that when the plaque was closed over the compartment again, the clasp would secure it in place.

I turned, careful not to knock over the beaker at my feet, and held my prize up to the light of the torch. Lying on my palm was a metal ring no bigger around than my fist. It took the shape of a snake swallowing its own tail.

An ouroboros. A symbol for wholeness. Or infinity.

The ring—the bracelet—was rigid and intricately molded, each individual scale distinctly visible. The snake's head was flared, its tail narrow where it fit between delicate metal fangs. The snake's eyes were tiny red jewels, shining like rubies in the bright white flame from the torch.

Stunned, I slid the bracelet onto my left wrist. It was warm against my skin and loose enough that it would clank against any work surface when I moved. And yet . . . I didn't want to take it off. Even though it didn't belong to me, and I'd vandalized yet more Alchemary property in order to find it.

The point was that I *had* found it. *I'd* found it. But the building had shown me how.

The building, and Past Amber.

And all I could think, as I closed the plaque and returned to Desmond's lab to seal up what was left in the beaker, was that there *had* to be a reason.

"Amber!"

As I stepped out of the Conservatory into the quadrangle, a familiar voice smashed through my triumphant haze like an adze through firewood, sending my splintered thoughts flying.

I looked up to find Professor Edmiston standing beneath the broad front portico of the Seminary, as if she'd just stepped out of the building. She looked both relieved and surprised to see me.

"Amber Fallbrook!" she repeated. "May I please have a few moments of your time?" Her voice lifted on the end of the question, implying that I actually had a choice in the matter, but her expression did not support that sentiment.

I nodded and began winding my way down the stone path, around topiary animals, past students who watched me with open curiosity. As I walked, I subtly pulled the ouroboros bracelet from my wrist and slid it into a pocket concealed in the folds of my cloak.

"What a delightful coincidence." Professor Edmiston looked back at me with every other step as I followed her up the front stairs of the Seminary. "I was just on my way to your Dormitory chamber to look for you, after failing to find you in the student laboratory." Though her smile held steady, her voice took on a censuring tone. "Most of your classmates have been hard at work at their stations all day."

"I had a late night," I mumbled.

She nodded as she pulled open the front door and held it for me, using her free hand to push back a poofy clump of silver curls. "So we've all heard."

"We?"

"This way."

I followed Professor Edmiston down the central corridor to the right, past torches flickering with a deep golden light, which lent the space a very formal and somewhat tense atmosphere.

We turned into another, narrower corridor on the left, between two of the larger lecture halls. A door at the end of the corridor stood open, and a jumble of whispered conversation leaked from it, the voices too muddled for me to identify or understand.

"Just through here." Professor Edmiston indicated the open door.

I stepped into a conference room dominated by a long, heavy table. Sunlight streamed through three tall windows, but a series of lanterns had been lit in a line down the center of the table as well, giving the room a surprisingly functional blend of only slightly flickering flame and strong, clean daylight.

Only a few of the heavy wooden chairs were occupied, but I caught merely an impression of several dark robes with distinctive collars, indicating both professors and staff researchers, before a familiar and unexpected form stationed near the door captured my full attention.

Cressa Baxter stood poised and silent with her wax tablet at the ready, and though she nodded at me, she did not offer an encouraging smile. And if *she* was in attendance . . .

I redirected my gaze toward the end of the table, and indeed, there was the Bluehelm, sliding her chair back so she could stand, her dark eyes piercing above pale, gaunt cheeks.

"Amber. Thank you for joining us," she said as Cressa closed the door.

I murmured a vague acknowledgment, despite my racing pulse.

Professor Edmiston took a seat, and as my gaze slid from her, the face to the Bluehelm's left came into focus.

Desmond.

No wonder he hadn't been in his lab; he'd been here, evidently discussing my future at the Alchemary, in my absence.

Across from him sat Professor Bollinger, who stared at me over the round frames of his spectacles. Next to the professor sat Dr. Winhoof, whose fine white hair looked virtually translucent in the bright daylight streaming into the room.

"It's our understanding that there was an incident last night in the third-floor student laboratory," the Bluehelm began.

I nodded, grasping for the best way to explain how and why I'd broken the stained glass, and when my silence only echoed throughout the room, Desmond broke it.

"Amber was assaulted by a fellow student, and I *demand* his immediate expulsion." He spoke firmly, without raising his voice, but I sucked in a deep breath, as shocked as if he'd shouted.

He'd reframed the issue so that it wasn't about me at all. It was about Pryce and what *he'd* done.

The Bluehelm turned to him. "As you know, the student in question has given a conflicting account of the event, and I'm afraid it doesn't cast Ms. Fallbrook in an entirely flattering light."

They'd already met with Pryce?

Desmond's coppery-brown eyes flashed with a quiet fury. "That's—"

"And as you *also* know, his parents are rather prominent alumni," the Bluehelm continued. "It seems to me that what would be in everyone's best interest is if we all proceed with an eye toward a cooperative outcome. A compromise."

"Compromise?" I said, despite my reluctance to draw attention back to myself. "Why? Who are his parents?" If they were alumni but not staff members, then they'd failed one of the Mastery-year trials. In all likelihood, they were accredited provincial alchemists like my mother had been—perhaps large donors to the school. Yet I found it difficult to believe that my mother, had she lived, would have had enough clout to keep me from being expelled if I'd assaulted a classmate.

Professor Edmiston cleared her throat and leaned toward me, tucking a silver ringlet behind one ear. "They both practice at court," she whispered, even though everyone could hear her. "One of the alumni in question is personal alchemist to the Crown."

No.

That was why Desmond had recognized Pryce's name. I'd managed to make an enemy out of the son of the most prominent alchemist in the kingdom, other than the Bluehelm.

"It seems clear to me that two things are true at once," the Bluehelm said. "This other student behaved abominably, in a manner unbefitting of the Alchemary. And Amber Fallbrook"—her gaze fell heavily upon me—"destroyed virtually irreplaceable, historically significant Alchemary property."

"That was an accident," I insisted, bolstered by the fact that she clearly understood the circumstances. "I was defending myself." I stood straighter, small but fierce flames licking the base of my spine. "And if I hadn't, you'd have an entirely different issue to deal with today."

"We cannot address what did *not* happen," she said. "Regarding what *did* happen, an offer has been made. The other student's family is willing to pay for the destruction of property, if you can see fit to move past their son's poor behavior. With the understanding, of course, that such behavior will not be repeated."

I took a second to process that offer. I could stay at the Alchemary, and I would incur no debt for the damage.

"All I have to do is . . . forgive him?"

"In a manner of speaking, yes," the Bluehelm said. "Though they are not requesting that you directly address him." She exhaled slowly. "I want to make it clear that they consider this a very generous offer, and if you were to decline, and I were forced to expel their son, I suspect they would put those same resources toward lobbying the Crown for your removal as well."

"So, we both stay, or neither of us does?"

The Bluehelm's brows arched at me. "You are a very bright young woman."

"Absolutely not," Desmond practically growled. He stood, and his chair squealed against the stone floor. "The boy is a brute, and he has no place here. Ms. Fallbrook cannot be expected to share classrooms and laboratory space with someone who is an objective threat to her person, and—"

"It is my understanding that she won't be sharing space with him," the Bluehelm interrupted with a glance at Cressa. "Have her supplies not already been moved to Desmond Gregory's private laboratory?"

"That is happening as we speak," Cressa said, without even glancing at her notes.

"An arrangement made without permission from or even notice to the Seminary faculty," the Bluehelm noted.

Desmond scowled. "Given the advanced nature of her work, the ambitious nature of her research, and the specific needs of her current . . . medical condition, it only makes sense that—"

"I agree," the Bluehelm interrupted, one hand raised for silence. "And since that arrangement was officially approved last year, I will let its extension stand. And that eliminates most of the concern with this other student, does it not?"

"It does not," Desmond insisted. "His character is not of a suitable caliber. He dishonors the Alchemary with his very presence. I want him expelled."

"That isn't your decision," I snapped, standing to confront him from across the table. He seemed truly outraged by the very idea of Pryce Wishart continuing his studies on campus, but . . . that wasn't the entire reason for his objection. Something familiar and infuriating lurked behind his coppery gaze—a coldly devious but effective tactic.

Desmond had realized that if he got Pryce expelled, he would no longer be dependent upon the Bluehelm to have me removed from campus. That decision would come from far above her head.

It would come from the Crown.

I glared at him, crossing my own arms over my chest to mirror his pose. "That choice is mine, as I understand it?"

The Bluehelm nodded, her attention shifting from me to Desmond, and back.

"Then I accept. The other student's family will pay for the window on my behalf, as restitution for his offense. I will move into

Des—into Mr. Gregory's laboratory. And the other student will stay on at the Alchemary, so long as he does not exhibit such aggression again."

"Amber—" Desmond said, and I shook my head sharply.

"I will not cut off my nose to spite my face," I insisted. "And I will not have it said that I only succeeded at the Alchemary by banishing my competition, or that I leveraged any personal advantage against another student." Whether he deserved banishment or not. The truth never spreads as faithfully as a juicy falsehood, and I would not be on the beneficial end of any gossip about me. "And *you do not speak for me*."

The Bluehelm's eyebrows rose. Over her shoulder, Cressa looked quietly amused.

Desmond's eyes narrowed. His intense focus on me seemed to be silently asking some question I had no way of understanding, much less answering. Finally, he sighed. "That does appear to be the case."

The ouroboros—a snake that devours its own tail—symbolizes the unity of mind, matter, and spirit, which assemble in a perpetual sequence of destruction and creation.

The "paradoxical serpent" represents the cycle of life, death, and rebirth. In alchemy specifically, it symbolizes wholeness, infinity, and eternity.

—from *Symbols, Imagery, and Metaphor in the Study of Alchemy*

Twenty

Monday was unseasonably warm for a fall day, and the heat only contributed to my stuffy feeling of frustration and discontent. And while the rhythmic whooshing of waves outside my window was peaceful, it also threatened to lull me to sleep.

After yet another night of low-burning candles and insufficient sleep, followed by two classes of my own and one of Professor Robard's, my brain felt like a swollen, overheated mass throbbing behind my skull. My thoughts churned with a maelstrom of facts, theories, and data. I would have given my left arm for another cup of tea, and the alertness it would surely bring, but I could not waste any more time going up and down the stairs.

Every day I understood more of my craft, yet felt less capable of using it. Less capable, even, of rising from my bed to face the day. I could not remember ever being more tired or less focused. Though, considering my circumstances, that really wasn't saying much.

Distracted as I was by exhaustion, my attention caught again on the metal ouroboros lying on my desk. Afternoon sunlight beaming from the open shutters caught its scales and glittered in its red eyes. As a hawk soared past the window, its shadow made the snake appear to be blinking as it worked to swallow its own tail. To continue the cycle of life, or learning, or the seasons, or anything else that could be said to begin the same way it ended.

I picked up the bracelet and studied it for the hundredth time in the past twenty-four hours. I had no idea why it had been hidden in the Conservatory wall, or who had been meant to find it. But the idea that someone there had secrets—beautiful, possibly symbolic secrets—made the cold, harsh Conservatory building feel more like a mystery than like the giant marble mausoleum it resembled.

With a sigh, I dropped the bracelet into the wooden chest, under my father's letter, where it encircled my mother's rose-cut ring, then pushed my chair back from the desk, careful to avoid the edge of an uneven stone that had caught the chair leg twice the night before. Desperate for a cross breeze, even if it fluttered my loose sheets of parchment, I rose and opened the door into the dark stairwell.

"Oh!" I jumped back from the unexpected face, practically glowing on the shadowy landing. "I didn't hear any footsteps."

Wilder laughed, lowering the fist he'd raised to knock on my door. "Buried in work?" he guessed with a glance at my desk. "All you do is study."

"Well, you *rarely* study, so I suppose, together, we achieve some sort of balance."

"I suppose." He crossed his arms over the front of his tunic, one brow arched expectantly. "May I come in?"

"Only if you've come to help."

"Actually, I've come to introduce you to the concept of daylight." Yet he stepped inside anyway. "They say the sun's rays have a medicinal effect on both the human body and spirit."

I blinked up at him. "You're here to save me from the gloom of my own dormitory chamber?" Despite the fresh breeze being pulled in from the glittering ocean view, now that the door was open.

Grinning, he stepped close and gently tapped the side of my skull, just above one of my braids. "And of this equally glum and much more mysterious chamber."

I rolled my eyes and turned back to my desk. "What I've learned—what I've *re*learned—today is that the sun can also have an effect on certain kinds of compounds and suspensions. It's something about the heat, or maybe specifically the light itself, though that's evidently quite difficult to replicate with open flame or direct heat in a laboratory setting, and—"

Wilder groaned as he glanced over my shoulder at the sheets of parchment I'd been studying. "You know, you used to spend time in places other than your own bedchamber. Not that this is an entirely unpleasant location, under the right circumstances." His gaze wandered toward my neatly made bed.

If only I could remember those circumstances... I thought, indulging the sudden warmth deep in my chest. "Where did I spend time before?"

"The library and the laboratory, mostly."

And the truth was that I would have loved to be in the library at that very moment, with a large selection of texts legitimately at my disposal, instead of merely the few I'd managed to sneak out of the building the week before. But I could not abide the stares. The whispers.

It wasn't only that they made me uncomfortable; they made it impossible for me to concentrate.

"Which laboratory?" I asked.

"Desmond's, mostly." Wilder's expression soured, as if the admission left an unpleasant taste in his mouth. "So, why aren't you there now?"

"I'll go tonight. I'm just... trying to study. While I still have daylight."

Wilder leaned against the front of my desk. "You're avoiding him."

"I am," I admitted. "I mean no offense to you, as he is your blood relation, or to my own memory of Desmond from childhood, but... he's not entirely pleasant to be around."

Wilder laughed, eyes shining with delight. "I've been saying that for years, yet everyone around here acts as if Desmond Gregory's name is synonymous with the term 'erudition.'"

"Is it not, though? I've heard his Mastery-year exam and trial scores were quite high." Keryth and Adria, another girl from our cohort, had said as much in the Refectory, at the midday meal, though they'd had no idea I was listening.

Wilder's blue eyes narrowed on me. "That is entirely beside the point. Scholarship and discipline are not the same as natural aptitude and cleverness—as *genius*, dare I say it?"

I rolled my eyes at him fondly. "I sense *no* hesitation in your willingness to say that."

Wilder paced the length of my narrow room. "Desmond is good at processing other people's ideas and extrapolating from them. Confirming, recording, and explaining them. Combining them in semi-novel fashion, in order to 'push boundaries' and extend the application of known theories. But at the end of the day, he is a noted scholar, *not* an innovator."

"*Not* a genius," I said, amusement lifting one corner of my mouth as I watched him pace.

"Exactly!" Wilder did not note my jest at his expense. "But everyone else seems oblivious to that distinction, and their misguided adoration has given him *quite* a high estimation of himself. And yet he marches across campus as if he does not know that women—and a few of the men—stare at him all day and no doubt contemplate his countenance when they are alone in bed at night." He huffed. "If a man is attractive, that man *knows* he is attractive, and I cannot deny that my brother is, based on his resemblance to me alone."

I snorted, but Wilder hardly noticed.

"And yet Desmond seems entirely unaware." He sank into my armchair, and finally his attention returned to me. His eyes narrowed. "Why are you watching me like I'm a buffoon dancing at court in a patchwork jerkin?"

My laughter broke free beneath the strain of that mental image. "Apologies. It's just that I've never seen anyone openly lusting after your brother on campus, though he *has* been afforded his own laboratory suite and seems to have earned his colleagues' deference. Is it possible you're viewing him through a skewed lens?" My brows arched. "Because you're envious?"

Wilder huffed. "*Of course* I'm envious. His contributions to alchemy are valued, while mine are disparaged."

"Indeed." I gave him a solemn, sympathetic nod. "Though my hesitance to avail myself of his lab space has more to do with the fact that he's still trying to have me removed from the Alchemary."

"Well, if you're hoping to use the lab while he's not there, you're out of luck. He works late." Wilder pulled at the end of my coat, which was draped over the arm of his chair. "Ow." He jerked his hand back and shook it, flinging a drop of blood across the room. "What . . . ?" He lifted the hem of my robe, angling it into the light from my candle, and frowned when that light glared off something stuck in the fabric.

"Glass." I carefully plucked the large shard of leaded glass from where it had evidently become embedded during my confrontation with the window in the student lab. The shard was half the length of my thumb and about a quarter as wide.

I set it on the edge of my desk, where it practically glowed in the flickering lamplight, reminding me all over again of the artwork I'd destroyed.

"Come." Wilder took my hand as he stood, trying to tug me toward the open door and the world that lay beyond the Dormitory. "Let's get you some air."

"I cannot." I pulled my hand from his grip and sank into my desk chair again. "Our first exam is on Wednesday, and if I don't pass, I'll be expelled." That knowledge had sat at the back of my mind for nearly a month, but it felt more like a weight on my chest now, slowly pressing the air from my lungs.

He rolled his eyes. "You're going to pass."

The dismissive tone of his voice lit a fire in my gut.

"You don't know that!" I snapped. "You can't possibly! I am not the girl I was a month ago." I lowered my voice, trying not to notice the hurt in his eyes. "The 'genius' is *gone,* Wilder. I count myself lucky that reading about a concept seems to unlock whatever understanding I once had. But it's a base-level understanding, and it doesn't tumble the next obstacle from my path. I have to read the next thing to relearn it, and then the next, and I don't have any understanding of how much I've forgotten. Of how much I still have to relearn. I can't remember what it is that I don't know, and while I read pretty quickly, there are only so many hours in the day. And the night."

My sigh seemed to empty not just my lungs, but my very soul. "And relearning the basic terms and concepts doesn't bring me up to the level of skill needed to pass a Mastery-year examination. Or to survive the first trial. And in case it's entirely slipped your mind, that's only a couple of weeks away."

"It has *not* slipped my mind. I just think that you need a break."

"What I need is a miracle. I can't keep studying night and day at the expense of my health. That's terribly inefficient. Especially given that I've *already* learned all of this, have I not?"

"Most assuredly," he said with a gesture at the sheets of parchment I'd scribbled all over. At the textbooks opened and stacked upon one another in inscrutable layers of information. "Better than anyone I've ever known. They know that."

They, presumably, were the leadership of the Alchemary.

"That's why they've kept you. That's why they're letting you move into Des's lab. That's why they're making Pryce pay for the window, when—"

"*They're* making him pay? I thought that was his family's idea?"

"I don't believe that for a second," Wilder said. "My guess is that the Bluehelm suggested it, so she could keep you both. They want the Wishart money, but they need the Fallbrook brain."

Something twisted deep inside me at his words. At the mention of a brain that felt more like lost legend than like a part of my own body.

"Well, to that point, so do I. And my time would be much better spent looking for a way to unlock the knowledge I already have. To find a cure for amnesia, rather than trying to relearn all of alchemy."

"And I promised to help . . ." he said as my point sank in.

"Indeed you did. Have you come up with anything? Any potential . . . elixir of memory?"

Wilder hesitated, just long enough for me to see the truth.

"You *have*! And you weren't going to tell me?"

"I found something *potentially* helpful, and I *was* going to tell you," he insisted. "In fact, I was going to ask you to help me with it in the lab the other night, but then . . ."

"Pryce," I said.

He nodded. "Pryce fucking Wishart."

"Did you know about this father? Or . . . maybe his mother?"

"Do you mean the Crown's personal alchemist? It's his father. And yes, we all found out during Fundamentals year, when the Wisharts showed up for Family Weekend. But my point is that you don't work in the student lab anymore, and I'm not welcome in Desmond's, so telling you what I'd found suddenly seemed a bit . . . complicated."

"What did you find?"

"There's a tonic on record in the library—just one—intended to help firm up memory in old age."

"That's not really my issue, Wilder."

"It's a starting place. There's also an elixir I was playing around with a while back, when I was having trouble memorizing about four million vocabulary words for Intro."

"I assume that's a hyperbolic estimate?"

He shrugged. "Who could say? I'm no better with numbers than I am with vocabulary words."

I rolled my eyes. "So, a tonic for dementia of advanced age, and an elixir intended to help students memorize new facts?"

"To be clear, I never perfected that elixir," Wilder said. "But with a little luck, some trial and error, and a good succedaneum for winter cherry, which isn't growing yet, I should be able to come up with some sort of boost for your brain, at the very least."

Not *exactly* a key to the lock on my memory dungeon, but surely it would be better than nothing.

"I'll work on it tonight. Ironically," he said, "we'd be much closer to the solution if you hadn't lost your memory in the first place." When I could only frown, he chuckled. "The Philosopher's Stone. If you'd actually created it, it could no doubt cure you now."

I scowled at him. "That may be the least helpful thing you've ever said."

"I assure you it is not." Wilder's gaze shifted downward, lingering on my thigh just long enough to make me squirm in my chair before it settled on my journal, which sat on the edge of my desk. "Has nothing in there sparked a memory?"

"No." I bent to grab the journal. "I can't read it. Though the writing looks familiar," I mused, flipping through the pages, oddly comforted by the whisper of dry parchment beneath my fingers.

Wilder frowned at the page I stopped on. "What is that?"

"You don't recognize it either?" Past Amber presumably understood what she was writing, but why would she have written in a language her best friend couldn't read?

He shook his head. "It doesn't look like a language, precisely. Some of those marks look more like symbols, but that isn't alchemical notation."

"This part isn't. But now that I've spent weeks studying alchemical terms, I can recognize the few that *are* written here. Everything else, though . . ." I could only shrug.

"What alchemical symbols?" Wilder scooted to the edge of the chair, and I tilted the journal so he could clearly see. Past Amber had written so much she'd run out of room and been forced to leave one final note running vertically along the narrow outer margin of the left-hand page.

The only part of that note I could read was the two alchemical symbols, which had been enclosed in a circle. A *perfect* carefully drawn circle, with no overlapping ends, rather than a hastily scribbled oval to emphasize a specific point.

"Cinis." Wilder ran one finger over a symbol like a three-tined pitchfork facing to the right, with a short handle extending from the left.

Only, in the one I'd drawn, the outer tines were rounded, curving in toward the center like a demon's trident, in my signature notation.

Any time I wrote the symbol, it appeared exactly like that on the page, my fingers forming those curves automatically.

"Cinis," I agreed. "Or ash." And what I'd relearned about ash spilled from my mouth as fast as the words blossomed in my head. "The word means *dust*, generally, and can mean anything from fireplace soot to incinerated human remains, but in alchemy it refers to the end product of the calcination stage: what is left after the prima material has been purified by fire. Symbolically, in the field of Apotheosis, ash is the incorruptible glorified human body that has survived the purifying ordeal."

"I understand that." Yet Wilder's soft smile looked distinctly impressed. "And I'm pretty sure you just quoted a textbook passage verbatim."

"I did."

"How many times have you read it?" His gaze scanned the texts open on my desk, evidently looking for the one I'd quoted.

"Once." I sighed. "I don't have time to read most of this more than once."

His eyes widened almost imperceptibly. "Amber." His voice was so soft it almost seemed to be coming from within my own head. "Most people can't read something once and remember it word for word." He took my hand and squeezed it. "The genius is *not* gone."

I looked up and found tiny versions of myself reflected in his eyes. "So, I could do that before?"

"I honestly don't know," he said. "We didn't talk about... alchemy."

"Then what did we talk about?" I regretted the question as soon as I'd asked it, suddenly certain that Wilder and I must have spent more time in bed than in the lab. Which might have been the only time we had together, if he'd spent nights in the student laboratory while I'd been set up in Desmond's space.

"Air," I said, feeling suddenly compelled to change the subject by a discomfort I could not explain.

Wilder blinked. "What?"

I tapped the other alchemical symbol circled in the margin, an upward-pointing equilateral triangle bisected by a horizontal line roughly half of the way down.

"In alchemy, air represents heat and moisture, in the form of water vapor, which is condensed from it. Because of that, the air symbol can also represent blood, which is a life-giving force."

"Ash and blood," Wilder said. "Any idea why you wrote those? Or circled them?"

"None."

A grin tugged at one corner of his mouth, his eyes flashing playfully in the light of the lantern. "Maybe you were talking about bodies. The glorified human form . . ." He stroked one finger slowly over the symbol for ash. "Hot and wet . . ." That same finger slid over the bisected triangle representing air. Or blood. "I think you made dirty notations when you got bored in the lab."

I arched one brow at him. "Without more context, I could just as easily have been talking about murder. About spilling blood from the human form, then burning the corpse."

He scowled. "Why do you always ruin my fantasies?"

Laughter bubbled up from my throat; he'd been giving me that look since we were children. "Every girl needs a lighthearted diversion."

"Tears," he said, snatching the journal from me so he could snap it closed.

"Pardon?"

"Tears are warm and wet. Maybe you were writing about making someone cry."

I rolled my eyes again. "Why would I have made someone cry?"

Wilder gave me a strange, sad look. "Maybe it's better that you don't remember everything."

Gazes followed us as Wilder and I stepped into the quadrangle, each burdened with an armload of my personal notes and supplies. He had practically dared me to stop wasting time and move into Desmond's lab, and when he'd offered to help carry my things, I'd realized I was out of excuses.

"What are they saying?" I whispered as we crossed the long axis of the lawn, headed straight toward the towering Conservatory. "What is the gossip?"

"About you? There's no gossip," he said.

I gave him a look. "I know you were at the Dusty Beaker last night." I'd overheard Yoslyn and Keryth as they'd walked down the stairs past my open door that morning, talking about how fetching he'd looked. How a couple of pints turned the younger Gregory brother into a charming and gallant libertine.

His gregarious reputation clearly had not suffered from his association with me, and I could not decide whether I was relieved by that or vexed by it.

"I was, yes. But you were not the topic on people's tongues there, like you are here."

"So there *is* gossip."

"Not really," he insisted. "What they're saying is surprisingly accurate, so I'd have to classify it more as conversation. Pryce told everyone about your memory. And about the window. Though he does not seem to have disclosed his own part in what happened to it."

"Of course he didn't."

"To be fair, he's hardly had the chance, considering that he has himself, just this very afternoon, become an irresistible topic of conversation."

"Has he?"

"If you'll glance subtly to your left—*subtly*"—Wilder elbowed me when my head swiveled too sharply as I resettled the tall stack of notes tucked beneath my arm—"you might notice that young Pryce Wishart is wearing a hat today. And if you were to squint across the quadrangle, and perhaps shield your face from the setting sun, you would further notice that the hair peeking beneath the brim of that hat is a robust shade of cobalt."

"What?" I *did* squint, and indeed, I found Pryce standing in the shade of the Seminary's front facade, all alone. Quite apart, in fact, from several of our classmates. As I watched, he tugged at the brim of a hat, and as he pulled it lower on his forehead, it rose on the back of his scalp. Where his hair was, in fact, a bright and vibrant shade of blue.

"In addition . . ." Wilder continued as we paused in our journey across the quadrangle, "if you were to move close enough to see his face and hands, you might notice that they, too, are now a particular shade of blue. As are his eyebrows. And his eyelashes. And his nasal hair. If you were to come up with a reason for him to remove his clothes—though I do not recommend such an adventure—you would further notice that there is not currently, nor will there be for the foreseeable future, a single hair or inch of flesh on that boy's body that is not some variation of the color blue."

I blinked at Pryce, then glanced away when he caught me looking, but not before I noticed two young women giggling from a few feet away while they stared at him.

"Oh *my*." I grabbed Wilder's arm with my free hand and tugged him toward the Conservatory, and I only let go when I noticed him struggling with the box he held. "Has he caught some contagion? My father said there's an illness that casts the flesh a strange shade of—"

Wilder's laughter caught me entirely off guard, but it took me only a second to understand.

"You . . . ?" I couldn't resist a glance back at Pryce. "You *dyed* him?"

"I know. It's petty and amateur. But it was also disappointingly easy, and I assure you, it's only the *visible* portion of his requital."

I stopped cold in the grass, a sick feeling churning in my stomach. "What else did you do?" I hissed.

He nudged me forward with his elbow. "I simply let the punishment fit the original offense."

"Meaning *what*, Wilder?" I demanded as we slowly navigated the stone pathway.

"I made sure he will not be able to demand the 'favor' he tried to extort from you from anyone else. For the foreseeable future."

A dark sort of satisfaction crept up from the pit of my stomach. "Pryce is . . . ?"

"Not feeling particularly virile," Wilder confirmed as we approached the Conservatory.

"He cannot . . . *perform*?" I whispered, eyes wide.

"Or assault. Though he may not have perceived that bit yet. *Oh,* to be a fly on the wall of Pryce Wishart's bedchamber . . ." He frowned, looking suddenly ill. "That is not a sentence I ever thought to utter."

"You rendered him *impotent,* for what he did to me?"

Wilder shrugged, the box bobbing in his grip. "I am simply using alchemy to slow the forces of chaos and make the world a better place, one violent clod at a time. Though, to be clear, I dyed him blue in revenge for having smashed my vials. And for generally being a squandering of organic material. Human detritus." Another shrug. "And because I had a new elixir in need of a test subject."

"Why would you have an elixir that tints the human form? Or that renders impotence?"

Wilder winked at me. "Because I don't always get it right on the first attempt. Trial and error is an inefficient yet vastly entertaining process, and sometimes the mistakes prove more profitable than what I intended to invent."

"Wilder Gregory." I turned on the second step toward the Conservatory's front portico so I could look at him at eye level. "Has anyone ever told you that you are *quite* the charming calamity?"

"You said something very similar to me once." He gave me a cheeky wink. "Only the word you used was 'disaster.' And you were not smiling when you said it."

"Well, I am smiling now."

Twenty-One

Desmond met us on the second floor and led us into his laboratory, where Wilder set my belongings on the nearest table. He shook his brother's hand, and I got an odd feeling—part nostalgia, part anxiety—as I watched them standing face-to-face. They said nothing to each other. Not a word. They seemed to have come to some sort of unspoken understanding, but it felt like the kind of compromise where both parties wind up not happy but equally disgruntled and resigned.

Wilder gave me a hug, then left the room. A moment later, his footsteps echoed as they pounded down the stairs.

Desmond and I faced each other in awkward silence from opposite sides of an empty lab table until Wilder's steps had completely faded. Until we heard the distant, soft thump of the huge front door, one floor below.

"I was afraid you'd revoke your invitation, after yesterday." After I'd stood up to him in front of the Bluehelm and my professors.

"I'm disappointed by your lack of faith in me. I would never go back on my word to you."

"You keep trying to get me kicked out, Desmond." I frowned up at him, unable to understand the series of contradictions that seemed to form his entire being. "That makes you difficult to trust."

He frowned. "Why would it? I've been nothing but honest about my efforts."

"Yet less than transparent about the reason."

"That is not the same as dishonest."

I couldn't fault his logic. But neither did I like it. "You are infuriating," I said, staring directly up at him from across the table, my hands splayed on the surface.

His left brow rose, and when the corresponding corner of his mouth matched it, I found myself unnerved by his resemblance to Wilder. "Well, we seem to have that, at least, in common."

Desmond left the laboratory door open while he showed me my work space, and I could only stare around the room. I'd been there before, of course, but being welcomed into the space felt different than sneaking in. Desmond's lab was as large as the entire student lab on the third floor of the Seminary, and he was allotting me a full third of it, when I'd only had a single table before.

He gave me a tour of the supply room—he had a large closet, where the students only had a wall cabinet—and showed me where my supplies had been stored. "But you're welcome to anything you need from my stores as well," he added, one hand propped against a wall hook from which hung several thick aprons. "Though I'd ask you to start making your own beyn. Not because I'm selfish with mine, but because distillation of one's own beyn is the hallmark skill of any elite-level alchemist, and thus it is a worthy pursuit."

Which I knew, of course. Just as he clearly knew that I had not yet begun redeveloping my own formula, since being struck with amnesia.

"Thank you." I stared at an array of equipment I hadn't even glanced at the day before, when I'd only needed what was laid on out his drying rack. This time, my gaze skimmed vials of brightly colored powdered ingredients and already-mixed, carefully labeled suspensions. Burners, and beakers, and vials. The immense athanor, which I would only have to share with one person.

And I burst into tears.

Desmond gaped at me, clearly perplexed, while I tried to reclaim my composure. "What . . . ?" he began, hands opening uselessly at his sides. "What is the concern? Is the supply closet lacking?"

"Quite possibly." I wiped tears from my face with the backs of my fingers. "But if so, I would have no way of knowing. And I'm fairly certain that even before I lost my memory, that wasn't the kind of problem I would cry over."

"That's accurate," Desmond said. "But you seem somewhat changed since then. Beyond simply missing your memory."

"I suspect I'm more than *somewhat* changed."

"No." He crossed his arms over his tunic, firmly anchoring his opinion with the display of authority. "You are only somewhat changed. The Amber Fallbrook I knew and"—he cleared his throat, his cheeks flushing slightly—"*respected* is still in there."

"And do you respect this version of me? This version that flounders, and breaks windows, and bursts into uncontrolled fits of emotion?" I'd had no idea that I cared about his answer until I asked the question. Then, suddenly, I seemed to hang on his silence, balanced on the precipice of it, arms flailing over the chasm as I waited for words that might pull me back from the edge.

Or send me plummeting over.

"As odd as it might seem to you, I think I respect this version of you even more. Though I admit I hardly know what to do with the tears." He frowned at my damp cheeks. "However *you* always seemed to."

I frowned up at him, clutching the strap of my satchel until the leather cut into my palm. "How could you possibly respect me, diminished as I've become?"

And what on earth had I done with tears?

Desmond sighed. "The Amber I knew a month ago was brilliant, in every sense of the word. She was clever and shrewd.

Vibrant, luminous, and intense. She was vivid, arresting, and *colorful*. You are still all of those things."

I shook my head, fully prepared to argue, but he went on.

"Yet that Amber Fallbrook had never faced a true hardship. Things came easily to her. Words. Theories. Experimental techniques." He paused, and his gaze seemed to retreat from mine. "Choices."

Choices?

"That Amber didn't have to struggle with anything, so she didn't have much sympathy for those who did."

"I was cruel?" My heart ached at the thought, and yet some angry impulse made me want to debate the premise.

Which was exactly his point.

"Not intentionally," Desmond said. "You were . . . driven. You saw everything in binary terms. Right and wrong. Efficient and inefficient. Worthy or unworthy."

"Worthy of what?"

"Of thought. Of your time. It made you an exceptional alchemist. The ideal, in many ways. And yet this Amber seems to embody an element the previous version was missing."

"Compassion?"

He nodded. "Or consideration, at least."

"I admit, I don't like the thought that I was cruel. Or even inconsiderate." Though my interactions with several of my classmates so far seemed to confirm Desmond's claim. "But compassion isn't helping me recover my skill. Or my memory."

He studied me, leaning with one hip against an empty workstation, his arms crossed over the front of his thick, stained safety apron. "Which is it you want? Your skill or your memory?"

"Am I limited to one?"

"I've never known you to be limited by anything." His focus narrowed intensely on me, and his gaze suddenly felt bottomless.

I sucked in a breath, shocked by the abrupt sensation of a plunge, as if the very floor had disappeared from beneath my feet.

"But even if you aren't able to recover your memory," he continued, "there's no real loss in being forced to relearn alchemy from the beginning."

Cold fear crawled up my spine. "Of course there is! There's lost time and lost skill! Both of which could lead to the loss of my life when the Black Trial comes. But you aren't thinking of that, are you? Because you don't think I should do it."

He blinked at me, calmly enough to be vastly irritating. "I *am* thinking of that, because I know you *will* do it. My point is that it is highly unlikely, statistically speaking, for you to learn alchemy the same way twice, and in relearning, you will gain techniques and aptitudes you missed or dismissed the first time around. Given your new understanding of the concepts of struggle and disadvantage, it's entirely likely that this time you won't undervalue the slower, less direct route to a solution, by which avenue you might discover entirely new ideas and options."

"You're saying I should let myself *meander,* in alchemy? That I should *get lost* in scientific theory?"

Or perhaps in life? That was a romantic notion, but...

"I'm saying that maybe this time you won't dismiss that idea entirely."

I nodded slowly. "That seems like a valuable lesson to learn, in certain circumstances. When one has time to meander. When one's life is not on the line." I lifted an accusatory brow at him. "Say, if one were a staff researcher with stable employment, a huge private lab, and bright career prospects."

Desmond somehow managed to scowl even as one corner of his mouth turned up.

"The most efficient route in *my* circumstance, however, seems to be to recover my memory, because with it would come all of my skill." I crossed both arms over my chest before adding, "Wilder agrees."

He scowled. "A bit of an irony, considering that his skill can mostly be attributed to instinct given free rein. Pure aptitude, both untempered and undisciplined."

"And yet he has already contributed quite a bit to the field of Panacea, whether or not the Alchemary recognizes his work."

"Indeed," Desmond said, and I could not contain my surprise. "And with that statement, you've made my point. While you wait for your memory to come back—or while you work actively toward that goal—would your time not also be well spent relearning alchemy with an eye toward paths and possibilities you likely did not take the first time?"

"That does make a certain sense," I finally admitted. "Learning alchemy via new pathways. And yet I am at a loss for how to begin."

"Well, if you will allow me to help you . . . ?"

"Yes. Please." I wanted to regain my former skill level and standing—to survive the trials—more than I wanted to be able to say I'd done it all on my own.

Though that was still true. I *had* done it on my own, before I'd been robbed of that knowledge.

"I understand that you've been quite literally burning the midnight oil in your studies. That you've largely caught up on vocabulary and concepts. On at least Fundamentals-year theory."

"Yes, but so far, that isn't unlocking an understanding of higher-level concepts."

"That's because you lack practical application. Which is where the lab comes in. And with any luck, your learning curve in here will be as steep as it has been with your textbooks. To that end . . ." He turned and marched quickly into his office, leaving me unsure whether or not I should follow.

Before I could decide, he was back with a stack of parchment, which he set on the nearest work surface. "These are my notes from my own Fundamentals year. I went through them and pulled out all of the lab experiments. They're all for basic, grade-one elixirs. You might notice that they're organized by date, which should help you start with the simplest. You might further notice that they get easier to understand midway through the year, when I started Bollinger's Records and Note-Taking practicum—or whatever it was called—and learned how to take proper notes."

I lifted the first sheet, and my eyes widened. Despite his claim, even from the beginning, he'd been a concise and thorough note taker.

"I've read through all the records from my own Fundamentals year, and they are nowhere near this thorough," I mumbled, still scanning the text. Noting, as I flipped through the sheets, when his alchemical notation began to develop its own signature style. "I must be missing some pages."

"I highly doubt that. You were quite an organized student, and I've never known you to misplace a thing. You simply didn't take copious notes in the early classes because you had no need to. You *did* take notes in the lab—last year, at least—but those are likely too advanced for you to understand."

"Quite so," I whispered, still turning over pages. "How many of these did I do each week, as a Fundamentals-year student?"

"Two, on average. They take between one and three hours each, so if you—"

"And how many could I reasonably run at a time, here in the lab?"

"Simultaneously?" Desmond blinked at me. For a moment, he looked surprised. Then a smile tugged at his lips, one brow arching high. "It would not be responsible of me to encourage—"

"How many?" I snapped.

His smile widened. He extended one arm to indicate my section of the lab—one-third of the total space. "One per work surface, I would surmise."

There were four tables in my section of the lab.

Numbers began to scroll through my mind. Tables. Parchment pages. Days. Nights. Weeks until the Black Trial.

There was plenty of equipment. There were plenty of supplies.

"I suspect that will be more than sufficient," I said. "I'll run the four simplest experiments tonight, and I'll set up for four more before I leave, to save time tomorrow."

I took the top four sheets of parchment and set one on the front right corner of each of my allotted tables, then I turned toward the supply closet, so focused on the list of equipment running through my head that I nearly missed Desmond's satisfied—almost greedy—smile.

Nearly.

It was after ten that night by the time I finished cleaning up and taking notes. Two of the four experiments had taken a little more than three hours, because my time was divided between them and because I was not able to apply lessons learned in the first two, since they were being conducted simultaneously.

Still, my learning curve was indeed steep. Desmond's lab was laid out *perfectly* logically. Every single piece of equipment and ingredient was exactly where I would have expected to find it, which cut down on what could otherwise have been a frustrating and slow search for supplies, even after the tour he'd given me.

And he was right. Concepts I'd relearned in theory become solidified in my understanding with the experience of their practical application.

Even better, I found myself anticipating the results, though I had no memory of having run the experiments before.

By the time I had reset my tables and equipment for the next day's work, I felt nearly intoxicated on both accomplishment—rudimentary though it was—and possibility. On comprehension and aptitude.

And my stomach had begun to growl.

A light still burned in Desmond's office. I moved quietly to avoid disturbing his work, but also because I had an inexplicable but undeniable desire to watch him when he didn't know he was being observed. To . . . understand him.

From a purely scientific perspective, of course.

I leaned around the doorway, expecting to find him huddled over a book or scratching out notes on parchment by lamplight. Instead, he was perched on his desk facing away from me. As I watched, he lifted something and tilted his head back, then heaved a full-body shudder, giving me a glimpse of a familiar vial as he lowered it, empty, from his lips.

I backed silently away from the door, the image burned into my eyelids as they fell closed.

That was one of Wilder's vials. I recognized the label he used for all of his illicit elixirs as well as the handwriting on it, which was entirely devoid of any signature notation. The symbols were all straight lines, benign curves, and right angles—as generic as possible, so that if the vial were discovered, its maker could not be easily identified.

Desmond had criticized Wilder for making those elixirs. He had warned me away from them, even though he did not deny his brother's skill and contribution to the field. Yet he was secretly taking one himself.

How could he possibly justify his own hypocrisy? And which one was he taking?

Wood creaked, presumably as he stood. I backed away from the door, and a second later, Desmond called my name.

"Yes?" I resumed my normal footsteps so they could be heard.

Desmond appeared in the doorway just as I did, and we collided rather gracelessly. Which led to awkward chuckling and mutual apologies, while we still stood much too close, until my heart began pounding in my ears and I stepped back. Then back even farther.

"You didn't have to stay," I said, hands clasped nervously at my spine.

"I did, actually," he said. "I couldn't very well leave you unsupervised with multiple experiments running at once, could I? It would fall on me, under that circumstance, if you were to burn the building down."

"Marble doesn't burn," I pointed out, trying not to be offended by the implication that I could fail so spectacularly.

"This building isn't entirely marble," he replied with a very slight smile. "And most of the furnishings are wooden."

"There is quite a bit of marble, though. And lead," I said, thinking of the heavy, fireproof roof tiles. "And glass. And bone."

"Bone?" Desmond arched one brow over his compelling copper-brown eyes.

"All of the plaques mounted to the walls. And my father mentioned that some of the door and window facings are also made of bone."

"Ah, the Toolkeepers' legends." He huffed. "Take most of that with the requisite grain of salt. This place was built long before Cornelius Fallbrook was born."

"Yes, but the Toolkeepers are just as likely to have passed down knowledge of their trade and practices as we are here at the Alchemary, are they not?"

Desmond nodded, one brow arched. "I suppose so."

We stood there for a moment, in silence. When his gaze lingered, and when I felt mine inclined to do the same, I looked off into a corner of the laboratory. "I should go," I said. "I should . . . sleep. I have class in the morning."

"But you will return tomorrow night, after the evening meal." He was issuing neither invitation nor request, but a direct order.

I nodded. "Evenings in the lab with you. Days 'meandering in alchemy' with your brother. As you suggested."

Desmond's expression shuttered so swiftly that I almost gasped at the sudden change. "That is *not* what I meant to suggest."

I indulged a small smile as I turned and left him standing in the office doorway, no doubt staring after me.

Twenty-Two

Wilder and I broke our fast together on Wednesday in the Refectory, and he noticed the elevation in my mood. He claimed to be as thrilled as I was that my evening with Desmond had gone so well, yet he scowled at his porridge as if its flavor were more bitter than usual.

His tea, it seemed, suffered from the same fault.

I still felt lost during our morning class, confused by concepts I had not yet caught up with, but I took notes studiously, and I found my mood buoyed by the opportunity to stare at the back of Pryce Wishart's cobalt head. Professor Bollinger seemed shocked to see his student's entire visage so startlingly blue, but even as his gaze slid less than subtly in Wilder's direction, he made no comment other than to compliment Pryce's "inspired devotion to his water affinity."

Wilder, for his part, also seemed more cheerful during class. His contributions to the discussion were characteristically droll, and afterward, I swallowed a sharp stab of jealousy to see him surrounded by several young ladies and one of the young men—Petyr Lorena—each looking fawningly up at him.

Had he not seemed so satisfied by the attention, I might have felt guilty about sneaking out of the classroom while he was distracted. Instead, I worried that he wouldn't even notice me missing, though we'd taken lunch together every day for the past month.

Today, I had no time for lunch.

Desmond had given me access to the Conservatory research library, and I *itched* to be among the stacks, reading about the Conservatory plaques and how they'd come to hold hidden alchemical symbols.

I could not have said for certain why I did not intend to tell Wilder about my plans.

When I'd woken with amnesia a month before, I'd had an overwhelming sense that I was forgetting something vital and specific, beyond my general memory loss. As if I'd been on the verge of completing some important task and could no longer remember what needed to be done.

That feeling came back every time I picked up my coded journal, and some latent understanding associated it with the fact that Past Amber had chosen, for whatever reason, to keep the journal's contents from both the Gregory brother I'd woken up beside and the one I'd evidently spent many long evenings of research with.

The people I'd clearly been closest to, for the past two years.

Past Amber must have had a reason to hide things from them, and without understanding that reason, I couldn't be sure I should share the hidden symbols and the ouroboros bracelet with them either. Though I had no real understanding of my motivation, either before the amnesia or now.

All I had was a gut feeling, and the hunch that following it might be the thing that wound up unlocking my memories.

The Conservatory's first floor was mostly taken up by the Panacea wing, behind its double doors. The second floor held suites of private labs: a semicircle of outward-facing spaces with exterior windows, as well as a cluster of oddly shaped spaces—including Desmond's—in the center of the building, all accessible from a single corridor that arced around the floor.

The third floor boasted an identical semicircle of outward-facing laboratory spaces, but instead of the central windowless cluster of labs, the interior of the top floor was entirely taken up by the research library, a perfectly round room lined by shelves that curved with the shape of the walls.

The room could be accessed by a single door at the rear of the building, opposite the three-story atrium. Like the spiraling stained glass windows of the atrium, the library felt distinct from the Conservatory's cold, straight white marble lines. It was a visually warm space full of endless arcs and curves, accented with dark, scrolling woodwork.

Above the bookshelves, the walls arched in a dome toward the ceiling, where a circle of clear glass—a window set into the roof—revealed a broad expanse of blue sky, clouds, and the sun, which was nearing the end of its morning arc.

Beneath the overhead window, a single large, round wooden table stood at the center of the room, surrounded by ornate and heavy-looking chairs, thickly padded with leather cushions.

Two researchers sat directly across from each other at the table, each half hidden by piles of books, scribbling swiftly on parchment with their quills. They ignored me just as pointedly as they ignored each other.

I walked past the librarian guarding the secure collection behind her desk, then past stacks of alchemical theory, history, and tome after tome containing records of practical application. Entire shelves were dedicated to the best practices in the procurement, processing, and preserving of every alchemical component known to mankind, and to the various general techniques for distilling beyn. Finally, I stood before a single shelf devoted to the history of the Alchemary itself.

The word *Toolkeeper* did not appear in any of the titles.

I pulled several successive volumes from the shelf, carefully turning the old parchment pages, breathing in the distinctive scent of the preserved paper. But none of them were . . .

There, on the third shelf from the top, far above my head. *The Historic Architecture of Alchemary Island.*

Standing on my toes, I snatched the book, then I settled into an armchair near the door to read, well back from the table and its occupants.

I already knew a bit about the history of the Alchemary, from the stories my mother had told me of her time on the island. But seeing the words written was a bit of a shock.

She'd quoted entire passages to me verbatim, evidently, and I found myself wondering how many times she'd read this very book.

Many, it would seem. Or once, perhaps, if she was the source of my own stalwart memory.

Then I found myself wondering how she'd read this book at all. She would not have had access to the research library while she was here. She *should* not have, at least.

And yet . . . I knew many of the words I was reading by heart, before my eyes even skimmed the page, because she'd spoken them to me, over and over.

I heard my mother's voice, echoing from the nostalgic haven of my childhood, as I read about the history of my current residence.

More than one hundred fifty years ago, the infamous Emperor Eldon had married a young woman named Avalona, a commoner he'd met during a tour of the empire. He'd fallen for her swiftly and unreservedly. So entirely that their love was still an oft-told legend across the empire, entirely aside from the history of the Alchemary.

According to that legend, Emperor Eldon was so besotted by his beautiful new bride that he'd endeavored to give her everything a woman could possibly want. Jewel-encrusted gowns and tiaras. Sculptures and paintings commissioned to immortalize her beauty. Fine furnishings and lavish balls. Exotic pets imported from kingdoms afar. Opulent castles built all across Aethermere, so that she could travel as she pleased, yet never be far from home.

Within a few years of the royal wedding, the nursery remained distressingly empty, and the treasury was headed swiftly in that direction. The royal accountant warned the emperor that his spending habits must change, but Eldon was a jealous and insecure man, loathe to disappoint his bride for fear of losing her. Whether that potential loss involved another man or the heartbreak of an empty cradle, the legend did not specify.

Eldon understood the problem, and he undertook an unexpected solution.

He commissioned a grand academy, initially funded by the Crown, and he tasked his confidant, Lord Calyx, the royal alchemist, to head the institution. Lord Calyx was charged with hiring a staff of accomplished alchemists and enrolling a class of promising young students, all with the goal of furthering the practice of alchemy in order to develop the Philosopher's Stone.

The Stone would allow the transmutation of base metals into silver and gold, which would fund both the Alchemary and the Crown, allowing the emperor to build limitless glorious tributes to his wife across the land.

"Greed," my father had declared, upon listening to my mother tell the story.

She had only smiled at him, her gaze soft and half amused.

"Love," she had insisted.

The emperor had risked it all—every coin he'd had, as well as the ire of his people—for a love that could be neither contained, nor defined, nor denied.

There was no record in any story I'd heard or text I could remember reading of whether the Queen Avalona had ever asked for such riches. Her desire, evidently, was far less important than the lengths to which her husband had been willing to go.

Whether he had acted for greed or for love, the emperor's story—like my parents' union—had no happy ending. Despite giving birth to one doomed son, Avalona died young and childless, and though the emperor married again and produced several healthy heirs, history rarely even mentioned his second wife's name.

Theirs, evidently, was not a legendary love.

The Alchemary had also failed him. Neither Lord Calyx nor his staff and students ever developed the Philosopher's Stone, and in fact, over the years, the very concept had taken on the overblown tenor of myth, much like the emperor himself.

Which was why I'd laughed when Wilder had told me that my research project had that very aim.

Interestingly, though the Alchemary failed to produce the Philosopher's Stone, it *had* become a storied and well-respected academy—the premier institution of higher learning in the kingdom. It had also become largely self-sufficient, financially. Though I'd learned that not from my mother or from any book but from Wilder, who went on at length about the contribution his commercially viable work could make to an institution so focused on profit. On returning to the Crown its initial investment, in order to be free of any royal opinions about the direction of its research.

According to *The Historic Architecture of Alchemary Island*, the Conservatory was the last major building erected on campus, and the only one Lord Calyx designed himself.

He gave up instructing entirely, turning the teaching arm of the institution over to his protégé, a woman named Iris, who started as dean of the Seminary but went on, after Lord Calyx's death, to become the very first Bluehelm, in charge of the entire institution. While she led the Seminary, Calyx dedicated himself to the design and construction of the Conservatory, a space devoted not to teaching alchemy students but to the elite-level study of advanced alchemical theories by a permanently appointed staff of the cleverest, most dedicated alchemists in the world.

Subtext in the official written account hinted at Lord Calyx's growing obsession and, toward the end, the decline of his lucidity.

I closed the book and stared at it, stunned.

The Toolkeepers' legend was true: Lord Calyx, the father of alchemy, *had* designed the Conservatory himself. Every window, door, and roof tile of it, according to the text. Every stair, bench, and shelf.

And, presumably, every plaque.

Was it possible that Lord Calyx *himself* had hidden the ouroboros bracelet and designed the code to its discovery? Could the hidden writing have survived that long?

Heart pounding, I turned to the back of the book and searched the appendix, but there was no mention of decorative or commemorative plaques. So I turned to the section of the book specifically about the construction of the Conservatory, scanning for any mention of the remains of alchemists used as building materials, making a mental note to go back and read more thoroughly.

At a glance, I found not a single mention of the bone plaques in the entire book. And yet . . . they existed. And they'd held a secret recipe, which had opened a secret compartment.

With a jolt, I noticed the angle of the sunlight shining through the curved pane of glass overhead. I'd been reading for far too long.

I slammed the book closed, ignoring the annoyed look from the scholars at the round table, and rushed across the room to stand on my toes and slide the volume back into place.

From the Conservatory portico, a glance at the Seminary's clock tower showed exactly what I'd feared: I had less than five minutes until Professor Robards would close the classroom door and begin Intro without me.

To my astonishment, however, a great commotion had taken over the quadrangle—the beating heart of our campus.

Burly workers swarmed all over the lawn in leather aprons and tool belts carrying planks of wood and clanking bags, presumably filled with iron nails. Several carts had been parked on the grass—mules were grazing at Queen Avalona's marble feet!—and they were full of folded bundles of thick, coarse fabric that could only be suitable for tarps and awnings.

At first, I could not fathom the occupation of our quadrangle. Then I noticed a cluster of staff members in their asymmetrical capes, huddled in front of the Conservatory with a couple of the workers—two men who were far older than the rest, and clearly displeased with the orders they were being issued.

And suddenly I understood: Family Weekend was only three days away. It would be half festival, half bazaar, and as such, it would need booths, stalls, and tables, all sturdy enough to be used, yet simple enough to be disassembled and stored away before the Black Trial, a scant week later.

Desmond was among the staff members evidently charged with imposing order upon chaos, and his gaze found me as I jogged down the Conservatory steps. I gave him a formal nod and was unnerved to realize that two of his colleagues—a balding man with a weak chin and a woman with wide-set eyes and a severe blond bun—were also staring at me.

But I had no time to parse through the interest two unfamiliar staff researchers might have in me.

With a groan, I lifted my satchel over my head and took off across the northwest corner of the quadrangle at a run, darting around animal-shaped shrubs and startled students, to whom I mumbled swift apologies. In the Seminary foyer, I stumbled to a stop to catch my breath, and when I looked to my right, I saw Wilder on a settee, his quill poised over a sheet of parchment on an adjacent tea table.

Yoslyn Savva sat perched on the edge of that table, beaming down at him as she fiddled suggestively with the edge of his quill while they watched the chaos through a window. Wilder looked up and met my gaze.

I frowned. Then the clock tower began to chime, and despite the bolt of irritation burning beneath my skin, I had no choice but to turn left and race down the corridor. Professor Robards raised one brow at me from the threshold of the lecture hall, but he let me slip past before he closed the door and began a lecture about the necessity of balance in any alchemical pursuit.

I hardly heard a word of it.

An hour later, I slid into my seat in Theories just as Professor Edmiston headed down the aisle toward her podium and the framed slate, fluffing her silver curls as she went.

"Where the devil were you?" Wilder demanded in a whisper as I began to unpack my supplies.

"Assisting Professor Robards. As I do three days a week."

"Before that." His gaze was trained on me as if he could see right through my skull. "You disappeared from Bollinger's classroom, and you never arrived for the midday meal." He frowned. "I was worried, considering there are two dozen strangers on campus today, and—"

"I was studying," I said, and technically, that was true, even if I hadn't been studying for class. "Which is more than I can say for *you.*" Yoslyn had clearly provided an interesting distraction from whatever concern he'd felt for me.

Wilder's eyes widened, hurt rippling in the cerulean depths. But he did not look guilty.

If he felt no guilt for flirting with Yoslyn . . . maybe he wasn't actually flirting. Or maybe he was, but he didn't consider that an issue.

Maybe I never had either, before.

Though Emperor Eldon commissioned and funded construction of the Alchemary—dedicating an entire island for its campus—his original commission was only for the Dormitory and the building that later became known as the Seminary, though at the time, it was simply called the Alchemary.

Construction on the Conservatory began almost five years later, after the tragic death of the queen Avalona. According to historical correspondence, following the loss of his first wife, the emperor also lost interest in his grand alchemy project, and he ceded both the funding and design of the final building to Lord Calyx, the royal alchemist. Despite the emperor's disillusionment with the magnum opus, public interest in alchemical medical and technological possibilities had blossomed, allowing for an expansion of both the staff and the facilities, as well as an increase in the number of students.

—from *The Historic Architecture of Alchemary Island*

Twenty-Three

"Varrah!" I called as I made my way across the Dormitory courtyard through a throng of milling students. Every bench was full, every stone archway of the colonnade filled with forms in student cloaks leaning against the stone columns. Students perched on the edge of the fountain, despite the cold spray, and slowly wandered the cobblestone patio, anticipation pulsing through the crowd like a shared heartbeat.

Classes had adjourned early for the underclassmen.

Family Weekend had arrived.

"Varrah!" I called again. She stood alone at the far end of the short northern wing of the Dormitory, having stolen a slice of shade from the overhang. Despite the crowd, her classmates had given her plenty of space. Of... solitude.

"There you are!" I came to a stop at her side, and she seemed surprised to see me, despite the fact that I'd been calling her name.

Varrah gave me a quick hug, but her green-and-brown-eyed gaze returned quickly to the quadrangle, which opened up from one side of the Dormitory courtyard. Everyone's attention was on the central lawn as students waited for a glimpse of their family members.

"Are your parents coming?" she asked softly, her bifurcated voice dancing eerily through my ears to tingle in the folds of my brain.

"Yes. I mean I hope so." I tucked my arm around hers, drawing her close despite the chilly looks from some of her classmates, who had yet to warm up to her. "Well, my mother died when I was an adolescent. But my father and his husband have promised to attend, if at all possible."

She turned away from the quadrangle to meet my gaze, her brows dipped low. "I'm sorry to hear about your mother. I didn't know."

I hugged her arm. "It was a long time ago now. What about you? Is your cousin coming?"

"Her letter said she would try, but that she was nervous to travel across Aethermere alone. Her husband cannot attend."

I could only imagine how difficult a time her cousin might have with hired coach drivers and innkeepers who were set on edge by her voice.

"Well then, I hope she makes it, as I look forward to meeting her."

"I—" Varrah suddenly stiffened. "Erikka!" She tore her arm from my grasp and launched herself across the grass and onto the quadrangle, where she threw herself into the arms of a woman with dark hair, ruddy cheeks, and . . . one eye that was dark blue, the other a pale green.

When the two women finally parted, Varrah tugged Erikka toward me. "Come meet Amber, my—"

"Friend," I finished as I held out my hand. "You must be Varrah's cousin. She speaks highly of you."

Tension seemed to ease from the woman's posture as her hand closed around mine. "Amber, it is an honor to meet you."

We chatted for several minutes while I kept one eye trained upon the festival that had unfolded in the quadrangle, and when I spotted Wilder winding through the growing crowd, twirling his blade over and under the fingers of his right hand, I excused myself with a reminder for Varrah and her cousin to sample the tricolor punch.

I followed Wilder, veering around people, food stalls, and vendor booths, ignoring merchants calling out for me to try meat pies and grilled sausages or to test the flow rate on a "new" no-flame wax seal. Wilder clearly had a goal in mind—I could hardly keep up with him—and I assumed he was headed for some favorite festival treat.

The frozen fruit vendor, maybe? I was curious about the alchemical process that could create ice in the middle of a sunny fall day. Or the cosmic grapes, which were coated in a sparkling syrup so that they resembled a sky full of stars?

Instead, Wilder sheathed his knife and disappeared behind a booth that sold novelty vials and beakers of every color. Those would have little use in true alchemy, because tinted glass disguised the color of its contents. And this glass was of poor quality, riddled with bubbles and uneven in places.

I peered into the booth, but when I looked disinclined to buy anything, the balding merchant gave me a polite goodbye, lifted the tarp at the rear of his stall, and ducked outside. Dimly, I heard whispered voices, so I peeked around the back of the booth, where I found Wilder and the merchant quietly . . . haggling.

My appearance caught Wilder's eye over the merchant's shoulder, but he did not give away my presence.

An agreement was made, coins were exchanged, and Wilder stuffed something into his trouser pocket, beneath his cloak.

I ducked out of sight again, and the merchant returned to his booth. When Wilder reappeared, I fell into step with him. "What was that about?"

"Clearly you've caught me in a secret dalliance with a traveling vendor. I took one glance at his novelty glass and knew he would be skilled with his hands," Wilder said, but the spark of amusement in his eyes was not enough to dispel the strained edge in his voice.

He was still hurt—maybe a little vexed—by the distance I'd maintained from him since I'd seen him flirting with Yoslyn.

"Funny." I'd been trying for two days to find a good time—and a good way—to explain my jealousy. To ask if it was warranted. But every time I tried, my tongue froze up, as if the words made no sense. And he'd made no effort to defend himself. "You bought something from that vendor."

"You are mistaken. I—"

I pretended to trip, and when he steadied me, I slid my hand beneath his cape and into his pocket, where my fingers closed around what felt like a wad of parchment. Triumphant, I pulled it out, and...

Wilder grabbed me by the waist and spun me behind a booth and out of sight of most of the crowd, in a move that no doubt looked like lovers stealing a moment alone.

But irritation was clear in the tight line of his jaw. *"Amber,"* he snapped softly, reaching for my hand.

I backed out of his reach, studying the bundle of well-produced strips of parchment. They were of a distinctive and familiar size and shape—thin, but sturdy, and cut so that they would spiral around three-quarters of a vial rather than sitting perfectly horizontal.

"These are the labels you use for your... *business,*" I whispered. "How *fancy*—"

"Yes. And Family Weekend has saved me a two-day carriage ride to retrieve them. Now, if you don't mind, this is not the only business I'm hoping to accomplish before—"

"Wilder! Amber! There they are!" a familiar woman's voice called.

Wilder groaned. Then he forced a smile as his gaze found something beyond my shoulder. "Mother!"

With a deft move, he waved, then lowered his hand to snatch the labels from me and shove them back into his pocket even as he spun me by my elbow.

Jon and Annora Gregory were headed straight toward us from one side of Conservatory, and the angle of their path had given them a glimpse of us that most of the crowd lacked.

"*Whatever* are you two doing back there?" Wilder's mother called as a breeze ruffled the thin, translucent veil draped over her dark blond bun.

"My love, you should not ask questions we might not want answered..." her husband scolded amiably as his assessing gaze roamed from Wilder's face to mine, which suddenly felt warm.

Wilder had his mother's fair, golden coloring and a lighter, clearer version of her blue-gray eyes, while Desmond took after their father, with his larger build, dark hair and eyes, and deeper skin tone. But both sons had inherited the shape of their mother's nose and their father's broad jaw.

It felt odd, looking at the Gregorys and suddenly seeing Desmond and Wilder in them, as if nature had made a game of selecting from their features. As a child, I'd never contemplated their resemblance to their parents. Or to each other.

Though I could not remember the past two years of my life, it felt like ages since I'd seen Wilder's parents, and having them at the Alchemary was particularly jarring. Especially considering the new webbing at the corners of Annora's eyes and the gray at Jon's temples. I might not remember the passage of time, but I could certainly feel and see its effects.

"Amber!"

I sucked in a breath as an even more familiar, and very welcome, form stepped out from behind Jon Gregory. "Martyn!"

"My darling!" My stepfather rushed forward to envelop me in a clove-scented hug, his slim-cut tunic flaring over snug, dark trousers. "I'm so delighted to see you!"

"And I, you!" I squeezed him tight, then let him go, unable to temper my broad smile. "Where is my father?"

His face fell slightly. "I'm sorry to say he could not make it. He's working on a project in the south, and it has run long. But I am delighted to see how disappointed you look, and I shall describe this moment to him in great detail." He leaned forward to whisper into my ear, "Your father has sent along a letter for you." He pressed a folded sheet of parchment into my hand, and I noted my father's seal.

"How kind of you to deliver it." I slid the note into my pocket. "Did you travel with the Gregorys?"

"Indeed. Jon and Annora were kind enough to offer me a seat in their carriage."

"Martyn is delightful company!" Annora declared. "And he kept us stuffed with a variety of pastries."

"Don't worry. I've brought some for you both as well," Martyn said with a wink at me and a smile at Wilder, who looked distinctly uncomfortable at having been located by our families. "Now, you must give me a tour of this *stunning* campus!"

I took Martyn to see my bedchamber, my classrooms, Desmond's lab, and the Refectory. I showed him my favorite bench by the Dormitory's courtyard fountain and my preferred table in the southwest corner of the student library, all while we ate rabbit roasted on skewers and dried fruit sold in wax paper packets. Finally, as the sun began to set over the ocean, behind the towering roof of the Conservatory, Martyn and the Gregorys said good night to me and to Desmond, whom we'd found in the quadrangle, then headed past the guards, through the gate, and over the bridge into Saltstrand, where they'd secured accommodations for the next two nights despite the crowd that had descended upon the small town.

"Have you any idea where my brother's gone?" Desmond whispered as we waved to them from the Seminary's rear lawn.

"He isn't exactly feeling forthcoming with me right now, but I could guess."

Wilder had likely snuck off to conduct his business as soon as Desmond had shown up to distract their parents.

"And that one?" Martyn leaned against the back of the bench and nodded subtly toward a student meandering through the quadrangle with an older couple who were clearly his parents.

"He's an underclassman. Fundamentals year. I only know him because he's in Professor Robards's Intro class."

"Where you're a teaching assistant?" he said, and when I nodded, he went on. "I see. What about that girl? She seems to have quite a bit of attention on campus."

I stifled a groan. "That's Keryth Malcom. She does not care for me."

He gave me a quiet smile. "Meaning that you are competition for her?"

"We are all competition for one another." But surely that didn't mean we couldn't be friends.

"And those two?"

I followed his gaze. "Petyr Lorena and Adria . . . something or other. They're in my cohort. They don't seem to care much for me either."

Martyn and I had broken our fast together on a bench in the Dormitory courtyard, looking out over the quadrangle, and afterward he'd seemed content to sit and ask about my classmates rather than drag me through the festival, as the Gregorys were currently engaged with both of their reluctant sons.

Annora was particularly enamored of the booth where people could fire arrows at a volunteer from the research staff, who stood against a wooden backdrop in only his trousers, his skin shining thickly with an embrocation that temporarily rendered his flesh impermeable to the projectiles.

She'd paid for four rounds so far and seemed to thrill at aiming directly at the poor man's bare chest. He maintained a good-natured smile, his arms propped on his narrow hips, and indulged her recreational bloodlust. As well as her repeated insistence that her son Desmond had helped develop the miracle elixir that made it possible.

She was not wrong.

Wilder would clearly rather have been drawn and quartered than hear the story again.

"And the azure-toned young man over there?" Martyn glanced pointedly at Pryce Wishart. "Is that something to do with the festival? Is there a booth for tinting skin?"

"In fact, there is." And that was likely what Pryce had told the elegant but dour-looking man and woman who were accompanying him across the quadrangle with their noses in the air. "But that boy's blue cast has nothing to do with the festival and everything to do with Wilder Gregory."

"Oh?" Martyn turned to me, brows raised. "Do tell."

"The story doesn't bear repeating," I insisted, well aware that if my father thought I was in any specific danger, especially from an influential family, he would redouble his efforts to bring me home. "Except to say that Wilder is the *last* student on campus with whom one ought to—"

"Interfere?" Martyn suggested, saving me the utterance of a particular profanity.

"Precisely."

"So, which of these students are your friends, Amber dear?" Martyn slid his arm around mine and squeezed. "With whom do you share your secrets?"

"Well..." There's never any good way to tell a parent you have no real friends. "With Wilder, I guess."

"So that's unchanged, since you were children?"

"I suppose."

"And yet yesterday it certainly looked... changed." His grip tightened on my arm, and I turned to see him eyeing me with one brow raised. "Would you say that your relationship has... matured?"

"Would *you* say you're gathering intelligence for my father?"

Martyn laughed and let go of my arm so he could retrieve the teacup sitting on the bench to his left. "At this moment? I am simply asking, as an interested parental figure."

"My relationship with Wilder certainly has changed. But at the moment, it is both difficult for me to understand and difficult for me to define."

"Because of your memory loss?"

"In part, at least. We have clearly bonded physically. But I can't remember that happening. And that has left me confused and unsure how I should feel."

"Regardless of how you *should* feel, how do you feel? Do you care for him?"

"Of course. I always have."

Martyn's brows rose. "Are you attracted to him?"

I shrugged, but the gesture was far more overblown than I'd intended. "*Look* at him!" I whispered, unable to resist a gesture in Wilder's direction. "Of course I am attracted. Who wouldn't be?"

Martyn chuckled. "You were possessive of both of the Gregory brothers, when you were younger. You considered them both yours—"

My face flamed like a bonfire. "I did not!"

"—and you would pout like a toddler if either of them so much as *glanced* at another girl."

"I do not recall the pouting," I mumbled. "But I *do* remember frequent roving glances." And more-than-glances. "That bit has not changed. Wilder is ravenous for attention, and it is becoming clear that mine may not be enough for him."

For a moment, Martyn sipped his tea in silence. My father was always quick to jump in with an opinion, which was no doubt where I'd inherited the trait. But my stepfather had a particular way of letting me stew in the echo of my own words. It was vexingly effective.

"Is that an objective assessment?" he finally asked. "Or might it be driven by overwrought sentiment?"

"You're asking if I could be overreacting?"

He smiled. "I would not quarrel with that phrasing."

"—cannot fathom what could have led to her acceptance."

The whisper floated to us on an ocean-scented westbound breeze, and I stiffened on the bench, loathe to turn and see who was speaking from the courtyard behind us for fear of silencing the speaker.

Martyn also went still and silent.

"No one trusts her," the voice continued. "Her voice is virtually painful to experience, and there's no telling what she can hear that we cannot, if her ears were altered as well."

Whoever it was, he was talking about Varrah.

A brief flash of relief washed over me when I realized I wasn't the target of such distrust and suspicion, but I felt immediately guilty for that.

"You think she's a spy?" another voice whispered.

"Or a scout?" There was a pause. "I can't imagine why else a citizen of the unified provinces would come to the Alchemary, when they don't acknowledge alchemy as a valid study. Perhaps she is an asset of the Crown. *Their* Crown."

"Unified Eria doesn't have a crown," the second voice said, and from my left, Martyn chuckled again softly. "It's comprised of half a dozen independent city states, each ruled by a figure of a different title. Some positions are elected, others are inherited. So even if she's an agent, it wouldn't be for *all* of Eria."

"I think you comprehend my point," the first voice grumbled. "It's difficult to trust someone who can hear things we don't intend to be heard, and who could be saying things we can't hear."

Finally, my patience wore thin, and I turned to find that the original speaker was a young man from Varrah's cohort. He was speaking to a woman a few years older who resembled him closely enough that she had to be a sister or a cousin.

He noticed me looking and tugged his relative off toward the festival.

"They're talking about a classmate from the provinces?" Martyn asked.

"A Fundamentals student. She's very sweet and shy. She shows a lot of promise, but most of her family disowned her for enrolling at the Alchemary, and her cohort hasn't been very . . . welcoming."

"How awful."

"Yes. That's her." I nodded at Varrah and Erikka, who sat on a blanket on the edge of quadrangle, watching the festival but largely removed from it. "The woman with her is her cousin, the only family member she still has contact with. They're from Reachan. She mentioned to me that she loves those little fried dough balls my father came home raving about when I was a child. Do you remember?"

"Do I remember?" He huffed. "I tried to replicate them for—" Martyn suddenly stood. "I have an idea. Would you mind distracting your friend, while I borrow her cousin?"

I arched both brows at him. "I hate to take her away from her family."

"It will be worth the sacrifice of a couple of hours. You have my word."

"And how is it made? This crunchy syrup?" Varrah bit into another celestial grape, smiling as she chewed. "It sticks to my teeth, and it's quite sweet, yet . . . I can't cease eating it!"

"It's novelty alchemy," I said, plucking one of the glittering orbs from her wax paper packet as we strolled slowly through the festival. "Like *that*."

I pointed to the booth where a female staff member from the Panacea division was applying a thin, clear serum to a young girl's arms and face. As we watched, her skin began to bloom a beautiful pale shade of green everywhere the serum had been applied.

"And like that," I added, nodding at a broad enclosure that had been built near the front of the Refectory. Within it, several small, wheelless carriages hovered several inches in the air.

"How does that work?" Varrah asked. "The hovering carts?"

"An alchemical solution has been applied to the floorboards, while a different solution has been applied to the bottoms of the carts. Those solutions utilize naturally occurring minerals that have repellent properties in relation to each other. Those properties have been enhanced through the alchemical process, of course, so that they can hold the weight of the passengers. But they exist in nature."

"Surely that isn't purely a novelty?" Varrah said. "Nor is the elixir that makes that gentleman's flesh impervious?"

"There are certainly larger-scale applications," I allowed. "But they're still in the developmental phase. These are all novelty versions of things the Alchemary is working on for other . . . reasons." According to what Desmond had told me, anyway. "You'll study the 'levitation' phenomenon next fall."

Which I knew because I'd just begun re-creating the experiments I'd worked on during my own Proficiency classes, having finally remastered the Fundamentals level.

I shrugged. "Who knows? Maybe someday I'll be able to 'levitate' all the way to Innswood, to visit my family!"

While Varrah watched children being tugged around on levitating wheelless carts, my gaze wandered, and I caught sight of Wilder behind one of the booths. As I watched, he handed what appeared to be several of his distinctive vials to a vendor, who gave him a handful of coins in return.

"I can't wait for the fireworks," Varrah declared, tugging me along the path again as she folded her empty wax paper packet and slid it into her pocket. "I've never seen—"

Her voice faded, and I followed her gaze toward the edge of quadrangle nearest the Refectory, where a new booth had been set up.

Or rather, a plain wooden table. Behind it stood Martyn and Varrah's cousin, Erikka.

"Whatever are they doing?" Varrah frowned, and we watched from several yards away as my stepfather dug a scoop of small, powder-coated balls from a lined basket on the table and gave them to a student in a wax paper packet.

Varrah gasped. *"Kokos!"* She turned to me, eyes alight. "They're selling kokos!"

"No . . ." I said as understanding dawned in my soul like the warmth of a candle's flame. "They're giving them away."

We rushed toward the booth, where a small crowd had formed. Varrah joined in to help her cousin give away packets of the small balls of fried dough—they'd made two varieties—while I pulled Martyn aside for an explanation.

He grinned. "I figured Erikka might be willing to show me how to make your father's elusive international treat, and that she might further like to introduce a taste of her culture to the Alchemary. On her young cousin's behalf."

"They're called kokos," Varrah explained from my left to a classmate whose eyes had nearly rolled back into her skull with her first bite. "This one is my favorite. It's filled with pear jam."

"This is the one your father described," Martyn said, handing me a packet full of the little fried balls. "Stuffed with cherry and a sweet cream made from goat's milk, rolled in fine-ground sugar and . . ." He shrugged. "Well, we didn't have access to the specific spice, but Erikka insists that anise is very close. Try one!"

He practically shoved one of the little spheres into my mouth.

I bit into the pastry, and an explosion of sweet, tart, creamy, and bitter flavors burst over my tongue. The sugar had crystallized, and I found the texture quite pleasing.

"It's delicious," I agreed.

"Do you think your father will like it?"

"I think the poor man will grow round and jolly from your efforts!" I assured him.

Martyn beamed. "I hope they survive the three-day carriage ride. But if they don't, I now know how to make more!"

"How did you do this?" I asked, plucking another kokos from the packet.

He gave me another humble shrug. "We begged some space and supplies of the Refectory staff and promised to share the recipe. A very pleasant woman in a brown apron was willing to oblige, since we promised to clean up after ourselves." He smiled. "She got the first taste."

The provincial donuts were a hit, and I was thrilled to see no fewer than three of Varrah's classmates gathered around her, asking for details on variations.

Martyn and I retreated to watch Varrah and Erikka enjoying their moment. "You're a very sweet old man," I said as I wound my arm through his.

"I am *two years younger* than your father, I'll remind you," he said with a laugh.

"A fact you never allow him to—"

A cry from the crowd spun me around, cutting me off in mid-sentence, but it wasn't coming from the kokos booth.

"Something's wrong with her!" an unfamiliar voice shouted, and I followed the sound to see a student I recognized from the Proficiency cohort trembling in a near panic next to a woman who could only be his mother. She stood, eerily still on one of the winding cobblestone pathways, staring into the distance as if she couldn't see her son, though his face hovered mere inches from hers. "She won't move! She will not speak!"

And as the setting sun shone on the poor woman's face—literally as I watched—her skin began to sparkle with an odd metallic tint. Not gold or copper, but . . .

I pressed my way through the crowd until I could almost see her clearly, just as two soldiers posted at the Alchemary arrived and blocked my view. Just as the Bluehelm, and Desmond, and a couple of his researcher colleagues—including the woman with the severe blond bun—appeared at the front of the crowd and began to whisper frantically to one another. Cressa stood at the Bluehelm's elbow, scribbling furiously on her wax tablet. When some movement parted the crowd, I could see the woman again. . . .

Bronze. That was the hue of the poor woman's flesh. Not the naturally occurring bronze that some skin has, but a true bronze. A metallic tone.

I could not hear what the researchers were saying, but one word buzzed up from the crowd at large, as the soldiers lifted the woman bodily and carried her toward the infirmary.

Aurum.

Twenty-Four

My Dearest Amber,

I lack adequate words to express my disappointment at being unable to see you this weekend, and I can only hope that Martyn's attendance in my place is a comfort. I suspect, given your fondness for each other, that you might even find his company preferable to mine. I hope with this correspondence to convey all of the heartfelt platitudes I am not there to deliver in person. And in that endeavor . . .

I keep thinking about how lovely your hair looked in plaits when I visited, not only for its beauty but also because I'm certain your mother would be delighted by your traditional Lysëan braids. I imagine your bedchamber is neatly kept, to your credit, and I hope that you remember to eat at least twice a day. I trust that you're enjoying the company of your friends, unless they are foolish enough to decline, in which case the loss is entirely theirs, and I trust that they will eventually come to that conclusion on their own.

The other day, as I was leaving work for the evening, a crowd had gathered on the edge of the construction site to admire our work. There was among their number a small child sitting in the dirt, drawing with his finger in the sand, and I was reminded of the child you were many years ago. You spent one spring dedicated to tracing various shapes in the dirt of your mother's garden, quite heedless, on occasion, of seeds she'd sown. I remember thinking, as

I watched you, that several of your forms resembled notation you'd seen in my masonry sketches. I had hoped, for a while, that you might follow in my footsteps. But I will admit to a different kind of nostalgic pleasure in knowing that a bit of your mother lives on in you instead. She would be just as proud of you as I am.

Love always,
Your father, Cornelius Fallbrook

Alchemary Island was quiet in the absence of visitors. The quadrangle felt virtually barren, without all the booths and stalls. Without the vendors and alchemy-themed diversions.

It had taken two days to clean up from the festival, but Mastery students had been exempt from the effort; we were expected to turn our attention to the Black Trial, now that it loomed just days away. The tension—the fear—was palpable.

Martyn hadn't said a word about it before he'd left, but he had squeezed my hands, then my shoulders, and he'd whispered into my ear a plea to make wise choices. Not to put myself into unnecessary danger.

But danger, I was coming to understand, was usually necessary.

The incident at the festival hadn't helped. The woman who'd become an aurum was being well cared for in the infirmary, in isolation, according to reports from Alchemary administration. But the fact that someone had come down with the mysterious malady on *our* campus, during the family festival, less than a week from the first trial . . .

The research staff in particular seemed bowed beneath the expectation. The pressure from the public—from the Crown—to identify the illness and develop a cure was intense. And since no one on our campus had any real faith in the Alkahest Institute—our rival alchemy academy—that duty seemed to rest primarily on the Alchemary's collective shoulders.

For my Mastery cohort, the appearance of an aurum on campus drove home the importance of the career we'd chosen, as well as the slim chances any one of us had of being selected to practice alchemy at the highest level.

The Black Trial represented the first step in winnowing down our cohort, and we each had a different way of dealing with that pressure.

Yoslyn Savva had taken to burning astringent-smelling incense in her room. Clouds of it occasionally wafted up the stairs to my landing, and oddly, I found that if I stepped out and inhaled them . . . I often felt better, at least for a bit.

Keryth and Lennox practically moved into the student lab, working through most of the night, much to Wilder's irritation, and even taking naps on the floor, bundled in blankets brought from their rooms.

Petyr, Adria, and Gavin studied in the student library, their heads ducked low over books of various poisons and remedies. Pryce and Cressa ignored everyone and everything, including the general sense of tension, as far as I could tell. And Wilder . . .

I caught him looking at me several times during class, and twice his arm appeared to intentionally brush mine at our shared table. But he seemed loathe to break my concentration by addressing our interpersonal concerns, so close to the first trial.

I found myself both relieved and frustrated by that development. I desperately needed the time to study. And yet, given everything that was going on, I certainly could have used a hug from a true friend.

"How long have Wilder and I been a couple?" I asked as I dipped my quill into an inkpot set into a divot at the corner of my workstation.

Desmond made a sound as if something had caught in his throat, and I looked up to find him staring at me from a table across the room, brows furrowed severely. "Pardon?"

I drew a tick mark beside the last task on my list, confirming that I'd performed the entire experiment and had recorded my findings. They were going faster now that I'd gained a modicum of experience, and my familiarity with both the laboratory and the equipment had developed very quickly. "I said, how long have—"

"I understood the question," Desmond snapped. "What I do not understand is why you posed it."

I tilted my head, displaying my confusion. "You said I could ask you about anything I don't yet understand. In fact, you encouraged that very process."

Desmond scowled at the journal open in front of him, where I knew there would be a meticulous record of his own accomplishments for the evening. "I meant that you could ask me about *alchemy*."

"Well then, you should have been more specific. The reality is that you made an open-ended offer, and I am availing myself of it."

He looked up again, and I could feel his gaze as I carried my equipment to the cleaning station. "Semantics," he mumbled.

"Precision," I corrected. "You've taught me that precise expression is crucial in alchemy, for accurate recordkeeping, and—"

"This is not alchemy. This is literally semantics." His grip on his quill was tight enough to strain the very structure of the tool. "You're asking about your private life, and—"

"Alchemy *is* life. You taught me that as well. And that, in a *literal* if esoteric way, life is alchemy."

He set his quill on the work surface and crossed his arms over the front of his laboratory apron. "Would you like it if I held you to the very letter of every word you said?"

"Yes." I nodded. "I think I should quite enjoy that. Of course, I'm generally more specific in my word choice than you are, but even in cases where an excited utterance fails me, being held to my word would no doubt teach me to be more careful the next time."

His dyspeptic gaze felt like glowing coals deposited directly into my bare hands. "I cannot tell whether or not you jest."

The truth was that I couldn't either. Needling him had become a rather amusing diversion from tidying up my workstations, independent of my original question.

"Why?" I struggled not to smile at his consternation. "Is that an activity we engaged in before? Did we jest with each other? Or was it terribly austere, all those hours alone together in your lab?"

Desmond turned away from me and began gathering his used supplies. "I do not care for this line of questioning."

I laughed, and I could swear he flinched. Which only made me laugh harder.

"Then I shall have mercy on you," I finally relented. "If you answer my original question. How long have Wilder and I been a couple?"

He sighed, copper-eyed focus burning into me. "Why do you ask?"

I had no interest in answering his question, but turnabout, evidently, was fair play. "Your brother and I have been embroiled in a lovers' spat for the better part of a week."

Desmond's expression soured. "I sincerely doubt that, considering the two of you are *not* lovers."

Fire blazed behind my cheeks. The more confused I felt, the faster I talked. "First of all, 'lovers' spat' is merely an artful turn of phrase, and thus exempt from the precise language stipulation. Second . . . it's none of your business whether or not your brother and I are literally lovers. Though we are not, given that I cannot remember the onset or development of our affair, and that he would never pursue something I could not—"

"He most certainly would," Desmond grumbled softly, and a private little shiver slithered up my spine.

"Just answer the question. How long have Wilder and I been a couple?"

Desmond turned to face me, and for a second, I worried for the beakers he held in each hand because of how fiercely he was gripping them. "It is my understanding that you and Wilder are not now, nor have you ever been, a couple. Defined as 'in a committed—or at least acknowledged—amorous relationship.'"

"I—" I gave my head a little shake, as if that would jar loose the proper words. "But he said . . ."

Had he, though? Had Wilder actually said we were together? I'd certainly asked, but he was just as skilled at avoiding the question as his brother was.

"Why on earth would he have been in my bed if we are not a couple?" I demanded softly, unsure whether I was asking Desmond or myself.

His grip on the beakers finally loosened. "I would *also* be interested in the answer to that question."

"You would—" Aggravation burned along my veins. "Could you possibly, just this once, give me a straight answer? Or tell me what you know, at least?"

He sighed. "To my knowledge, the two of you were nothing more than good friends on the night before your memory vanished, six weeks ago. At the point when I last saw you, anyway. But I could not say what happened—what might have changed—after you left my lab that night." His gaze narrowed on me, and I felt the weight of his attention like a vest made of iron, pressing me toward the earth. "Have you not asked him to clarify that point?"

"Of course I have."

His brows arched expectantly. "And?"

"And . . . that led to nothing more than a few salacious implications and some alchemy metaphors . . . which . . . I now realize served to distract me from the original question."

Amusement broke through his scowl. "No doubt that was the intent."

"No doubt."

"Regardless, it does not matter," Desmond declared, slamming his journal shut. He fixed me with a pointed look and cleared his throat, as if some further declaration were forthcoming.

"It matters to me," I insisted.

"I assure you it does not. What matters is the Black Trial, and the fact that it is in less than one day."

I could not argue with his point. And yet, I felt argumentative. "Believe it or not, it has not slipped my mind that I could be expelled from the Alchemary tomorrow." Or wind up in a coffin, being shipped back to Innswood. "That's precisely why I've already spent half of the day—a Sunday, no less—in the lab." I hadn't even broken my fast, beyond the tea I'd made in a beaker over a flame, and hunger had no doubt contributed to my quarrelsome temperament.

"I assume you understand what the trial entails?" he continued. "That's why you've been focused on poisons?"

I nodded. "I can't be sure what kind we'll be given, so I've spent the morning creating half a dozen of the most likely poisons, based on the obvious criteria." I ticked them off on my fingers. "The poison must be ultimately and somewhat efficiently fatal. But it must be slow acting enough to allow students to identify it and concoct an antidote. And that antidote must be concoctable using only common alchemical ingredients that students have had regular access to and experience with."

"Logically sound conclusions." Desmond's eyes lit with a soft flame I'd come to recognize as mild approval.

"Thank you. Working backward from the possible antidotes that could be formulated, eliminating poisons that work too quickly or too slowly, or that are not fatal, I came up with these." I gestured at the six beakers lined up at the front of my primary work surface. They were of various dull shades of green, brown, and a watery yellow, any of which would appear almost entirely colorless at the concentration of just a few drops.

The poisons were wholly unsatisfying to concoct, given that they lacked the bright colors of most alchemical potions and elixirs. I'd come to recognize and count on—to *thrill* at—the transition of a decoction from one vivid color to the next as the ingredients went through various stages of calcination, dissolution, putrefaction, congelation, sublimation, etc.

But like life itself, alchemy was really only beautiful when it was resisting entropy. Fighting the uphill battle toward order and progress. Poisons introduced disorder and chaos.

Desmond peered at the labels I'd carefully printed, nodding as he went down the row. Approving of my deductive reasoning and, presumably, my creation of the poisons themselves.

"Of course, I'm not going to ingest them."

One of my classmates—a young man named Kornell—had tried that two weeks ago, in his own trial preparation. Wilder had told me the story in great, dramatic detail I'd have been tempted to assume was largely hyperbole had I not later heard a similar version from Yoslyn. In the student laboratory, Kornell had undertaken a test run at an antidote to the poison he believed we'd be ingesting.

No one seemed sure what he'd concocted and ingested—he'd maintained secrecy, loathe to give up his "advantage"—so our classmates could only watch as he broke out in coin-size dark splotches, which rapidly calcified, rendering them hard as stone. One of these patches grew over his eye, blinding him, while others robbed his fingers of mobility, which led him to drop his antidote, which shattered on the floor. He'd sobbed as he'd collapsed next to it, seizing, his teeth snapping uncontrollably. The theory circulating among our classmates was that those dark calcifications had also formed beneath his flesh, on parts of him not visible, and had done damage that could not be readily understood.

He'd lingered for a week in the infirmary, puzzling the staff and terrifying his classmates—missing the festival entirely—before they'd finally found an effective treatment and returned him to his studies.

I, for one, had learned from Kornell's mistake.

"Instead, I shall apply the antidotes—the formulation and production of which is my afternoon's work—to drops of the poison in a glass dish, working on the theory that if the antidote is effective outside of the human body, it will likely be effective inside as well."

"That is not a guarantee, of course," Desmond said.

"Of course not. Concoctions and elixirs occasionally react in baffling and unexpected ways when ingested," I acknowledged. "But I cannot succeed in the trial if I do not live to *attend* the trial."

His left brow rose, revealing more amusement than I suspected he'd intended. "Indeed." He nodded. "Carry on."

He pivoted to return to his own work, his thoughts shielded by his typical inscrutable expression.

"Wait!" I called, and Desmond turned, eyeing me expectantly. "I won't ask you to tell me what the poison will be, specifically. That would be cheating, and I am not a cheater. But can't you at least tell me if it is *one* of these?" I gestured again to the row of beakers.

It would be good to know that I wasn't striking off down an erroneous path that could get me killed. Or at least fail to save my life.

"No, I cannot."

My heart plummeted into the cold depths of my stomach. "But—"

"Amber," he interrupted. "I mean that quite literally. I cannot tell you what poison will be administered to the students because I do not know. I am not involved in designing the Black Trial."

"But you've endured it."

He nodded. "I also worked as an official observer of last year's trial. Which is how I know that the poison used during my trial year was not repeated with last year's students. The trial changes every year. I do not know specifically how it will go this year."

"Could you make an educated guess?"

Finally, he gave me a small smile, his eyes crinkling comfortingly with the expression. "I could, and I have. But . . ." He gestured at the row of poisons I'd created. "So have you."

With that, he turned back to his workstation, leaving me alone with my theories and projects.

Twenty-Five

At first, I had enormous fun, despite my anxiety about the trial. I practically danced around Desmond's laboratory, a song ringing through my head while I mixed, and lit, and timed, and measured, and adjusted, and recorded. I flitted from table to table, one eye on the hourglasses, the other on the height of flames and the softly bubbling contents of half a dozen suspended beakers and rounded vials.

Yes, my classmates had been preparing for the Black Trial for a month and a half already, while I'd essentially had only one week, because it had taken me more than the first month of class just to relearn what I'd spent two years learning in the first place. What none of them had forgotten.

But while I'd had to fight for that base-level knowledge—not just for the alchemy skills themselves, but for understanding of what skills I should even be trying to reacquire—knowledge fit into place quickly for me, and self-evaluations had assured me that retention was no issue.

I felt relatively good about my prospects, going into my own trial preparation, despite the tense anticipation from the entire Mastery cohort.

Until my first antidote failed. Utterly and terrifyingly. It had absolutely *no* effect on the drops of poison I applied it to.

I rallied, mentally, and had already adjusted the formula and started slowly heating fresh ingredients before I tested the second antidote on its poison.

It, too, failed, and my confidence bruised as surely as my tailbone had the time I'd fallen from the fourth rung of the loft ladder as a child, on an errand for my mother.

My smile disappeared. The song faded from my thoughts.

I dug in and tried harder, pulling textbooks from Desmond's office for reference. Double-checking my measurements, and heat levels, and timing. Making careful, detailed note of each failure.

Wishing upon every star in the sky that I'd made up with Wilder and snuck him into his brother's lab long enough to help him with my memory elixir.

Ignoring the concerned looks I could feel coming from Desmond, even as I refused to look up and acknowledge them.

But then the third antidote failed, and I could only clutch the edge of the worktable, breathing in and out slowly as I held in a scream of frustration, shocked by the sharp pain like a thousand knives stabbing the inside of my throat.

"Amber?" Desmond's voice was a cold wash of reality against the white-hot roar of my own frustration. Of my *humiliation*. I'd learned so much, *so* fast. Despite my exhaustion, I'd loved the process and had felt, up to that very moment, that every second devoted to studying was time well spent.

"I'm fine." I spun away from him, swiping tears from my eyes before they could fall, and hurried into the supply closet, where I snatched my satchel from its hook. I dug into the inner side pocket and felt an instant modicum of calm as my fingers brushed the smooth, cool, rounded glass of a slim vial.

Desmond appeared in the doorway just as I tipped the uncorked vial up to my lips.

A snarl rumbled up from his throat as he snatched the vial, spilling several precious drops on the floor.

I swallowed the half that had made it into my mouth as I whirled on him, anger blazing from my eyes, burning in my very veins.

"*What* do you think you're doing?" I demanded, reaching for the vial.

He stepped back and turned the vial to read the distinctive label, coming perilously close to spilling more of the contents. "What is this?" He frowned at the writing, and I realized he did not understand Wilder's product code. Which meant this elixir was not the one I'd seen him take that night in his office.

"If you don't know what it is, why would you feel justified snatching it from my hands?" I demanded.

"Because I recognize Wilder's diagonal label, and none of his elixirs have been properly tested or approved for production and distribution."

"And yet, you avail yourself of them. Hypocrite," I could not resist adding. "I *saw* you drink from one of Wilder's vials."

"I—" His mouth snapped shut. A maelstrom of conflicting thoughts swirled behind his eyes, and I watched him struggle, clearly grasping for a response that would defend his honor and prove me wrong, yet also be truthful. "You do not understand what you saw," he finally said, speaking through teeth clenched not in anger, but in . . . something more complicated. Something that looked very much like a struggle for control. "And frankly, that is none of your concern."

"As *that* vial is none of *yours*." I grasped for it again, and again he lifted it out of reach. When I rose onto my toes, I found myself pressed against him, one hand curled in the fabric of his shirt while the other pulled at his arm like a small child losing a game of keep-away with an older sibling.

And I *was* losing. Desmond was too strong and too tall to be moved.

But . . . he did not feel like my sibling. Not with his firm, broad, warm chest pressed against mine, his shoulder grazing my cheek as I stood on my toes.

"Give it to me," I demanded, and to my dismay, my voice sounded breathy, less like I was demanding what I wanted than like I was . . . begging for it.

Desmond's breath hitched. He groaned, but the sound died in his throat before I could even be sure I'd heard it. Though . . . I'd felt it. I could *still* feel it, caged up in his chest, echoing against every shallow breath he took.

I uncurled my fingers from his sleeve and lowered my arm as I stepped back, desperate to reclaim poise as I smoothed the front of my dress. As I composed my expression.

Desmond stood like a statue three feet from the closet doorway, his arm in the air, his gaze fixed on me with an intensity I'd never seen in my entire life.

That I could remember, anyway.

If he was breathing, I could not tell.

He stared at me as if I were a spirit returned from the grave to haunt him. As if he could not be certain *what* I was, or whether I was real.

As if moving might break the spell and banish me from his presence.

Shame flooded me as I regained myself. I cleared my throat. "I apologize for—"

"*Don't* . . . apologize." His words were sharp, but not cruel. He lowered his arm but did not offer me the vial. "What is this?"

"It . . . it elevates the mood."

His brows rose; evidently that was not what he'd expected to hear. "Why would you require such a service?"

"Because I'm frustrated." I huffed, dropping my gaze. "This afternoon has been an *utter* failure, and—"

"We all get frustrated, Amber. That's no reason—"

"No," I said, my gaze snapping up to his. "Don't trivialize this as the standard academic strain. I'm in an extraordinary situation, and you know that. I'm not the Amber I used to be, and—"

"Yes, you—"

"Desmond!" My fists curled in frustration. "Stop assuming you know what I'm going to say, and *just listen*."

He blinked at me. Then he exhaled. "I apologize. Please go on."

"Maybe the Amber I used to be got everything right on the first try, or maybe she had plenty of time to work through her mistakes, if she made them. But neither of those is true for *this* Amber. Tomorrow, I'm going to swallow poison. And if I can't identify it in time to make an antidote—which I must *already* know how to make—I will die. In an inglorious pageant of failure that will outlive me and likely become Alchemary legend. My humiliating legacy."

I smoothed my hands down the sides of my skirt, resisting the urge to clutch the material. "I thought I had a handle on this. I thought I'd at least gotten *close* to the level of my classmates. But every antidote I've made today has failed, and I haven't the *slightest* idea why, or how to fix it. And all I want in the whole wide world is to rant, and cry, and throw things. To break every vial and beaker in this room. But alchemy isn't about how I feel."

Desmond's expression went suddenly, startlingly blank. Not as if he had nothing to add, but as if he wanted to hide his thoughts on the matter. Likely because I'd told him to just listen, for once.

"Frustration will not serve my ambition," I continued. "Which means I cannot afford to waste time wallowing. I need to rally so I can focus on something other than the greater-than-average chance that by this time tomorrow, my corpse will be in the back of a carriage headed straight for Innswood. And Wilder, for all his unapproved and unorthodox methods, is the most practical alchemist I've ever known."

One corner of Desmond's mouth quirked upward. "You're a student. The only alchemists you've known are your professors."

And my mother. Had he forgotten about her?

"And yet I feel like my statement has merit," I insisted. "And I *know* Wilder's elixir does. So kindly return it."

"Amber—"

"It works."

"I know." He sighed. "I am not saying it doesn't work. I'm saying that even if it accomplishes the desired effect, every elixir also functions in some unexpected manner."

"I haven't noticed—"

"And you may not, or you may not immediately. But that doesn't mean that the undesired effect isn't . . . happening."

"Okay, well, if it helps me live through tomorrow, I'm perfectly willing to deal with these 'undesired effects,' later."

Desmond glanced at the vial, then his gaze returned to me. "How about *I* help you live through tomorrow?"

I blinked up at him, trying to ignore the sudden jump in my pulse. "Can you promise that *you* don't come with 'undesired effects'?"

Though, truth be told, I was more worried about him causing *desired* effects, even if I wasn't willing to say such a thing aloud.

Desmond laughed, and the coppery glow in his eyes lit a fire deep in my belly. "If I do, we can deal with that tomorrow, too."

Twenty-Six

"Four out of six. A sixty-six percent success rate." I blinked at my notes, silently commanding the numbers to change. Willing the letters to rearrange themselves and spell out my victory. My survival.

They did not change.

"That's a vast improvement," Desmond noted from his stool across the table, where he held the beaker containing my latest antidote up to the light, examining the particulates.

"Yes. As long as one of these four poisons is the one administered tomorrow, assuming I'm able to make the antidote in time, I should be able to survive." But there was no guarantee that one of the six I'd focused on would be chosen, much less one of the four I'd managed to cure.

And... it had taken me far too long to make each one.

On the bright side, however, I had no concern that I would forget the formula. I rarely forgot anything once I'd read it or written it—ironic, considering my current affliction—and we were allowed to bring notes.

My concern, aside from the possibility that I'd be presented with a poison I could not identify, was the time it would take to make the antidote with a poison already running through my veins, compromising my ability to concentrate and potentially my physical capabilities.

"I'm going to try those two again." I gestured at the two beakers at the end of the table.

For all I knew, Desmond had known the exact recipe for each one before we'd even gotten started. If so, he'd resisted any urge to give me the answers—to potentially save my life—because he knew, as I knew, that the Alchemary had no use for a scientist who could not save herself with the skills she intended to spend her entire life practicing.

This trial was intended to weed out weak alchemists, and however terrifying I might find that fact personally, I had no quibble with that goal.

If I could not pass on my own, I should not enter the trial.

"You need a break," Desmond insisted as he set the beaker down. "You missed the midday meal, and the Refectory will stop serving the evening meal soon."

"I'm fine."

He sighed. "Then *I* need a break. And a meal. And a walk, or something." He stood, arms extended behind his back to flex his shoulders.

"Go ahead." I dismissed him with the wave of one hand as I carried yet more supplies to the cleaning station.

"Amber—"

"I don't have time to waste eating and exercising. If I don't figure this out, I could die tomorrow."

"I know. And repeating that won't help you come to terms with the fact. But taking a break could help you approach the next round with a fresh perspective. Clearer thoughts."

"I can't—" Frustrated, I set the beakers down too hard, and when I turned, I gasped to find Desmond right behind me. "I can't figure out what I'm doing wrong with those last two. And I've made a second list of possible poisons, in case none of these six are the right one. The smart thing would be to at least write up notes on some antidotes for them, even if I don't have time to brew or test them. And—"

His brow furrowed, and a wave of guilt washed over me. "You don't have to stay. This is not your burden."

"I'm not going to leave you here alone."

"I promise I won't burn your lab down."

He chuckled softly, and I found myself smiling, despite the fear growing like a tumor inside me. "I meant that I'm not going to abandon you here."

"You don't even think I should be doing this."

"In part, because I don't want you to die." His voice deepened in a way that echoed through me, triggering quakes like the rumble of the earth itself before entire towns heaved into collapse. "Leaving you to struggle alone would be counter to that goal."

"Of keeping me alive?"

Desmond nodded and stepped back, his copper-eyed gaze holding mine. "Exactly."

"Do you go to this much trouble for all of your childhood friends?"

He blinked, and something visceral passed behind his eyes, swallowing his smile like a beast leaping from the ocean to devour a bird. "No one has *ever* been as much trouble as you are, Amber." But then he seemed to brush the thought aside. "Also, I have no other friends."

"You . . . ?"

He shrugged, as if that statement meant no more to him than announcing that we had run out of clean beakers. "Alchemy—the Alchemary, at least—does not prize personal relationships. You might have noticed that the staff researchers are all unmarried? The theory is that relationships get in the way of true science. They serve to distract."

"I see." In truth, I *could* see that concept reflected in interactions I'd observed but never truly considered. And in the fact that while many of the professors were married, none of the staff researchers, as far as I knew, had spouses or children. They all lived in dormitory-style on-campus apartments.

Students, however, clearly weren't yet expected to cast off personal relationships in order to better serve alchemy. So, why did I feel so isolated among them?

"Is that why, aside from Wilder, my cohort seems to want little to do with me?" I asked. "Did I simply take alchemy more seriously than the rest?" Had I already chosen my craft over camaraderie?

Desmond gave me a strangely assessing look, as if he were trying to divine the origin of my question in order to know how to answer. "No. And yes. Respectively. Most students take alchemy seriously, but most also have friendships and other personal relationships." He turned abruptly back to my primary workstation. "You're getting in your own way."

I frowned as I followed him to the table. "What do you mean?"

"You're second-guessing yourself. Depending too much upon what you know and not enough on your instincts and memory. You've done all this before, whether you remember it or not."

"But I *do not* remember it, so those experiences are of no use to me."

"That's not true." Desmond's quiet smile burned in me like the spark from a flint strike. "Do you remember the day you woke up with no memory? You and I left the Dormitory together, to go see Dr. Winhoof."

"Yes." I remembered, but I had no idea what point he was making.

"You turned directly and specifically in the direction of the Conservatory that morning, all on your own, though you had no memory of ever being on the Alchemary campus."

"I—" I frowned, trying to remember that moment. My memory since that morning was virtually unimpeachable, but I had little recall of events that hadn't made enough impression on me to form a memory.

"The same is true of my lab space."

"I turned in the right direction?" I guessed with a smile, to cover the flustered feeling chewing on my very nerve endings.

"Essentially," Desmond said. "From the first moment you stepped into the space, you seemed to know where everything was stored. You haven't once struggled to find a component or a piece of equipment, though I didn't point them all out during the tour."

"That's likely because this space is impeccably organized. I give you credit in that regard. I could not imagine a more logical and better organized storage system, and—"

"*You* organized this lab," Desmond said, this time with a broad, almost gloating smile.

"I . . . ?"

"Yes. When you moved into the space last year, you declared my organizational skills to be utterly subpar, and you set about remedying that. Without asking permission, I might add."

My cheeks burned like banked coals as embarrassment overwhelmed his point entirely. "I do apologize for overstepping."

"Don't. You were right. Your system was much better. And a couple of weeks ago, you stepped back into this lab and walked around as if you remembered organizing it."

"I didn't," I insisted. "I still don't."

"And yet, your instinct functions as if you do. Because your instinct *is* a form of memory, letting you call upon experiences you don't consciously remember."

"Stars above," I murmured. Was he right? Was I subconsciously remembering things I had no active recollection of?

I turned in a slow circle, and with every drawer or cabinet my gaze fell on, I recited its contents. Even the ones I had no memory of ever opening. Then I rushed around the room, opening drawers and cabinets. Verifying my hunches.

They were all correct.

I turned to Desmond, astonishment probably shining on my face like a freshly polished pane of glass.

He granted me a quiet smile. "My point is that that same instinct is likely available to you in other aspects of alchemy." He hesitated for an almost imperceptible instant. "And of life."

Because life *was* alchemy. And alchemy was life.

"All you have to do is trust your instincts." Desmond stepped closer, his voice lowered to a near whisper, as if he were letting me in on a very special secret. "Which essentially just means trusting what Past Amber already knows."

My instincts . . .

What did Past Amber know?

An impulse seized me. I wrapped my hands around fistfuls of his shirt, rose onto my toes, and kissed him directly on the mouth.

For one heartbeat, Desmond stood stiff and unyielding, and my mistake—my horrifically erroneous *instinct*—loomed over me like the guillotine, hungry for the crunch of my spine.

What in the name of entropy was I doing?

I let go of his shirt and dropped onto my heels, intending to flee the room, and the building, and the Alchemary, and my own humiliation.

But then Desmond's hands curled around my hips in a bruising grip, pulling me closer, higher, until I was balanced on the very tips of my toes. He made a primal sound at the back of his throat, like a half-starved dog tearing into a steak suddenly dropped in front of him, and a blistering need unfurled deep within me, hot tendrils curling low and tight. Gripping me with a desire I recognized on a bone-deep level but could not remember ever having felt before.

Desmond's mouth crashed down upon mine. His tongue plunged into me with greedy, demanding strokes. His hand slid up my spine and splayed across my back, the heat from his palm burning into me as if the sturdy material of my frock were as insubstantial as a fleeting thought.

My fists tightened again around handfuls of his tunic. My head tilted, granting me greater access to his mouth, and that one long kiss fractured into a dozen more, urgent and reckless, until we were feeding from each other with each salacious flick of his tongue across my lips, with each ravenous tug of his lip between my teeth.

I did not think.

I *could* not think.

This moment was not about thought. It was not about analysis, or reason, or planning. A fire burned between us, white-hot and blistering.

In alchemy, fire represented strong emotions such as passion, love, anger, and hate. Fire was yellow, orange, and red: bright, vibrant, flickering colors, constantly in flux as they released energy. Fire, written as an upward-pointing triangle, was considered hot and dry.

Hot, yes. Definitely. But *dry* seemed *wholly* inaccurate.

Fire was considered masculine, based on its destructive power alone, yet I'd never felt more like a woman in my life than I did with this blaze burning inside me, changing me as surely as flame changed every alchemical ingredient it touched.

Fire is alchemy. And alchemy is life.

This was my life.

I had no memory of it, and if I'd stopped to think about it, I would not have been able to identify a single bit of empirical evidence, but I knew—*knew*—that this was right, even if it had never happened before. Desmond's hands on my body . . . his lips on mine . . . his tongue—the wet heat and the taste of him . . .

The fire burned, and it *would* consume me, as every flame consumes without thought—without reason or restriction—until its fuel is used up.

I *knew* that.

And I reached for it anyway.

I let go of Desmond's tunic and slid my hands over his chest, my fingers finding familiar comfort in smooth planes and hard angles I had no memory of ever touching, until my hands slid behind his neck and locked there, anchoring my body to his.

Desmond groaned and turned us toward the empty workstation on my right. He lifted me onto the countertop, where I yipped from the cold seeping through my skirt.

He caught the sound. He devoured it, his hands trailing up my bodice, now that I sat higher. Now that his hands were both free.

I moaned when his mouth trailed from my lips toward my jaw, then down my neck. I leaned back on the table, my neck arched, and his left hand slid behind my head, fingers plunging into my hair, loosening my coiffure as he cradled my scalp.

My breathing felt ragged, every sensation heightened, as if one of Wilder's elixirs had left my skin sensitive and my nerve endings ablaze. But there were no chemicals at work here. There was only Desmond.

And instinct.

"Why, in the name of *utter* anarchy, do you taste so good?" he murmured against my skin as he worked his way back up my throat toward my mouth. We kissed again, hands wandering, desperate, as I tugged his tunic up over his waistband.

He moaned as I ran my hands over his chest, beneath the material. Greedy, I pulled him closer, even as I nibbled again at his lips, hungry for something I could hardly even name. My hands slid around his back, then down, until my fingers dug beneath the waist of his pants.

Desmond pulled away, imposing a cold gap between us, staring down at me with his lips swollen and his gorgeous copper-brown eyes dilated. Breathing hard. Powerful muscles bunching beneath my hands as he resisted the same tension—the same *need*—driving me. "Do you want this?"

I nodded as my gaze trailed toward his chest, then lower.

"Amber." He took my chin in his left hand and drew my gaze back to him. "Are you sure?"

"Yes," I whispered. "Assuredly, yes."

The truth was that I wasn't even sure what I was asking for. Certainly I *knew*, in theory. I also knew that I'd likely already done this. Though I could not remember it, the feeling was an instinct housed deep in my flesh.

In the moment, *that* seemed the real tragedy of my lost memory, alchemical theory be damned. I'd forgotten more than just schooling. I'd forgotten my own experiences. My *life*.

With a vast carnal ache driving me toward a culmination I could not remember ever having reached, all I really understood was that I wanted more. I wanted to keep touching him. I wanted him to touch *me*. I wanted to kiss him, and taste him, and I wanted the conclusion to this throbbing that pulsed within me, in scandalous places.

"Yes." I said it firmly, holding his gaze.

He made that sound again, that hungry growl deep in his throat, and this time it tugged at something low and sensitive in my own body. It made me crave things I lacked the vocabulary to express and the boldness to demand, and . . .

Desmond lifted me from the counter and set me on my feet, leaning down so he could kiss me again, long, and hard, and deep.

Then he stood, pulling away from my mouth. Leaving me panting. Urgently sucking in more oxygen to feed the flames. He met my gaze, his burning with passion like I'd never seen from him. Like I'd never imagined could exist in Desmond Gregory, with his stoic scowl, censuring gazes, and the intimidating breadth of his shoulders.

An ache throbbed between my legs, and my feet moved with an understanding—an *instinct*—my mind lacked.

I turned, my heart racing, and bent over the workstation, a bit in awe of my own bold invitation.

Desmond groaned. His hand caressed my lower spine, and suddenly I felt the warmth of him against the back of my thighs. Lifting my skirt.

My pulse roared in my ears.

My legs felt chilled, exposed so suddenly to the air, but then Desmond's very proximity gently warmed me, as if his flesh glowed like banked coals through his own clothing. His hands felt scalding as they slid my linen undergarment down, letting the thin material pool at my feet.

I stepped out of the garment, gasping as his hot hand caressed my backside, then dipped between my thighs. He stroked my most sensitive parts slowly, gently, and my thoughts scattered like leaves tossed by a fierce breeze. The maelstrom refused to settle, each thought seized from my attention before I could interpret it, leaving me with only fleeting, primal impressions, entirely subjugated by an explosion of sensation far too intense to be sorted.

What I felt could not be understood. It could not be analyzed.

It could only be experienced.

"Close your eyes," Desmond ordered in a fierce whisper, as if he knew exactly what I was thinking.

I obeyed, and my entire existence narrowed to what I could feel.

The cold, smooth table leeching warmth from me through the front of my frock, cooling my overheated cheek. The hard, straight edge of the work surface, cutting into my palms as I grasped it, anchoring myself to this last semblance of the real world as everything else churned around me, a seething storm of sensation.

And Desmond. I could feel him. The warmth of his body against my legs, and his palm on my back. His fingers . . .

"Oh," I breathed as he stroked faster, circling. Teasing. He was diligent, certain of his task, and in no hurry, and yet I groaned, squirming with impatience. Arching toward him, too ravenous to be humiliated by the exhibition of my own need.

"More," I demanded in a husky voice I'd never heard before. A voice I'd had no idea my throat could produce.

Desmond groaned. His fingers plunged inside me, and his groan deepened into an inarticulate plea.

Then, suddenly, he was gone, and I was left panting, arching toward him. I started to rise, and his hand landed firmly on my spine again. "Don't . . . move," he growled.

I heard the rustle of fabric, and suddenly he was back, his fingers stroking again. Teasing. Testing. He exhaled, a strange, needy sound, and his fingers were gone.

He slid inside me slowly, steadily, and for a single second the world seemed to still around me. As if all of existence had been distilled into this one moment. This one sensation.

Us.

In that moment, I was satisfied. Fulfilled, in a way I simultaneously craved like a habitual dependance and yet could not remember ever before feeling.

In the next moment, I was entirely *un*satisfied.

"More," I demanded again, pressing back against him. And with a moan, Desmond began to move.

His hands curled around my hips, guiding my movements until I understood—until my body remembered what my mind could not.

He gasped as I clenched around him, clutching the table. Arching up. Grinding back against him. Try though he might to take it slow, to draw pleasure out, my body would have none of it.

I needed something—I needed *him*, now—and it did not take long for him to understand.

He moved faster, stroking into me over and over, bruising my hips on the edge of the table, pushing me closer with every thrust. We raced toward a crest building quickly, mercilessly inside me, and yet the peak remained brutally out of reach.

"Please," I groaned, frustration rivaling my arousal, and Desmond bent forward. His hand snaked around the front of my thigh, and with his next thrust, he stroked my tenderest, most aching bit of flesh, drawing a groan from deep in my gut. Altering my understanding of the sensations building within me.

My body clenched around him, and my breathing hitched. My very existence narrowed again to a single point of focus as pressure—*pleasure*—built toward a blistering peak, and then suddenly . . .

A single, infinitesimal point of ecstasy abruptly exploded into a million sparks burning brightly, followed by another wave of sparks, and another, and another, each pulsing within me even as the next burst forth.

My cry echoed through the room.

Desmond leaned over me, thrusting deeper, harder, even as his hand clamped over my mouth.

I bit his finger, still riding out the explosions, and he grunted as he released into me.

For a moment, we both lived in a still, quiet moment of post-release, a cluster of damp flesh and pounding hearts. Tangled clothing and gasping breath.

Then Desmond stepped back, and air cooled my overheated skin. He perched next to me as I lifted myself onto the unused workstation, primly tucking my skirt around my legs. He stroked damp hair back from my face and leaned forward to murmur something I could not clearly make out. But it sounded a bit like "You are a burst of light in a dark room."

I considered asking him to repeat it. To clarify.

Instead, I leaned back so I could see his face, searching it for something I might recognize. Any hint that I should have seen before, that any of this was possible. That Desmond Gregory, the distinguished Alchemary researcher, the surrogate older brother from my childhood, could also be this man.

This explosive *force.*

Looking at him from this close was a blistering sort of intimacy unlike anything I'd ever experienced, including the act we'd just shared. The brown of his irises was shot through with bright copper striations, which seemed to flicker with the lamplight.

He blinked lazily. He was not smiling, but he wasn't scowling either.

He looked . . . exposed. Vulnerable.

I leaned forward, and he leaned in to meet me. "Again," I whispered in his ear, and Desmond laughed, a deep, throaty chuckle.

"We cannot do that again here. We shouldn't have done it here at all. Suppose someone had come in?"

"No one comes to your lab." I'd worked there daily for two weeks and had yet to see another soul.

He frowned. "That is true, though I have no clear understanding of why."

"It's because they do not like you. You are gruff and severe, and your face is fixed in a permanent scowl."

He scoffed, as if I were teasing. "That is not true."

"It is. But I am unconvinced that it matters. The researchers *all* scowl, as if that's the only expression their faces will form. This is a cold, soulless building. It sucks the very joy out of what we practice. So we *should* do that again, here. *Everyone* should be doing that here. Because joy is life. Pleasure is life. And *life* is Alchemy."

He stared at me as if gibberish were my native tongue, and I'd just lapsed into it.

"Why are you looking at me like that?" I demanded, tangling my fist in the loose tail of his tunic. Touching him, because I couldn't *not* touch him.

But he seemed to have no answer. No words, in fact, at all.

I slid one hand behind his neck and pulled him down until I could whisper in his ear once more. "Again. I demand that you do that to me again, but . . . different."

He groaned, and his breath hitched. "Different? An *intriguing* word, and, in this context, one which requires elucidation."

My brows rose. "I have theories, about this act we've just performed. About the possibilities. And they need testing."

"You have a theory." One of his brows rose, briefly casting his natural skepticism as amusement. "About sexual congress."

"Theories," I corrected as his gaze locked intensely onto mine. "Plural. And you shall *have* to pay attention. Details matter."

"Of *course* you have theories." He slid from the surface of the workstation, holding my gaze even as he fastened his breeches. "Will you be taking notes?"

"Copious," I assured him, sliding off the counter to reclaim my undergarment. "Someone wise taught me that accurate record-keeping is vital."

He laughed, gravelly and sincere, and the sound bounced around inside me, setting off an unspeakable ache at every point of contact. "Very well, then, Miss Fallbrook. But this kind of experimentation requires a different sort of laboratory." He offered me one hand, and I took it. "Follow me."

Twenty-Seven

I awoke in Desmond's bed, and I could not tell, at first, whether I was relieved or disappointed to find myself alone.

The other side of the fine wool-and-feather-stuffed mattress was cold, as if he had not been abed in hours, and a shower of possible reasons flooded my thoughts.

None were pleasant.

Contrition. His regret about what we'd done was so strong that he could not pass the night at my side, yet he was too much of a gentleman to send me home, my thighs still damp, after our passion was spent.

Disgust. His needs sated, he now looked upon me the way I once looked upon an empty jug of ale Wilder had pilfered the morning after we'd drunk the entire thing when we were far too young to imbibe, any memory of my joy eclipsed by nausea and head pain.

As the possibilities chased each other through my thoughts, I rose and pulled on my clothing, shivering in the cold, empty room. Though I'd hardly gotten a glance at it the night before, Desmond's apartment was much finer than my own Dormitory room. It even had a stone fireplace built into one wall. But it was unlit, and though I knew very well how to build a fire, it was not my place to do so in someone else's private space.

Instead, I stepped into my shoes and glanced around the chilly room for my satchel. But it was nowhere to be found.

The obvious conclusion—I'd left it in the Conservatory—triggered fresh panic as I turned toward the window, where I could see the sun just peeking over the eastern horizon, glowing across the top of the forest stretching down the slope of the island toward the southern shore.

Desmond's view was different from the one visible from my own window, but no less beautiful. Yet I had no time to truly consider it.

Monday morning. The day of the Black Trial.

Fear swelled inside me like a gust of cold air, swirling up from my gut, blossoming into gooseflesh on my arms and legs.

I hadn't finished my preparation.

I'd followed Desmond back to his apartment and rolled around in his bed until the early hours of the morning, lost in a passion that had been all-consuming for hours on end, but that now felt . . .

Like a death sentence.

Air rushed in and out of my lungs without lingering long enough to perform its function. The room swam around me. I sank onto the edge of the unmade bed, fists clenched around the bedclothes, listening to my chest rattle and wheeze as I hyperventilated yet was unable to stop it.

"Amber."

Desmond had said my name at least three times before I was able to process the syllables. Before I could draw his face into focus as he knelt on the woven carpet in front of me. "Breathe. *Slowly.*"

But it wasn't his advice that brought the world back into clarity and unlocked my lungs. It was *rage.*

"You left me." My words carried the sharp, hot edge of a blade gleaming in firelight.

"I had to run an errand."

"You left me. On *Black Trial* day. I'm likely going to die today, and you left me here to wake up alone." Never mind the fact that if I'd slept in my own bedchamber, I'd have woken up alone anyway. Fear had swelled within me, leaving little room for logic.

"I went back to the lab to make this." As he stood, he dug into his pocket and pulled out a sealed vial, just like the ones Wilder used. Only there was no handwritten label, and I did not recognize the color—the pale, sickly yellow—of the contents.

"What is it?"

"You need to drink it."

"I will not, without knowing what it is."

Desmond sat next to me on the bed, a puzzled, disappointed expression swirling slowly behind his eyes. "It is . . . a remedy. For a problem that only may exist. Because of last night. I swear on my soul that it will do you no harm. It will only prevent . . . conception."

And suddenly the reality of what we'd done—of the potential consequences—hit me with the impact of the clock tower collapsing directly onto my unsuspecting body. Crushing me swiftly and terribly.

"Most women buy these in Saltstrand, which we have no time for. Or they get them from Wilder. Which is equally out of the question, for obvious reasons."

I groaned, scrubbing one hand over my face as guilt rose like a behemoth to overshadow the other facets of my misery. "Wilder. What have I done?"

"No," Desmond said firmly as he pressed the vial into my hand. "I do not know what passed between you and my brother the night you lost your memory, but I know for certain that you were not then, nor are you now, together as a couple."

And yet . . . Wilder had been in my bed. I'd spent the past six weeks at his side—I *cared* for him—and—

"You have done nothing wrong, Amber."

"And yet you brought me here in secret."

His sigh carried the weight of the entire planet. "Because while you have done nothing wrong, the same might not be true of me."

I frowned at him. "What does that mean?"

"It's . . . complicated. Amber, drink the remedy. Please."

"And if I don't want to?" I stared down at it.

"That is your choice. Entirely yours. But I wanted you to have the option, and I strongly suspect that if you were thinking clearly right now, you would have already swallowed the entirety of that vial."

He was right. I did not want a child. Not right now. Not when I had yet to graduate—to even survive—the Alchemary and could remember little of the past few years.

I thumbed the cork from the vial and swallowed the contents, grimacing as the bitter taste and viscous texture lingered at the back of my tongue. "That is *loathsome*."

"So I've heard. If I could take it for you, I would. But despite the Alchemary's attempts to perfect the human form, men are as yet incapable of conception."

"I don't understand what happened last night."

He turned from his desk to give me a wry smile. "At the time, you understood well enough to have *theories*."

I flushed at the memory of what I'd said and done. Of what I'd asked *him* to do.

Of his unflinching willingness—eagerness—to oblige.

I closed my eyes, and I could feel the ghost of his touch on my skin. I could still taste him. I could feel the firm strength of his form pressed against me. Over me. Arching beneath my hands, between my thighs.

No.

I shook my head, rattling the memories loose. Banishing them to the abyss that had swallowed more than two years of my life.

"I don't have time for this. I have to find my satchel. My notes. I need to go back to the lab and—"

"The Conservatory is closed," he said. "For the trial. That's why I had to leave so early—to get out before they posted attendants at the doors."

"*No* . . . I need my notes, I can't—"

A familiar plane of leather swung in front of my face, and I looked up to see my satchel dangling from Desmond's left hand.

"Thank you!" I snatched it from him and threw open the flap. Everything appeared to be in order, though I had no memory of repacking my notes before we'd rushed across campus to his apartment, drunk on lust. Blind to all other concerns.

What in the name of eternal chaos had gotten into me?

"Amber, there's something else."

The solemn tone of his voice stilled my hand. I looked up.

"The Bluehelm met me on the path. She was headed this way, and if I hadn't caught her, she would have shown up here at my door."

"Why?" Unease churned in my belly.

"She wanted my opinion on whether you should be allowed to undergo the trial."

"So, you got another chance to plead your case for my dismissal."

"Yes. And so I did," he confessed, holding my gaze.

"Even after . . . ?" I glanced at his bed, where the bedclothes were still rumpled.

"Yes. You already know my opinion on this matter, and last night has no relevance to it."

Of course it didn't. Desmond was far too logical to let pleasure get in the way of his rational opinion. Or even affection, should that actually exist. Though I was starting to believe that the older Gregory brother and I were saltpeter, sulfur, and charcoal—destined to explode upon contact, yet unable to enjoy each other's company.

I understood that his opinion wasn't personal, and he'd been honest with me about that from the start. Thus it should not have stung. Yet a brand-new ache had formed just beneath my ribs, clutching me like a vise.

I inhaled slowly. Bracing myself for the inevitable. For a loss that would surely rival the loss of my memory.

"So then . . . I won't be allowed to compete?"

"On the contrary," he said. "I gave my opinion, but her next question was quite specific. She asked if you would be in greater danger than any other student in the Black Trial, and I had no choice but to truthfully answer that in my opinion, after six weeks of study, you are not the least proficient member of your cohort. At which point I was informed that you are passing both of your classes and your professors are both quite impressed with your progress." He cleared his throat and looked distinctly displeased. "You will be allowed to compete."

A jolt of anticipation fired throughout my entire body, lighting it on fire.

"I have to go bathe." I stood and dropped the strap of my bag over my head, onto my shoulder. "And change clothes." I stepped toward the door, but then Desmond's left hand closed around my arm, before I even realized he'd stood.

"Just because you are not the least proficient does not mean there is no danger."

"I am aware." I pulled my arm from his grasp.

"Amber, you could *die*."

"I—"

"You could just withdraw. There would be no shame in it, considering your memory loss. And I know you didn't get to test all of your antidotes."

I blinked up at him, anger firing through my veins. "Was that your plan all along? Distract me with carnal pleasures so that I am unprepared for the trial and *have to* withdraw?"

His eyes narrowed, his brows dipping in a look of censure that hurt all the more, considering how he'd looked at me just hours before. "*You* are the one who kept demanding more."

The truth of that stung. "Well, that won't be a problem again. Even if I survive." With that, I marched out of his apartment and slammed the door, grateful not to see any other staff members in the small, forest-facing courtyard.

I managed to hold back tears until I'd rounded the building and set off down the stone path, but they burst forth, uncontrolled, the very second I stepped out of sight from Desmond's window. And the worst part was that I could not rightfully identify the cause.

It wasn't just fear or frustration, though those were certainly among the villainous emotions battering the ramparts of my soul in that moment.

There was a deeper affliction. An ache with no source I could identify, as if I'd poked at a bruise and reawakened the pain but could not recall the initial impact.

I was *angry* at Desmond, as I had been weeks before, and again, I could not remember why. I was angry at myself for forgetting that long enough to enjoy the pleasures of his bed.

And worst of all was the fact that every step I took away from his apartment seemed to widen a chasm opening deep inside me, spilling forth a cold emptiness that I could not understand.

What was wrong with me?

Swiping tears from my face, swallowing hiccupping sobs, I hurried down the path through the woods, my gaze catching on various brightly colored and distinctive plants. To distract myself from the maelstrom of unpleasant emotions storming inside me,

I quizzed myself on their names, and to my utter surprise... I knew them all.

Fevervine, with its scarlet-hued veins twisting along plump, leathery, bluish ropes of plant material.

Devil's root, arcing up from the ground in gnarled, charcoal-colored knots and twists.

Spiky hibiscus, with its bright pink leaves and deep, greenish-purple thorns.

When he was bored, Wilder sketched these plants in the margins of his "notes."

The Alchemary woodlands had been cultivated carefully and deliberately in order to grow plants that were useful in alchemy—mostly to the Panacea division. More than a century ago, according to my mother, special soil had been brought in by the cartload and mixed with the loamy earth of what was then a sloping field sparsely dotted with hardy trees. The soil was sown with seeds from plants specially bred by the Alchemary, and since that time it had been constantly monitored by staff gardeners.

Within a few decades, the forest had exploded with trees and exotic plant life. Plant life that was nurtured by soil infused with alchemy-specific nutrients so that the vegetation could be dried and ground, or boiled and reduced into specialized and concentrated versions of the very chemicals they had been grown in. No other alchemists in the world had access to these ingredients. To beyn and common formulas made from them.

Wilder often came to class with dirt beneath his fingernails and fresh scratches on his arms from harvesting elixir components in the middle of the night, and my interrogations about his illicit activity inevitably had shifted, at some point, into him good-naturedly quizzing me on the usage of the plants he'd purloined from the Alchemary forest.

Thinking about Wilder sent a fresh pang of guilt like a sledgehammer through my very soul, and I hurried through the woods, my steps clicking rapidly on the stone path, my breath puffing in the cold morning air.

At the end of the trail, I veered around the back of the Refectory and let my path arch toward the cliffside the long way, avoiding the quadrangle entirely.

I could not be seen like this.

I managed to avoid both students and staff members until I snuck up the steps at the center of the Dormitory's ladies' tower.

A figure stood at my door, fist raised to knock, and I knew who it was even before he turned at the sound of my steps.

"Amber?" Confusion crinkled Wilder's brow. "Where have you been? Have you been crying?"

"It's just nerves," I told him. "I was in the Conservatory until late, then I just kind of . . . fell asleep."

An omission of details wasn't the same as a lie. Not technically. And there was no reason at all for me to feel guilty about that, considering how many details of our relationship he was *still* withholding from me.

And yet, I did feel guilty.

"How do you feel?" he asked as he followed me into my room. "Are you prepared? Has Desmond been generous with his experience?"

I flinched and could only hope he hadn't noticed.

"I mean, he may not think you belong here, but he doesn't want you dead," Wilder continued.

"He's done absolutely everything he can for me," I confirmed, stung by my own unintentional double entendre. "I . . . um. I need to get ready. I'll see you at the Conservatory, okay?"

Wilder frowned. "No, that is not okay. I don't understand why you're angry with me, and I can't let that stand, when either of us could die today. You *must* forgive me, for whatever I've done."

"I'm not angry." I settled onto my desk chair and stared up at him. "I was a bit piqued, but with no real cause, I must admit, so . . . it is *you* who must forgive *me*."

His smile burst forth like the sun breaching the horizon. "Then consider the matter settled. Meet me in the Refectory in half an hour, and I will have food and tea waiting. We can go over theories and strategy."

In fact, we could. Though most of our cohort would not. The competition for a permanent position at the Alchemary was fierce, and most of our classmates would never give up their edge by working with a competitor. Not even for a friend or lover. But Wilder was not selfish.

He was also not particularly helpful, a fact he confirmed half an hour later, over porridge and tea, when his theories all amounted to guesswork and an alchemical instinct I could not understand. He had written none of it down, and his explanations leapt from point to point in no logical order I could discern.

He would likely be the only Mastery student in the history of the Alchemary to carry precisely zero notes into the trial.

The Black Trial challenges students to distinguish themselves from their cohort not simply by demonstrating their burgeoning alchemical expertise but also by confronting both physical death and the shadows within their own souls, as well as by enduring and overcoming the symbolic alchemical steps of purification and decomposition.

During the trial, students are expected to confront and conquer forces of fear, chaos, despair, and disillusionment in order to continue to the next phase of their personal transformations.

—from the *Alchemary Student Handbook*

Twenty-Eight

At the entrance to the Conservatory, a small queue had formed made up entirely of my Mastery-year cohort. My pulse raced as Wilder and I came to a stop at the end of the line. Anticipation buzzed around our peers like flies on a ripe corpse, and my head pounded so fiercely I worried the top of my skull might erupt from the pressure.

"It's going to be fine," Wilder whispered, squeezing my hand.

And it would be. For him.

His grades might have historically hovered just above the median, and the Alchemary research board might have had no respect for his work, but Wilder's skill—undocumented though it was—would easily get him past this first hurdle. In fact, I suspected he was better prepared than any of our classmates, by virtue of time spent in the laboratory alone. To say nothing of how many of those hours had been spent experimenting with medicinal elixirs.

"For those of you just arriving," a voice called, and I leaned out of the line to see one of the attendants Desmond had mentioned addressing us from her position to the left of the door. It was his colleague with wide-set eyes and the severe blond bun. "Mastery students will be admitted promptly at ten in the morning. The trial will be explained, then it will convene, and it will continue until all students have either passed or been rendered unable to compete. That is expected to take no more than two hours."

Yoslyn Savva shuddered, directly ahead of me in the queue.

"What time is it?" Cressa Baxter asked from two spaces ahead of me. Keryth and Lennox were at the very front of the line, with Pryce's still-blue head right behind them.

"Quarter till." Yoslyn pointed behind us, at the Seminary clock tower.

A couple more students fell in behind Wilder, and as we waited, nerves simmering, feet shuffling, a cluster of staff and faculty members arrived. Desmond was among them.

They gave their names to the attendants and were admitted into the building one at a time, and as their number trailed down the steps, forming a line parallel to ours but longer, I could practically feel Desmond's gaze on the back of my head.

As his line shortened, he stepped even with me briefly, and when he turned to offer a devastatingly formal nod both to me and to Wilder, it took every fiber of self-control I possessed to keep from reaching out. To keep my fingers from trailing down the sleeve of his staff cape to curl between his.

It seemed ruthlessly unfair that I could not touch him now.

Two hours ago I'd woken in his bed, then stormed out. But the instinct remained.

The line moved again, and he stepped ahead of me. Maybe he could feel my gaze now. But he did not turn.

The Alchemary amphitheater was at the very back of the Conservatory, accessible only by walking through the entire Panacea wing and past the infirmary. We marched the length of the building like ducklings following their mother, a role played by the researcher with the blond bun.

At the end of the main hall of the Panacea wing, she opened a tall, thick set of double doors and led us into a huge chamber like nothing I'd never seen.

I was certain of that, even with more than two years of my life missing.

We entered the space at the top row of seating tiers, in an aisle that led down past six flights of bench seating into a venue that had been dug deep into the ground beneath the Conservatory. Most of the benches were already occupied by staff researchers and faculty, as well as alumni who'd been invited to observe the trial.

The centerpiece of the amphitheater was a stone-floored circular chamber, set up with twelve workstations and a substantial supply cupboard. Those I had expected, based on the very concept of the trial.

But I had *not* expected the glass wall surrounding the entire center chamber.

At least ten feet high, it was comprised of the largest individual panes of glass I'd ever seen, each half as tall as I was, affixed to the others with thin lead frames. The effect was like a transparent honeycomb. Spectators would be able to observe the trial without being affected by anything that transpired inside the arena itself.

Though I could not imagine that the Black Trial—the administration of individual doses of poison—presented much threat to the spectators.

My hands clenched around the strap of my satchel as I followed Yoslyn down the broad, steep steps, watching my own feet to make sure I didn't trip and send all of my classmates careening to the gallery.

At the floor level, I followed Yoslyn as our line of student competitors curved in front of the lowest level of seating, facing into the glass arena, to the right of the aisle. A second line of twelve individuals curved to the left of the aisle, each holding a journal, a quill, and an inkwell. These would be the official observers:

volunteers from among the staff researchers, each assigned to one of the trial participants and tasked with recording that student's every movement.

Desmond had been among their ranks the year before.

The blond attendant stepped forward and opened a glass-paned door into the arena, then gestured for the observers to go in. When they had set up their quills, inkwells, and stools, each at one of the twelve workstations, we were allowed to file in, in reverse order, beginning with the last student in line.

Wilder was the third to step into the arena, and I was the fourth, my heart racing, with Yoslyn behind me. He wound up at the workstation to my right, and she was directly in front of me.

My observer, as it happened, was another of Desmond's colleagues: the man with a bald head and a receding chin.

When we'd all taken up our positions, the Bluehelm marched into the arena, formal, gold-trimmed robes swishing, and addressed us in a commanding voice, her hands clasped at her back, her dark-eyed gaze shifting from face to face, pale skin practically gleaming in the glow of at least a hundred torches.

"Welcome to the Black Trial, the first in a series of four competitions that comprise a hallowed yet pragmatic Alchemary tradition." Her voice echoed around the arena in a formal cadence. "Every Mastery-year cohort for more than a century has been where you now stand: in this same arena, facing a very similar test, awash in same trepidation and excitement likely racing through your veins at this very moment. I want you all to know that regardless of the outcome, it is quite an accomplishment to have made it this far."

Her focus seemed to snag on me for a moment, and my pulse spiked painfully.

"The Black Trial symbolizes spiritual death," the Bluehelm continued. "By enduring and overcoming the symbolic alchemical steps of purification and decomposition, you will shed your old ways of thinking so that you can take the next step on your journey toward a higher state of being."

She paused, her hands sliding down the long, gold-trimmed lapels of her robe, as if out of habit. "In a moment, each of you will ingest a poison administered by your official observer. Each poison is identical, brewed all in the same batch by a panel of your professors, using an officially approved formula. You must drink every drop, and only once you have will you be released to the supply cupboard."

No one dared speak, but a tense sort of restlessness worked its way around the arena as feet shuffled against the stone floor and stances shifted uncomfortably.

"At that point," the Bluehelm said, "you will have access to all of the available supplies and equipment, though no student will be allowed to take anything from another."

That likely wouldn't be necessary anyway because the cupboard held plenty of every ingredient I could imagine, as well as a collection of surplus equipment, in case something broke in mid-trial.

"Students must each identify the poison administered, then formulate, produce, and consume an antidote. Those who manage all of that in time to nullify the poison before it does irreparable harm will be considered to have passed the Black Trial."

More anxious fidgeting erupted among my classmates.

"Those who fail to find and consume an antidote in time to avoid irreparable harm, and those who do not survive the poison, will fail the trial."

What she did not mention, though we were all well aware of it, was the likelihood that one of us would die this day. Or that even those who survived but failed would be expelled from the Alchemary, severed from the power and prestige of the academy.

Like my mother.

"You may not help one another, nor are you allowed to observe and replicate another student's technique or formula. Are there any questions?" The Bluehelm's voice echoed eerily around us.

There were none.

She wished us all luck, then exited the arena to take her position in the first row of spectator seating. The best view in the venue.

An attendant pulled the door closed behind her and stood in front of it. To make sure no one tried to enter? Or that no one tried to leave?

A wave of nausea washed over me as the Bluehelm lifted her arm into the air. All of the official observers turned toward her, silent and attentive. When she lowered her arm, they each reached into a pocket of their cape and withdrew a narrow, corked vial.

My observer offered me his vial, and I took it with trembling fingers, staring at the pale, almost colorless fluid it held.

From my right, something crashed with a high-pitched shattering sound, followed by an anguished cry.

Kornell had dropped his vial, spilling his poison across the stone floor. His observer fixed him with a pitying look, then escorted him out of the arena, through the door the attendant opened for them.

Just like that, his time at the Alchemary was over.

I tightened my grip on my own vial, my heart slamming against my sternum.

At the front of the room, with a touch of bravado, Lennox tilted his head back and swallowed his poison in one gulp. He shoved the empty vial at his observer, then raced toward the cupboard, dark curls flopping as he ran, clearly eager to get first choice of the equipment and supplies.

Keryth was right behind him.

I resisted the urge to follow their example, even as three other students raced after them, one stomping on the empty vial he'd dropped in his haste.

Instead, I held my poison up to the lantern suspended directly above my work surface. With the bright, unnaturally white flame shining through the glass vial, I could make out thousands of particulates suspended in the fluid.

I turned the vial over and watched the substance flow toward the cork, noting its thin consistency. Mentally eliminating several possible poisons from my list before I'd even opened the container.

As my observer watched, scribbling madly in his journal, I thumbed the cork from my vial and sniffed the damp end as if it had come from a fine bottle of wine. I noted the scent, and with the vial carefully held in my other hand, I dipped my quill in ink and scribbled all of my observations on a sheet of the provided parchment.

And finally, while several more of my classmates ran to select their equipment, I took a sip of the poison.

Rather than gulp it, I held a few drops of liquid on my tongue, noting the smooth texture and the fact that the particulates were too fine to feel. Noting the acrid taste. I swallowed, then immediately inhaled, in order to analyze the aftertaste—as much scent as true taste—as it bloomed with the inhalation.

I made more notes, while the observer watched me with a thoughtful arch of his brows. Then I took a deep breath and swallowed the rest of the liquid.

My observer accepted the empty vial, corked it, and slid it into his pocket. He scribbled in his journal again, lamplight shining on his dark, bald skull.

I . . . bent in half beneath a wave of pure panic.

A muted murmuring traveled around the otherwise hushed audience.

My hands clutched my knees, nails digging into my flesh through the layers of my cloak and skirt. My back arched as I sucked in great gulps of air and stared at the floor.

I'd just poisoned myself. Voluntarily.

A ticking echoed in my head like the hands of the Seminary clock, counting down toward my demise, and with every mental click, I flinched.

Get. Up.

The voice was mine, and yet it wasn't. It was Past Amber shouting at me through the fog of amnesia. I could practically feel her disgust, not just at my ignorance but at my inaction. I could feel her pacing through the dark, inaccessible recesses of my mind, itching to show me what she would do in my position.

Past Amber could yell at me. But she could not help me.

Finally, I stood, and my gaze locked immediately on the official observer, quill poised over the half-full page in his journal, where he'd clearly meticulously noted my panic.

I blinked. Then I raced toward the supply cupboard with the observer at my heels.

Wilder was still there. He turned to me with a smile as I reached for a set of beakers and a burner. We weren't allowed to speak to each other, but he took a moment, before turning toward his workstation with an armload of equipment, to give me a saucy wink.

The scoundrel was having fun!

I returned his smile—a subtler version—and gathered my initial load of supplies, then carried them to my workstation. My official observer did not help, but he did make note of everything I selected, as well as everything I added on my second trip to the supply cupboard.

I arranged my equipment, setting up beakers and burners, but I still had no idea what ingredients I would need. What format my antidote should take. And since I'd ingested the poison later than everyone else, I would be last to feel its effects, thus last able to analyze those effects on others. A disadvantage, to be sure, when everyone else would be able to use their own symptoms to help identify the poison well before I could. However, Lennox and Keryth had taken very little time to study the poison before they'd swallowed it, and as far as I knew, they had taken no notes on the details of its initial presentation. Which was potentially a disadvantage to them.

We'd chosen different methods of analysis, and I could only hope mine was not in error.

While I waited for the poison to take effect, I went back through the notes I'd taken in preparation for the trial. None of the six potential poisons I'd focused on looked exactly like what we'd actually been given. But it was possible that some small variance in the composition had given the poison its particulates. Or its pale color.

It was also possible that variance was introduced on purpose, to throw the students off. That those details were cosmetic in nature and unrelated to the function of the poison.

Of course, it was just as likely that they'd chosen a poison I'd never even considered during my preparation.

I flipped through my notes, searching for anything with even marginal similarities to the taste, scent, and consistency of the poison, and while a couple were vaguely similar, nothing truly stood out.

Fighting panic over the utter blank slate in my mind, I set aside my trial preparation notes and pulled a large stack of loose parchment from my satchel: Past Amber's research notes. They were copious and meticulously organized. And detailed. They could also take an eternity to go through, especially considering that I had yet to feel any effects from the poison.

This trial was a deadly gamble. I could not identify the poison, nor could I start devising the remedy, until the sickness emerged. But the sickness itself would likely impede my ability to think, and perhaps to physically perform.

Until it killed me.

A groan from the front of the room caught my attention, and I looked up to find Lennox bent over his workstation, clutching his stomach. Even from where I stood, across the arena, I could see sweat glowing on his forehead.

I was not allowed to copy a classmate's technique or recipe, but the officials couldn't stop me from using what I happened to notice about someone else's symptoms. Right? So long as I wasn't watching anyone blatantly enough to be accused of cheating?

Abdominal cramps. Sweating. Common symptoms, which could come from almost any poison.

A pleasant humming came from my right, and I turned to see Wilder smiling as he added ingredients to a beaker suspended over an unlit burner. He seemed unaware of the solemnity both of the event and of his fellow students. He'd blocked it all out. Evidently effortlessly.

I had no such luxury.

I surreptitiously studied my classmates, beginning with those who'd taken the poison fastest. Lennox was the first, and . . .

Keryth suddenly pivoted away from her workstation and vomited on the stone tiles. A soft gasp rose from the audience.

Keryth had taken the poison after Lennox, but she was smaller—half his weight, maybe—so she was feeling the effects faster and likely more severely than he was.

She stood, turned resolutely back to her workstation, and picked up a beaker. But she only stared at it.

I frowned, trying to understand why she stood seemingly frozen, holding the beaker. I needed a closer look, but any observation of my fellow students and their methods would have to be covert. So I headed for the cupboard again, taking a path that took me by her station. And as I drew closer, I understood the problem.

Her hand was shaking so badly that she was clearly afraid to try to use the beaker—or even set it down—until the tremor passed, for fear of shattering the equipment.

Neurotoxin. Whatever they'd given us affected the brain and its control over the body. That should narrow things down.

Lennox, I noticed, had also developed a slight tremor, but his shaking was nowhere near as severe.

Women, it seemed, would get the worst of this challenge, by virtue of being generally smaller. Which meant I had mere minutes before I'd be in the same position as Keryth.

I rushed toward the cupboard and grabbed the most commonly useful elixir ingredients.

I still had no symptoms. Wilder, however, had stopped humming. Sweat had broken out across his forehead, and though he wasn't clutching his stomach, he seemed distinctly uncomfortable. And more than a little irritated by that fact.

I flipped through Past Amber's notes again, pulling out every page on poisons. Then I sorted through them, plucking out pages that detailed symptoms like those my classmates seemed to be suffering.

Nausea, vomiting, and abdominal distress were quite common among them, but the tremor was distinctive. That narrowed the field to four. All were neurotoxins.

At the front of the room, Lennox began to cough, spraying his workstation with spittle. Keryth was bent over, clutching the edge of her table with both hands, gasping for breath. And though the audience remained respectfully quiet, I could practically feel the weight of the gazes trained on us.

I added respiratory distress to the list of symptoms and turned back to Past Amber's notes just as the first wave of nausea rolled over me, a tidal wave of queasiness and dizziness that left me clammy and unsteady on my feet.

I bowed my head for a moment, breathing through the discomfort. Then I focused on the list again. Sheets of parchment shook in my hands. My fingers clenched unexpectedly—my very body betraying me—and crumpled the pages.

With a groan, I set my notes on my workstation and flattened them.

Four possibilities. One was a snake venom, one was secreted from a poisonous frog, one was from a spider, and one was distilled from a variety of spiky hibiscus grown on this very island.

The antidotes to all four used three of the same ingredients, so I began measuring those out, moving slowly, to avoid dropping or spilling anything.

That was it. That was all I could do, until I knew for certain what I'd ingested. Until I understood what other specific ingredients should be added. How rapidly the solution should be heated, and to what temperature. Whether or not it should be condensed, purified, or diluted. How much of the provided beyn to use.

I turned to look at Wilder, hoping for some clue about technique—though he and I rarely approached any assignment the same way—but before I could process the setup of his equipment, my gaze snagged on his face, which was bright red and appeared a bit puffy.

My own face began to burn, but without access to a looking glass, I couldn't tell whether or not I was imagining that symptom simply because I'd seen it in him. But I was *not* imagining the sudden pins-and-needles sensation in the tips of my fingers.

My heart racing—the room spinning—I turned back to my notes and scanned them for mentions of numbness, redness, or swollen skin.

None of the four remaining toxins listed any of that. Frustration lit a fire in my belly.

I was missing something.

Nausea rolled over me again, and I clenched my jaw against the forcible return of my breakfast. My hands shook, my fingers still tingling, and . . . did they look a little red?

Directly in front of me, Yoslyn gasped. She coughed, spraying her workstation with spittle, just like Lennox had, drawing more soft reactions from the crowd, but she was close enough for me to notice the crimson tint of her saliva. Was the blood from her lungs? Or from her mouth? Were her lungs filling with fluid? With blood? Or had ulcers developed on her tongue?

Focus! Yoslyn would be fine. Or she would die. Either way, her struggle was no different than anyone else's. We'd *all* consumed poison. Every member of my cohort was likely less than an hour from death—by design. The only way to walk out of the amphitheater, for any of us, was to maintain focus and put our skills to work.

Wilder had two elixirs going, each over a lit burner, each boiling at a different intensity, based on the height and color of the flame. But I could not tell what he'd put into his beakers, nor could I understand why he was making two different antidotes.

All I knew for sure was that the symptoms I was experiencing didn't match anything in Past Amber's research on toxins.

With a groan, fighting another brutal wave of nausea, I dug back through her notes, reading as fast as I could, desperately scanning the text not just for the word *toxin* but for the symptoms I'd seen and was beginning to truly suffer. Finally, the second time I went through the pages, forcing myself to slow down and process the words, one stuck out.

Tremors.

I kept reading.

Respiratory distress with the production of bloody sputum. And . . . *swollen red skin.*

My gaze snapped up to the top of the page, where the subject she'd expounded upon was written in large, scrolling print and underlined twice. The top line was thin and wispy, done in a hurry. The second, lower line, however, was thicker and darker. As if it had been written with more intentionality, with a freshly dipped quill.

But it was the words themselves that captured my attention: *Acute ingestion of base metals.*

Metal toxicity.

I hadn't included this page among the poisons because metal wasn't a poison. But it *could* be a toxin.

My gaze dropped again to the section with the symptoms that matched the ones I was feeling. The ones I was seeing all around me.

Arsenic.

I'd swallowed a vial full of arsenic.

Twenty-Nine

Normally, acute arsenic poisoning would take several days to become fatal, but this was the Black Trial. Whatever the administering team of professors had done to the toxin had clearly accelerated its impact, for the purposes of the event.

I'd swallowed not just arsenic, but *alchemically compounded* arsenic.

Shit.

Hands shaking, I swept my notes on toxins and poisons off the edge of the workstation and into my open satchel, distantly noting my official observer as he scribbled in his journal from his stool at the end of the table. Then I flipped the page on metal toxicity over, hoping against hope that Past Amber had taken notes on a remedy.

And she—*I*—had. Copious, prolific notes, full of concepts that strained the level of knowledge I'd managed to reacquire and exceeded my post-amnesia experience entirely. It would take me hours just to read through all of it and determine which parts were relevant to this specific scenario, much less identify the formula for an antidote, and . . .

Wait. The alchemical symbol for arsenic was underlined, in that same bold style as the second line beneath the title of this section of notes, trailing downward on the left end of the stroke. As if the writer had started on the right and moved her quill to the left.

As if she—no, *he*—were left-handed.

Desmond.

He'd been in the lab that morning, making a remedy for potential conception, for me. While he was there, he'd gathered my notes into my satchel and brought it to me. Had he also done this? Underlined the relevant bits of Past Amber's research on metal toxicity?

Why? He'd said he had no idea what the poison would be.

A cough billowed up from my chest and exploded from my throat, spraying pink-tinged droplets all over the notes, and distantly, I heard another murmur from the crowd.

Panicked, I swiped the sleeve of my robe across the page, leaving pink smears across the ink. Smudging the print.

There was no time to wonder how or why Desmond had decided to help me, or to feel like I was getting an unfair advantage. Yes, I wanted to survive on my own merits. But more than that, I wanted to *survive*.

I scanned the text, homing in on each underlined word and phrase, reading just enough of the surrounding bits to understand the context. Then I raced back to the supply cupboard, grabbed what I needed, and got to work.

Keryth was blinking blearily at a vial as she carefully swirled it, watching the contents separate, then recombine. Vomit had dried on her shoes and the front of her robe.

Lennox's light brown cheeks had been overtaken by a swollen red rash. The fingers of his left hand were spasming, and he was compulsively clearing his throat.

Cressa looked fairly composed, though she coughed into the billowing material of her cloak as she worked, heating a bright pink substance to a slow boil over a low flame while she crushed something else to powder in a stone mortar.

Wilder looked triumphant, if nauseated, as he held a vial up to the white-flamed lantern suspended above his workstation.

A second vial—its contents a vibrant moss green—hung in a stand at the end of his table.

At least half of the class had finished a first attempt at an antidote, and they likely would not get time for a second. Which meant I was running behind.

I measured, ground, and diluted as carefully as I could, given the tremor in my fingers. Clenching my jaw until it ached fiercely, in order to avoid contaminating my workstation with vomit. When my elixir was finally bubbling softly, I took a moment to lean against my work surface, pretending to double-check my notes while I caught my breath. While I surreptitiously spied on my classmates.

Lennox had just swallowed his antidote, and Keryth was eyeing her own somewhat skeptically. Lennox's observer stood in front of him, journal open, quill poised in one hand, and pulled down his student's lower eyelids to peer at the whites of his eyes.

Finally, the observer nodded, made one final note, and gestured to the attendant to let him out.

Keryth watched him go, panic firing behind her eyes. Tensing the line of her spine.

She threw her antidote back, wincing as she swallowed, and I realized she had not let it fully cool.

Wilder tapped his workstation, drawing my attention. I turned, and he raised his vial in my direction, as if he were proposing a toast with a glass of wine. He looked utterly confident, highly nauseated, and terribly worried. That last sentiment was likely on my behalf, as his gaze shifted to the elixir I'd just begun to heat.

He swallowed his bright pink antidote, then turned to his observer, who paused in her scribbling to assess the antidote's effects.

The other vial still rested in its stand, but at some point he had corked and labeled it, though I could not read the print from my own workstation.

Minutes later, Wilder's observer nodded and released him from the arena.

As I watched him leave, jealousy sliced me with all the pain and drama of a knife right to the heart, despite my relief for him and my pride on his behalf.

And to my amusement, as he passed the dignitaries seated on the front row, he paused to not-so-subtly pass the corked vial of moss-green fluid to one of the men to the left of the aisle staircase.

I laughed, though it earned me several strange looks from my competitors. But I couldn't help it. Wilder had struggled so little with the trial that he'd had time to concoct one of his unsanctioned elixirs *while* he made his antidote. Right there in full view of our professors, the staff researchers, honored alumni, and the Bluehelm herself.

My kingdom for an ounce of his confidence. And just a dollop of his skill.

Or, preferably, the return of my *own* skill.

Two more students cured themselves and were allowed to leave while I waited for my antidote to bubble to the right consistency, and a third left while I waited for the elixir to cool. While I coughed, spraying my entire workstation with blood-tinged spittle, and prayed that none had fallen into the open vial.

Or, if some had, that the elixir was still hot enough to boil off any impurities.

Cressa glanced back at me as she left the arena, just in time to see that last scientific transgression, and she gave me a sympathetic smile.

No matter. The technique didn't have to be perfect, as long as the result was functional.

There were three of us left by the time my elixir had cooled enough for me to pour it into a preheated vial without cracking it.

Three still by the time that vial was cool enough to touch without an iron vial clamp.

Yoslyn stood hunched over her workstation, her forehead pressed to her folded arms. The flame was too low beneath her beaker. The liquid inside had yet to start bubbling, and I worried she would not have time to finish her antidote before the poison had progressed beyond repair.

Heartache gripped my chest like a set of overheated beaker tongs. Squeezing. Burning. She was not going to make it, and there was nothing I could do about that. I wasn't sure I would make it out alive myself, even with Past Amber's notes and Desmond's surreptitious underlining. I could not worry about a classmate. Especially considering that we were not allowed to help each other.

The third remaining student was Petyr Lorena, at the front right table. His face was bright red, and as I watched, he shoved his spectacles back up the sweaty slope of his nose. I could feel all of the eyes trained on us from the spectators beyond the honeycomb of glass panels. Some looked concerned, others coldly clinical in their silent assessment.

Fighting a crippling wave of nausea and a vicious tremor in my left hand, I gingerly touched my cooling vial. The fluid inside was still hot, but not scalding. So I snatched it from the stand, holding it as firmly as I dared, given that my hand could spasm at any moment. Then I took a sip. When the hot liquid did not burn my tongue, I tilted the vial back again.

I'd swallowed half of the elixir when Yoslyn collapsed to the floor in front of my workstation, startling my observer so badly that he nearly dropped his quill. The vial Yoslyn had been holding had shattered, and even from where I stood, I could see that the spilled liquid had scalded two of her fingers and her thumb. She lay on the ground, unmoving except for the twitch of her right arm.

I rushed around my workstation, still holding my own vial.

"Ms. Fallbrook!" my official observer snapped, his stool squealing behind me as he stood. "You are not allowed to intervene with another student."

I knelt next to Yoslyn and used the edge of my cape to wipe scalding elixir from her hand. Blood lined her lips, and as I tried to lift her head, she coughed, spraying a foamy, pink-tinged spittle all over us both.

Vaguely, I was aware that several members of our audience had stood from their seats in order to see us over Yoslyn's workstation. They whispered fiercely to one another, but no one tried to stop me when I brushed hair back from her forehead. Or when I pulled her chin down and poured the last half of my elixir into her mouth.

I had no idea whether or not I'd made the right cure. Or whether half of a properly brewed antidote would be enough to save either of us. All I knew was that I wasn't dead yet, and that I could not step out of the arena and let her die, if there was any chance I could help her.

Yoslyn's observer, a woman with hair as dark as her eyes, contrasting harshly with very pale skin, pulled me up by one arm. My own observer scribbled furiously in his journal. Then he turned to me, while Yoslyn's observer knelt to examine her, journal and quill at the ready.

"It'll take a few minutes," I said to the balding man as he pulled my chin down to peer into my mouth. And yet . . . I'd stopped coughing.

He pulled my lower eyelids down, one at a time, then looked into my ears and peered intently at my face. He turned me around, and I felt something hard and round pressed against my back.

"Breathe," he ordered softly.

I inhaled, then let the breath out. Had the rest of the cohort been examined this thoroughly?

"Cough," he ordered, so I forced a cough.

Nothing came up from my throat. I tasted no blood.

The hard circle left my back, and when I heard the scratch of quill on parchment, I turned to find him writing in his journal once again. But when I tried to read the words, he retreated to his stool. A moment later, he set his quill on my workstation, stood, and gave a nod to the Bluehelm through the glass panels. Then he gestured at the attendant to open the door for me.

"Wait," I said as the attendant waved me forward. "What about Yoslyn?"

"She is none of your concern," her observer insisted.

Yoslyn was sitting up. She coughed softly, but I saw no blood. Her eyes looked clear, and though she had not yet stood, she looked steadier by the moment.

With an exhalation that emptied my lungs, I crossed the arena, avoiding both shattered glass and a sour puddle of vomit, and stepped through the open glass doorway. Many members of the audience were still standing. Some stared at Yoslyn. Others stared at me. But the only look I returned as I climbed the steps, following a path already trodden by nine of my classmates, was Desmond's—not of relief, but of pure and utter pride.

Thirty

"Amber! Thank every force of order in the known world!" Wilder appeared in front of me like a wild-eyed apparition the instant I stepped into the Conservatory atrium, and his hug was like an embrace from the universe itself. "I knew you could do it!" he declared, but the relief in his expression and the exaggerated volume of his voice said otherwise.

He'd thought I was going to die. That, at the very least, it was a strong possibility.

I hugged him back, happy as ever to prove him wrong, which had been a specific pleasure of mine since we were hardly old enough to talk.

"Where is everyone?" I asked when he finally let me go. When I could look around the atrium and note only five of our classmates were seated on benches built into the walls. Keryth and Lennox were huddled together closest to the staircase, arms around each other. Cressa sat nearest the exterior door, and Pryce and Gavin had claimed isolated spots across the atrium, along the opposite wall.

Wilder made six, and he was the only one standing. Everyone else looked exhausted and still nauseated.

I was the seventh to emerge into the atrium, and Yoslyn and Petyr were still in the amphitheater. Which meant three were missing.

"Adria?" I said. "And Raelah? And . . . Kornell." But then I remembered. "He failed, didn't he?"

Wilder nodded. "We haven't seen him. But Adria and Raelah are in the infirmary. Did you not see them on your way back?"

I hadn't looked. I'd hardly noticed a thing on my walk through the main corridor of the Panacea wing, other than the fact that I was alive. That my nausea was abating, my hands steadying, and my lungs clearing. The absence of illness had left me floating in a vaguely pleasant fugue state, a cloudy oblivion in which my feet carried me forward with little help from my mind.

"Will they survive?" I asked, clutching at Wilder's hand. I found that I needed the contact—the warmth—to ground me in this moment. To assure me that I was real, and that this wasn't all some reverie of my dying mind as I lay unconscious on the floor of the glass-walled arena. "Will they *pass*?"

"I suppose that remains to be seen." Keryth sounded a bit breathless, and my gaze found her over Wilder's shoulder as he turned toward her voice. She was still cuddled so close to Lennox that they seemed to comprise one form with two heads, each with one arm lost to sight around the other's back.

Lennox frowned up at me, his cheek pressed to hers, his eyes narrowed. "How did *you* pass?"

"She survived the same way you did," Wilder snapped. "With a lot of talent and hard work."

"And no memory at all," Lennox added, his voice hollow and echoing with danger, like a plunge down a long, narrow shaft.

I waited for his words to hit the watery grave at the bottom. For the splash of my dignity into the well of his anger and resentment. But I never heard it. His ire at me, it seemed, was bottomless.

At last he added, "Or was that a lie, told to lull the rest of us into complacency?"

He stood, divorcing himself from Keryth's comfort, glowing

with rage as if someone had struck a match to his very veins. "Was this all an act? Another cruel aspect of your mad science? Are we all still lab rats in your moonstruck alchemical conjecture?"

Keryth stood and put an arm around him, drawing him back toward the bench with her. "Forgive him," she said while I stared at them both, wide-eyed, guilt churning in my newly calmed gut, though I could recall no offense on my part. "His antidote produces some unpleasant secondary effects. A short tempter and unmeasured words seem chief among them."

And yet she did not deny the truth of his rant. Nor did she appear particularly concerned that I had heard it.

What *moonstruck conjecture* was he referring to? What mad—

"Amber!"

I spun toward the doorway at my back just as Yoslyn burst from the Panacea wing into the atrium, and before I could brace myself for impact, she threw herself into my embrace, arms tightening around me like a corset made of human flesh and bones.

"Thank you!" she sobbed into my ear, her tears wetting my cheek, chin digging into my shoulder. "I should be dead." She suddenly lurched away from me, hands clutching my shoulders so that I had space but lacked freedom. "I would have died, right there on the floor of the arena, if you hadn't . . ."

Fresh tears formed in her eyes, and suddenly her gaze tore away from mine as she realized we were not alone. That the rest of the Mastery cohort was staring at her through gazes that felt equal parts bewildered and . . . frosty, as if a winter chill had drifted down from the mountain to blanket us all.

Because if she'd needed my help . . . she should be dead right now. That was the rule. Students who could not save themselves should not have entered the arena.

"What happened?" Wilder asked, and even his voice lacked its usual jovial warmth. "Amber?"

"She shared her antidote with me," Yoslyn said. "She gave me half, as I lay dying on the ground."

Wilder's brows furrowed, more in confusion than in irritation or anger.

Footsteps shuffled slowly toward us, and though I didn't turn, I could feel our classmates closing in on us. Waiting for me to explain. To deny her claim that I had helped her cheat.

"You survived on *half* a dose?" Cressa Baxter asked, and I turned to find her studying me with narrowed gray eyes. Suddenly she lurched forward, reddish ringlets swinging as she reached for my face. I stumbled backward, my heart racing, but Wilder was at my back and he had no time to retreat. Cressa seized my chin, and while I clutched at her wrists, she pulled down my lower left eyelid and peered into my eye.

I forced myself to relax, both because any movement could result in my injury and because there appeared to be no malice in her examination. She seemed viscerally curious and astonished, but not angry.

"How?" Cressa let me go and swung toward Yoslyn, who back-pedaled out of reach.

"I don't know," I admitted.

"Oh, did you *forget*?" Keryth snapped. "Because that's starting to sound terribly convenient."

"No. I mean, I know what recipe I used. But I don't know why my antidote was enough for us both. Maybe the observer can—"

"Did you pass?" Lennox cut me off, staring daggers at Yoslyn. "Even though she saved you?"

Yoslyn's hesitant nod tugged at my heart. "The observer said my antidote would have worked. I—" She swallowed thickly. "I got it right."

"But not in time to save yourself," Keryth snapped, and heads all around us bobbed in agreement.

"Take that up with the officials," Wilder insisted. "It's their call. I, for one, am happy she's alive!" But then he frowned and turned back to Yoslyn. "What about Petyr? Was he still in the arena when you left?"

She shook her head slowly, lips pressed together, green eyes damp. "He's in the infirmary. It . . . doesn't look good."

Pain flickered behind Wilder's eyes, deeply lining his forehead. Then, in the solemn silence that had settled over our entire cohort, he stood a little taller, making an obvious effort to shield his thoughts. He put one arm around me and one around Yoslyn and ushered us toward the front door.

As he pushed it open, I turned to look over the disapproving faces staring back at me, fiery islands of anger in a sea of cold white marble.

Pryce had stood from his bench near the door to the Panacea wing. The blue skin and hair that had saddled him with an absurd look—had turned him into the very farce of a serious student—suddenly gave him a fierce and menacing edge.

He was glaring right at me.

"Are you sure about this dress?" I pulled my shawl tighter around my shoulders, shielding my décolletage from the frigid night air.

"I am entirely certain." The giggle in Yoslyn's voice told me she'd bolstered her own courage with a precelebration glass of wine. Or two. As did the warm breath that washed over me when she clutched at my arm.

She'd found the dress pushed to the back of my wardrobe and had seemed surprised that I did not recognize it, until she remembered my condition. At which point she'd assured me it was among my favorites.

But Present Amber *truly* had no memory of Past Amber's favorite dress, or of how bold she must have felt, walking around with the upper curves of her bosom exposed.

It wasn't just the dress, though. Even before I'd lost my memory, I'd evidently rarely left campus, and I hadn't realized how much I'd depended upon my "instinctual" understanding of the Alchemary's geography, as Desmond put it, until I'd let Yoslyn tug me through the gate and onto the bridge. Past the soldiers standing guard, the Crown's crest emblazoned upon the front of their black uniforms.

Saltstrand was only half a mile from Alchemary Island, but that distance felt interminable in my heeled boots, with the cold, humid night breeze slicing like a knife through the thin fabric of my unfamiliar attire. With the ocean churning beneath us, night-black waves crashing on the piers beneath the bridge and against the cliffside of both the island and the mainland.

Moonlight glinted on the water, and looking down made me feel dizzy, though I had yet to touch a drop of alcohol. I let my right hand trail over the cold stone bridge railing as I walked, steadying myself just from the light touch.

"You really don't remember anything, do you?" Yoslyn gripped my left arm as if we were sisters. As if we'd spent every waking moment of the past six weeks glued to each other's sides.

As if we were friends.

"Not a thing," I repeated for at least the fifth time. "I've been forced to relearn it all from scratch, and I'm as grateful as I could possibly be for the notes I took before I lost my memory."

"How'd it happen?"

"I have no idea," I admitted, staring past the end of the bridge at a sparse scattering of cottages and long stretches of farmland. Sheep bleated in the night, and I found the sound oddly comforting. It reminded me of Innswood and my childhood, despite the addition of the salt-tinged air. Farmland reminded me of a time when my parents had lived together, I'd had many friends, and I'd known exactly who I was.

"You don't know how you lost your memory?" Yoslyn asked, and I shook my head as we stepped off the end of the bridge onto firmly packed dirt, squinting at the dark road as I tried to avoid falling into a hole in the ground or tripping over a rock. "I bet it had to do with your—"

Her mouth snapped shut.

I stopped, pulling her to a graceless halt alongside me. "My what? My research?"

The quarter-moon rode low in the sky, doing little to light her features, yet I could see regret written into every line of her expression.

"It doesn't matter. Truly. I'm forever stuffing my foot into my mouth, and I'm eager to wash away the taste of my own toes with a good, stiff ale. Let's—" She tried to tug me toward town, her long curls bobbing with the motion, but I held my ground.

"Are we friends, Yoslyn?"

"The very best of," she confirmed. "I owe you my life."

"You owe me nothing." I let go of her arm and tugged my shawl tighter. "I did nothing any decent person wouldn't have done."

"That isn't true." Her eyes widened, displaying her gratitude with an exuberance that made me distinctly uncomfortable. "You could have *died,* sharing your antidote with me, and no one else—"

"No one else saw you collapse. Any of our classmates would have—"

"No," she insisted. "They would not have. I can't swear that *I* would have done that for a classmate, at the risk of my own life. And six weeks ago, neither would you. You would have said that of the two of us, you had more to contribute to the world through alchemy, and risking your life wouldn't be fair to alchemy in general, to the Alchemary specifically, or to the world itself."

A cold current churned through my veins, drawing gooseflesh across my arms. "That is both callous and *categorically* arrogant."

Yoslyn nodded solemnly. "It's likely also true. And yet you saved me, with no regard for your own life. Which is why, as far as I'm concerned, we are the very best of friends, from this point forward."

"I don't want your camaraderie out of any sense of obligation," I said, careful to moderate my tone so she heard no insult in the statement.

"That's not what I'm offering." Yoslyn shifted to fully face me from inches away, her dimly lit expression fierce and determined. "I'm saying that in my judgment, anyone who would make such a sacrifice must be a good person, and thus worthy of staunch friendship."

I blinked at her in the dark, hoping she couldn't see the sudden shine of tears in my eyes. "Very well, then. Friends." I took her arm again, and we moved forward together, boots crunching on dirt and stray rocks.

Ahead, flickering lamplight and boisterous conversation leaked from a low-ceilinged, wood-paneled establishment that could only be the Dusty Beaker, though I could not yet read the sign attached to the front wall, gently swaying from two short lengths of chain.

"Tell me, then, friend, why you believe my research is responsible for my amnesia."

Yoslyn's arm stiffened in my grasp, but I only hugged her tighter and kept moving forward, to assure her that I was curious, not angry.

"I truly want to know. Do you know what I was working on?"

She shook her head. "No one in the cohort knew. Wilder, maybe. But no one else."

"Then why would you think—"

"Because it's all you did. Other than eat, sleep, and a couple of visits to the Dusty Beaker—just a couple, in two years—all you did was research. So unless you woke up with a head wound or a festering fever, there's simply nothing else that could account for what's happened to you."

As badly as I hated to consider her theory, I could not deny that it made sense.

"Why do our classmates hate me?"

Yoslyn huffed over my change of subject. "They don't—"

I stopped walking again and turned to frown at her.

She shrugged, dragging my arm up with the motion. "You weren't *cruel*. Not *truly*. But it's possible their views diverge from mine on that matter."

"And your view?"

"You did not intentionally cause pain, that I know of. But neither did you go out of your way to avoid causing it. And when pain *was* felt, you capitalized on what you called a resource, insisting that it was in the name of science. Of alchemy."

"What, in the name of all discord, does that mean?" And how had I never heard this from Wilder? "What did I do?"

Another shrug. "The incident that ruffled the most feathers was when you allowed Adria and Pryce to labor under a misunderstanding that led them to cease their relationship."

"Led them to . . . ?"

Yoslyn sighed, displaying her reluctance to rehash what was, to her, old news. "You contrived a scenario that made it *appear* as if Pryce might prefer your company to Adria's. And you encouraged her to believe that was the case. According to Pryce's telling of it, anyway."

Pryce's angry countenance flashed to the forefront of my memory. *You are reaping what you've already sown—it's not my fault you don't remember the original sin.*

Guilt crashed over me like waves against the cliffside. "Why would I do that?"

"I don't know. You seemed, at the time, to be comforting her. You even lent her your handkerchief for her tears. But I was with her, when she came upon you and Pryce at the back of the library, and . . ." Yoslyn sighed. "Pryce certainly contributed to the dissolution of his own relationship. But you . . . Well, you appeared to be entropy incarnate that day." She glanced at my exposed cleavage. "In that very dress, come to think of it."

"Why on *earth* would I have done such a thing?" In addition to being cruel, driving a wedge between two lovers was in *direct opposition* to alchemy's goal of fighting chaos and imposing order upon the natural world.

No wonder this dress had been shoved to the back of my wardrobe.

Yoslyn's silence spoke volumes. "Adria never forgave you," she finally said. "Neither did Pryce."

In fact, Pryce considered his assault upon my dignity to be a seed I'd sewn, and Adria had not said one word to me in the past six weeks.

A cold gust brought with it the hoot of a distant owl, and I glanced toward town again as I shivered, eager for a warm respite, but reluctant to quit the most informative conversation I'd had in weeks. "What could that debacle possibly have to do with my research?"

"I honestly could not say." Yoslyn shifted from one foot to the other in the middle of the dirt road, trying to stay warm. "All I know is that when Adria left, you asked for your handkerchief back, then you sat there in the library and took notes, as if you'd just concluded a lab experiment."

I'd come across no such notes among the sheets of loose parchment in Past Amber's collection. But it was the handkerchief that stood out in Yoslyn's story, for no reason I could understand, except that it struck a harmonic chord with a newly formed memory.

When my father had visited, upon hearing of my strange ailment, he'd wiped his damp eyes with a handkerchief of his own, which had fallen onto the bench unnoticed as he left.

I'd kept that handkerchief, with no real thought of calling after him to return it. And I could not say why—either then or now—that impulse had struck me.

"What format were the notes in, do you happen to recall?" I asked. "On parchment?"

Yoslyn frowned. "No, in a journal. I remember that you set an inkwell on the table, and you were taking *true* notes, as if you were in a lab setting, rather than light notation with a lead stylus, like most people would utilize for quick reminders."

I *was* running an experiment. I had no memory of that incident, or of the others that had clearly led my cohort to distrust me, yet I knew that. And not just because I recognized my own documentation methods. I *felt* the truth of it, in the same way I'd known where to find supplies in Desmond's laboratory.

"I'm sorry if this has upset you," Yoslyn said, squinting at my expression in the dark.

"Don't be. I dragged the information from you, and unsettling though it is, I needed to hear it."

"You're not that person anymore," she insisted. "If you were, I wouldn't be here."

Uncertain I was worthy of her assumption, given that regaining my memories might turn me back into Past Amber, I started us both down the road again in lieu of a response.

"They don't want me in there," I whispered as we came to a stop in front of the Dusty Beaker. And for the first time, I understood why.

Yoslyn huffed. "They don't want me in there either. Not anymore. But that doesn't mean we should cower in our bedchambers or bury our heads in our notes. We deserve a night off as much the rest of them do. We survived!" She spun toward me and took my hands, her exuberant expression lit by the flickering glow from the tavern window. "Let's celebrate!"

The village of Saltstrand began as a base camp and bunkhouse for builders—mostly Toolkeepers—during the initial construction of the Alchemary. As the university continued to expand, Saltstrand grew into a vital support system for the school, storing and providing all manner of resources and labor. Local farmland grows the food served on campus. Local seamstresses produce students' uniforms from locally grown, specially dyed wool. Students and staff members spend their coin in the local tavern. Their guests room in local inns. Everyone in Saltstrand either works on Alchemary Island or in support of the academy, in some way.

—from *The History and Economy of the Alchemary*

Thirty-One

I followed Yoslyn from the cold, dark dirt road into the warm, crowded tavern, and at first, I could only stand in the doorway, letting the voices and the flickering light wash over me. Listening to the cordial cacophony, as the clink of tin ale mugs rose through the buzz of overlapping conversations.

My mouth watered at the scents of brown bread and mutton stew, and I noted that several people were dipping crusts into half-full bowls. But *everyone* had a mug of ale.

"They're all from the Alchemary!" I said directly into Yoslyn's ear.

She nodded. "The locals won't set foot in here after dark unless they work here. We tend to suck up all the air. The whole town's like this," she half shouted, evidently unconcerned with being heard. "Every house in the village becomes an inn during Family Weekend, graduation, accreditation testing, and any trials week, and they can charge whatever they want, because the demand for lodging is greater than the supply."

Trials week. *This* week. That's how so many alumni had been in the audience. I looked around, studying ale-flushed faces. Were they in the crowd as well?

"Half our professors live on this side of the bridge," Yoslyn added.

Business was clearly booming, yet the harried staff of the Beaker didn't seem entirely enamored of their patrons. I could not blame them.

The front room was crowded, and though I recognized many underclassmen, I couldn't find a single member of the Mastery-year cohort.

"Through that door!" Yoslyn shouted.

I followed her pointing finger toward a private room, just past the long plain-board table where a dozen or so professors and staff researchers sat on simple wooden stools with their tankards.

"Staff and faculty usually gather in there, but after each trial, they relinquish the space for the Mastery-year celebration. Come on!"

Yoslyn pulled me through the crowd, and I muttered apologies as my shoulders and elbows collided with no fewer than three patrons.

"Amber!" Wilder called from the doorway to the private room.

Desmond's head swiveled my way from the staff table, and I gave him a nod as I was swallowed by his brother's ale-scented embrace.

Wilder tugged me into the small, warm room, and Yoslyn followed.

"That's everyone!" Wilder declared, practically shoving me onto an empty stool. His eyes were glazed with drink, his smile sweet but sloppy.

Despite his gregarious greeting, no one else seemed to care that Yoslyn and I had joined the group, and I accepted their indifference as the lesser of two evils, considering the animosity I'd been expecting. My classmates were too drunk to be angry. Except maybe Pryce, who sat on a stool in the corner, gulping morosely from a dented metal mug.

A headcount revealed nine Mastery students including Yoslyn and me. Out of twelve. No, out of eleven, since Kornell had washed out. "There are still two in the infirmary?" I whispered to Wilder as he pushed a mug of ale into my grip.

His smile faded. "Just Adria," he said. "Petyr didn't make it."

A pall fell over me, like a cloth pulled over a corpse. But before I could demand to know how everyone could feel so celebratory, knowing that a classmate had died, Wilder turned to the room and lifted his mug. "To Petyr!" he shouted.

"To Petyr!" the chorus echoed, and everyone took a drink. Including me. And that's when I understood that this gathering was as much a memorial as a celebration.

And that it would not be the last.

Would they toast to me, if I'd died in that glass arena?

Yoslyn took a mug from a tray in the center of the table and raised it in my direction, her eyes alight with the glow of the bone-and-candle chandelier, as well as the triumph of survival. Then she veered across the room, presumably to take advantage of the drunken goodwill of our classmates.

"I wasn't sure you'd come." Wilder leaned in to be heard over the crowd.

"I had no plans to," I admitted. "You can thank Yoslyn for dragging me from the Dormitory tower."

"I certainly shall." His gaze held mine. "You were amazing in there today."

"I most assuredly was not. I accomplished the bare minimum required to pass—to survive. Literally the bare minimum. And I very nearly didn't, truth be told."

"But you *did*. And Yoslyn can attest that it was far more than the bare minimum. How did you know you'd have enough for her as well?"

I had no answer for him. None at all.

"You didn't." His smile faded. He seemed suddenly, blisteringly sober. "Amber, you could have—"

"I'm fine."

"Yes, but you could have . . ." He cleared his throat and set his mug on an unoccupied stool, unbothered when it wobbled on the weathered wood. Then he placed his hands deliberately on my knees and boldly parted them so he could step closer, his body warm between my thighs. Straining the material of my skirt.

"I could have lost you," he said, and I caught my breath as his hands found my waist. "Losing any member of our cohort is bad enough. Losing Petyr is . . . awful. But I *can't* lose *you*. Amber, I don't care whose life is in danger. I don't care if it's the Bluehelm herself, or an entire carriage full of mewling kittens and chubby babies. Don't you *ever* do that again."

He kissed me. Gently. Softly. Slowly, as if he had all the time left in eternity to explore this connection.

As if he had every right to do so.

As if this were expected, and no one at all should be shocked, least of all me.

"We're not supposed to be back here," I whisper as his lips trail down my throat toward the expanse of skin exposed above my bodice. My head falls back, and I revel in the heat of his mouth as my gaze finds the bone-and-candle chandelier. It's unlit, and the empty tavern back room swims in darkness.

I hardly hear the din of voices from out front. I hardly smell the stew, or the bread, or the ale. All I can see—all I can hear, and taste, and smell—is him.

"Wait," I moan, my thighs clenching around his hips as the stool rocks beneath me. "Don't stop. Just . . . wait."

His lips disappear from my throat, and I sit up as he looks down at me. In the light spilling into the dark room through the cracked open door, I see his coppery-brown eyes, his irises dilated with lust, his lips damp and slightly parted. . . .

I shoved Wilder back, and his blue eyes widened.

"Amber? Are you okay?"

No one else noticed. They were all lost in their own drunken revelry.

I didn't know how to answer. Panicked, I slid from the stool and rushed into the crowded front room, around the professors' table and into the kitchen.

A rough voice shouted for me to get out, but I kept pushing forward, past a large pot bubbling over a fire and a sweaty woman scrubbing metal ale mugs in a wooden tub full of cloudy water.

I burst through the door into the cold, quiet alley, and only once I stood there with the wood-paneled wall at my back, shivering even as I welcomed the frigid air against my overheated face, did I realize I still held my mug, and that some of its contents had sloshed over the side to run down my hand.

I lifted the mug and drained the ale in several long gulps.

"Amber?"

My eyes fell closed at the sound of Desmond's voice. His footsteps echoed toward me from the open kitchen door.

The tin mug hung from two of my fingers, its bottom edge scraping the wall at my back with every deep breath I took.

I did not open my eyes until he stood in front of me, so close I could feel his warmth.

"You're shivering."

"It's cold," I whispered. Though truth be told, I hadn't noticed.

"What's wrong?"

I sidestepped him and started down the alley without answering, and he didn't try to stop me. But then, just before I stepped out of reach, Desmond's left hand captured my free one. He didn't pull me back. Neither did he let me go.

My mug clattered to the ground, tin ringing against roughly paved stone.

"You survived," he whispered. "Against all odds, you made the antidote, and you survived, and you saved another student. What could possibly be wrong?"

So much was wrong. And I felt all of it, deeply. But there was no way to put a single bit of it into words without sounding like an ungrateful wench.

"You gave me the answer," I finally said, turning slowly to face him. "I'm sorry if that sounds ungracious, and it's certainly not the only source of my current mood. But . . . I didn't save Yoslyn. *You* saved us both, by underlining the relevant parts in my research."

"No—"

"Yes," I insisted. "I would never have figured out the antidote—the formula—in time without that, and if anyone finds out—"

"Amber. You saved *yourself. You* did that research. *You* took those notes. *You* came up with those antidotes, six months ago. Today, amnesia was the only thing locking you out of work you have *every right* to understand and to utilize. You should be able to access your own skills, memory, and research, just as the other students can. All I did was point you in the direction of work you'd already done."

I blinked up at him, studying the way shadow sharpened his cheekbones. Deepened the copper flecks in his eyes. "You showed me exactly what to do."

He nodded, accepting my accusation in a manner that almost felt gracious. "I showed you what to do *with your own research*. With *your* theories and formulas. And if you hadn't figured out what the toxin was on your own, you never even would have seen the lines I left in the notes. The before version of you doesn't get credit for that. *This* version does."

It wasn't his words that convinced me. That loosened the vicious grip my rib cage had claimed over my lungs, and my heart, and my soul. It was the conviction echoing in his voice. Glowing behind his eyes.

"This was not my victory," he whispered, leaning down until his forehead rested against mine, his warm breath brushing my cheek. "It was yours. And you earned it not just today, but over the course of the past two years, with every class you attended, every experiment you performed, and every note you took. Don't let whatever happened to you six weeks ago strip away everything you've *damn well* earned."

His hand slid into my grip, fingers winding around mine in a touch that felt desperately reserved. Intimate, and yet guarded. Restrained.

I clung to his palm. My free hand slid over his tunic, beneath his waistcoat, and clutched at a handful of the fine material, wrinkling it brutally.

"Does that mean you want me here now?" I whispered.

"I want you"—he let the first part of the statement linger, while I could feel the rest of it coming like the swift drop of the guillotine—"*anywhere* but here."

Frustration clenched my teeth. So I changed the subject.

"Wilder passed easily." No need to mention what else Wilder had done—the kiss that had propelled me out of the tavern and into the alley.

Desmond nodded. "Yes. He does that."

"He had time to make *two* elixirs. One of them wasn't even for the trial. How is he so good at Alchemy when he hardly takes notes? When he hardly listens in class, that I can tell?"

Desmond sighed. "Alchemy is about harnessing nature's inherently unpredictable and destructive forces and repurposing them. Redirecting them. Wilder *is* an inherently unpredictable and destructive force. When you and I say that Alchemy is life, the statement is aspirational. For Wilder, it is *absolute fact*."

"He operates on instinct. Pure instinct." My words were so soft, I wasn't sure Desmond even heard them.

Until he replied, "And that instinct is rarely ever wrong."

His words rang through me like a striker through a giant bell, leaving me trembling all over. Thrumming with the implication.

If Wilder had kissed me on instinct, and his instinct was rarely ever wrong, what did that mean for us? For the *three* of us?

I shook my head, blinking to clear the thoughts from my expression before Desmond saw them. In their place, I let him see something just as personal.

"I don't understand how I did it," I admitted, laying the greater truth bare before him. Flaying my very soul open, to show him the wound festering deep inside. "I shouldn't get credit, if I did it by accident."

"What do you mean?" he took a step back, but our hands remained joined, and suddenly, robbed of his body heat, I *did* feel the cold.

"I mean that I followed the formula, and presumably that would have saved me. But how did it also work on Yoslyn? Why was one dose enough for both of us? And why did it work *instantly*?"

Desmond didn't look surprised by the question. But he didn't answer it either.

"They're discussing that, aren't they?" My hand tightened around his, silently demanding a response. Demanding the truth. "What did my observer say? He's your colleague?"

"Yes, and likely assigned to you specifically by the Bluehelm. His name is Osric Irving, and he's one of the seniormost Apotheosis researchers." Desmond sighed, but he held my gaze. "Osric has no idea how your antidote worked like it did. The formula was correct. It was one of the correct approaches, anyway, though he was openly impressed with the ingenuity of it. As was *I*, for the record. I hadn't seen your work on metal poisoning until this morning, when I went back to the lab and grabbed your notes."

"Desmond, please. Just tell me." I didn't feel like I could claim the work I'd done, considering that I couldn't remember doing it.

"But they all agree," he continued. "Osric, and the assembled panel of professors and researchers. One vial shouldn't have been enough for both you and Yoslyn. And it shouldn't have worked so quickly. And . . ." He exhaled heavily. "It shouldn't have reversed the damage."

"What do you mean?"

"I mean . . . at half a dosage, the most your antidote should have done was neutralize the poison. By all rights, you and Yoslyn should both be in the infirmary right now, waiting on the Panacea's antidote to reverse the effects, like your classmate Adria. She suffered mild lung damage and will likely be breathing viable air"—a remedy produced by the Panacea staff and sold by the Alchemary as a treatment for various lung illnesses—"for several days. Though they've deemed the damage minor enough that she will pass."

Suddenly the chill I felt seemed to be coming from beneath my skin rather than from the cold night air.

"So then, how did it happen, Desmond? *How* did I earn this? Me *or* past me?"

"I have no idea. And they've certainly asked. They crawled all over my lab this afternoon, looking for some hint of an ingredient you could have snuck in, or some way you could have preprepared the antidote and exchanged what you pretended to make for what you'd brought with you, though Osric swears no such thing happened." He sighed. "A couple of my colleagues have even accused me of telling you what the poison would be, but that idea was dismissed, because I'm not on the committee this year. I didn't know it would be a metal toxin."

"Then why did you underline that antidote?"

He frowned. "I underlined several of the ones you didn't get a chance to practice, to make sure you could understand your own notes quickly."

“Truly?” I asked, and he nodded. I hadn’t noticed any others. Likely because I didn’t spend much time on the ones that didn’t fit the symptoms.

“I didn’t give you the answer, Amber. I didn’t even *know* the answer.”

I exhaled slowly, letting the truth of that settle into my soul. “So . . . what was the conclusion?” I whispered. “From that panel of professors and researchers?”

His thumb stroked over the back of my right hand, his coppery gaze holding mine with remarkable steadiness. “They have no idea. But they desperately want to understand. They’ll do *anything* to understand, in fact.”

“That’s why Yoslyn wasn’t expelled.”

He nodded. “They’re studying you both. They’re already set up in the arena, with two teams of researchers, trying to replicate what you did. Following every step Osric wrote down.”

“Any luck?”

“Not so far.”

“Will I be . . . questioned? Interviewed?” The very idea made anxiety twist in my gut.

“I sincerely doubt it,” Desmond said. “That would mean admitting that they don’t understand how a student got professional-grade results from an intermediate-grade recipe. They think . . .” He exhaled heavily. “The *Bluehelm* thinks you’re back. The old Amber. Or at least that this is evidence you could be. She’s convinced the Alchemary can benefit from your research. If you ever manage to finish it.”

“Or even remember it,” I mumbled.

He nodded. “Either way, it appears that I’ve lost this battle. She will not send you home. And if you will not leave on your own accord—”

“I will not.”

"—then it seems we are still lab mates. If that is still what you want."

I took a deep breath. "The situation is complicated," I admitted.

"Amber, I do not regret what happened between us. I should. Yet I *do not.*" His coppery gaze flashed fiercely at me in the dim light, and a heat began to build low, low in my center.

Saltpeter, sulfur, and charcoal.

"But I understand if you do."

"I—"

A commotion swelled from inside the Beaker. Panicked shouting. For the second time in a week, one word carried above the others in a crowd.

Aurum.

Desmond squeezed my fingers, even as he turned toward the open kitchen door. "I'm sorry. I have to go." Then he released my hand and disappeared into the chaos.

As I exited the alley, I saw several Alchemary staff members carrying a motionless, gold-tinged man out the front door of the Dusty Beaker on a litter made of coarse material stretched over two poles. A crowd had gathered. Professors and researchers were examining the man by the light of several lanterns, while a cluster of students watched.

I snuck through the dark on the edge of the crowd and headed for the bridge alone.

Thirty-Two

Yoslyn popped up off a weathered wooden bench when I stepped out of the ladies' tower and into the Dormitory courtyard. "Amber!" she called as she crossed the expanse of cobblestone between us, scattering crunchy brown leaves with every step. "I've hardly seen you in days!"

Days was a bit of an exaggeration. I had snuck home alone thirty-six hours earlier during the chaos caused by the aurum—an employee of the Beaker—because I had no idea what to say to Wilder.

Unfortunately, slipping out of the alley without even a word to him after he'd kissed me—in public—had left me crawling with guilt and smoldering with embarrassment. I'd spent all of Tuesday in my room, studying, drinking cold tea, and nibbling on stale bread I'd snuck out of the Refectory during my trial prep.

Poorhouse food, Wilder would have called it. But any pauper would be grateful for the warmth and luxury of my private room and soft bed, so rather than feeling sorry for myself, I'd buried myself in studies. I had one month until the White Trial, which took some of the pressure off and gave me time to continue relearning the alchemy basics alongside my trial prep.

"Shall we break our fast?" Yoslyn fell into step beside me as I headed out of the paved courtyard into the quadrangle. "You like to eat in the morning, do you not?"

"I do," I conceded. "But if that isn't your custom . . ."

"Honestly," she whispered, leaning closer, "I would love to. I always thought I'd appear a glutton, eating the moment I rolled out of bed, but you've inspired me to indulge my more fleshly appetites. And not just with food." She waggled her eyebrows at me salaciously, and my face warmed when I realized what she was referring to.

Wilder's kiss.

"Food is fuel," I said, ignoring her implication. "You need food in the same manner that a fire needs kindling or oil. If you eat in the morning, you will find that your stamina is robust and your thoughts flow faster and more clearly, like the current in a strong river, rather than the stagnant waters of a pond."

"Well!" Yoslyn huffed, eyes wide. "Food is fuel," she repeated. "Both fire and water. What a beautiful, alchemy-themed metaphor as an excuse for our morning indulgence!"

"Life is alchemy," I told her.

And alchemy was life.

Wilder did not appear in the Refectory, but that did not stop Yoslyn from talking about him as she sipped her tea and nibbled almost reluctantly at an edge of toast.

"Of course, it's not unusual to see him pay special attention to someone at the Beaker. You certainly don't remember this—and I hope I'm not speaking out of turn—but he has been known to drink to excess, and the forces of chaos know there is no limit to the man's charm. He was quiet as a Fundamentals-year student, but by Proficiency year, he was the very *life* of the party. And there was that thing, briefly, between him and Petyr. Which Petyr was always trying to rekindle."

She frowned with her teacup halfway to her mouth, and I doubted she would manage a single sip before it went cold.

"I wonder how poor Petyr's death is affecting Wilder? Maybe that's why he was a bit excessively merry last night. As a method of coping, I mean. My point, though, is that while it's not unusual to see Wilder enjoying himself in the company of a particularly attractive classmate"—her gaze flashed briefly, pointedly at my entire visage—"it *is* unusual to see him leave the Beaker alone."

I drank the last of my tea and gathered our dishes onto the wooden tray, doing my best to scrub all emotion from my face. She had no way of knowing how guilty I felt, or how unsure I was about how I would normally have reacted to a kiss from Wilder. And for one careless moment, I almost asked her. I almost asked a classmate whether or not Wilder and I had been an acknowledged couple before I'd lost my memory.

Just because Desmond didn't know about it didn't mean it hadn't happened.

My mouth opened, and I could feel the traitorous question clawing its way up my throat, where it sat heavy on the back of my tongue, waiting to pounce.

"Yoslyn," I said as I backed slowly away from the table, clutching the tray tightly enough to press splinters into my palms. "Are you aware of the secret code written into the bones of dead alchemists bolted into the walls of the Conservatory?"

I hadn't meant to tell her. Even three hours later as we stood on the second floor of the Conservatory, eschewing a midday meal with our classmates in order to stare at a plaque at the back of the hallway, I could not entirely understand how the revelation had come forth.

The mind was a complicated thing, and sometimes it reacted in defense of the body—of the psyche—in ways we were not prepared to fully understand.

At least, that was the closest I could come to understanding the defensive impulse that had spewed a secret to a classmate I hardly knew. One who refused to leave my side, despite her repeated assertions that she did not want to bother me or keep me from my studies. Maybe it was because my burgeoning friendship with Yoslyn was less complicated than my relationships with Wilder and Desmond.

Or maybe it simply felt nice to finally have a female confidante.

"This is bone?" Yoslyn leaned in to peer at the blank plaque, standing on her toes with one palm pressed against the wall for balance, long curls tumbling over one shoulder of her cloak. "How can you tell?"

"I can't. Not really. But my father taught me a lot about the construction of various buildings at the Alchemary when I was a kid. It's a bit of a . . . passion."

"Construction technique is a *passion* for your father?" She dropped onto her heels and gave me an amused look. "What is he, a Toolkeeper?"

When I didn't answer, her smile faded. "Wait, he is *in fact* a Toolkeeper. I'd forgotten."

"Indeed."

Yoslyn's gaze narrowed on me in a careful version of the suspicion most alchemists had for my father's guild. "A Toolkeeper by trade, or a member of the Toolkeepers' Rebellion?"

"He's a master stonemason, by trade. Guildmaster of the Stonemason's Guild, since I was fourteen or so. At least, I think he's still the guildmaster." The truth was that I hadn't asked, when I'd seen him the first week of the term, and I couldn't be sure he would have shared any of his own troubles, considering that he had come to see to mine.

And because my father considered his problems to be his own.

I let the second half of her question go unanswered. My father was, in fact, a member of the Toolkeepers' Rebellion—the cross-guild political movement, which was officially and staunchly anti-alchemy—but I saw no reason to verify that. Even for my new confidant.

Her green eyes widened. "And he let you attend the Alchemary?"

"I don't recall asking for permission." I shrugged, turning back to the plaque. "My point is that he taught me about the construction of this campus long before I came here. Including the fact that some of the plaques are formed from a paste made from the ground bones of alchemists who died in service of the Alchemary."

Yoslyn made a strangled sound at the back of her throat. "That's horrific."

"It's an honor," I insisted. "They dedicated their very bodies to the craft they practiced, and they were rewarded by being allowed to remain a part of the Alchemary even in death."

"That is certainly a poetic way to put it." She turned back to the plaque, hiking her bag higher on one shoulder. "And alchemical symbols were hidden on these?"

"Not on this one. This one was blank, and that led me to conclude that it was a different part of the puzzle. Once I'd identified the compound based on the components, I applied it to the back of this plaque, and..." I slid my smallest finger behind the bone scroll, and to my relief, it fit just far enough to release the metal clasp. The plaque swung away from the wall, revealing the empty compartment.

Yoslyn's brows arched, displaying her surprise: evidence that she hadn't truly believed me until that moment. She peered into the dark, square hole. "What was inside?"

I slid my hand into my pocket, where my fingers curled around the bracelet, and for one long, heavy moment, I said nothing. Then, with a sigh, I withdrew the bracelet and showed it to her.

"Wow," she breathed. "That's beautiful. An ouroboros. What do you think it means?"

"The ouroboros represents the cycle of—"

Yoslyn rolled her eyes. "I know that. I meant, what do you think it means that it was stuffed into a secret hole in the wall, on the second floor of the Conservatory? Who could have put it there?"

Instead of answering, I took another deep breath.

Yoslyn frowned at me. "Why do you keep your thoughts prisoner, when they so clearly want to be free?"

"Because they cannot be trusted," I whispered, my voice dwarfed by the gravity of a truth I had not intended to reveal. "Once, they escaped entirely, as you well know, and I have yet to recapture them. And the ones that remain . . . I'm not entirely certain of their lucidity."

To my surprise, her eyes shone with amusement. Or excitement, perhaps. "Mad thoughts are the *best* sort to run free, Amber. Release this one, and let me share in the lunacy."

I couldn't help but smile, despite the doubt creeping up my spine like an army of spiders. "I think it was Lord Calyx. The histories say he was intimately involved in the design of this building, and I think he's responsible for this hidden compartment. I think he may have placed this bracelet inside with his own two hands."

"Lord Calyx, the father of alchemy?" Yoslyn's green eyes widened. "The very founder of the Alchemary itself?" Her voice rose into a squeal of excitement, and I shushed her with one finger over her lips. "That *is* madness, and almost certainly untrue," she whispered. "There have been any number of researchers over the past century and a half who could have done this, long after Calyx was dust in his grave, but I will say, when you theorize, you reach for the very stars."

I frowned, running one thumb over the snake's scales. "You don't believe it?"

"Not one bit," Yoslyn said, almost gleefully. "And yet . . . they say he was quite mad by the time he died. Driven over the edge by his own failure." She reached for the bracelet. "May I?"

I placed the metal snake in her palm, and she held it toward the wall torch, examining it as light flickered off its scales and gleamed in its crimson-jeweled eyes. She turned it, angling the snake's head toward the light, and I assumed she was studying the red stones, until suddenly she was gripping its triangular-shaped head between her thumb and forefinger, tugging at its tail with her other hand.

"No, I assure you the little beast is quite rigid," I said. "It won't—"

"There's something in its mouth," she insisted.

I huffed. "Yes. Its tail. That's the defining characteristic of the ouroboros."

She shoved the bracelet so close to my face that I started to back away out of instinct. Then the flicker of the white torch flame shone on something just past the snake's tiny fangs.

"It's just the end of the tail," I said. "Looks like it might be tipped with a jewel, like the eyes."

"But why bury a jewel where it can't be seen?"

I shrugged. "The entire bracelet was hidden."

"Yet intended to be found," she noted. "Thus the formula for revealing it. Whoever orchestrated this little adventure appears to have been hiding clues in plain sight, waiting for someone observant enough to notice them. To see what's there."

She had a point. Whatever had gone wrong for Yoslyn in the Black Trial clearly had nothing to do with deductive reasoning.

I took the bracelet and examined it in the light, letting my attention linger on every detail. Each individual scale. And finally I realized that one of them was raised just enough that I could wedge my fingernail beneath it. When I did so, my heart pounding with the fear that I was about to ruin yet another priceless work of historic art, the scale rose a mere fraction of a millimeter and spun ninety degrees. Which allowed me to spin the one next to it. And the one next to that. When I'd spun four tiny scales in a row on the snake's back, the resulting gap loosened the scale pattern just enough to allow flex in the ring.

Gently, I tugged the tail from the snake's mouth, and indeed, the tip was crowned with a tiny red jewel. And just beyond where that jewel had rested between the metal fangs, I found the end of a minute piece of parchment, rolled up like a scroll.

Yoslyn shuffled her feet with uncontrolled anticipation as I carefully unrolled what was likely a very old document, no longer than the width of my smallest finger. But then her feet went still as a disgruntled sigh slid from her throat. "It's blank."

I nodded. "Or . . . it *appears* that way."

"Invisible ink? Like on the bone plaques?"

"That seems likely, given that this paper unrolled into the same shape the plaques were molded into."

"Do you have any more of the solution that reveals the print?"

I nodded. I had not told her that solution was blood.

Carefully, I replaced the tiny scroll and tucked the snake's jeweled tail back into its mouth. Then I rotated the scales to hide the seam again and slid the bracelet into my pocket.

"I will let you know what it says," I told her as I retrieved my satchel from the floor and lifted the strap over my head. "You have my word."

"...And finally, don't forget that essays on your personal struggle with the universal forces of entropy are due on Friday," Professor Robards said. "And with that—" He frowned at the class, and I followed his gaze to the third row, where Varrah sat at a work surface shared with a classmate, her hand in the air. "Yes, Varrah?"

"I just thought that before we dismiss, we should all congratulate Amber on passing the Black Trial."

"Yes! Thank you, Varrah!" Professor Robards's eyes lit up as he turned to me. "Congratulations to our class teaching assistant for making it through the first of her Mastery-year trials! A triumph indeed!"

The class burst into heartfelt applause, which likely had more to do with their own ambitions than with my success—if I'd survived, surely they all could!—and I aimed a smile of thanks at Varrah.

"One down, three to go," I said as I stood, and the class laughed politely.

Professor Bollinger was writing something on the large framed slate when I arrived for our afternoon class. Wilder gave me a tight smile as I slid into my chair next to his.

I returned the expression with as genuine a smile of my own as I could muster.

I'd managed to avoid this awkward moment that morning in the Ethics and Advancement of Alchemy because Professor Edmiston had sent us all to the library to find sources for an upcoming paper. It had been easy to steer clear of Wilder in the stacks.

But now...

"Are you okay?" he whispered. "I apologize if I startled you the other night."

"No, I—"

"I hadn't intended to kiss you, and I regret going back on my word. I just felt, in that moment, that we were having a chemical reaction." He nudged my knee with his. "Remember? Two reactants introduced into the same space, resulting in a change of energy?"

I recognized my words. I remembered saying them.

"But maybe that was the ale talking," he conceded.

I exhaled slowly and lowered my voice to as soft a whisper as I could manage. "I'm sorry if my reaction worried you," I said. "I'm just . . . I've only had flashes of memory, and I don't know whether I can trust them, and—"

"What have you remembered?" Something in the sharp slant of his gaze set me on edge.

He must have noticed, because his expression changed, like fluid poured from a short, wide beaker into a tall, narrow vial. The same contents suddenly seemed to take on a different shape—a more amenable form.

"Nothing, really. Just flashes," I repeated. "They're . . . addled. Disorienting and . . . not possible, frankly. It's like my mind is gifting me with shards from a mosaic but placing them in the wrong locations, so the image doesn't make sense."

His brows furrowed deeply over eyes that seemed a darker shade of blue than usual. "What images?"

"You, sometimes. And sometimes . . ." I shrugged.

"Des."

I nodded. Wilder was the only one I'd ever heard use that nickname, and the fraternal relationship it implied felt at odds with the suddenly shuttered nature of his expression.

I was a bit relieved when Professor Bollinger's chalk screeched against the slate, and he apologized as he turned to begin his lecture.

On Friday after the evening meal, as had become my habit, I crossed the quadrangle not toward the Dormitory or toward the Seminary, as many of my classmates did, but toward the Conservatory. I climbed the spiral stairs, staring up at the stained glass panels, noting how the dim glow of the waning moon painted dully colorful scenes on the smooth, curved plaster walls above my head.

The royal wedding. The royal nursery. Queen Avalona's funeral. All of it both beautiful and tragic.

Desmond was in his office, working by candlelight with half a dozen thick tomes spread open on his desk and a half-used journal balanced on his knee for note-taking.

He stood the moment he saw me and set his journal on one of the open texts. "Hello. What are you working on this evening?"

I rounded my primary work surface and ducked into the supply closet, where I hung my satchel on its usual nail. When I reemerged, I found him standing at my preferred workstation, waiting for my reply.

"Tonight, I begin preparations for the White Trial."

"Rebirth," he said.

I nodded. "Which could, naturally, mean just about anything."

A smile tugged at one corner of his mouth, but it was gone in an instant. "I cannot tell you what to expect at the White Trial, but I do want to share one other bit of . . . conjecture regarding the Black Trial."

Pressure mounted within my chest, and I fought the yawn that would force my lungs to expand for fear of appearing bored or tired. "Please tell me they haven't decided to expel me after all, for helping Yoslyn?"

"It's not to do with you, actually."

"Oh?" I folded my arms over my chest and watched him from across the table. And this time, Desmond's smile was wide, and true, and full of a bitter sort of joy.

"Pryce Wishart, as it happens, should not have passed the Black Trial at all."

I frowned. "How so?" He'd beaten me to an antidote and had suffered little ill effect from the poison.

"Upon further examination of his official observer's notes, it has been discovered that his formula was flawed. What Wishart concocted in that arena should not have saved his life."

Questions swirled among the cacophony of my thoughts. "Well then, how—?"

"The prevailing theory is that he'd ingested something else, recently, that prevented the metal toxin from entirely affecting him and perhaps bolstered the effects of a flawed antidote."

"The board thinks he cheated? That he took an antidote in advance? Or that—"

Suddenly the meaning of Desmond's bittersweet smile settled into place.

"Wilder," I said. "It was Wilder's concoction."

Desmond nodded. "The prevailing theory is that whichever unnamed miscreant slipped something into Pryce Wishart's morning tea dyed every inch of his flesh blue—and saved his miserable, unworthy life in the process."

When Desmond was well absorbed in his own work, weighing out an endless series of ingredients bound for the athanor, I angled my body away from him and used a clean scalpel to prick the tip of one finger.

Carefully, hidden by my satchel, which I'd propped up on my own workstation, I smeared a drop of blood across the tiny little scroll, which I held open at the top with the handle of the scalpel and the bottom with a small pair of laboratory tweezers.

I would have preferred to perform the task alone in the storage closet, but I knew from experience that if I was gone from his sight for too long, some odd instinct led Desmond to call out for me.

This tendency had grown more noticeable in the days since I'd shared his bed, and I'd consciously decided not to study the impulse. In fact, I was pretending not to have noticed it, as I pretended not to notice when he snuck into his office every few days to hypocritically avail himself of whatever elixir Wilder was selling him.

By the time I had pressed a cloth to my finger to stop the blood welling from the small cut, words had appeared on the tiny scroll.

Unfortunately, they were too small to be clearly read.

Swallowing a sigh of frustration, I took the scrap of parchment into the supply closet, where I pulled a glass magnification lens from its drawer. The light was dim in the closet, but there were no prying eyes, so I held the scroll carefully in my palm, angled toward light spilling in from the doorway, and fitted the clear glass lens over it.

From beneath the convex disk of glass, the words appeared *just* large enough to read.

My sun, never again shall she rise.
Beautiful, but frail.
Now the moon shines.
When the ouroboros bit off its tail.

Thirty-Three

The heavy door of the Seminary library swung slowly shut behind me, and I exhaled as my gaze settled on the grand table—the focal point of the large room. Somehow, I'd never noticed that the chairs surrounding it numbered twelve. That was likely because I'd never seen our entire cohort gathered there before.

Three of the chairs stood empty.

"Amber!" Yoslyn waved at me from across the open space, gesturing at the empty one next to her.

Several of our classmates, as well as a couple of underclassmen seated at smaller tables, glared at her for shattering the reverent feel of the room.

Wilder's head pivoted in my direction, and he scooted his chair abruptly farther from Raelah, who seemed disappointed by his sudden disinterest.

Wilder and I had hardly spoken since class the previous Wednesday. We weren't ignoring each other, exactly. I was giving us both some space to think through what had happened at the Black Trial celebration, and as far as I could tell, he had the same intent.

I avoided his gaze as I rounded the table toward the seat Yoslyn had claimed for me with her satchel. Which was wholly unnecessary. Our classmates didn't dislike her as vehemently as they disliked me, but they seemed much less eager to sit next to her now than they'd been before the Black Trial.

Pryce seemed to have suffered no disgrace from the fact that he, too, should have failed the trial. Likely because no one else here knew that.

As I sat, the remaining two empty chairs suddenly seemed tragically conspicuous. I did my best not to look at them. Not to think about Kornell's failure. About Petyr's death.

Adria had been released from the infirmary that very morning, after five full days of treatment, but she still looked a bit . . . peaked.

"Thank you all for coming." Keryth Malcom stood from the far end of the table, running one hand over the green ribbon braided through her long blond hair. She let her gaze skip over those gathered with an air of self-appointed authority. Most heads turned her way, but Cressa looked bored as she doodled surprisingly skilled beakers, tongs, and alembics around the edge of a sheet of parchment with her lead stylus.

Gavin sat to Cressa's right, followed by Pryce, who seemed to be going out of his way to avoid eye contact with me. Adria, Raelah, and Wilder sat across from them.

Wilder was staring at me. I could see that on the edge of my vision, but every time I turned to confirm it, he'd evidently *just* decided to focus on Keryth and the reason she'd called this meeting of our entire cohort, in the middle of a Saturday afternoon that could have been better spent studying.

"Having spoken with several of you privately, it's come to my attention that while we all knew at least vaguely what to expect from the Black Trial, we stand in utter ignorance of what we'll be facing in three weeks at the White Trial. Does that sound accurate?"

Mumbles of assent made their way around the table as students shifted uncomfortably in their chairs, and I could practically feel the underclassmen in the room leaning in. Trying to hear.

"So, my suggestion is that we concentrate on what we *do* know and work together to ascertain what we may be up against."

Pryce frowned. "It's a competition. Why should we help one another?"

"I am by no means suggesting that we help one another come up with strategies or solutions," Keryth explained. "Only that we put our heads together at this phase and try to figure out what we'll need strategies *for*. And," she added, her pitch rising on the word, "this is *one* of the things we know: The White Trial is a competition in a different way than the Black Trial was."

"How so?" Raelah asked, and I realized with some measure of relief that I wasn't the only one in the dark on that matter.

"In the Black Trial, everyone who survived was allowed to move forward." Keryth's gaze fell heavily for a moment upon Yoslyn, who—to her credit—stared right back at her. "Not so in the White Trial. This time, only the eight fastest times will move competitors forward, even if all ten of us succeed in our task. The two slowest, even if they survive, will fail and be expelled."

A discontented rumble echoed around the table as the shock of that information sank in.

"How do you know that?" Wilder demanded softly. "I've heard nothing of the sort."

"We uncovered that information the same way any of you could have," Lennox said from Keryth's right. "Through observation and research. Skills we should all be perfectly capable of, at this stage in the game."

"I went back through my notes," Keryth clarified. "I've kept record of which Mastery-year students succeeded in each trial for the two years we've all been here, and only eight made it past the White Trial both years. That seemed like more than a coincidence, so we looked into it." She aimed a glance at Lennox, and I noted that it was somewhat less warm than usual.

Was competition getting in the way of their bond?

Lennox pulled something from the bag at his feet, then stood and dropped a heavy leather-bound book on the table. "It's a ledger. Turns out the Alchemary keeps a record of trial participants, as they keep records of everything else. This one is the White Trial. It was right here in this library, free for the looking."

For a moment, we all stared at the book. Then Yoslyn leaned forward and dragged it across the polished surface of the table.

"They're correct." Cressa didn't even look up from her doodling.

Yoslyn opened the thick ledger to a page marked by a gold ribbon, about a third of the way through hundreds of sheets of fine, thin, delicate, *expensive* parchment. The right-hand page was blank.

The left-hand page was labeled with the date of last year's White Trial, and below that was a numbered list of the participants, including the time it took each to complete the trial.

Eleven had begun. Three names were crossed through. One of them had no completion time.

"Ten survived," I said, staring at the crossed-through names. "But only eight moved on."

Yoslyn flipped the page. "It was the same the year before. Nine of ten survived, but only eight moved on."

Keryth nodded. "It's been eight for every one of the past twenty-three years, except for two years when only seven survived. At no point in almost two and a half decades have more than eight Mastery-year students gone on to the third trial."

"We're guessing some new policy was put into place that year," Lennox said. "Before that, everyone who survived moved forward."

Yoslyn closed the ledger and slid it into the center of the table.

Keryth aimed a magnanimous look at our entire group. "We've chosen to share this knowledge with you all, when we did not have to."

"How long have you known?" I asked, staring at the ledger.

Silence descended from every direction as chatter and nervous fidgeting ceased. Several heads turned my way.

"Pardon?" Keryth asked.

"I said, how long have you known?" When neither of them answered, I met her scowling gaze. "A while, right? Maybe since last year? And you're just now sharing that information."

"This is a competition," Lennox said, his voice hard. Defensive.

"As is my point," I said. "You're not sharing information to be generous. You're sharing, months after you came by this knowledge, because you need help. Because you haven't been able to figure it out for yourselves."

Cressa smiled down at her drawings.

"That doesn't change the calculus," Keryth insisted. "Helping one of us helps all of us."

I nodded. "But you're misrepresenting your intentions. You aren't trying to help us. You're *using* us."

"Well, you'd certainly know all about that," Lennox snapped, glaring at me from across the table.

"So, what else do we know?" Keryth set her right hand on his shoulder. "What do we have to work with?"

"Theme," Lennox said.

She rewarded him with a smile. "Yes. Purification and rebirth."

"And color," Wilder said. "Alchemy is about colors as much as it's about anything. This is the *White* Trial."

"Yes," Yoslyn said. "A theme and a color. White. Purification and rebirth." She glanced around the table. "So . . . what could that mean?"

"Transmutation. Rebirth into something new," Gavin spoke up. "This is a Transmutation trial, where the Black Trial was Panacea. They're testing us in each of the three disciplines."

"But there are four trials," Lennox pointed out.

"Of course," Gavin conceded. "But the fourth trial could be something entirely different. Like a final exam that covers the entire course, while smaller exams cover specific portions of class."

"Maybe . . ." Keryth seemed unconvinced.

I leaned back in my chair, listening as the discussion took hold, individual contributions running wild like piglets in a pen.

Cressa continued to doodle, as if she could not care less about the discussion. Had she overheard something in the Bluehelm's office? If so, why not share her intelligence?

Because this *was* a competition, after all?

"So, what could we possibly be asked to do to prove our alchemy skills, considering a theme of purification and—or—rebirth?" Keryth seemed to be asking herself as much as she was asking us.

But no one had an answer.

Not one they were willing to share with their competitors, anyway.

Light, rapid footsteps echoed up the tower stairs, and I tensed as they stopped at my landing. A fist tapped softly on my bedchamber door, and I looked up as it opened, though I had yet to reply.

"What does it say?" Yoslyn stepped inside, and with her came a whiff of the incense usually kept burning in her room. Her green eyes shone wide and eager in the daylight streaming from my open window, her hands clutching great fistfuls of her own cloak, which contrasted the stiff blue cuffs of her sleeves. "The miniature scroll?"

I ignored the breach of etiquette because only a good friend would rush uninvited into someone else's private chamber, and in what I could remember of my adult life, no one other than the Gregory brothers had even tried.

A warm sensation flowed over my skin, like bathwater heated over the fire, at the realization that Yoslyn must *truly* consider herself my friend.

"It's a riddle." I held the scroll up carefully between my thumb and forefinger as she closed the door and leaned against it. "But it makes no sense."

Yoslyn grinned. "That's the entire point of a riddle, is it not? Reckoning sense from the nonsensical? Let me see!"

I handed her the scroll, and she carefully unrolled it against her palm. But she could only squint at the print. "It's too small. I see four lines, but I can't distinguish the letters."

"I used a magnification lens in the lab. Here." I handed her a sheet of parchment where I'd written the riddle, and she returned the scroll, which I carefully rerolled and returned to the gullet of the metal snake.

Yoslyn read from the parchment, backlit by the window, and the rhythmic crash of waves far below seemed to accompany her words like music played behind lyrics.

"'My sun, never again shall she rise. Beautiful, but frail. Now the moon shines. When the ouroboros bit off its tail.'"

She frowned and repeated the four phrases, and finally, she looked up at me, eyes narrowed. "What in the name of entropy does it mean?"

"I've been working on that." I laid one hand over another sheet of parchment on my desk where I'd scribbled my own thoughts, both meandering and analytical. "But I want to know your initial impressions, before I share my own, to avoid bias."

The left side of Yoslyn's mouth quirked up. "Then we're approaching this like science?"

"Like alchemy," I confirmed.

She sank into the green armchair to the left of the window and closed her eyes, mouthing the words of the riddle silently. Then her eyes popped open. "He was in love. With a woman. A beautiful woman, who was frail. And yet . . . he calls her his sun, which is odd, because—"

"In alchemy, the sun is a masculine figure."

"Exactly. The fiery spirit. The divine spark of man. Nobility and incorruptibility. It's associated with kingly imagery. Although . . . it's also associated with gold—the most perfect of all metals. The very goal of inorganic transfiguration. The stated goal of the Alchemary itself—by its founder."

"Lord Calyx," I said.

Yoslyn sat straighter. "You still think he left the bracelet. And that he wrote the riddle."

I nodded.

"You think that Lord Calyx was so in love with this woman that he associated her with the very state of human perfection that alchemy seeks to achieve."

I nodded again. "Metaphorically, at least."

Yoslyn leaned back in the chair, brows scrunched together. "But Lord Calyx was famously unwedded. He established the very archetype of the scholar-bachelor. He wrote that 'alchemy cannot be perfected if alchemists are distracted by material comforts or intimate companionships.'"

"Actually . . ." I spun toward my desk and snatched an open text, which I handed to her. "I found the origin of that theory, and the quote is attributed not to Lord Calyx but to Iris. The first Bluehelm."

"Calyx's protégé." Yoslyn scanned the text. "I remember that she ran the original Seminary, teaching while he pursued the creation of the Philosopher's Stone." She looked up. "Though I'll admit I did not remember her originating this theory. But . . . surely, even if the words were hers, they were inspired by her mentor. Lord Calyx was practically a recluse, especially by the end, and—"

"But what about the beginning?" I sat at my desk chair, putting us at eye level, and I found myself entirely unable to hide my excitement. Not even to avoid biasing her conclusions. "By the time he wrote this riddle, his love—whoever she was—was clearly dead. He calls her the sun, despite the masculine imagery, because he found her powerful. Incorruptible and unassailable. Beautiful. Fiery and likely passionate. The golden ideal."

Yoslyn frowned. "You're making a lot of assumptions."

"That's what you're meant to do with a riddle. Extrapolation and interpretation are the only way to solve it."

"Indeed, but even if you're right. If Lord Calyx—before he was the original scholar-bachelor who famously failed in his mandate from the crown—was in love with a fiery, golden ideal of a woman, who was she? There's no mention of a courtship in any of the histories of his life and work. He isn't even associated with a woman, in any text I've ever studied, except for Iris. His protégé. About whom we know virtually nothing, except that she can't have been his tragic lost love because she outlived him and famously went on to run the Alchemary for who knows how long."

"That is *almost* accurate," I conceded, and Yoslyn's brow arched at me. "He is associated with one other woman, in the histories."

"No, he—"

I snatched the text from her, my movement sharper than I'd intended, and I flipped carefully through the pages to a place I'd marked with a scrap of my own rough parchment. On the right-hand page was a very old, very sparsely detailed sketch of five people, their faces just nose- and mouth-shaped smudges, their sizes indicating distance and position to form a familiar ceremonial tableau.

"The royal wedding," Yoslyn said.

"Yes. This is the officiant." I tapped the vaguely male figure in the center, who was turned away from the reader. "The emperor." I tapped Emperor Eldon, standing to the officiant's left, facing him.

"And Lord Calyx." To his emperor's left, where he had been drawn slightly smaller to indicate that he stood back a distance from the royal couple. "And—" I tapped the maid standing on the far right, next to the bride, at the same distance as Calyx.

"You think he was in love with the queen's witness?"

"No, I think the queen's witness was Iris."

"How do you—?"

"There's a portrait of Iris in a book about Alchemary history in the research library. It's much more detailed than this, but she's wearing a hooded robe with this same distinctive shape, which is also shown in the stained glass wedding image. History has largely forgotten who she was, but in her day, people would have recognized that hooded cape as the uniform of an alchemist. In the stained glass version, you can see that Lord Calyx has one, too, but his hood is folded back. When this was drawn, people would likely have recognized her."

"Even so," Yoslyn said, "Iris could not have been Calyx's golden woman."

"But Iris is not the only woman in this image."

Yoslyn squinted at the drawing, as if she might have missed a hidden sixth figure. "Yes, she is. Other than"—her gaze snapped up to meet mine—"Queen Avalona. *No . . .*" She shook her head slowly. "Avalona was—"

"Noble and unassailable. Incorruptible, by all accounts. Beautiful and frail. The golden ideal. We don't know what her personality was like, but she clearly captured the emperor's undying devotion, so my assumption leans toward 'fiery and passionate.' And she certainly suffered a tragic, early death."

"You think that Lord Calyx, the father of alchemy, was in love with the queen? With the wife of his best friend and sovereign?"

I let the power of her own words sink in. "I think that love may be warm and sweet, but passion is madness and angst. It is push and pull. It's an insatiable, covetous craving, equal parts adoration and vexation. I think it is a powerful force that can drive a man to obsession and grief. Be he the ruler of an entire kingdom or just a simple laboratory alchemist."

Yoslyn smiled. "You sound like you know whereof you speak."

I blinked, startled not just by her words but by the deeply assessing nature of her gaze. As if she could see through flesh and bone into my very thoughts. "Do I?"

She nodded. "You sound as if you've fought and died in the same trenches you describe."

My throat felt suddenly tight. "I'm afraid I would not remember, if I had."

Finally, Yoslyn's expression relaxed into its standard half smile, and some of the tension eased deep in my belly. "Well, anyway," she said, "I'm starting to see why the first Bluehelm decided that personal relationships were, in fact, antithetical to the practice of alchemy."

I could only shrug. "Maybe that's why Lord Calyx failed to create the Philosopher's Stone—because he was distracted by matters of the heart."

Was that why I had *also* failed?

"So then, what about the last two lines? They make no sense, even if we've uncovered the meaning of the first two. And I am not convinced we have."

"Because of the tense?" I asked.

Yoslyn nodded. "'Now the moon shines' sounds like it's still happening. But 'bit' is clearly in the past, so the ouroboros biting off its tail—whatever that means—has already happened. How can the two of those be related, if one's still happening, and the other is not?"

"That, I don't yet understand," I admitted. "But we know that the ouroboros is a symbol of the cyclical nature of life and death. Of birth and rebirth."

"As are the seasons, cycling year after year. And the sun, rising and setting every day. But if 'she' will rise no more, then she has passed on. Which we've already surmised. The ouroboros biting off its tail seems to be a repetition of the same theme—an end to the cycle of life."

"Or to *one* life. Avalona's."

Yoslyn scowled at the parchment where I'd written the riddle. "But no individual's life is cyclical. It's humanity in general that observes the cycle of life and death, not any one person."

"So . . . maybe the ouroboros *isn't* the repetition of a theme. Symbols in alchemy often have more than one meaning or interpretation. Maybe in this instance the ouroboros represents not a cycle but infinity. A life that does not end."

Yoslyn shook her head. "But Avalona's life *did* end."

I nodded, my thoughts spinning. "But it wasn't supposed to. Or Lord Calyx didn't *want* it to. Maybe *Emperor Eldon* didn't want it to. The ouroboros biting off its own tail would sever the loop and end the cycle. That could mean the end to a life that was supposed to last forever."

Yoslyn looked up from the text. "How can one life last forever?" Then her eyes widened, and I saw the moment she came to the same conclusion I had. "The Elixir of Life."

I stood from my chair so quickly that my head spun. "That was my very thought. What if Lord Calyx wasn't only working on the Philosopher's Stone? Or, what if he gave up on that?" His notes certainly seemed to hint that he considered it, eventually, to be an impossible endeavor. "What if he was actually working on the Elixir of Life?"

Yoslyn stood, practically buzzing with the potential of our hypothetical. "To keep his true love alive forever?"

"And, presumably, to keep himself alive with her." I sucked in a deep breath as my gaze wandered toward the wedding image still visible in the book open on my desk. "Emperor Eldon immortalized his love for his bride in books, and statues, and buildings bearing their names. In songs, and in plays, and in legend. But Lord Calyx . . . Yoslyn, I think the father of alchemy tried to immortalize Avalona *herself*."

The Alchemary campus is known throughout the world for many stunning displays of stained glass, each handcrafted by master alchemists, most more than a century ago. Across campus, numerous works illustrate the various processes, procedures, and phases of the alchemical process, their vibrant hues reflecting the colors an alchemical elixir typically transitions through from one stage to the next. These distinctive, complex works of art exist as door lights, sidelights, transoms, and true windows, but perhaps the most famous example of all is the spiral-shaped skylight of the Conservatory atrium. A masterpiece of form, function, and design, it reportedly took a team of four alchemists nearly two years to complete and set into place.

—from *The Historic Architecture of Alchemary Island*

Thirty-Four

"Amber!"

I turned toward the sound of my name, my pulse spiking at the anticipation bouncing through each syllable. At the enthusiasm of the greeting.

Too late, I recognized the voice, and though unease washed over me when my gaze fell upon Wilder heading across the quadrangle toward me, my pulse did not slow.

He cut a daring figure, jogging in his waistcoat and breeches, his cloak tossed over one broad shoulder, moss-colored knife sheath rhythmically brushing his hip, blue eyes shining in the setting sunlight.

I'd spent three weeks avoiding further discussion on the subject of our kiss, while not avoiding him specifically, and the effort required to walk that particularly fine line—to keep a natural-sounding change of subject at the ready, at all times—had begun to take its toll.

I did not dread seeing him. But I did wish, fervently, that I could simply stare at his handsome figure unnoticed from across the quadrangle, free from the burden of talking, when I had no idea what to say.

He fell into step beside me, breathing easily despite his exertion. The dirt beneath his nails and a stray hibiscus blossom caught in his hair told me that he'd been in the forest again, and that his satchel was likely full of carefully plucked and sorted plant matter, waiting to be dried and powdered or distilled into usable alchemical ingredients.

His recipe for beyn, I knew, was plant-forward.

Wilder was the only student, as far as I had heard, who collected his own elixir components, and while that was not strictly forbidden, it was plainly frowned upon by certain members of the faculty.

He grinned down at me as we rounded the statue of Eldon and Avalona at the center of the quadrangle. "So, I know I'm not supposed to ask, but have you given it any thought?"

"Naturally, I know precisely what you're talking about, given that in addition to being a gifted alchemist, I can *read minds* . . ." I teased, careful to keep my tone light and approachable. Too late, I realized that if he was talking about that kiss, I'd walked face-first into my own doom.

Wilder laughed. "The White Trial, of course. It's next week, Amber. How could there possibly be anything else on your mind?"

"There isn't," I lied. "I just . . . I didn't think *you'd* be worried, considering how easily you managed the Black Trial."

It took me a moment to interpret his silence, along with the intensity with which he held my gaze as we walked, as if he had no concern for where his feet would land on the path. "Oh. You're worried for me, not for yourself."

"That is not what I was going to say." He pulled his knife from its sheath and began to twirl it between the first two fingers of his right hand and into his palm over and over as we walked. "Not precisely, anyway. I'm *certain* there's a less offensive phrasing. . . ."

"And yet probably none more accurate," I insisted. "Don't fret. I'm not offended." I was concerned for myself as well, and the truth was that the trial had never been far from my mind. It just wasn't the *only* thing occupying my thoughts, with Wilder's kiss in my memory, his brother waiting for me in the laboratory, and the mystery of Lord Calyx's riddle providing a welcome if not exactly helpful distraction from everything else.

"And yes," I added. "I've given it considerable thought. But I have no idea how the trial will interpret the concepts of purification and rebirth in order to put us in mortal peril while challenging us to do our very best alchemy."

"Succinctly put." He hesitated, his blade going still, and the tension in his arm as it brushed mine said that there were more words waiting on his tongue. "Has my brother said anything?"

"About . . . ?" I hadn't told Desmond about the kiss, and he'd been very busy in the lab, working on something for the Bluehelm. Something to do with the mysterious contagion causing aurums, to which the Alchemary had vowed to devote considerable resources.

"About the White Trial."

"Oh. Not a word. He told me before the Black Trial that they're different every year, so he couldn't—"

"Not the White Trial," Wilder interrupted. "The Black Trial yes, and maybe the Red one. I'm not sure about that. But the White and Gold Trials require equipment and some sort of momentous setup that keeps them static, year after year. That's why there's such secrecy around them. Last year's Mastery students were required to take a temporary draught of memory drain after they passed so they couldn't tell the rest of us what had happened."

"A temporary . . . ?" My pulse spiked again, so strongly that the quadrangle warbled out of focus for a moment.

He sheathed his knife. "It's precisely dosed to only take a few hours of memory, and it wears off after a few months. But by then, they're all either gone from the Alchemary or they've taken oaths as permanent members."

"Could that be what happened to me?" I asked. "Someone slipped me a draught of memory drain?"

Wilder shook his head. "I did consider that at first. But a draught that took years of your memory and has lasted this long would have had other noticeable effects on you."

So either it was not a memory drain, or it was a very *skilled* memory drain, which did not seem beyond the realm of possibility, considering the expertise of every alchemist in residence on the island.

"But I am planning to take advantage of the fact that we'll be forced to take one."

"How so?"

"I have a client among our instructors who has agreed to get me an extra dose of the draught they're going to make us take since I've assured him I won't be using it on anyone. Instead, I'm going to essentially engineer it in reverse, in order to develop a new elixir for you. To try to *recover* your memory."

"Oh!" I seized his arm and squeezed it, unable to conceal my excitement. As desperate as I was, I'd felt too guilty to remind him of his promise to help. "Thank you!"

"I'm sorry it's taken me so long. My initial attempts were utter failures."

"I appreciate those attempts anyway, and you owe me nothing," I assured him.

"Thank you. Clearly Desmond believes that's true for him as well."

I let go of his arm. "Meaning?"

"He *knows* what the White Trial is, Amber. At least, he understands its basic construct. And I thought he might . . . I'm not asking for information for myself," Wilder clarified.

"You just want me to know that he could be helping me more than he is."

He frowned. "That isn't precisely how I would have phrased *that,* either."

I sighed. "He took an oath, Wilder. He can't just tell me what's going to happen in the trial any more than he can tell you."

"Those are two different scenarios. You're still operating at a memory—and thus a skill—deficit. He has the ability to keep you safe."

"It's not that simple."

Wilder nodded, a little too hard. "I know. I know he took an oath, and I know that knowing what's coming would be cheating, technically. But I could not care less. If *I* had information that could save your life, I would give it to you."

I spent four hours in Desmond's lab, struggling to concentrate on my own work instead of surreptitiously observing his confidential task before the seed Wilder had planted—whether intentionally or unintentionally—grew roots too big to be ignored.

"My wheels are spinning freely, Desmond," I finally said as I replaced the last of my freshly washed beakers on the shelf, a task that required me to stand on the counter in order to reach.

He looked away from his work, his eyes still glazed with concentration, his nose crinkled rather fetchingly as he frowned at up me. "To what wheels are you referring?"

"In this metaphor, I am a cart stuck in the mud, and though my wheels may spin freely, they will not find purchase."

He snorted and turned back to his work. "That is a rather laborious way to say that you feel you're wasting your time."

I lowered myself to sit on the countertop with my heels dangling against the cabinet doors. "And do you intend to address the heart of the matter or simply to criticize my phrasing?"

He looked up again. "What have your spinning wheels to do with me?"

"In this scenario, I am a cart with spinning wheels, and you are—" I hopped down onto the floor and crossed my arms over my chest. "Well, truth be told, I don't know enough about cart construction to say what you would be, but it has come to my attention that you know at least approximately what I can expect in the White Trial, and you have been keeping that from me. Do you deny it?"

"Of course not. The very point of a secret is the keeping of it."

"I know of several gossipy classmates who would disagree."

Desmond's gaze narrowed on me from across the room. He crossed thick arms over his broad chest, still holding a set of calipers. "Are you suggesting my solemn oath to the Alchemary shares some equivalence with the late-night whisperings of a schoolgirl?"

"I am not, but neither do I appreciate your condescending tone." I mirrored his pose with my own arms crossed over my lab apron. "There isn't a thing wrong with being a schoolgirl, and girls are not the only ones who gossip."

"Point taken," he assured me solemnly.

"I take your point as well: The information you have is far more vital than gossip. Still, you have a choice to make, and that choice could save my life."

For a moment, Desmond regarded me in absolute silence, so unmoving that he could have been a statue in the quadrangle. Then he slowly, deliberately set down the calipers and planted both palms flat on his work surface.

"It seems to me that you are *also* facing a choice that could save your life. No one is forcing you into the White Trial, Amber. And as I've said repeatedly since the first day of this term, if you do not feel ready for a trial, you *should not undergo it.* And you know that. Yet somehow you feel justified in blaming me for keeping my oath to the institute to which I've devoted my entire life. You would evidently rather see me throw away my career and any benefit it could bring mankind than face a choice you don't want to make."

"I . . ." I could see the fire in my own cheeks like the sun on the horizon of my vision. "No. I apologize. You're entirely correct. Just because you helped me last time doesn't mean that you owe me that same help this time. In fact, you owe me nothing."

Desmond blinked, and with that one small motion, he suddenly looked as startled as if I had slapped him. "I did not tell you what you would face at the Black Trial, and I would not have, even if I'd known. I only highlighted research you'd already done for yourself. I get no credit for how you performed, or for any of your work. And that must be the case with the White Trial, else you will not have truly passed, and the Amber I know and respect would never be able to live with herself under that circumstance. And you are not so changed that you are not still *that* Amber Fallbrook. No matter what you may have forgotten."

There was something in his words. Something stalwart in the bulk of them, and something heartbroken in the last sentence, the combination of which brought stinging tears to my eyes. A maelstrom of emotion swirled within me, stemming not just from what he'd said but from the unshakable certainty that he was referring, at least in part, to some event or circumstance I could no longer remember.

There was something he was not telling me.

And suddenly, it was all—every bit of it—too overwhelming to bear. Not just that I was unprepared for the trial, but that I should *not* be unprepared. That I'd been robbed of my preparedness.

Not just that I could not remember any important event from the past two years of my own life, but that *he* remembered much of what I'd forgotten.

It wasn't just that he knew what I would face at the White Trial when I did not, it was that I'd asked him to compromise the very ethics that made him a stellar alchemist in the first place rather than working to earn my own place alongside him.

And more than all of that, it was the fact that I was compromising myself by asking. And that he knew it.

The laboratory blurred behind my tears, and I swiped them away, which gave me a clear view of the sudden helplessness in his expression.

He had no idea what to do with tears.

I grabbed my satchel and rushed toward the door. Desmond's steps shuffled behind me, but I waved him off without a glance back. "Don't!" I snapped. "I'm fine."

The shuffling ceased and I slammed the laboratory door behind me, but I only made it halfway down the grand spiral staircase before I realized that it would be unbefitting and dramatic of me to run across the quadrangle crying like a small child. Especially considering that nothing had actually happened. I was neither ill nor injured, and not a thing had changed in my life or circumstance since five minutes before, when I'd been respectably dry-eyed.

So I sank onto the stairs for a moment of solitude in which to gather my wits. And as I concentrated on breathing slowly and calming the irrational impulse deep inside me—which seemed directly and frustratingly tethered to my tear ducts—a soft wash of color caught my attention.

I blinked to clear my vision, and I realized that the refraction of light through the stained glass above was not from the sun but from the moon. The weaker light source left the colors washed out, yet . . .

There was one strong flash among them, like the glint of bright sunlight through a magnification lens. The scene itself was stretched and blurred, though still recognizable as Queen Avalona on her deathbed, and when I looked up at the stained glass, I understood what that flash was.

It was moonlight streaming through the multifaceted surface of her legendary ring. The light was bright and starkly colorless, painting a single sharp beam of light on the wall to stand out against the other softly blurred colors.

That beam was centered directly over the tread my feet rested on. In another hour, as the moon shifted, it would likely fall on the metal plate serving as trim just above the stairs. Or maybe on the trim of the step below.

How had I never noticed before that the stair treads were trimmed with metal?

A dull sort of epiphany stole over me, like the day's first ray of light spilling over the ocean. It was indistinct, but I could feel it *wanting* to come into focus, like the tiny words on the scroll in need of a magnification lens.

Queen Avalona had died, despite Lord Calyx's best efforts to the contrary, and every day and every night, the sun and moon shone through the memorial glass, painting her death on the wall of the building he'd designed every single line of . . .

Now the moon shines.
When the ouroboros bit off its tail.

The moon shines . . . through the scene of her death. Through the very *moment* the ouroboros bit off its tail.

Thirty-Five

"Yoslyn!" I hissed, knocking as loudly as I dared on her door. Hers was the lowest room in the women's tower, which cut down on the number of classmates who could possibly hear me. Still, I was loathe to wake anyone else. "Yoslyn! Open the door!"

Wood groaned from within her room, and I stepped back as soft footsteps shuffled toward me. The door opened, and Yoslyn blinked at me, her pale, freckled face stark against the dark interior of her room, her curls standing out in frizzy disarray.

"Were you sleeping?"

She nodded blearily. "That has become my habit, in the middle of the night. I do recommend the custom, if you've grown weary of assaulting closed doors."

"Yos . . . I figured it out!"

"You've figured what out?" She rubbed at her eyes, and I brushed past her into the room, vaguely aware that I had become the friend barging in uninvited. And that her room smelled pleasantly of some incense I could not identify.

"Shush and close the door." I fumbled at her desk for a candle, which she took from me. Her eyes were better adjusted to the gloom, so she carried the candle onto the landing and lit it from the torch mounted there, then she set it on her desk. I closed the door behind her. "To be accurate, I haven't *entirely* figured it out.

But I've found the right path, and I thought you might want to be involved."

"With what, Amber? What could possibly—?" She blinked, and I saw the very moment sleep faded from her visage. "The White Trial? You've figured out what we'll be facing, or— No! The riddle!"

"That very thing!" I seized her hand and tugged her to sit with me on the bed. "I was on the staircase in the Conservatory, and I noticed that when moonlight shines through the stained glass depiction of Queen Avalona's death, there is a single colorless ray of light reflected among the muted hues, almost as if it's pointing at something on the staircase."

"Colorless?" She frowned. "Avalona's ring was an emerald. The light from it should be green."

I could only shrug. "Her ring is a diamond in the stained glass illustration. I suppose that's so the beam of light will gain notice." As it had. "Further, the stairs are trimmed in hand-hammered metal plating, which I never took note of before."

"Moonlight, like in the riddle. And Avalona's death, which is the biting off of the ouroboros's tail!"

I nodded. "That is my thought."

"We're meant to use the solution you made that dissolved the metal behind the plaque? You think we're meant to dissolve one of the metal plates?"

"I'm afraid it's not that simple."

She frowned. "You already tried it?"

"I couldn't resist," I admitted. "I was right there, and I had the solution in my bag, but it didn't work. My conclusion is that 'when the ouroboros bites off its tail' isn't simply referring to that scene. It's—"

"The anniversary of her death."

I nodded. "Likely the exact time. We won't know where that beam of light will shine—and which metal plate to treat with the solution—until that day and time."

Yoslyn's shoulders slumped. "I don't remember what time of day the queen died, but it was definitely in the spring. All of the images of her funeral—all the paintings and such—show fresh spring blooms sprouting at her graveside."

"We can get the date and time. It's recorded with all of the other royal records, and there's definitely a copy in every library. But . . . I can't wait until spring."

I didn't even know if I'd still be at the Alchemary by then.

I couldn't even swear I'd still be alive.

It took us no time at all to discover that Queen Avalona had died on the fourth day of the third week of spring, at approximately a quarter past midnight. But it took two full days of searching after class and before my laboratory time to find a record of the moon's cycles that went back far enough to be any use to us.

The mathematics took another couple of days. But finally, after several sheets of parchment and a couple of hours spent checking our calculations, we felt ready to predict where the moonlight would cast that bright white beam on the anniversary of Queen Avalona's death. And if I was right, there was no need to wait for that anniversary to show us the way.

Four nights after I'd sat crying in the laboratory stairwell, I returned, with Yoslyn at my side.

The second and third floors were empty; I'd checked. But someone was always at work in the first-floor infirmary, so we would have to be quiet.

I paused on the second-floor landing, and my gaze was pulled toward Desmond's lab. The thin gap beneath the door was dark. Hidden behind a shrub in the quadrangle, I'd watched him leave nearly an hour before.

Yoslyn crept past me, mumbling beneath her breath, and it took me a second to realize she was counting. "Here," she whispered from three-quarters of the way up the second flight of stairs, just feet from the third-floor landing. "If our calculations are correct, this is where the beam of light would hit just after midnight on the anniversary of Queen Avalona's death."

"Are you sure?" I asked.

"Of course not."

Our calculations were approximate, at best. The brightest astrological minds in the world were yet unable to account for all of the moon's movements—they blamed the celestial body herself, as the very personification of a woman's temperamental nature. Yoslyn and I were *not* among the brightest astrological minds, but we just had to get close, because there were only so many metal trim pieces on the stairs.

"Do you have the solution?" Yoslyn asked.

I pulled the capped vial from my satchel.

"What if this doesn't work?" she whispered as I knelt on the tread she'd indicated, facing the stairwell wall.

"Then we try again."

I uncorked the vial and carefully poured the solution onto the metal trim piece at the juncture of stair tread and wall, but at first, nothing happened.

Yoslyn made a disappointed sound over my shoulder, where her shadow was layered over mine on the wall. "Maybe we—"

"Shh!" I leaned closer to the floor, drawn by a soft hissing sound. Hoping I wasn't imagining it entirely. A second later, I heard a soft pop, and the metal trim piece shuddered, so slightly the movement could easily have been a play of light and shadow on the wall.

I reached for the trim piece, and the decorative metal rectangle came off easily in my hand.

Behind it was a wooden knob, shaped a bit like a bolt or a gear.

Yoslyn gasped. "Turn it!" she practically squealed into my ear, gripping my shoulder so tightly that her fingers dug into my collarbone.

I reached into the rectangular opening and carefully twisted the knob clockwise. Because everything my father had ever made turned clockwise, in the Toolkeeper tradition.

The knob settled into some groove I couldn't see, and something clicked from my left. Yoslyn jumped, so startled that she almost tumbled us both down the stairs. I grabbed her arm to steady her, and we knelt together as the riser to our left slid open, revealing a small hollow beneath the tread above the one we sat on.

There was something in the space. Something glinting in the red-tinted wash of moonlight shining through the stained glass overhead.

As I reached inside, my hand brushed another tiny lever, and again I marveled at Toolkeeper ingenuity, though at first, I could not tell what the lever had triggered. My fingers closed around a warm bit of metal, and I pulled a square from the dark space. It was small—about half the width of my palm—and the front side had been cast with highly detailed swirls and swooping lines, as if it were meant to frame a tiny portrait, in the corridor of a very well-to-do doll's house.

"What is that?" Yoslyn took the small frame from me, and while she examined it, I picked up the metal trim piece. And suddenly I could see what the lever in the hole had done.

The knob, with its distinctive shape, had popped a fraction of an inch beyond the stairwell wall, where it appeared to be in the way of the curved metal trim piece.

I turned the trim piece over, and sure enough, there was an indention in the back of it that was the very shape of that knob.

The trim piece popped into place, locking around the knob with a satisfying click that also functioned as a trigger to slide the riser back into place, covering the hole beneath the stair tread as if it had never been there.

Toolkeeper ingenuity at its finest.

"Well, I'll be damned . . ." Yoslyn said, staring at the unmarred staircase. "It's like it never happened." And if not for the metal square nestled in her palm and the ouroboros bracelet hidden in my bedchamber, I'd have to question whether any of it really had.

Thirty-Six

On the morning of the White Trial, I woke up alone, as on the morning of the Black Trial. Only this time I was in my own bed, as if it were a normal day.

It was not.

Keryth had not called another meeting in her self-appointed roll of cohort chancellor. Yoslyn and I had not discussed the trial, in an unspoken yet mutually-agreed-upon decision to ignore the fact that either or both of us might soon die. Instead, in the moments we'd stolen from academia, we'd postulated the purpose of the bracelet and the frame, tossing out absurd theories over late-night snacks. Yet coming to no real conclusions.

Wilder and I had discussed the White Trial at length. He was openly willing to help me, despite being my direct competition, and though I felt certain I had less to offer, I was just as willing to help him. As far as I was concerned, until the trial actually began, we were in it together, as we'd been in nearly everything together since we were small children.

We did not revisit our kiss. We did not even acknowledge it.

Wilder seemed convinced that the White Trial would involve fire, because purification in alchemy was almost always through flame. I could not disagree with his logic, but neither could I help pointing out that rebirth was rarely ever through fire, and the White Trial was just as likely to take rebirth as its theme.

Because we had no specific task to focus on, we'd spent the last week before the trial refreshing ourselves on every theory we'd ever studied—some of which I could not remember studying in the first place—and every formula we'd ever been taught or come up with. Wilder was generous with his invented formulas, as I was with Past Amber's notes.

Yet on the morning of the trial, I woke up covered in sweat, in the middle of a panic that had evidently begun in my sleep. In my very dreams.

I bolted from bed and rushed to throw open the shutters, then stood staring out the window, hyperventilating, letting the frigid ocean breeze dry my damp skin. Counting on the rhythmic crash of waves against the cliffside to calm my racing heart.

Death felt only hours away. And as loathe as I would have been to admit it, humiliation seemed just as likely, and far more horrible.

Everyone would eventually die. I did not want my legacy, like my mother's, to be the humiliation of failure.

I rinsed myself at the washbasin and got dressed, and as I stared at myself in a smoky handheld glass that had been my mother's, an odd sense of foreboding washed over me—a quieter, more somber version of the fear that had woken me.

For a moment, the resemblance to my mother was so strong in the glass that I did not recognize my own face. When had I grown to look so much like her? Had I forgotten that, as well as two years of memories?

With a sigh, I set down the glass and opened the wooden box where I'd found her ring. Where I had stored both the bracelet and the ornate metal frame. If I didn't survive the White Trial, someone would find them among my things. Yoslyn, perhaps, if she fared better.

Otherwise, Wilder. Or Desmond, if he packed up my belongings for my father.

Soft steps echoed on the landing, and a knock sounded on my door. I snapped the box closed and set it on the corner of my desk.

"Come in," I said as I stood.

Wilder pushed the door open, and an instant later, I found myself swallowed by his embrace.

"Are you afraid you won't get a chance to hug me after the trial?" I asked as I laid my head on his shoulder, amazed to find that he still smelled exactly like he had as a child. Like herbal tea, and the sweet, earthy smell of a childhood spent outdoors, and most of all, like a whirling tempest that will not settle for any force in the world.

In fact, I could feel his very soul raging, barely contained by his flesh and blood, as I returned his embrace.

"On the contrary," he said into my hair, and I had the distinct impression that he was breathing me in as well. "I'm just a selfish boor who refuses to wait that long." Finally, he stepped back just far enough that I could see his face. That I could see he was examining mine. "Are you ready? Did you sleep?"

"Too long," I admitted. "I intended to wake early and study."

"If you aren't ready, it isn't for lack of studying," he said. "In fact, we studied *too* much for my personal preference. I'm a bit afraid of jinxing myself."

"Because you didn't study at all for the Black Trial?"

Wilder grinned. "Precisely. If I fail this time because there's too much knowledge clanking around in here, jamming up the gears"—he tapped the side of his skull—"I shall blame you entirely."

I laughed. "Fortunately for me, too much knowledge has never been your problem."

"And on that note..." He held out his arm, crooked at the elbow, inviting me to take it. "May I escort you to our doom?"

He made such a joke of it, with his formal posture and indefatigable grin, that I could not help but return his smile. And take his arm.

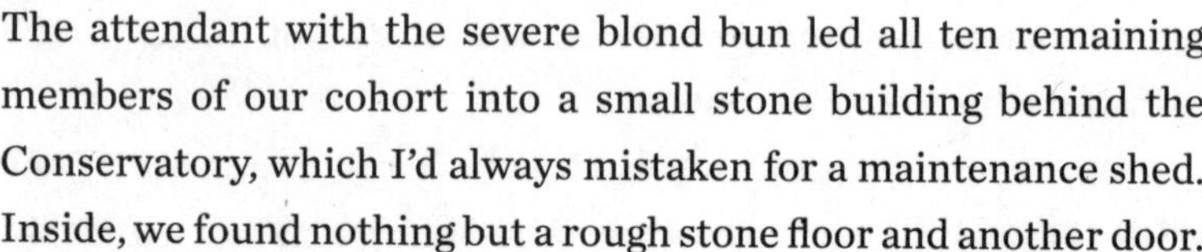

The attendant with the severe blond bun led all ten remaining members of our cohort into a small stone building behind the Conservatory, which I'd always mistaken for a maintenance shed. Inside, we found nothing but a rough stone floor and another door.

Beyond that second door was a broad set of smooth marble steps, leading deeper into the earth than I'd ever been. As I descended, my pulse pounding, I reached back to grip Yoslyn's hand and forward to squeeze Wilder's shoulder, unburdened by my satchel, because we weren't allowed to bring any notes into the White Trial.

The white arena was a thing to behold, and if I weren't preparing to face my own purification and rebirth—or die trying—I probably would have been in awe of it. The round competition space itself was much larger than the amphitheater and was entirely paved in white marble stones, cut and polished to a slick mirror finish. The arena was sunken below the audience seating, so that spectators—far fewer than in the Black Trial—could observe the competition from above.

Desmond sat among them, on the row behind the Bluehelm and several senior professors and staff members.

My Mastery-year classmates and I were led into the arena and stationed just inside its perimeter, at ten workstations equidistant apart. An eleventh and twelfth stood empty: reminders of Kornell's failure and Petyr's death.

For this trial, there were no official observers. No one other than the competitors had entered the arena, and that fact made my very bones ache with nervous anticipation.

When the spectators had all taken seats, the Bluehelm stood, and all eyes turned her way. Bright white torchlight flickered across her taught alabaster skin, which made her cheekbones look sharp, the hollows beneath them deeper than usual.

"There are no specific instructions for the White Trial." Her voice boomed across the huge space, no doubt aided by specially designed acoustics. "The trial has two stages, and at a certain point, anyone who has not found their own way into the second stage will be given access to it. You may use any materials at your workstation. Your only goal is to exit the arena. But to pass the trial, you must be one of the first eight to do so." She glanced around the arena, briefly looking at each of us. "You may begin."

With that, she took her seat.

Startled by the stark brevity of her speech, at first I could only stare at her, waiting for more. But no more came. No words of history or tradition. Of comfort or encouragement. The Bluehelm was all business today, and I took that as an indication that I should be as well.

I glanced at Wilder, who occupied the station two to my left, then at Yoslyn, who was directly to my right. The workstations were angled to face the center of the arena, so we could all see each other, but the spacing was so great that it would be difficult to understand what anyone else was actually doing.

My gaze strayed to the marble wall behind Wilder. The surface of the stones was too smooth to grip, and they were so cleanly cut and so tightly packed that the seams were hardly visible. My fingernail would not fit into a single crack. There was no hope of climbing out.

The door we'd entered through had closed neatly behind us, and I'd lost track of it when I turned to claim my station. Wherever the door was, the gap around it was now indistinguishable from the seams in the stones themselves, and I had no doubt that even if I could find it, it would not open.

It was unclear how we were intended to escape the arena, or how alchemy would aid in that endeavor. So I turned to the workstation in front of me to see what had been provided.

The supplies were basic, but plentiful: The usual array of ingredients and equipment. Three burners, an entire rack of vials in several shapes and sizes, and a generous allotment of beyn. I would have preferred to distill it myself—I'd tried out several basic recipes over the past month—but the time required for that would cost me. Not that I really understood the challenge yet, and . . .

A great grinding suddenly echoed, seemingly from everywhere at once, and several of my classmates gasped. I looked around for the source, even as the ground trembled beneath my feet, and I noticed that while my entire cohort looked startled, not one of the spectators did.

Yoslyn stood with both palms pressed to her work surface, as though it might shake apart without the extra stability, and Wilder stared, wide-eyed, at the ground.

Keryth and Lennox both backed away from their tables, directly across the arena from me, their arms outstretched as if for balance. Cressa had also stepped back, but she seemed to be looking not at the ground, or the spectators, or her work surface, but at her competitors. As if our actions were of more interest to her than the terrifying rumbling.

Then motion on the floor to my left caught my eye, and I understood why Wilder was staring at the ground.

Unlike the walls, the white tiles at our feet had been fitted together with thick mortar joints. The floor tiles were uneven, and some had clearly been chipped into angles in order to fit into odd shapes. And as I studied them, I noticed that the mortar was thicker in some places than in others, and that a line of it on my left had begun to . . . tremble.

A length of mortar suddenly bulged up from the floor, stretching oddly, as if something were pushing against it from beneath.

I dropped into a squat and pressed my finger into a line of mortar between my feet, and to my surprise, it was not hard and granular, like the grout between the stones of the ladies' residential tower. Rather, it was gummy and soft. Something between a paste and a wax, like a sturdier version of the substance used to seal vials for long-term storage.

All around the arena, lines of mortar had suddenly popped up from the floors, stretching, leaving thin threads stuck to stone as something beneath them pushed upward in a pattern I could not yet comprehend.

The strange protrusions did not involve all of the mortar but just the thicker lines, which stretched for a bit, then seemed to turn at right angles and to join other lines, almost like . . .

A maze.

Walls were rising from the floor, creating barriers between each of the workstations and stretching into the center of the arena, forming winding paths on the way. The walls were glass, formed of the largest, clearest panels I'd ever seen—a mastery of craft that would have required the work of both a master alchemist and a master Toolkeeper to produce. There were great, huge squares of it, with seams of metal, and within a few seconds, they'd grown to the height of my waist. A second after, that of my shoulder. Then they were over my head, and I was staring at Yoslyn through a massive pane of glass.

I turned left, and when Wilder looked a bit distorted, I realize I was seeing him through at least two panes, and that it was no longer easy to trace the lines of the maze. To see the paths. They had become a jumble of glass and thin metal frames, difficult to distinguish beyond the ones immediately walling me in.

How was alchemy supposed to help us through a *maze*? Were we meant to concoct a formula that would dissolve the front wall and let us into the labyrinth?

I turned back to my station and had just grabbed a burner and a single vial when a new sound from behind me made my heart thump too hard and my throat tighten. I spun toward the wall at my back to see that a gap had opened between two stones near the top, and that water was rushing into the arena.

Godfather of all chaos.

Yoslyn squealed, and I looked to my right to see that water was pouring in behind her as well. Soon it would reach her feet, and then it would begin to fill the cell that had formed around her, as it would fill the one I found myself trapped in.

A hole had opened in the center of the arena floor, and water rose from it as well, to fill glass passages still unavailable to us.

Yet another grinding sound—a deafening cacophony—drew my gaze upward, where a massive panel made of panes of glass was slowly being lowered toward the arena. It was perfectly designed to provide a cover for the giant container we found ourselves in, enclosing us with the rushing water, with no way out . . . except through a single hole in the center of the glass ceiling.

And finally I understood. We were rats in a maze, scurrying to escape our watery grave.

"We're going to drown!" Yoslyn shouted, her voice muffled by the grinding and by the glass between us.

"No, we aren't!" I shouted back. Then I pointed to her workstation. Ordering her to focus. To get to work. There was no way for me to help her—no way for anyone to help anyone else—with glass walls separating us.

We were *truly* on our own, at least until our cells opened, releasing us into the labyrinth.

Even worse, I now realized, once the rising water reached the surface of our workstations, it would put out our burners, ending any alchemical pursuit. At that point, anyone who had not found a way to survive would simply be waiting to die. In full view of both spectators and competitors.

My pulse rushed so fast that the entire arena seemed to warp around me. I gripped the front of my table in both hands, squeezing hard enough that the corner cut into my palms. Forcing myself to concentrate.

Panic would only get me killed.

When good sense had returned, I squatted to examine the supplies stacked on the shelf beneath my work surface, which would flood even before the water reached my burner.

Desmond had faced this trial. The Bluehelm and all of my professors had faced this trial. All of the observers had faced this trial.

Even if she didn't finish in the top eight, my mother had survived this trial and gone on to marry and give birth to me. And if *they* could all do this, I could damn well do it, too.

Now I understood why we hadn't been allowed to bring any notes; the parchment would be destroyed by the water.

Water, not fire. Purification by giant bathing tub. Rebirth after swimming in fluid, through a single narrow canal.

I glanced to my left to find Wilder laughing, watching me as he peeled off his cloak, then his vest, as if he'd been thinking the same thing—how very wrong he'd been. As if he found his own erroneous assumption too amusing to dwell on.

He was right about the clothing, though. The more I wore, the more weighed down my limbs would be when they got wet, and the slower I'd move.

I folded my cloak and set it on the shelf beneath my work surface, out of my way. My frock was much bulkier than his shirt and trousers, and it would have to come off, too, despite the frigid temperature of the water now seeping through my shoes to soak my feet.

After a moment's hesitation, I unfastened my frock and stepped out of it, ignoring the scandalized gasps audible through several panes of glass as I folded it atop my cape.

Shivering now, in only my thin undergarments, I went over my options.

We were clearly in the first stage of the trial. The second stage, presumably, would open our cells and admit us into the labyrinth, though that was unlikely to happen before water had filled the arena.

So, I could try to get free of my cell early and make my way to the center of the maze before it filled, or I could work on a way to breathe underwater while I waited for the cell to open. My classmates seemed equally split in their efforts. Some were examining the glass walls, assessing the composition of the panels. Others were already mixing components at their stations.

Several had laid out bits of their own clothing, and their goal was clear: to coat the cloth with something waterproof and use it as an air bladder, from which to breathe on their way through the maze once the doors opened.

Attacking the glass was a risk. If I failed, I'd be stuck until the door opened, with no way to breathe underwater, and if it took me longer to get through the maze than a single held breath could last, I would drown.

I decided to focus on not drowning and trust myself to get through the maze quickly. I only needed to beat two of my classmates to the center.

The obvious option was to create one or more air pockets, as several of my classmates—including Yoslyn—had opted to do. That seemed simple, in theory, but the risks were that the pocket wouldn't hold enough air, and that breathing from it would let out too much air at once.

Still, the waterproofing substance would be easy enough to work on in the background. I mixed a potion I remembered from Past Amber's triumph with a rainproof cape and set it over one of my three burners. Then, as the water rose above my ankles, I turned my efforts toward a more complicated—but hopefully effective—solution.

It had long been known, through alchemical experimentation in sealed jars, that the substance we called air—which was invisible and omnipresent—was actually made up of several different gaseous substances. One, called noxious air, had been proven to suffocate rats in a sealed box. One, called fixed air, was heavier than the general atmosphere, would not burn, and would, in fact, put out a candle's flame.

And a third, called viable air, was highly flammable and yet very efficiently consumed by the human body. Viable air could be isolated in an alchemical reaction—in fact, it was the very treatment the Panacea's doctors had offered Adria for her damaged lungs after the Black Trial.

Excited by this idea, I set up my second burner and began mixing everything I could remember from Past Amber's notes on a hyperefficient candle flame, which involved dipping the wick in a tarry substance that interacted with regular environmental air to off-gas viable air, which made the flame burn brighter.

If I could reproduce her tarry substance and coat the inside of my air bladder in it, that substance would react with the trapped environmental air to create a higher concentration of viable air, which would make my breathable supply more efficient. Which would make it last longer.

By the time the water had hit my knees, my waterproof coating was cooling in its vial, and I had cut a large circle from my cloak with a pair of shears I'd found among the provided equipment. While the coating cooled, I monitored the tarry substance that would be my viable air catalyst, and for the first time in at least half an hour, as I shivered in the cold water, I glanced around the arena, through the glass panels.

Several students were painting the insides of air bladders like mine with the coatings they'd created. Keryth had lit two of her burners and was carefully examining the transparent panel blocking her cell from the rest of the maze. Wilder had all three of his burners alight, and he was also studying the panel at the end of his cell, but he was examining not the glass itself but the metal frame attaching it to the perpendicular walls of the clear corridor.

Brilliant, I thought as I watched him slosh through water not yet up to his knees, since he was several inches taller than I. The alchemical formulas that would weaken a metal frame would surely be much simpler and faster to concoct than anything that would affect the glass itself. And I was uncertain the transparent panels actually *were* glass, given that two of our classmates—both men—had already tried to shatter them. Both had wound up with broken equipment for their troubles, which no doubt limited the functionality of their workspaces.

If I were certain that Lord Calyx's metal-melting fluid would work on the labyrinth frames, I might have taken an approach similar to Wilder's. But I was far from sure of that, given that it had not dissolved the metal trim piece on the Conservatory staircase.

When my waterproof substance had cooled, I spread it generously over the outside of my air pocket and blew to dry it. The finished product was rough and rubbery, but waterproof and airtight, and flexible enough to let me close the circle of material into a pouch.

By the time the exterior coating had dried, murky water was lapping at my thighs and my entire body was covered with gooseflesh. My hands shook as I worked, and water had just begun to slosh onto the shelf below my work surface. Tiny waves rocked unused vials, pulling them back and forth with a motion that grew more aggravated by the moment, both from the rising of the water level and from every sluggish movement I made.

I snatched up my frock and what remained of my cloak and made room for them on a corner of my work surface to keep them dry, in case I found myself in need of more material.

The rising water had slowed me down, both from its natural resistance to motion and from the cold. Men seemed to have the advantage again in the White Trial because they were generally taller, so less of their bodies was submerged. But there was nothing I could do about the lack of physical equity.

Regardless of size or gender, those who wore spectacles would have even more difficulty once we were fully submerged.

By the time my tarry catalyst had reached the proper color and consistency—denoted by a sudden bright green flare rippling through the vial—the supplies on my shelf had been washed away. Some floated around my waist, and others had sunk to the floor, where they rocked in the water with every move I made.

The catalyst was still too hot to use, but I was running out of time. I needed to know immediately if I'd made the solution properly, because if I hadn't, I'd have to start over, and there was no guarantee I'd have time to complete a second batch.

Shaking from the cold, I grabbed a candle from the edge of my workstation and snuffed out the flame with two fingers, then inverted it into the vial, coating the wick in the still-hot, bright green substance. I blew on the wick to dry it quickly, then poked it into the flame of a lit burner.

The candle flared brightly. *Extraordinarily* bright. So bright, in fact, that I heard a gasp from my left and turned to see Raelah staring at me from her transparent cell.

It worked.

Though the catalyst was still hot, I poured a generous blob of it onto the inside of my still-flat air bladder and used the dull side of a scalpel to spread it over the entire surface. It dried quickly into a smooth, thin, greenish layer, and I immediately gathered the edges of the double-coated cloak material and tied the air pocket closed with the lace from the neck of my cloak.

With one viable air bladder complete and hopefully functional, I found myself with several extra minutes, a dry and otherwise worthless frock, and nearly half a vial each of both coatings.

So I grabbed the shears and cut out a second bladder. I painted it as quickly as possible with the waterproof coating, and while I was waiting for that to dry, nervously eyeing the rising water as it now actively threatened the surface of my workstation, I accidentally knocked my candle off the edge.

I gasped, horrified by the loss of light—until I realized that the candle was still burning. *Under* the water.

Thirty-Seven

W*hat in the name of all chaos . . . ?*

I stared at the bright white glow as it sank toward my feet, drifting back and forth with the current.

My viable air coating, which I'd tested on the wick, was somehow allowing it to burn underwater!

With a jolt, I remembered a line running up the margin of Past Amber's notes on her candle experiment, noting that her candle had stayed lit in the rain and reminding herself to test that particular side effect for its cause and limits.

Its limit, evidently, would blow right past complete submersion in water.

Suddenly inspired, I turned and sloshed through waist-high water to grab the torch mounted on the white marble wall at my back. It was still burning, and for the first time, I noted that its flame was the normal yellowish color of every stove and fireplace I'd ever seen, rather than the stark white glow of the torches mounted in the halls of the Conservatory.

On impulse, and despite the risk that I'd be unable to see well enough to finish my second air bladder, I slogged three slow steps back to my workstation, where water now sloshed over the edge with every move I made, and smothered the torch flame with my miraculously still-dry frock.

This particular torch appeared to be constructed of resinous wood and fabric scraps soaked in animal fat, to extend the length of the flame. I added several scraps from my dress, binding them tightly to enclose the remaining original fuel. Then I carefully poured half of the remaining viable air catalyst onto the cloth binding the fuel and poked at it with a set of laboratory tweezers to compress the material in strategic places, spreading the catalyst and helping it soak through the fuel. While the torch dried at the center of my work surface, I spread the remaining viable air catalyst in a thin layer over the inside of my second air bladder and blew it dry, then tied it closed with a strip of material torn from my dress.

Then, just as the water rose fully onto my work surface, I snatched up my still-burning candle and lit my treated torch.

The flare of light was so bright that even I gasped.

As water washed supplies and equipment from my work surface, extinguishing my burners, I climbed onto the table, where I sat shivering in my drenched and somewhat translucent undergarments while water lapped at my legs. I held my torch in one hand, and as my inflated air bladders floated past, I snatched them, fumbling with cold, stiff fingers to tie them together with a strip of material from my drenched dress while I balanced the torch between my knees.

"Are you ready?" Yoslyn asked, and I turned to see her standing chest deep in murky water, facing me through the transparent barrier, dressed only in undergarments that clung to her thin form. Which was when I realized that water was now pouring into our cells much more rapidly than before.

Now that the work surfaces had been submerged, effectively putting an end to the performance of alchemy, the trial had been accelerated. The arena was filling quickly.

I slid off my work surface and gasped as water washed up to my chest. My air bladders bobbed on the surface beside me, tethered to the strip of fabric wrapped around my left palm, while I held the torch in my right hand. "I don't think any of us are truly ready for this."

"He is," Yoslyn said, and as water rushed over my shoulders, I turned, following her gaze, to see a form at the center of the arena, staring up at the hole overhead.

It was Wilder. He'd gotten his cell open and was ready to let the water lift him from our labyrinthian womb, ostensibly purified by the murky water. Though I had serious doubts that even the White Trial had challenged him.

As I stared at him, treading water now that the level had risen above my chin, he turned, still evidently flat-footed, to look at me.

And I swear to the stars that he grinned right at me.

"Can you see the path?" Yoslyn asked. "I can't tell where it goes. It's impossible, since the walls are transparent!"

She was right. I could see the light of my torch—the only light left in the arena—reflecting from the tops of dozens of translucent panels, but I could not see where any of them turned, diverged, or merged.

"Get a deep breath!" Yoslyn shouted as the rising water lifted me.

Wilder was swimming now, treading water directly beneath the opening in the ceiling, and I could no longer feel the ground even when I pointed my feet.

Suddenly, a great grinding noise startled me. I gasped and sputtered when water washed into my mouth.

My cell was opening, the translucent panel sinking into the floor, causing fresh ripples that rocked me back and forth as they lapped against the other walls of my watery cage.

I moved toward the opening, and my head brushed the translucent ceiling. There was less than four inches of air left above the water, and the door hadn't opened far enough to let me out yet.

Panic crashed over me. I felt like I was suffocating, even as I tilted my head back to suck at the last of the air.

"Amber! Let's go!" Yoslyn shouted, and I turned to see her suck in one last, great breath. Then she pushed through the water toward the widening gap at the end of her cell, tugging a single air bladder of her own.

I took a moment to calm myself. Then I dragged in as deep a breath as I could get and plunged beneath the surface.

It took a bit for me to orient myself as I blinked in the cloudy water. The torch blazing on one edge of my vision sent a triumphant bolt of glee through me, and it was hard not to open my mouth and shout for joy.

But then I saw Yoslyn's bare toes kicking ahead of me, and I lurched into motion.

I'd made it several feet through the translucent corridor, blinking constantly against the burn of water in my eyes, carefully analyzing the reflection of my flame in the glass walls, when something brushed my leg.

Startled, I kicked, and I heard a muffled oof behind me, along with a burst of air being released. When I turned, I caught just a glimpse of Raelah's furious face before she grabbed my ankle and yanked, hard.

I felt myself sink through the water as she used my body as a launchpad to kick off of, and suddenly she was swimming away from me down the corridor.

I struggled to reorient myself in a world where there was no up or down. No forward or backward. Then Raelah was gone, and I was alone in water I could hardly see through. I grabbed my largest air bladder and used my teeth to loosen the cord. Despite my desperate lungs, I forced myself to move slowly as I pressed the opening of the bladder to my mouth, forming a seal against my skin before I loosened my grip on the neck of the bladder. If I lost air to a bad seal, I might run out.

With the bladder pressed against my mouth, I inhaled deeply.

The burning in my lungs eased, and I squeezed off the neck of the bladder again. With that relief, I was able to focus. I waved my torch slowly until I found the marble floor of the arena, then reoriented my body so that my head was up. And I pressed forward into the corridor again.

I was pleased with my progress, until I turned the corner ahead—and found myself back in my original cell.

I'd gotten turned around during the collision with Raelah, and I'd wasted both time and air going the wrong way!

My heart pounding, fear burning through my veins and into my lungs, I spun around and swam as fast as I could in the other direction.

Two lefts and a right later, I finally saw a set of bare feet churning swiftly through the water. I kicked as hard as I could, but I had to stop when my lungs began to burn again. As I was sucking from my larger air bladder, a shadow appeared in the bright glow from my torch. I turned just as a familiar, bluish silhouette swam toward me, and alarm tightened my chest. I clutched the air bladder closed and verified that the smaller one was still tethered to it. Then I mentally pleaded with Pryce Wishart to just swim on past.

He had no air bladder, nor any other equipment that I could see, but there was a strange mask tied over his mouth, and his blue skin had an odd glint when he swam into the light of my torch.

For one terrifying second, his face appeared in front of mine, close enough to be clear in the cloudy water. His eyes were narrowed, his brows drawn low. His navy-tinted hair floated around his face, shifting with the underwater current. And for a moment, I thought he would just . . . go.

Then his hand shot toward me through the water.

Some irrational instinct made me close my eyes in defense of a blow, even though the water denied him any real momentum. An instant later, the torch was tugged from my grip.

My mouth opened in a rage-filled shout that water rushed in to douse, and I found myself coughing, choking on water as the light *I'd* crafted, through a formula *I'd* developed, swam away. Leaving me alone, disoriented, and still choking in water too dark and murky to clearly see through.

Near panic, I gritted my teeth and forced water out of my mouth with my tongue, then I sucked at my air bladder, careful to keep the marble tile beneath me and the light of my own torch ahead. With my lungs again refreshed, I followed that light, flinching every time I passed an open cell door, both fearing and hoping for the sight of a fellow competitor.

If there were none left, then I was last. I'd failed.

But if I was ahead of anyone, that person was unlikely to survive.

The light moved swiftly, and twice it doubled back, but I was unable to keep up. Once, as my largest air bladder began to lose its shape from being emptied, I put on a burst of speed and crashed directly into a translucent wall. Pryce had managed to put several panels between us, and . . .

Something swam in front of the light. Another competitor.

I felt my way along, slower now that I couldn't follow the torch, and I turned when I got to the end of the corridor. Another shadow—or the same one?—swam in front of the now-distant light of my torch, and suddenly, the light lurched upward.

My gaze rose, following it, and I realized that Pryce had found the center of the arena. He'd gotten out, thanks to *my* work!

As I pressed forward again, my free hand trailing along the wall, the murky shadow that had been following Pryce pushed upward toward the surface, only to suddenly reverse course and plunge toward the floor. The shadow looked too big. It . . .

The shadow splintered into two silhouettes, a tempest of flailing arms and legs, and I realized that something had just fallen into the watery arena, colliding with the competitor who'd been about to emerge.

Then, as I watched, still making my way slowly toward the center of the maze, frustrated when my path led me ninety degrees in the wrong direction, a third form plunged into the water, feet first and deliberate, and this form was carrying my torch!

Even in the murky water, even blurry across the distance, I would have known that form anywhere.

Wilder.

He'd taken my torch from Pryce—he'd thrown Pryce back into the arena—and *he was coming for me*.

My heart leapt into my throat, and I kicked harder, despite the exhaustion in my legs and the ache in my empty lungs. I lifted the air bladder to my lips and tried to inhale, but it was empty. A fit seized my stressed lungs, and I coughed into the bag, sucking my own used air in and out rapidly until it eased. Then I let go of the deflated air bladder and quickly seized the smaller, still-full one. As I struggled to untie it, the empty bladder floated in front of me, still tethered to the first, the viable air coating giving off a faint green glow.

Finally I got the second bladder open and took a deep breath from it, then I kicked off against the nearest wall and felt my way forward again. Heading for the light.

But the light hadn't found me. I could tell from the crazed way Wilder was waving it back and forth as the two shadows at his back swam up toward the surface, fighting each other sluggishly and silently for the right to climb out first.

I wanted to shout for Wilder. I wanted to wave my arms to catch his attention, but that would have been a waste of time, effort, and breath, so I kept swimming, working my way around corners and past intersections, gleeful every time I turned toward the center, devastated every time a path took me the other way.

But finally, just as I sucked the last of the air from my second bladder, I emerged from a transparent pathway into the broad center of the maze. Wilder was just emerging from a corridor he'd taken in error, and he saw me. He lurched across the open area, pulling in powerful strokes against the water as I kicked toward him, exhausted and slow. He got to me before I reached the center, and his free arm wrapped firmly around my waist. He hauled me forward, my lips sealed against a breath I desperately needed.

We made it to the opening just as another form reached it, his movements sounding muted and sloshy to my submerged ears. Wilder pushed the poor man aside and shoved me upward, toward the surface. Toward a crown of light and the silhouette of a familiar head peeking over the opening in the glass ceiling. Toward a hand reaching for me.

I reached up, and Yoslyn grabbed my wrist.

My head broke the surface, and I sucked in a great breath, bringing in a spray of tiny droplets with it.

"Amber!" she shouted, and vaguely I was aware of a form behind her, pushing past her.

Desmond grabbed my arms and pulled me effortlessly from the hole in the glass, water streaming from my drenched form. I collapsed on his lap, soaked and shivering as he ripped off his cape and wrapped it around me.

"You're okay," he whispered. "You did it. You *survived.*"

I dragged in breath after breath, and as the world came back into focus, as forms regained color and clarity, I realized that half of the audience was staring at us. At Desmond, who held me tucked neatly into his formidable embrace, and Yoslyn, who stood staring down at us, still dripping from her own ordeal and draped in a drying cloth.

The other half of the spectators were staring from their seats at the hole in the glass.

I turned just as Wilder lifted himself onto the glass floor, drenched, his underclothing clinging to his every trim plane and well-developed cord of muscle, and that was when I realized that he wore Pryce's mask. That he'd been breathing through whatever Pryce Wishart had come up with to allow air into his mouth while keeping water out, and that . . .

I turned and counted my classmates, who sat shivering, wrapped in thick drying cloths, on the lowest level of spectator seating, just above the glass-covered surface of the arena. Directly below the Bluehelm and the highest-ranking professors and staff members, who stared at us, unmoving. Unspeaking.

And I began to count.

Keryth Malcom sat in the first position, but there was a gap on the bench to her left, which told me she hadn't been the first out. Wilder had.

Lennox Pettigrove sat on her right, in third position, and next to him sat Adria, then Cressa, who stared at Wilder, dumbfounded. Number six was Yoslyn, who stood right in front of me. Then Gavin, number seven, who'd been collateral damage when Pryce was thrown back into the arena. He'd made it out but had yet to take his seat.

I was the eighth.

Only I wasn't, because Pryce Wishart had beaten me out of the arena.

Wilder had pushed him back in, without his mask, though he would have been able to swim right back up through the hole if he hadn't tangled with Gavin on his way down.

Yet . . . Pryce was still in the water, along with Raelah, who must have gotten turned around after she'd passed me.

Wilder tore the mask from his face and marched across the glass ceiling toward his spot on the lowest bench. In first position. He glanced at me, and when our gazes met, the fury in his eyes faded. He grinned. Then he winked.

I pushed myself upright, out of Desmond's warm grip, and raced across the slick surface toward Wilder. He stood, frowning at my dangerous speed, and I crashed bodily into him, heedless of my drenched, largely transparent clothing. Of my stringy, soaked hair and the tears streaming down my face. Of my very dignity.

"Amber? Are you—"

I shot up onto my toes and kissed him, right there in front of everyone. In front of Desmond, who I could practically *feel* watching us.

Wilder kissed me back, long and hard. His fingers dug into my hips, and I slid my arms around his neck, burrowing into the warmth glowing through his cold, wet clothing, and in the end, it was only the low, solemn voice of the Bluehelm that broke us apart. That brought me back to myself, and to the ongoing trial.

"They've been submerged too long."

I let Wilder go and stepped back to see that the Bluehelm had stood.

"Let's get the victors somewhere dry and warm," she said, stepping down onto the glass. "And let's begin the recovery effort."

Her words chilled me all the way to the bone, and I turned, Wilder's hand warm in mine, to stare down through the transparent panels at the water below. It was too murky to see more than a couple of feet in, but somewhere down there, two of my classmates had—

"Look!" Keryth shouted. Her arm bumped mine as she stood.

Yoslyn gasped, and I followed their gazes to see a hand pressed to the glass. Clawing at it.

"Someone's still alive!" Desmond shouted. Water splashed through the opening, and suddenly he was gone, and it took me a second to realize he'd jumped in.

He'd stood on the glass ceiling while I nearly drowned, but he'd jumped in without hesitation to save *someone else.*

A moment later, he bobbed to the surface of the water, framed by the hole in the glass, and shoved Raelah to safety.

Wilder grabbed her—I'd had no idea he'd disappeared from my side—and pulled her onto the glass, where she coughed up what seemed like buckets of water. She'd failed. But somehow, despite the fact that she'd lost her air bladder and had been down there far too long, she'd survived.

"How...?" Wilder asked, and someone stepped down from the spectator's benches to hand him a drying cloth. He draped it over Raelah, and Yoslyn knelt to pound on her back. "How do you think—"

A pounding cut him off, and I jumped, whirling to look for the source. The sound echoed again, and this time I saw a fist hit the underside of the glass, several yards from the opening.

"There!" I shouted, pointing.

"Pryce is still alive!" Adria yelled while Cressa stared in stunned silence beside her.

Desmond dove under the glass again, and I watched the blur of his movement. His form met the other one, and he hauled a coughing, choking, still-blue-tinted Pryce Wishart into the air.

A buzz had begun among the spectators as they voiced quiet disbelief and confusion. As they made soft conjecture, while Pryce coughed up absolute *leagues* of water, shivering in a puddle.

No one had offered him a drying cloth.

He coughed again, then looked around in utter confusion, all animosity washed from his expression by the shock of survival. He was trying to say something, but the words seemed stuck.

Pryce spit out more water. Then more. He cleared his throat. Then he said something, the syllables cracked and broken. Disjointed.

"What was that?" the Bluehelm demanded, lifting the hem of her robe out of a puddle as she stepped carefully closer.

"I said, you can breathe it!" Pryce shouted. He pushed himself unsteadily to his feet. "You can breathe the star-cursed water!"

Silence descended across the arena.

"He's delirious," a professor said softly at my back. "Mad from the experience of near death."

"No, he's right," Raelah said. "And it's the *damnedest* thing. I ran out of air, and I couldn't find the center of the arena, and I thought I was going to die. I held my breath as long as I could, but then . . . my mouth opened. I couldn't help it. And water . . . I was choking on it. Sucking it into my lungs as if it were air, because that's what lungs do, whether you want them to or not, and—" She blinked, staring at the glass beneath her feet. "I didn't die. I was breathing the water. It was thick, and it was hard to push in and out, but it *worked*."

"You can breathe it . . ." Pryce repeated, his eyes wide, hair plastered to his skull and trailing down his cheeks.

And finally, as we all stared at one another, and at the hole, and at the glass surface in wonder and astonishment, but mostly in confusion, the Bluehelm stepped down from her place in the stands and cleared her throat.

"I don't yet understand how it happened, but today, for the first time in the history of the White Trial in its current incarnation, *all* of the participants have survived!"

Despite years—decades—dedicated to the pursuit of the tincture—the Philosopher's Stone—I have today been forced to admit my own utter failure in the occupation. I remain convinced that the *prima materia* is true and precise, which can only mean that the failure is mine alone. I cannot, despite the number of years consumed by this specific portion of the task, conceive of how to combine the spirit with this glittering yet otherwise ineffectual decoction of mind and matter.

If such a substance as the Stone can in fact be created, it will not be by me. Not, at least, in the measure of years I can still claim on this earth. That leaves me with but a pair of options: retire in shame, or revise my focus to the lengthening of my own life and, with that pursuit, perhaps the time needed to *finally* square the circle.

—from the private notes of Lord Calyx,
the father of alchemy

Thirty-Eight

"Number eight was Pryce," Keryth said, clearly unaware that I was sitting at the Refectory table behind her, shielded from view by a large potted fern. "That's really all there is to it."

"But he cheated," Lennox insisted softly, punctuated by the sound of him sipping from his teacup. "We all know who made that torch, and she would *never* have given it to him. Amber Fallbrook wouldn't spit in the mouth of a man dying of thirst, especially if that meant *she* would die of thirst, and if that man were Pryce Wishart, she would pour his mouth full of sand instead."

I scowled into my own tea. I would *not* let a man die of thirst, if I could possibly help him. Though I *did* wish upon Pryce Wishart the biggest metaphorical mouthful of sand one could imagine.

"To rebut, I have two points," Keryth said. "First, Amber saved Yoslyn during the Black Trial—"

"She had a *reason* for doing that," Lennox insisted. "She needs Yos for something related to her research, or she wanted to show off the fact that her elixir, while slow to produce, was by far the most effective."

A sick feeling churned in my stomach. Had I shown *no* kind sentiment to my classmates before I'd lost my memory?

"And *second*..." Keryth continued, her tone combative in a way it often was to defend her opinions in class. "There were no rules for the White Trial, so it is not possible for Pryce to have broken any."

"But he went *back* into the water after he came out, and—"

"He didn't *go* in," Keryth snapped. "Wilder stole his breathing mask and *shoved* him in."

"Which is not breaking any rules, according to your own logic," Lennox concluded, somewhat smugly. "And *my* point is that Pryce was still in the water when Amber came out, making her the eighth victor."

"The seventh," Keryth said. "According to *your* logic, Wilder would have been eighth, since he reemerged after her. And I'm not sure even *that* is accurate, because Amber did not emerge from her own efforts. Not exclusively."

"Neither did Pryce," Lennox insisted. "He used Amber's torch."

"Well then, I suppose your point stands," Keryth conceded, and I grinned into my porridge. "Ultimately, Pryce was tenth out of the water, after Raelah, and whether or not we take into consideration that he stole Amber's torch, both making use of her efforts and robbing her of them, as tenth, he should be eliminated from the competition."

"Indeed." Lennox sounded very pleased with himself. "And yet, a week has passed with no announcement."

A great frustration to the entire Mastery cohort.

"That's not about the victors," Keryth whispered, lowering her voice until I could hardly hear it above my own slow chewing. "It's about the breathable water. Cressa says the Bluehelm has put great pressure on the staff and faculty to figure out how that was accomplished and who did it. They expected one of us to take credit, but obviously no one has."

"I truly thought Pryce would," Lennox mumbled.

I snorted, then froze, afraid I'd been overheard until Keryth replied.

"There is no way Pryce Wishart is capable of—"

"Agreed." Lennox huffed. "But he *is* capable of lying about it."

"He may not be brilliant, but he isn't a fool, either," Keryth insisted. "Anyone who takes credit will be expected to prove the skill, and when he can't, he'd be expelled for lying."

"So . . . who do you think did it?" Lennox asked, and I found myself leaning backward, into the plant, so I could hear better.

"I have no idea," Keryth admitted. "No one in our class has that kind of aptitude."

"Not even Wilder?"

"Not even Amber, back before her fall from grace."

I bristled at the label. I'd been struck with amnesia. How was that disgraceful?

"So then . . . ?" Lennox left the unspoken question dangling.

"A professor, maybe? Or a researcher? It had to have been a staff member. My father says there have always been conscientious objectors to the trials. To letting students die to prove their worth." She hesitated, and I could practically see her shrugging. "Maybe someone decided to do something about it."

I stood so suddenly I nearly knocked over my teacup.

Maybe she was right.

Maybe Wilder wasn't the only Gregory brother who'd tried to help me. . . .

I was halfway across the quadrangle when I spotted Wilder heading directly for the Conservatory, absentmindedly weaving the handle of his blade through the fingers of his right hand, and my pulse spiked so hard that the world swam before my eyes for one swollen instant.

He was looking for me.

There was no other reason he'd go into the Conservatory, considering that he and Desmond were hardly on speaking terms.

Mastery-year classes had been suspended for the past week, ostensibly to give students ample time to recover from the White Trial, but the truth, I suspected, was more in line with Keryth and Lennox's supposition: Our professors were trying to understand what had happened in the arena and which students should move forward.

That was no doubt also why we had not been given the expected draught of memory drain; one could not claim credit for what one could not remember.

Instead, we'd been sternly instructed not to reveal details about the White Trial and to spend missed class time working on our personal research and studying for exams. I'd spent much of that time in the Seminary library, sharing a table with Wilder and Yoslyn, all three of us avoiding several pressing topics, while I seemed capable of privately contemplating little else.

Which is to say that Wilder and I had not discussed our second kiss, just like we'd never fully discussed the first. Just like we'd never truly discussed the nature of our relationship before I'd lost my memory. And the last thing I wanted was for him to rush up to the laboratory looking for me and come face-to-face with his brother instead.

So, as he stepped into the Conservatory atrium, I raced across the lawn, mumbling apologies to students I brushed abruptly past, then I stormed up the front steps, rushed across the Alchemary creed in its triangle on the floor, and headed up the steps.

I was prevented from running up the first flight of stairs by two researchers who were on their way down, embroiled in a debate about the ethical uses of a temperament-enhancing elixir, so by the time I got to Desmond's office suite, the door was already swinging shut.

I pulled it open, but Wilder had already crossed the outer office and entered Desmond's private laboratory space. The door stood ajar, and I could see Wilder's elbow and the satchel he carried under one arm.

I should have said something. But his words stopped me cold.

"You know, you still owe me for the last dose."

Surprised, I lurched to the right, out of sight from the door, as the familiar soft creak of leather told me he was opening his satchel. Vials clattered together, then clinked distinctively as they were set on a hard surface.

"I apologize. I was running short on several things last time. Amber goes through quite a bit of my inventory. But it's all there."

I heard more clinking, along with the rustle of fabric and another soft creak of leather, and I understood, suddenly, that Desmond was paying Wilder in supplies for whatever elixir he'd provided. Whatever it was that he snuck into his office to take, at least once a week.

"How long do you anticipate needing my services?" Wilder's voice was thick with arrogant amusement.

"Only as long as it takes me to replicate your formula for myself." Desmond didn't sound the least bit shamed by his admission.

"Naturally," Wilder said. "And have you had any luck?"

Desmond exhaled heavily. "Panacea is not my area of expertise, and I will admit that your mind and mine do not tread the same scientific pathways. But I am confident in my own abilities. I will eventually unlock the functionality of your elixir, even if I wind up using a slightly different recipe."

"Best of luck." The door creaked open an inch, and with a jolt of panic, I scooted even farther away, glancing around for some place to hide in the empty foyer. But Wilder didn't emerge. "Was it you?"

"Was what me?" Desmond asked.

"The water. In the arena. Did you make it breathable? And as a brief follow-up query, *how* did you do that?"

"It wasn't me," Desmond said, and I found myself easing closer to the door again, drawn by something in the almost unnaturally tranquil tone of his answer. I'd come to recognize that tone and to understand what it meant: He was telling the truth, yet leaving something else—something relevant—unsaid.

"There's no one else who has the skill for such a thing who also had a reason to demonstrate that skill, in that manner, at that time."

Desmond huffed. "So, you believe you've sorted it all out."

"You were trying to protect her." Wilder sounded tense and insistent, each word tightly wound and ready to explode. "That's why you didn't jump in. You didn't go save her because you knew she wouldn't drown in that water."

"I didn't go save her because she didn't need saving."

"I thought she was going to die—"

"But she *didn't* die. She made it to the center of that maze on her own, and she deserved the chance to emerge without anyone else interfering. *You* jumped in and created the appearance that she couldn't do it on her own."

My heart thumped so hard my sternum felt bruised.

"Everyone *knows* she can do it, Des," Wilder insisted. "That's never been in question. She's at an unfair disadvantage because of her memory, but she's the best alchemist in our cohort, and it would be unfair for her to flunk out just because she's temporarily lost some of her previous skill set."

"That would *not* be unfair," Desmon practically growled. "She *has* lost knowledge, and that has weakened her, and the board has to be sure that she can contribute to the Alchemary, because whether or not you want to admit it, she may never get back what she's lost. She needed to prove she could do this on her own—to herself, and to everyone else. She needed everyone to know she is worthy of the victory. And you jumping in to save her only tells people that you don't think she can do it. Which allows them to suffer the same delusion. You *stole* the moment from her, Wilder."

"And *you* were going to let her die."

"I would not have—"

"Then why didn't you jump?" Wilder demanded, his shadow gesticulating angrily through the crack in the door. "If you didn't know she could breathe in the water, why didn't you jump in? You were *right there*, on the edge of the hole, even though all of the staff and faculty were staring at you. You had already shed the thin veneer of your objectivity like a snake casting off its own skin. But you didn't jump. I know how you feel about her, so *why* were you willing to let her die?"

I pushed the door open, and they both turned to stare at me, silence heavy and horrible between us.

"He wasn't going to let me die," I finally said, my voice echoing with a truth as cold and as deep as the sea. "He was just going to let me *fail*. Desmond would have jumped in to save me if you hadn't pushed Pryce back in and jumped in yourself, because then I would have been the ninth competitor out of the water.

"He doesn't want me dead." I shifted my focus to Desmond, who met it without any hint of an argument. "He just wants me far away from here."

Desmond nodded, holding my gaze. "I've been honest about that from the beginning. You should not be here. But if you'd needed help, I would not have let you die."

I blinked slowly, anger and a grief I could not understand swirling in my gut like eddies on the surface of a murky pond. Then I turned and walked away from them both.

"Amber, wait." Wilder's footsteps clomped behind me. His hand closed over my bicep, pulling me to a graceless stop halfway through the outer office, and I turned to find myself alone with him. Desmond had not followed.

"I . . ."

I had no idea what he'd intended to say, and he seemed somewhat unsure of that himself.

"He's not wrong, you know." I gently tugged my arm from his grasp. "As sweet as it was"—as well-intentioned, and kindhearted, and *fiercely* charming—"you should not have jumped in after me."

His forehead crinkled, confusion warring with something deeper and more painful. "I jumped because I couldn't let you die."

"No." My heart cracked open at the words—at what was still to come—but it had to be said. "You jumped because you didn't believe I could save myself. And now no one else does either."

I left Wilder staring after me in the outer office, and instead of going down the stairs, I went up. Desmond would not follow me, and there was only one other place where neither Wilder nor Yoslyn would be able to.

To my utter surprise, I found as I stepped into the grand, warmly but imposingly furnished research library that the space was completely empty. Even the librarian was absent, a likely momentary state I attributed to the very odd atmosphere that had settled over the Alchemary campus like a spiritual fog in the week since the White Trial.

Maybe Keryth was right; maybe the Bluehelm really had tasked most of the staff with figuring out who had altered the water in the arena, and how. Considering they were still also looking for a treatment for the odd aurum pestilence popping up all over

Aethermere, *tense* didn't come close to describing the ambiance on the island.

Regardless, with the entire stately room to myself, I had access for the first time ever to the shelf of rare books behind the librarian's desk, which I was absolutely *not* supposed to touch. But I had unanswered questions about the father of alchemy, and the rare books shelf held a volume comprised entirely of his handwritten personal notes, compiled along with commentary by some of history's finest alchemical theorists. . . .

Given that, and the fact that if Pryce were not disqualified, I would be considered ninth in the White Trial, which put me on the precipice of expulsion for the third time in two months, and given the fact that I'd just been betrayed in two entirely different ways by my two oldest friends and recent lovers . . . I was feeling more than a bit daring and reckless.

Especially considering I would likely never get a chance like this again.

With another glance around the perfectly round bookcase-lined space, I snuck behind the librarian's desk and plucked the volume from the shelf where I'd spied it weeks ago. Worried that she would reappear at any moment, I adjusted the other books to close the gap between the spines, then I took the stolen book to a chair on the opposite side of the room, where I opened it inside one of my textbooks to disguise what I was reading in case anyone came in.

I will admit that I felt quite daring and clever.

The pages of the historical volume were thick but delicate, and very, very old. I thumbed through them carefully, staring in awe at Lord Calyx's signature notation, noting that his flourishes were subtle and austere, which wasn't surprising, since he was writing before the practice became widespread. That he was, in fact, the source of it.

I read the first few notes word for word, and I found myself in awe of his thought process and of his plans for the Alchemary. He spoke respectfully of Emperor Eldon, who had given him both funding and a mandate, but he rarely mentioned the queen.

After that, worried that my time alone with the book would soon elapse, I began to skim, searching the text for mentions of the Philosopher's Stone. There were no specific formulas listed, but Lord Calyx documented failure after failure in his quest to accomplish his mandate, and finally, three-quarters of the way through the text, he wrote the actual words, expressing his utter frustration with his own lack of progress.

The lines of the triangle in the symbol for the Philosopher's Stone, which he had traced over and over in the margins of his notes, represented spirit, mind, and matter. The goal of the Philosopher's Stone was to fuse all three in an effort to perfect the human form in all three aspects.

The spirit is the problem, he'd written at the bottom of the page. *Unification. The outer circle.*

According to his notes, even with all the right ingredients, catalyzing the Philosopher's Stone with only mind and matter had created an inert stone. Calyx considered it beautiful and multifaceted, like alchemy itself.

He believed it to be highly valuable and virtually flawless in form, and yet it was not functional. His inert stone was both precious and worthless at the same time. He described it as a token bestowed but not treasured.

I could practically feel his heartbreak bleeding onto the page with each word, and I could not blame him for giving up.

The rest of his notes detailed a shift in his focus from the Philosopher's Stone, which Emperor Eldon had once been obsessed with, to the alchemist's own personal passion, which he was clearly reluctant to name.

But it *had* to be the Elixir of Life.

Calyx was careful, even in his private notes. He was circumspect and sparse with specific details, likely because he knew that after his death, everything he'd ever written would be collected and studied, his soul flayed open and consumed by generations of alchemists with their theories and assumptions. With their awe and their judgment. He must have known that he would live immortalized in history books, shaded by bias and perspective. He would have known that truth is all about perspective.

He would have held his secrets close.

Or . . . he might have hidden them. He might have designed a series of secret—

"You!"

Startled, I snapped the book closed and looked up to find the librarian staring at me from the open doorway, having returned to her post on virtually silent feet. Her scowl was severe, her hands propped on generous hips beneath the slate of her dark cape.

"Yes?" I half whispered, guilt warming my face.

"Just studying, are you?" She did not wait for my reply. "I will never understand why they allowed you back in here."

"*Back* in here?" I stood, and when she turned to round her desk, I carefully set the rare volume on the table beside my chair, blocked from her immediate view by a bronze sculpture of a set of scales.

"After the disaster you visited upon this sacred space this past summer."

"The disaster I . . . ?" I slid my textbook into my satchel and crossed the floor toward her, stopping when she gestured at the table in the center of the room, directly beneath a skylight of the same size.

"You set the place ablaze, child!" Her gesture grew more frantic, and I turned to scan the table. "And when everyone came running, you just stood there, covered in ash and your own blood. You may have everyone else fooled, but I don't for one moment believe you've forgotten that."

I caught my breath.

Ash and blood. Written at the center of a perfect circle, in the margin of Past Amber's journal . . .

The librarian looked ready to expel me, despite my permission to be there, and that's likely what she would have done if not for the entrance of two staff researchers at that very moment, heading right for her with a question.

While she was busy with them, I bent across the table to peer at the center, at whatever she'd been pointing at.

Someone had done a good job of refinishing it, but the damage was still visible beneath a clean, glossy coat of wax. The very center of the table had indeed been burned, and the fire had exposed the shape of an inlaid circular panel of wood, no bigger in circumference than my palm. I wedged my fingernail into the crack and pried the panel out, holding my breath in anticipation.

Another secret compartment. A circle, no doubt opened with ash and blood.

But it was empty. Whatever it was—whatever Past Amber had found—she had taken it with her.

Thirty-Nine

Yoslyn sat alone at a small table in the student library on the first floor of the Seminary, tapping a lead stylus against a sheet of parchment, and for a moment, I felt bad for having skipped our study session. Especially since Wilder clearly hadn't shown up either. But I was as relieved by his absence as I was by her presence, despite the fact that half an hour earlier, I'd wanted nothing more than to be alone.

"I think I found another secret compartment," I whispered as I slid into the chair across from her, flinching when it skidded on the stone floor and several gazes snapped toward us.

She blinked at me. "Why are you cross with Wilder?"

"I . . ." I frowned, thrown by the change of subject. "Pardon?" I whispered, leaning over the table toward her.

"That man jumped into an underwater labyrinth to try to save you, and he's been walking around here for a week like there's nothing but clouds beneath his feet, until you both failed to show up for our study session." She narrowed green eyes at me. "Then, half an hour ago, he came in here looking like someone had ripped his heart out and devoured it right in front of him."

Yoslyn nodded subtly to my left, brown ringlets falling over her shoulder, and I turned to see Wilder sitting alone in a chair across the room, angled away from us, the corner of a textbook visible on his lap.

"There's only one person on this island with the power to make Wilder Gregory look like that," she said. "And you *do* have a history of leaving your classmates in tears. So don't try to tell me you didn't just carve open his chest and leave him bleeding."

I leaned back in my chair, and the wood creaked conspicuously. "It's . . . complicated, Yos."

"I'm not certain it is."

"I didn't need him to save me," I whispered, well aware that we weren't supposed to talk about the White Trial in public. Specifically, near the underclassmen.

"And he didn't. But he was willing to. *Demonstrably* willing. He was *further* willing to land a blow atop the skull of the pig gizzard of a boy who's been bullying you for weeks now. For the second time. And you're *cross* with him because of it? For caring about you and being willing to act on it?" Her perplexed frown practically begged me to explain.

I swallowed a groan and leaned forward again. "The problem isn't that he cares," I insisted softly. "It's that he doesn't believe in me."

Yoslyn slammed her textbook shut with a sharp thunk that made me cringe. "That is categorically false. He *does* believe in you. He just also knows that Pryce Wishart's moral decay could very well have killed you, and he wasn't going to let that happen."

My hands tightened around the arms of my chair. "Even if it cast me in the role of the helpless damsel, in front of the entire Alchemary board?"

Yoslyn nodded. "Even if it vexed you so badly that you'd never speak to him again. He'd rather have you alive than happy." She reached across the table and poked my arm with one finger. "What was it you said about love? That it's madness and angst? That it's insatiable and covetous, equal parts adoration and vexation?"

I swallowed a groan. "Actually, I said that about *passion*."

She laughed softly. "I believe my point stands."

For a moment, I could only stare at her, struggling against uncooperative lungs for a deep breath. Then I twisted to sneak another glance at Wilder, who was definitely *not* actually reading a textbook.

I lowered my voice even further as I turned back to Yoslyn. "You think he loves me."

She rolled her eyes. "I do, but only because that is patently obvious. I also don't think it's fair to hold that against him."

I sighed again. "I will take that under advisement."

"Good." She leaned back in her seat, arms crossed over the front of her gray frock, blue cuffs standing out stiffly. "Then let's revisit what you just said. You *think* you found another hidden compartment? Where?"

"In the research library. There was a hidden panel in the center of the table, and evidently I set it on fire and bled all over it at some point over the summer."

"What?" She shot forward again in her seat. "I never heard a word about that.... But then, most students go home for the summer, and it's not as if the staff would broadcast the fact that the one who didn't turned out to be an arsonist."

I arched one skeptical brow. "I'm not—"

"What was in it?"

"I haven't the faintest. It was empty. I think Past Amber—"

"Past Amber?"

"The me I was before I lost my memory. I think Past Amber found that compartment first, and she took whatever was in it."

"Which means that Now Amber—*you*—must have it."

"Or . . . I hid it."

Yoslyn's brows rose, her green eyes shining in the light from the candle at the center of the table. "You left yourself a secret?"

"I left myself nothing *but* secrets."

She leaned over the table, eyes wide and eager. "Okay, then, let's go search your bedchamber."

"I searched the whole room, from top to bottom, when I woke up with no memory and was trying to figure out who I am and what I was studying. Whatever was in that compartment is not in my room."

Yoslyn arched one eyebrow at me, pointedly. "Well then, we really have no choice but to call in reinforcements."

"Reinforcements?"

"Someone who knew you well, when you were Past Amber. Someone who might know where you used to hide things. Someone you might even have told about the compartment, when you found it." She nodded to my left again, and this time I did not turn to look at Wilder. "Letting him in on this little mystery might be a good way to show him that you're no longer cross. That it was, in fact, unreasonable of you to have been angry with him in the first place."

I groaned and lay my head on the table, my cheek pressed into the cool surface. Then I sucked in a deep breath, grabbed my satchel, and headed toward Wilder's chair, motioning over my shoulder for Yoslyn to join me.

"You two have been opening secret compartments all over campus for weeks, and you're just now telling me about it?" Wilder sat in my green chair, where the ocean breeze from the open window had given his blond waves an adorably tousled look.

"It was mostly her." Yoslyn had reclined on my bed, her arms folded behind her head against the simple wooden headboard. "And it wasn't all over campus; it was just in the Conservatory. And to be fair, it was really only two puzzles, until today." She frowned.

"Though evidently Amber was doing this long before even she knew about it."

"Am I to assume," I said, "based on your reaction, that I did not tell you about the first one, this past summer?"

"You did not," Wilder confirmed. "You stayed here for the break, but I went to Innswood, and I'd only been back on campus for a single day when you lost your memory, so I *like* to think you *would* have told me. If you hadn't forgotten yourself."

I let him labor under that delusion, despite the fact that I'd clearly been keeping coded secrets from him in my journal. "So . . . do you know of any place I might have hidden something I'd found?"

Wilder laughed. "I *wish* I knew where you hid your secrets. I do not. But . . . maybe *you* do."

"If I knew, I wouldn't have to ask you."

He shrugged. "Desmond says you often act on memories you can't consciously recall. That you'll put away equipment in the very same drawer you put it in before you lost your memory, almost as if you remember storing it there."

I scowled up at him. "Do the two of you *frequently* discuss me when I am not present?"

Instead of answering my question, Wilder pulled his blade from its sheath and commenced his habit of winding the handle in and around his fingers as he thought aloud. "I'm assuming that's what made you pursue these puzzles in the first place: Some latent memory of having found one over the summer made the first one feel familiar and interesting. Or it showed you where to look. Or . . . *how* to look."

"I did find myself a bit preoccupied with it," I admitted.

"Okay . . ." Wilder leaned forward, pinning me with direct eye contact. "So, what did you find in the two latest compartments, and where did you hide *those* little treasures? Because it's entirely possible you hid them in the same place as—"

"No," I interrupted, twisting to retrieve the wooden box from the far corner of my desk. "I found a bracelet, and then Yos and I found this tiny little frame, and I put them in this box that used to be my mother's."

"I remember that box. Your mother kept dried herbs in it, right?"

"Yes. But there was nothing in the box when I opened it save for my journal, which I still can't read, and my mother's ring."

Wilder sheathed his blade and lifted the metal ouroboros and the square frame from the box. "Wow..." He examined them, turning them over and holding them up to daylight streaming in through the open shutters. "These are beautiful. A bracelet, and... you think this one's a frame? For what? The world's smallest portrait? Can anyone even paint something this small?"

Yoslyn shrugged. "Lord Calyx wrote in print too small to read without a magnification lens. Maybe he also painted?"

"There's no record of that," I said. "But then, there was no record of these compartments, either."

Wilder set the snake and the frame on my desk. "May I see the box? You are a clever girl, as was your mother. Maybe there's a false bottom?"

"I don't think so." Yet I handed him the box.

Wilder went entirely still as he stared down into it. "Where did you get this?"

His voice sounded oddly hollow as he took my mother's ring from the box. He held it between his thumb and forefinger, and light reflected from a dozen different facets of the large stone, illuminating my bedchamber with bright white reflections.

"I told you. It was in the box. It belonged to my—"

"This is not your mother's ring, Amber." He turned it, and Yoslyn gasped as the reflections shifted and flickered all over room. "She was buried with the only ring I ever saw her wear."

"The one my father gave her." She *was* buried with it.

Could he be right? Was that why I had no memory of her wearing such a large stone?

"So then, where did I get this one? Do you think *this* was in the table compartment?" My heart began to thump almost painfully. "Do you think Lord Calyx hid it in the research library, one hundred fifty years ago?"

Yoslyn made a strange, awed sound as she rose from the bed and came closer, staring at the ring.

"Amber," Wilder said, and he was looking directly at me now, rather than at the brilliant stone. "This is Queen *Avalona's* ring."

"No," Yoslyn said. "Her ring is famously green, and it's an oval cut. It's on display in the palace historical—"

"Not that one." Wilder handed me the ring and stood to pace between my bed and the chair. "There's a portrait of Avalona in the Panacea wing. In it, she's heavy with child and smiling radiantly. Her hand is on her belly, and she's wearing *this* ring. Dr. Winhoof has a theory that it was given to her by—" He shook his head. "That doesn't matter. The point is that as far as I know, that's the only time she was ever pictured wearing it, and no one's entirely sure where it came from or what happened to it, since that portrait is from *after* Eldon gave her the emerald."

I held the ring up to the light again and was nearly blinded by the reflection.

And suddenly one of my new memories slid into place with an almost audible click of my mental gears. "This is the ring from the stained glass tableau."

"What?" Wilder frowned.

Yoslyn's hand slapped over the O her mouth had formed. "It certainly is! The light through her ring in the spiraling Conservatory ceiling showed us where to find the tiny frame. And that ring is *clear*. Not green."

His frown deepened. “I never noticed.”

“It’s the same one,” I insisted. “It has to be. If you’re sure *this* ring is the one in that other portrait?”

“It’s pretty hard to mistake,” he said. “That stone is huge, and clear, but I don’t think it’s a diamond. And . . . well, you can come see for yourself. That painting is in the main corridor of the Panacea.”

I glanced at Yoslyn, and she nodded.

“Let’s go.” I set the bracelet and frame back into the box, along with the ring, but before I could close the box, I found my attention strangely captured by the shape the three objects had formed.

The frame was entirely encircled by the bracelet: a square inside a circle. When I’d set the ring down, it had fallen half into the frame, and I now realized something I’d overlooked before, distracted as I was by its luster.

The stone was a perfect circle.

My hand trembling, I picked it up again by the band and placed it stone-surface-down inside the frame. It was a perfect fit.

A circle inside a square, inside a circle.

All that was missing was the triangle.

Forty

"That's it," I whispered as I gazed at the framed portrait. "That's the ring." I stared in awe at the stone I held up to the painting, comparing it to the one Queen Avalona wore on her right hand as it caressed her pregnant belly.

"Do you think Lord Calyx gave it to her?" Yoslyn blinked against the glare of light reflected in the ring.

"How could he have?" Wilder asked, his feet shuffling on white marble as he stepped closer to examine the portrait. "He came from famously modest means, and that's a huge stone. Emperor Eldon funded the Alchemary, but I can't imagine Lord Calyx found room in the budget for a ring made to seduce the emperor's wife from her marriage."

"We don't know that was the purpose of the ring," Yoslyn pointed out. "And—"

"He made it," I said.

"Lord Calyx was not a jeweler," Wilder said. "And again, I don't think he had the means to—"

"He made it," I insisted. "'Beautiful, but inert. Multifaceted, like alchemy itself. Both precious and worthless at the same time. A token bestowed but not treasured.'" I turned to find them both staring at me as if I'd elapsed into a foreign tongue. "He must have thought so, since this is the only portrait of her wearing it."

"What are you talking about?" Yoslyn asked softly.

"I read about it just today, in a bound collection of Lord Calyx's notes. This gem was a failed attempt to create the Philosopher's Stone. This inert but beautiful jewel is the result of his inability to combine spirit with mind and body."

"How can you be sure of that?" Yoslyn said. "We don't even know that the Philosopher's Stone actually *is* a stone. Right?"

I nodded. "We don't know what its true form will be, but *this* form is an alchemist's failure. Yet it is beautiful, so he gave it to his beloved, and as far as we know, she only wore it once. 'Bestowed but not treasured.' At some point, it was returned to him, and he used it in this puzzle." I opened the box and rearranged the pieces again so that they could see. "What does this look like to you?"

Yoslyn gasped as understanding dawned.

"It's the symbol of the Philosopher's Stone," Wilder whispered. "Just missing the triangle."

He was correct, on both counts. For whatever reason, Lord Calyx had hidden in the Conservatory—a building he'd designed himself—three of the four shapes necessary to form the symbol for the Philosopher's Stone.

"We must have overlooked a compartment," Yoslyn said.

"I don't think we have." I'd been mulling it over since we'd left my bedchamber. "I think we're looking for a triangle hidden in plain sight. An indication of where these pieces are supposed to be placed."

"For what purpose?" Wilder mused.

"You think they open something?" Yoslyn asked. "Another compartment?"

I shrugged. "Only Lord Calyx knows what this puzzle is about." Though the truth was that I had a theory.

Considering that the puzzle had taken the shape of the Philosopher's Stone, and that he'd worked on it for years, there seemed at least some chance that he'd hidden his formula—imperfect though it was—in this very building. There was even some chance—albeit a much smaller one—that he had gone back to his magnum opus and actually finished it.

The Philosopher's Stone—or a formula that would get me close—might be the only thing in the world that could restore my memories. And even if it didn't, finding the Stone would be . . .

Well, it would be an *enormous* accomplishment: the completion of the Alchemary's original mandate and the culmination of one hundred fifty years of effort by the greatest alchemical minds in the world. Finding the stone, or a valid path to creating it, wouldn't just keep me enrolled, regardless of my rank in the White Trial. It would render me a *legend* in the field. It would lead to job offers, and grants, and my name in the history books. It might lead to statues and paintings of me, on these very grounds.

And yet, while Yoslyn's eyes were alight with the thrill of a fresh mystery, Wilder seemed . . . quiet. More solemnly determined than I'd ever seen him.

"So, you think we're looking for a triangle we've already seen somewhere," he said, sounding oddly thoughtful.

Had he come to the same conclusion? Was he hoping to leverage the Philosopher's Stone to his own advantage as well? After all, if the board wanted an excuse to get rid of him, he'd given them one at the White Trial by pushing Pryce into the water. By jumping back in himself.

"Yes, but it needs to be small," I said. "It would have to fit inside the ouroboros, and the frame would have to fit inside it. So, a triangle no bigger than my palm." I held up my free hand to demonstrate as I tucked the box beneath my right arm.

"There are triangles *everywhere* around here," Yoslyn moaned. "There's literally one on every uniform."

Our school motto. *Mind, Matter, Spirit*—the three aspects of human nature, which the Philosopher's Stone sought to elevate to a higher form. The Alchemary's seal was all three words, written in the shape of a triangle, in beautiful, scrolling print. And it *was*, in fact, embroidered over the heart of every student wearing a school-issued cloak.

"Well, we're not looking for a uniform, clearly," Wilder said. "So, maybe on a plaque? Or painted on a wall? Carved into one of the doors? Or—"

"Oh!" I breathed as the epiphany struck me. Then I spun and raced down the Panacea's main corridor toward the iconic white marble atrium.

"It's been here the whole time," I whispered as Wilder caught up with me, Yoslyn panting at his heels. "I walked across it every time I entered the building, but I hardly gave it a second thought because Yos is right; there are triangles everywhere. And the stained glass is so stunningly distracting."

I knelt on the floor at the center of the atrium, where the mosaic tile spiraled outward from a version of our school's creed that was just smaller than the palm of my hand. Yoslyn and Wilder knelt on either side of me.

"Mind," I whispered as I pulled the ouroboros from the box and laid it over the triangle. It was exactly the right circumference to surround the triangular seal, with only the points touching the inside of the circle. When nothing happened, I twisted the bracelet, and something clicked. The ouroboros dropped from my fingers, sinking into the floor in a ring that had formed in the mosaic until it was almost flush with the tile.

"Body..." I placed the small metal frame inside the triangle, and another soft click echoed through the foyer.

Yoslyn squealed and grabbed my arm.

Wilder picked up the box and handed me the ring. He seemed to be holding his breath.

Though I could not imagine it was necessary for the puzzle to work, I slid the ring onto my middle finger. I couldn't help it. How could I *not* wear it, now that I knew what it was and who it had belonged to?

With my hand curled into a fist, I pressed the stone directly into the space inside the square frame, and it sank into the tile with another click.

Then . . .

Nothing.

"Turn it," Yoslyn whispered, as if someone might overhear us.

I twisted my fist, unconvinced that would do anything, considering that the stone was perfectly round, but then I heard another click . . . followed by a deep groaning rumble.

The tile beneath us began to tremble, and Yoslyn squealed again as she retreated toward the benches built into the atrium wall. I grabbed the bracelet and the frame and scrambled back, just as the floor began to fracture at its center, right where we'd been standing. Only it wasn't *truly* fracturing. It was shifting, the marble stones sinking in a pattern. . . .

Stairs.

The stone tiles around the central symbol were settling into the ground, each a little deeper than the last, to form a narrow spiral staircase leading below the floor of the atrium.

"Stars alight!" Yoslyn exclaimed, grabbing my arm.

Wilder held out the open box, and I dropped all three pieces inside. I took the box from him and he grinned at me, excitement gleaming in his eyes, but there was something else there, too.

He looked oddly . . . relieved.

A strange feeling rushed over me, foreboding and eerie, and it flushed the excitement entirely from my form.

"Wait." I reached for Wilder's arm, but he was already in motion, and my fingertips hardly grazed the sleeve of his tunic.

"No time," he insisted, already three steps down. "Everyone in the building will have heard. They'll be on the way to claim our discovery."

Panic spiked my pulse, and I rushed down the steps after him, into the dark, my gaze trained on his silhouette. But I'd gone only six or seven steps, my head still protruding above the floor of the foyer, when I heard a sharp crack, then the crash of clay shattering. A hissing echoed up the steps toward me.

Startled, I retreated two steps toward the foyer, my heart thudding in my throat, my fingers scrabbling at the tile floor, now at the height of my shoulders, as I fled from what sounded like a snake about to strike.

From the dark stairwell below, Wilder gasped.

The hissing faded, and he coughed as he stumbled up the steps toward me, reaching for the edge of the floor.

On the edge of my vision, Yoslyn backed away again, one hand covering her mouth, her eyes wide in horror. Shouting echoed from behind her, from the depths of the Panacea wing.

Wilder was right. They had heard.

"Am-ber." Wilder croaked the broken syllables of my name between wet, hacking coughs, and as he turned to me, crawling slowly up the steps, his face pale, lips stained with blood, light fell beyond him to reveal the shattered remains of two small clay pots—and a thin white cloud bubbling up from the contents that had spilled from them to combine on the stairs.

"Go!" Wilder coughed again.

Instead, I rushed down several treads and grabbed his arm, my pulse racing in my ears. I pulled as hard as I could to tug him to his feet, but he was too heavy.

"Yos—" I shouted over my shoulder, but a fit of coughing swallowed her name as I pulled on Wilder's arm, terrified to see him struggling to lift himself. To watch his arm shake beneath the weight of his torso.

"Yoslyn!" I tried again. "Help!"

But she only backed away from the recessed stairwell, eyes still wide and panicked.

Wilder coughed yet again, spraying my sleeve with blood, and Yoslyn screamed. She turned and raced in the direction of the Panacea wing, toward the forms thundering toward us, footsteps heavy on the marble tiles.

Sobbing, I sank onto the second step and tried to pull Wilder up with me. To get his head above the creeping white cloud of whatever noxious fume the broken pots had released. I pulled as hard as I could, but I'd only tugged him over one tread by the time blurry forms knelt on the edge of my tear-fogged vision, distorted arms reaching for us.

Someone lifted me, and the movement triggered my own fit of coughing. I tasted blood, and my vision darkened.

When it cleared, I lay on my back in the atrium, on the cold marble tile. Someone knelt above me, shouting orders, and though I could not draw his face into focus, I recognized Dr. Winhoof's voice.

I turned my head, ignoring the ministrations of a woman with one finger pressed to my pulse, and saw Wilder several feet away, being tended by two more Panacea staff members. He blinked at me slowly. Blood trickled from his mouth, but his lips turned upward in a grin I would never, for the rest of my days, forget.

Then his eyes lost focus. His chest stopped rising.

I screamed, despite the hands tending me—I screamed until the entire world went dark.

Forty-One

"She's waking up."

Yoslyn's voice haunted me like a ghost, hovering just on the edge of comprehension, but it took me a couple of heartbeats to make sense of the words.

I was the one waking up. And she was there. Wherever *there* was.

"Amber. Open your eyes."

Desmond. And surely that was his hand, warm on my arm. My cold, cold arm. All of me was cold, in fact. Utterly freezing.

"Amber." His voice was sharp. Demanding.

My eyes opened—just a crack to let in the flicker of my candle. And I knew it *was* my candle by the clear, bright quality of the light, from the coating Past Amber had dipped her wicks in.

I blinked, and my eyes opened wider. My vision narrowed on the thin wooden planks lining the ceiling of my bedchamber. On the stacked-stone walls.

Shadows shifted, and Yoslyn's face appeared over mine. "Thank all that is good in the universe," she whispered. "She's awake."

A hand took mine from the opposite side of the bed, fingers warm and strong. "Amber." Desmond's voice was softer now. "Amber, look at me. How do you feel?"

I turned my head, and my neck crackled, as if I hadn't moved it in ages. Desmond's face came into focus, first his silhouette, broad but hunched, then his features, and I wondered if my eyes were out of practice, too.

"What happened?" My voice creaked like an old wooden chair. I tried to push myself upright, but the world spun.

Desmond helped me sit up slowly while Yoslyn fluffed my pillow, and when he leaned back to get a better look at me, I noticed that his eyes were red. "What do you remember?" he asked.

"I . . ." I shook my head.

A ring. A portrait. A staircase descending into the floor. Then . . .

"Wilder!" I sat up straight, and the room spun again.

"Get her some water," Desmond ordered as he pressed gently on my shoulders, forcing me to recline against the pillow. I had no strength to resist. "You'll have to go slow," he said. "You've been unconscious for most of a day, and you spent the first several hours breathing viable air through a medical air bladder. We'll get you some food shortly, but first . . ."

Yoslyn pressed a wooden cup of water into my hand, and I sipped from it. The water burned my throat, and Desmond tensed when I coughed. But then I sipped again without incident, and the tension in his form eased.

"Where's Wilder?" I asked as I handed the cup back to Yoslyn.

She made a wounded sound deep in her throat, but it was Desmond's face that told the story: the pained crease at the corners of his eyes and the firm, defensive press of his lips together, before he even opened his mouth.

"He didn't make it."

The room swam around me.

"From what we've been able to ascertain, based on what we found and what Yoslyn told us, you three uncovered a staircase hidden in the floor of the Conservatory foyer. Wilder rushed down first—naturally—and stumbled into a trap. He broke two clay jars, the contents of which combined to form a poisonous gas.

Fortunately, that gas is heavier than air, so it hasn't risen above the staircase, which spared Yoslyn entirely. But Wilder . . ."

"Didn't make it," I finished, my voice brittle. Fragile.

Desmond swallowed, and his steady gaze was a seawall holding back the tide of grief. "You were on the verge yourself, for a few hours. But then you made a sudden recovery."

"From the viable air?"

He shook his head. "That was all they could think to give you, but it can't account for your recuperation." He exhaled, his gaze holding mine. "There's been a lot concerning you that no one can seem to account for lately."

"Where is he?" I demanded softly. I couldn't process the rest of it. The unanswered questions and Yoslyn's curious, heartbroken expression. "Where is Wilder now?"

"I . . ." Desmond frowned. "In the morgue, I assume. They've isolated his body, in case any of the natural postmortem processes were to release any of that gas from his lungs."

A sob burst free from my chest. "This is my fault. It's all—"

"No." Desmond flinched, as if the word tasted bitter. "Wilder rushed down the stairs, into the unknown. He's always been reckless, and it was bound to catch up to him eventually."

"You don't mean that."

"I do," he insisted. "It brings me no pleasure to say. In fact, I would give anything for the opportunity to have been there. For the chance to have seized his cloak and knocked some sense into the back of his skull. I wish he were here to scold, and I swear to the stars that this time I'd make him hear me. But I *do* mean it. My brother made his typically impulsive choice, and this time, for perhaps the first time in his life, his instinct failed him."

I closed my eyes, and Wilder's face flashed across the dark expanse of my vision. Not his usual grin, but the way he'd looked right before he'd rushed down the stairs.

Relieved. As if somehow, even though he'd had no idea Yoslyn and I had even found a puzzle, he'd already been desperate for the solution and afraid he'd fail to find it.

But that made no sense. And now I would never know the reason. I would never again get to . . .

"Tell her the rest." Yoslyn sank onto the edge of my bed, her hands clutched in her lap.

I turned to Desmond, my stomach twisting, though there couldn't be anything for it to reject, considering how long it had been since I'd eaten.

"What's happened?" I demanded softly. "What more could there possibly be?"

He sighed, regret flashing in brief lines across his forehead. "You've been expelled."

Numb, I nodded.

I'd dreaded those very words for weeks, since the moment I'd decided to stay, despite the odds stacked against me. Despite the dense fog that my memory had become. And now that I'd heard them, they meant . . . less than nothing.

What was the point of staying, of rising to the highest possible ranks of alchemy, when those already there—the very top of their craft—used it to kill and manipulate, but could not save a life?

When the very father of the art had confessed his own inadequacy, failed to save his true love, and used his talent to set up a series of puzzles that had killed my best friend in the world—a man who'd loved me, for no reason I could understand.

Why in all the universe would I want to be an alchemist now?

"How is she?" a familiar voice asked, and I looked up to find Keryth peering at me from the doorway, her face half shrouded in shadow from the dark landing. Her pinched expression was equal parts concern and curiosity, and I got the distinct impression that she already knew about my expulsion. That it was only the fact that I was no longer her competition that allowed her to feel any concern at all.

"Get out," I croaked at her. "Drown in a sea of your own false tears, for all I care, but do it out of my sight."

Yoslyn gaped at me. Keryth huffed, standing straight and stiff, and clearly mortally insulted. From behind her, I heard a chorus of gasps, from which I understood that several of our female classmates loitered on the landing.

"I'm no longer a student?" I said as footsteps clomped softly down the narrow spiral stairs.

Desmond nodded.

"Then get me out of here. Please, please, get me out of here."

He stood and crossed my room in two long strides, a soldier relieved to have orders.

"Pack her things," he commanded Yoslyn as he slammed my door shut. Then he turned back to me. "Your father has been summoned. It will take a couple of days for him to receive the correspondence, and a couple more, at best, to come retrieve you. You will stay with me until then. They cannot deny me that now."

For the rest of the day, I drifted in and out of sleep in Desmond's bed, and every time I woke, I remembered Wilder's death with a fresh pain like a blade plunged straight into my gut. Each waking wound cast me into a paroxysm of grief—and guilt-fueled weeping, leaving me curled into a limp form in the center of the wool mattress.

Desmond offered me tea to calm my tears, but the third time, when I was inconsolable, he climbed into the bed and lay behind me, holding me close with one hand around my waist, his head sharing my pillow.

As I drifted into a teary sleep, I could swear I felt him shaking at my back. Silently sobbing. And I realized with no small amount of shame that I had thoughtlessly let him care for me while he was still mired in his own grief.

I'd lost far more than a friend, in Wilder. But Desmond had lost his brother.

When I next woke, the sun had set. Desmond's chest was still pressed against my back, his breathing as steady and calming as the ocean waves outside my own bedchamber window.

I rolled onto my back, and though he shifted a bit, he did not rouse, and I wondered at his unconscious comfort. At the fact that he was not startled awake by my presence.

I turned carefully to face him and found myself captivated by his sleeping expression. By the relaxed cast of his features, which were so often sternly set in his waking moments. In his sleep, he seemed like another person.

Or . . . maybe he was only vexed in my presence.

I should have been grateful that he'd found peace, however temporary, in rest. Yet something tugged painfully at my bruised heart while I watched him.

As I ran one finger gently down the bridge of his nose, then over the generous bow of his lips, it finally occurred to me that in his sleep, he looked uncannily like Wilder, who'd rarely, in his entire life, worn a frown.

Fresh tears slid down my face as I stretched forward to press my mouth against his, beset by an irrepressible urge.

Desmond's eyes flew open. "Amber?" he whispered, and I burst into sobs.

His eyes widened, his forehead crinkling in a helpless expression. Then he kissed me. Quickly and desperately, as if he could think of no other solution and yet understood that this was not it.

Surprised, I gasped, stealing the breath straight from his throat.

Desmond slid one hand over my jaw, plunging strong fingers into my hair, loose and free from its typical braids, and instead of giving me space, he closed the scant inch between us and fed from my mouth as if I were the source of all life. As if I were the sustenance of his very soul.

I fell into his touch as if he were the earth itself, pulling me toward his center with a force I could not see, yet could not fight. I could feel him—every single part of him—even where we were not touching. He broke free from my lips and kissed away my tears. His hands roamed over me slowly, both a comfort and a slow, hot torment.

A reminder of our grief and a blistering, bruising way through it.

Desmond removed my thin nightdress without a word, though his eyes seemed to speak volumes in the weak flicker of a low-burning candle. I clutched at him, starving for comfort and solidarity. For warmth and for touch. For any sensation with the power to obliterate thought. Memory.

After weeks of desperately trying to remember what I'd lost, I wanted nothing in that moment but to forget.

I touched every inch of him I could reach as he stripped off his own clothing, then I pulled him down over me, seeking to block out the entire world with his body. With his touch and the very force of his presence, like a shield brandished against all of existence.

I sank my teeth into his earlobe, and Desmond groaned. He parted my thighs and slid fully inside me with no preamble, urgency drawing a cry from deep in his throat.

My body tightened against him, holding him for a moment. He murmured senseless syllables into my ear, breath hot against my neck, and I arched upward, drawing him deeper, captive to my own desperate need.

He moved inside me wordlessly, slowly at first, then faster when I tucked my ankles at his back. When I dug my fingernails into his arms, demanding more. Faster. Deeper.

We moved in a frantic rhythm, trying to outpace grief and memory, and something deep inside me began to loosen—to unwind—even as that intimate tension steadily built.

Finally, Desmond drove himself into me frantically, and his need pushed me toward a blistering edge.

Fresh tears slid down my cheeks as release washed over me, and I clung to him with my arms, and my legs, and all of my very being. I could not let go, even when he brushed hair back from my damp face and tried to withdraw. When I refused to release him, he rolled us onto our sides and tucked my leg over his hip.

We held each other, my face buried in his shoulder, and I pretended I could neither interpret his rough sniffles nor feel the warmth of his tears as they soaked into the pillow.

Sleep claimed us both, and I clung to that release as well.

It was still dark when I woke again. Desmond was dressed, scribbling haltingly on a sheet of parchment with his back to me, but he turned the very moment I opened my eyes, as if he'd sensed my waking.

He smiled, but the expression was more pain than joy. "I have to go," he said. I opened my mouth to object, but he spoke over me. "I'll be back shortly. The Refectory has finished serving the evening meal, but I've requested that they pack something for us. I will retrieve that, and I must stop by the lab to mix up an elixir for you as well."

I could not argue with his reasoning. "Mix up a double batch," I said. "I cannot fathom how we will get through this, if not together."

He nodded, and something heartbreaking flickered briefly behind his eyes. "Please do not leave this apartment." And then he was gone.

I slept all evening in Desmond's bed, waking only to drink the elixir and the broth he offered and to relieve my bladder. By morning, I felt much better, physically, and though I still had no urge to rise from the bed, when he left to get more food at midday, I forced myself to tread several small circles around the room, to test my stamina. Then I washed myself with the rag and the bowl of fresh water he'd left for me.

Clean again, and feeling stronger than I had since waking, I pulled fresh clothing from the bag Yoslyn had packed for me, and when my fingers brushed a familiar smooth wooden surface, I realized she had included my mother's box. When I opened it, I further understood that in the chaos of Wilder's death and my injury, she'd thought to shove the box into my satchel and bring it to my room without anyone discovering how we'd managed to open a secret staircase beneath a floor that generations of the world's best alchemists had trodden for more than a century and a half.

Dear, dear Yoslyn.

I'd been too distracted by grief to ask if they had expelled her, too.

I folded my worn frock, and as I was about to stuff it into my bag, I noticed in the corner of Desmond's apartment a wooden crate that appeared to contain a bundle of material. I knelt next to it, certain that must be where Desmond kept his soiled clothing, and was surprised to find one of my own handkerchiefs lying atop the pile, neatly folded, with my mother's embroidery visible in one corner.

All of the material in the crate was folded, and though I couldn't say it was all clean, precisely, very little of it appeared obviously soiled. I removed each piece, one by one, and found several of my own handkerchiefs—two stained with blood—and three whose ownership I could not ascertain. I found a pillowcase, neatly folded, an unfamiliar linen tunic, and an entire set of bedsheets, also of linen, though of a finer weave than the fabric on my own bed.

At the bottom of the crate, I found a journal I recognized from my own childhood.

My heart thumped as I opened it to see my mother's handwriting. It was a volume of notes from her time at the Alchemary, written in a mixture of my native tongue and her own, which she'd spoken to me when I was a child, until I'd become embarrassed by the differences between the other village children and myself.

As I was scanning the book, surprised by how much I could still read, the door opened behind me and Desmond stepped into his own chamber, carrying a fragrant cloth-wrapped bundle of food.

"Are these mine?" I asked as he set the bundle on the table in one corner of the room. "The things in this crate?"

"They are." And though he looked pained by the admission, he hadn't hesitated to admit that he'd had a crate of my belongings this whole time yet had never mentioned them.

He'd never lied to me, that I could tell. Not even when a little white lie might have made me more pleasant to be around.

"Why do you have these things? Why didn't *I* have them?"

Desmond exhaled so long and hard that the loss of breath seemed to deflate him. "Will you sit and eat?" He pulled out a dining chair for me, then he sat in the other.

"Will you *answer* the question?" I returned as I sat, willing myself to ignore the scents of cheese and roasted meat, as well as the needy grumble from my stomach.

"I will, and though I've been dreading it for weeks, after all that's happened, I suspect this discussion will come as a relief. Amber, your things are here because you left them here."

Forty-Two

"Why would I have brought those things here in the first place?"

Instead of answering, Desmond only held my gaze, waiting for me to draw the obvious conclusion.

I sat straighter as it sank in. As embarrassment and a strangely intimate fascination warred within me. "We were embroiled in an affair, were we not?" I finally said, and the verdict felt somehow familiar and yet wholly startling. As if I'd known the truth all along, deep down, yet could still hardly believe it.

Desmond scowled, crossing his arms over his chest. "We were not."

"We most certainly were!" I was *convinced* of the truth now that I'd discovered it. "That's why my 'instinct' was to kiss you in the laboratory that day. That is why you felt entitled to walk into my room without knocking, and why you refused to discuss my relationship with Wilder, and—"

"You *had* no relationship with Wilder beyond friendship," he snapped, eyes flashing copper in the light from the fireplace. Arms crossing over his chest. "Not before the night you lost your memory, anyway. And as I've said, I would *very much* like to know what changed that night."

My eyes narrowed as I studied his face. "I was not in a relationship with Wilder, and yet he loved me?"

Desmond nodded solemnly.

"I assume that was a source of tension for all three of us?"

"For Wilder, certainly. And increasingly for me, though I will admit I was not terribly concerned until I discovered that he'd spent the night in your bed."

"And for me? I felt the tension?"

Desmond shrugged his left shoulder. "You had alchemy, and you had me, and you had Wilder, and you seemed cognizant of little else in the world. I'm not certain you truly realized that the nature of his affection for you had changed."

Could I possibly have been that oblivious? "You insist you and I were not having an affair, yet I have had flashes of very intimate . . . moments." I stared at the food growing cold on the table in front of me, avoiding his gaze. "With you. From before I lost my memory."

"I am not denying that we were often in bed together," he said, and my gaze snapped back up. "I simply reject the characterization of that state as an *affair.*" Desmond leaned forward, piercing me with an almost righteous stare from across the table. "Amber, you and I had been embroiled in an emotional and psychological entanglement since virtually the day you arrived at the Alchemary, at the beginning of my Mastery year. We were a couple. You and I. *Not* you and Wilder."

The thudding of my heart in my ears threatened to drown out his next words.

"I've spent almost three months waiting for you to remember on your own." He leaned back in his chair, his jaw stiff for a moment before he continued. "Hoping you would, because I'd convinced myself that if you *did* remember, then our relationship must have held some value for you."

"We were in a relationship," I said, as if I were auditioning the words. Trying on the concept like a new frock. "For almost two years. Despite the fact that relationships are frowned upon for staff members of the Alchemary. Yet you're not sure it actually meant anything to me?"

"I *was* sure, for quite a while. But then that night—the night you lost your memory—you did something that destroyed my faith in . . . in *us*."

"Did that something have anything to do with Wilder?"

His face paled, but he did not look away. "No. For the last time, I don't know what happened with Wilder. And for the record, relationships are not entirely unheard of for staff members, but they are certainly . . . discouraged."

"And between a staff member and a student?"

"*Highly* discouraged," he admitted, picking a bit of crust from the hunk of bread on his plate. "But the administration looked the other way, because—" His mouth snapped shut.

"Because what?"

"Because you were *so close*." He leaned over the table again, his voice fervent, each word coming faster than the last. "Because you were so *inconceivably* brilliant, and driven, and . . . You were like Wilder, with his *tremendous* instinct for alchemy, but with a disciplined and analytical mind like—"

"Yours."

"Yes," Desmond admitted, not the least bit embarrassed by my glimpse of his ego. "You were the perfect combination of his type of alchemy and mine. Yet you were entirely your own beast. And a *beast* you certainly were. You were a light shining brightly in the dark and endless cave that the craft of alchemy can so often feel like. We've only managed to light one small corner of it, all of us—the greatest minds in our field—over the past century and a half. But then you came along, and you lit a candle in some other corner, and we could all see you from across the yawning, inky gulf. *Everyone* was watching you, Amber. We were hoping that your little candle flame would flare and light up the whole world. And it could have. You were so close that no one—not even the Bluehelm—was willing to interfere with your methods. They gave you whatever you wanted."

My heart pounded as a strange pressure built deep in my chest. "And I wanted you?"

He nodded, and in the golden flicker of the fire, I saw just the hint of a flush in his cheeks. "I thought you did, in any case. And no one was very worried about that, because you were still—" Again, his mouth snapped shut.

I did not like this habit of aborting his sentences. Of cutting me off from his thoughts.

"I was still what?"

"Young." But he had that look again, as if he were only telling me part of the truth. "You were still young, and no one considered me more than a fleeting fancy for you." His jaw clenched. "A diversion you would outgrow. As most serious alchemists eventually put aside such diversions, in order to focus on the work."

"They thought you were humoring me," I said. "Enduring a childish crush while you encouraged my alchemical pursuits." It wasn't a question. I could see the truth of my conclusion burning in his eyes.

"They were wrong," he said. "They didn't understand that I would have razed the whole world for you. For *us*. I would have left the Alchemary with you to start our own laboratory. Or academy. Or whatever you wanted. And by the end, I was ready to do just that."

"By the end." I mulled those words over, searching for their true meaning. "By the time you realized I was a danger to the Alchemary." He'd said that several times, yet he'd always refused to elaborate.

"And *it* to *you*. You had a terrifyingly clear understanding of the alchemical process—of its potential—and the Alchemary was *designed* to exploit students like you. Not that there's ever been a student like you. And that's exactly what the Bluehelm would have done, if you'd finished your project. She would have fed your ambition and corrupted your purpose, and—"

"You can't possibly know that—"

"I *do* know!" he roared from across the table, shooting to his feet so abruptly that his chair skidded backward. "That's what happens to everyone here. It's part of the process."

I stared up at him, stunned by the outburst. Desmond did not get upset without cause. "What process?" I asked.

"I just mean..." He sat again, visibly composing himself. Shielding more of his thoughts from me. More of the *truth*. "It happens to all of us."

"It didn't happen to you."

"Of course it did. *You* are what pulled me back from that. And that's exactly what they don't want. If a relationship is important to you, it could come to mean more than alchemy. More than the Alchemary. And they can't have that. They would eventually have pulled us apart. I think..." He frowned, anger dripping from every word. "I think maybe they already have."

"You think the Bluehelm is responsible for my amnesia?"

"Not intentionally," he admitted. "That doesn't benefit her. I think memory loss is an unintended side effect of whatever they did to you. Whatever they gave you."

Every elixir has an unintended side effect.

He'd warned me of that more than once.

"I've often thought back to the day your hand was cut by the stained glass, when I saw something in your blood. At the time, I attributed it to Wilder's elixir, but..." He hesitated, as if carefully weighing his next words. "The Alchemary has ways of getting what they want out of their alchemists, and of repressing any part that isn't valued."

A chill washed over me. "You think that that night, the Bluehelm gave me something, and it backfired."

He nodded. "I don't know what else could have done this to you. I don't know where you went when you left, or what happened. And that has plagued me ever since."

"What happened that night, Desmond? Tell me what you *do* know of the night I lost my memory. I left those things here?" I gestured at the crate full of material.

"No, they were already here. You did not come to my apartment that night. The last I saw of you was when you gathered your things and stomped out of the lab, your face flaming with anger."

"Why was I angry?"

"Because we'd fought."

"About what?"

Pain churned behind his eyes for so long that I did not think he was going to answer.

"The night before that—two nights before you woke up with my brother and without your memory—I told you I loved you."

The ache in my chest threatened to swallow me whole. "And . . . what?" My voice held almost no volume. "I didn't believe you?"

Desmond held my gaze, pain churning behind his eyes. "You didn't believe in *love*."

I could not speak. I could only inhale the rich scents of my untouched meal, my fingernails digging into the woodgrain of the table while I tried to make sense of his bewildering statement. While I waited for him to explain.

"I told you I loved you, and you laughed," Desmond finally said. "But you were not amused. You looked sad, as if you *pitied* me. You said that the perception of love, like any other emotion, was just alchemy of the human body. That it was all to do with micro-volumes of various metals in our body's fluids. In sweat, and blood, and tears, and other secretions. You said you had proven it. You had distilled all of what we call emotion into various solutions and had proven that they react like elements in alchemical experiments. That, you said, was the secret to your uniquely effective distillation of beyn—the inclusion of specific combinations of micro metals collected during moments of strong human emotion."

I sat straighter, gaze narrowed on him from across the table. Something tugged at my memory, like the plucking of a harp string echoing deep into my brain. "*That* was how I made beyn? The formula Wilder said I would not let anyone else see?"

"Yes."

Frustration stirred inside me like a storm gathering strength. "Why have you never told me that?"

Desmond exhaled slowly, appearing distinctly uncomfortable with what he was about to say. "Telling you would have done no good, because even if I wanted to return that ability to you—and I do not—I couldn't have. I don't have your formula," he said. "I cleaned out your lab space, but there wasn't a single note relevant to your research. As far as I can tell, you kept it all in that journal, which—it turns out—is written entirely in some code even you can no longer interpret."

"That is accurate," I mumbled.

"And because I did not approve of your methods."

Irritation narrowed my gaze on him. "They were not yours to approve of!"

"Yet I stand by my judgment." His jaw clenched with an echo of the frustration I'd seen in him weeks ago, when he'd declared that I did not deserve my place here, even if I'd earned it.

"You owe me an explanation," I insisted. "So that I can judge my methods for myself. How did I collect these emotions, in order to distill them?"

With a sigh, he glanced at the wooden box on the floor. "What did you find in that crate?"

I shrugged. "Folded cloth, of various sorts."

"A set of bedsheets? Did you see those?"

I nodded. "They seemed of a very fine quality."

He picked at splinter in the tabletop, and when he met my gaze again, his held the odd weight of a bittersweet memory. "I bought them from a shop in Saltstrand, when we'd been together for a year. You loved them. We spent quite a lot of time in them. And then, two nights before you lost your memory, I made a declaration I've since come to regret."

"You said you loved me."

He nodded. "And *you* said that love was a delusional state—a sort of hysteria—induced by a collection of micro metals produced by the human body. You said *ideas* were the most powerful thing in the world. That everything else was just alchemy, and that if people are really just giant petri dishes—walking solutions of metals in various imperceptible quantities—then they could be manipulated by ideas."

"I said people could be manipulated?"

"You said some people *should* be manipulated."

A sick dread twisted in my gut.

"And I saw then that the Alchemary was already changing you. You weren't yet a staff member—you hadn't even started your Mastery year—but it had sunk its claws into you like a hungry cat, and I knew it would not let go."

That dread swelled to fill me like smoke in a closed room, and my throat burned from the acrid bite of it. "I had let myself be corrupted."

"No." He seized my hand, and my gaze with it. "You were *scared,* because you loved me, too, and that made you feel out of control. You couldn't explain it. And you'd convinced yourself that if you felt something you couldn't explain with alchemy, then you had failed as an alchemist. You were *not* corrupted. Not yet. But I could see, in that moment, the angle the Alchemary would use—the angle it was already using—to change you. To turn you into what it needed, at the expense of what *you* needed. Of who you were. So I tried to make you see what was happening. What you were becoming. But you misunderstood. You thought I was doubting your theory, and you felt compelled to prove you were right."

"How?"

His exhalation seemed to entirely deflate him. "I didn't understand what you intended until I came into our lab the next night. You were working, completely embroiled in what you were doing, your hair in total disarray, braids unraveling at your temples, your lip pinned between your teeth. I had come to try to put things right between us. But then I saw that you had boiled my sheets."

"I . . . What?" An ache blossomed deep in my chest. "Why?" But I knew. On some level, be it memory or scientific instinct, I understood before he even answered.

"You wanted to distill everything we'd shared the night before, to prove that what we felt for each other was nothing more than a series of alchemical reactions taking place in our bodies. As if we were ourselves merely components thrown into a human beaker and placed over a psychological heat source. That's how you described passion. Lust."

The storm broke inside me. "I'm *so* sorry." I reached across the table for him, palm up, but he did not take my hand.

He waved my apology off, eyes only half focused, still caught up in the memory, so I tucked my hand back into my lap.

"I thought emotion was worthless?"

"On the contrary," Desmond said. "You thought it was invaluable—as an alchemical accelerant, of sorts, for your beyn. Your theory was in direct opposition to everything the Alchemary teaches. Alchemists are instructed to eschew all strong emotion because it distracts from science. That theory goes all the way back to Lord Calyx's teachings, late in his life."

Late in life. After he'd been heartbroken by the loss of his only love? After Iris had written about the same theory?

"The Alchemary has based its most foundational theories on the idea that the less emotion an alchemist indulges, the closer they are to a higher form. But *you* . . . You decided, halfway through your Proficiency year, that everything you'd ever been taught was wrong. You thought we should be *harnessing* emotion, not suppressing it. You wanted to utilize it. So you started . . . triggering it, for lack of a better term. Inducing emotions of all kinds in your classmates. Joy, pain, rage—"

"Envy," I finished as Pryce's and Adria's faces flashed behind my eyes. I leaned forward with my elbows on the table, my head cradled in my hands. "No wonder my cohort hated me." I stood, suddenly seized by the need to move, and paced across his room toward the bed.

"That is putting it mildly." Desmond's gaze followed me as I paced toward him again. "They had no idea what you were doing or why. They only knew that you were cruel. That usually when something bad happened to them, you were there."

I snatched a cube of cheese from my plate and chewed it absently as anxiety buzzed beneath my skin. "But did I not also make good things happen?" Even if only for my own benefit?

"Sometimes. But people are less likely to notice that, because—"

"They aren't looking for someone to blame for their happiness." I bit into another cube as I sank back into my chair. "So . . . I induced strong emotions, presumably through unethical means?"

He nodded. "And then you would soak them up. You'd offer your handkerchief or steal a piece of clothing. Anything that had been cried on, or bled on, or sweated into at the height of some great emotion. Then you would distill that excretion, in whatever form it took, and use it in your formula for beyn. You harnessed human emotion, when the rest of the alchemical world considers sentiment nothing more than a distraction from what matters."

"But I used people. I used our relationship. I used *you*." I stared into his eyes, desperate for some sign that he didn't hate me. "No wonder you wanted me gone from the Alchemary."

"No, that's . . ." He looked heartbroken as he leaned toward me, over the table. "That isn't the reason. Yes, I was hurt. But I would not have tried to remove you from your life's work over my own bruised feelings." Desmond sighed again, a somber weight settling into his expression. "Amber, there's something else I have to tell you." Yet for a moment, he only held my gaze, as if trying to measure what he saw there. How much I was ready to hear. Then he exhaled again, long and steady. And he stood. "Do you feel up to a walk?"

"You said I shouldn't leave the apartment."

"I did." He circled the table and offered me his hand, and his next words were very quiet. "But I share walls with two other staff members, and we cannot risk being overheard." Then he conjured up a smile, as if with a sudden thought. "Have you been to the southern dock?"

Forty-Three

The very moment we emerged from the woods onto the beach at the south end of Alchemary Island, I wondered why I had not, in fact, been there before.

Whereas the northern and eastern sides culminated in steep cliffs like the one the Dormitory was perched upon and the one spanned by the bridge into Saltstrand, the island sloped gently to the south, specialized soil giving way to a smooth-pebble beach and a single long dock.

"What is this for?" I asked as we traversed the wooden planks above gentle waves washing toward us, glittering in the afternoon sun. A cool breeze lifted the ends of my hair and the hem of my frock, raising gooseflesh on my arms and legs. "I thought supplies came over the bridge from Saltstrand?"

"Most do," Desmond said. "But some come via ship and are carried up the trail through the woods, to the Refectory."

"Or the infirmary?" I said, thinking of the path at the rear of the Conservatory.

"Mmm," he said, and I noted his lack of a true answer.

I'd grown accustomed to the salty scent of ocean air that blew through my bedchamber daily, and I'd grown to love that view. But this one was just as stunning, if different. From the dock, I could see the sea at eye level.

Somehow, that made me feel even smaller.

Desmond sat at the end of the dock and let his legs dangle so that spray from the waves lightly splattered his shoes. He patted the spot beside him, and I gathered my skirt and sat. Under normal circumstances, the moment would have felt peaceful. But the current churning in my mind was much more turbulent than the midafternoon waves gently washing over the pebble beach.

He cleared his throat, an obvious preamble to a discussion that necessitated complete privacy. "There are some things you don't know about alchemy."

I huffed, running one hand over the loose braid stretching back and down from high on my temple. "Desmond, I'm still a student. Despite my purported skill, I suspect there are quite a few things I don't yet know about alchemy."

He nodded but betrayed no amusement as he shifted away from the sun to face me, folding one leg beneath himself on the wooden planks. "But I'm not referring to the theory or the craft of alchemy. I'm talking about the practice of it. The organizational structure. The . . . hierarchy. You don't yet understand where the real power and influence lies, in the alchemy community. Nor can you possibly understand the scale of it."

A thread of unease wound around my spine.

"I know that the Alchemary is the oldest, most prominent and influential alchemy institution in the world, and that the Bluehelm is in charge of it. So wouldn't that place her at the top of the hierarchy?"

"It would, in theory," Desmond acknowledged. "But not comfortably or safely so, given the growing influence of the Alkahest Institute as our academic rival and the fact that the Crown has its own private alchemist."

"Pryce's father."

"Yes." He looked as if he'd just swallowed a bitter clod of dirt.

"So, you're saying there are . . . what? Threats to the Alchemary?"

"Yes. And I'm saying that the Alchemary, in return, poses its own reciprocal threats. As does the Toolkeepers' Rebellion."

"My father would never—"

"And that because those reciprocal threats have been escalating for years. For generations"—Desmond continued as I squinted into the sun shining over his head—"much of the true power of the Alchemary has retreated into the shadows, where it has been allowed to grow—and to advance—unseen. Largely unchecked."

Unease stewed in my gut like laundry bubbling over the fire. "Meaning what?"

"Meaning that there is very little that the elite practitioners of our craft are not capable of. And even less they are not willing to do."

"In pursuit of the greater good of mankind?" I prompted, as if speaking the words might somehow make them true, despite my understanding that he would not have needed complete privacy in order to tell me how *virtuous* the alchemical elite had become.

"In pursuit of great power."

Desmond let me sit with the words. With the implication.

I turned toward the north for a glimpse of the beautiful campus I'd come to love, trying to picture it in this new light. Or rather, cast beneath this new shadow. To my surprise, despite their height, not one of the grand buildings was visible beyond the forest, from our position. I felt isolated and protected by the woods and the peaceful churn of ocean waves.

And yet, the rest of Alchemary Island had not *truly* disappeared.

"These elite have veered from the true goal of alchemy," I murmured.

"Some have truly diverged," he acknowledged. "Others believe that accumulating power is the only way to protect and enforce the true goal: bettering the world through resisting entropy. Yet regardless of their original intent, people who gain power are rarely wiling to relinquish it. Or to limit its reach."

Chills washed over me, unrelated to the cool breeze. "Who are these people? Professors?"

"Only a few. Most of the Alchemary researchers are among the elite, though, as well as the Alchemary board. And a few distinguished alchemists in private practice."

There were very few distinguished private practitioners, as far as I knew. Most notably, the royal alchemist.

"They call themselves scriveners," Desmond added.

"Scriveners? Why?" The word meant simply *those who write.*

"The title refers to their mastery of grade-five elixirs."

"There *is* no grade five," I said, but I knew before the words had even left my mouth that I was wrong about that. "Very well, *what* is a grade-five elixir?"

Because it was very clearly something entirely apart from the first four grades.

It would have to be, if the majority of the alchemy community wasn't allowed to even know it existed.

Desmond twisted to look up the length of the dock and peer into the shadowy depths of the woods, as if to assure himself that we were truly alone. Finally, he turned back to me, a new, quiet sort of tension drawn in the stiff line of his shoulders. Echoing in the depth of his voice. "Grade-five elixirs require only one ingredient."

"Beyn," I guessed, and he nodded. "But how is that possible?"

"The most elite practitioners of alchemy have developed a technique for imbuing the writing of a formula—the symbols, specifically—with the *intent* of the ingredients. With the will of the alchemists themselves."

"They only have to write the formula?"

"And paint the symbols with their beyn." Desmond hesitated. "There are other . . . details. Complications of the process. But yes, in reductive terms, they write, instead of laboring over a lab table and refining tangible ingredients. The art is called scrivening, the practitioners scriveners. And they're only capable of doing this because they have done the true scientific labor of alchemy thousands of times over. They have become so adept at it that they can now mentally perform the same art."

"They have achieved a higher state of alchemy," I whispered. "An elevated form. In a way, the very goal of alchemy itself."

"Indeed." Yet there was something tense and distant in Desmond's voice.

"But with 'complications'..."

He gave me a tight smile. "Yes."

"How does this craft afford the scriveners power? What do they do with their alchemy?" I asked.

Desmond exhaled slowly. Heavily. "There is very little they cannot do. Scriveners have developed advances in medicine, entertainment, and cosmetic application beyond imagination, though they do not make those advances known to the masses for fear of exposure. But the most prominent use is the production of alchemy-based weapons."

"Weapons?" Horror flowed across my flesh like a slow dunk into a cold pond. Weapons were the very agent of chaos and disorder. Of violence and oppression. The antithesis of the goal of alchemy.

"Weapons," Desmond repeated. "Ostensibly–and often legitimately–to protect both the craft of alchemy and the Alchemary itself."

"From what?"

"From the threat of control by outside forces. To protect the autonomy of the institution. And the right for alchemy to exist, as an art."

"To protect the Alchemary from the Toolkeepers?" I guessed.

Desmond nodded. "Yes. But not exclusively."

"What kind of weapons?" I'd never seen an overt threat to the Alchemary, at least that I could remember. There had been no soldiers attacking the gates. No navy assaulting our shores.

Another sigh. "Scrivenings can stun, paralyze, burn, and shock. They can blind, deafen, and even kill. But that is not the worst of it."

My heart pounded painfully. "How could killing not be the worst?"

"Killing one person usually has a limited scope of impact. But *influencing* one person—or, ideally, a handful of strategically positioned people—can have limitless impact."

"You're talking about large-scale manipulation. Not of one person's emotion, but of many people's behavior."

"In any number of ways, on every possible level," he confirmed. "Through mechanisms that may never be acknowledged or discovered. All with a few strokes of brush or a quill, dipped in a specialized beyn."

Every muscle in my body seemed to seize at once, freezing my breath in my lungs until I cracked them open with sheer willpower. The scope was almost inconceivable. The benefits . . . The *consequences* . . . And . . .

I sat straight, stuck with a sudden cold and paralyzing fear, at odds with the soothing pulse of ocean waves. "Can scrivening cause memory loss?"

"Yes." Desmond shifted, and the boards beneath him creaked. "And I've given that hours of consideration, over the past three months. But I haven't come up with anyone who would benefit from visiting such a calamity upon you, considering how much the scriveners—how much *everyone*—stood to gain from your work."

But his eyes had that look again. He was leaving something out.

"Desmond . . ." I insisted. "Who would benefit?"

He sighed. "The Toolkeepers. They would benefit from keeping *any* strong alchemist out of the scriveners' ranks. But your father would never stand for your injury—"

"Unless he believed he was saving me from *greater* injury or corruption."

"Precisely." Desmond's eyes fell closed, and when he opened them again—when he met mine frankly—I understood.

"That's why you wrote to him."

"No. I wrote to him before I knew you'd lost your memory. I wrote to tell him you were in danger as soon as I realized what the Alchemary was doing to you. How it would corrupt you."

That was how his correspondence had arrived so quickly. And why it hadn't mentioned my amnesia . . .

"But I will admit that when your father arrived I studied his reaction, because I needed to be sure that he'd played no part in what had happened to you. And he seemed wholly and legitimately shocked to hear about the state of your memory, and truly concerned."

"So if the Toolkeepers are responsible, my father played no part in it."

"That is my conclusion, yes."

"And you don't think it was a scrivening?"

Desmond shook his head. "I can't find any motive there."

And yet the scriveners could do—and evidently had done—*unspeakable* things.

He studied the horror evidently written across my expression. "Did you *truly* think it was all levitating carnival carriages and skin-tightening creams? That the Alchemary would ever be satisfied with such a small scale?"

"No. I thought alchemy was medicine and altruistic advances." I paused, tears threatening to spill. "And things like Wilder's elixirs."

"He was very skilled. But Wilder could not be controlled, and that would eventually have made him a threat to the scriveners, which would've outweighed the benefit of his skill. Especially considering he'd begun to perfect his own versions of some very expensive elixirs scriveners reserve for their elite customers. And he was underpricing them."

No wonder the board wouldn't approve his research project.

"And I thought alchemy was pursuits like your effort to improve the human form."

"The *soldier's* form," Desmond corrected. "I am tasked by the Alchemary with creating a stronger, faster soldier. A more efficient and deadly defender of the craft of alchemy in general, and the Alchemary in particular."

"You . . . ?" Shock rolled over me. I'd thought he was *studying* soldiers to understand the physical ideal. The peak of human health and ability. But . . . "You're creating human weapons."

He nodded. "Through alchemical advances. I am increasing the efficiency with which they utilize air when they breathe. Fuel, when they eat. I am strengthening muscles and increasing the speed of reflexes."

"And armored flesh?"

Another nod. "What you saw at the carnival was a parlor trick. The real version of it is . . . well beyond."

"But it's for defense." My voice felt soft and hollow. I couldn't be sure whether I was stating or asking.

Desmond gave me another nod, but this one was short. Stiff. "For now."

"What has any of this to do with my beyn?" I finally asked, resisting the urge to stare out at the ocean and let it calm me. "And with the reason you wanted me removed from the Alchemary?"

"That is all to do with the complications I mentioned. It is true that scrivening requires only one ingredient. Beyn. But the production of that beyn comes at a great cost."

I waited, but for several seconds, he seemed either unwilling or unable to continue.

"A symbol can only be imbued with the power and intent of the element it represents if that intent is anchored—some say *bought*—with a portion of the human soul."

"What?" I could not quite understand what he was saying, yet I felt the weight of it—the bitter wrongness—like a spot of rot in a bite of fresh apple.

"A very small portion," he clarified. "Very, very small. So small that for a long time, the cost to an individual scrivener went unnoticed. Until it began to accumulate. To . . . change them. Now that they understand the cost, most scriveners are unwilling to pay it. Yet they are equally unwilling to give up the power of a grade-five elixir. So they foist that cost onto someone else."

"How?" I asked, and it sounded like I was speaking from the end of a long, dark tunnel. Because some vague understanding was tugging at my mind, trying to bridge this new, horrifying concept with . . . something else. Something hidden in the dark recesses of my memory.

"The beyn necessary to create a scrivening must use some small part of the human body. In the past, scriveners have used a piece of their own hair, a stray eyelash, or fingernail trimmings. Occasionally a drop of blood or saliva. But when the cost became clear . . ."

"They began taking those parts from other people," I concluded.

Desmond nodded. "Stealing bits of other souls, to fuel their alchemy. The theory was that if they spread the cost out, no one person would be noticeably affected." But again he had that look, as if he were leaving something out.

Those scriveners, I understood, weren't just taking stray eyelashes and fingernail clippings. They were . . .

But then that vague understanding was suddenly brutally overshadowed with another, more personal one.

"Chaos incarnate," I swore as the truth crashed brutally over me. "That's what I was doing, with my beyn."

"Amber." Desmond took my hand, trying to comfort me, but the truth shadowed his eyes like clouds rolling over the sun.

"I was stealing my classmates' souls!"

"Yes," he conceded. "But only a very, very small portion of them. Nothing that would cause damage. And you did not know. You had *no concept* of the consequences of what you were doing."

"That makes it *worse*, not better!" I scrabbled back from him across the wood, heedless of splinters and damage to my frock. "I acted recklessly, with no way of truly understanding what I was—"

"You had no intent to steal any portion of anyone's soul." He did not reach for me, but he looked like he wanted to. "You developed your technique independent from the scriveners, and for an entirely different purpose. A separate but eerily parallel procedure, born of your sheer gift for the craft."

"But you saw what I was doing. And you knew that if they figured it out . . ."

"They would never have let you go," he said. "If the scriveners knew that you'd come up with their technique on your own, without their training or permission, they would either have whisked you into their folds—beyond my reach—or—"

His face paled with fear.

"Killed me."

"They would have considered it the elimination of a threat. But yes. If they could not secure your cooperation and secrecy, they would have done you harm. And I couldn't let that happen."

"So, I stole and consumed portions of my classmates' souls, and instead of telling the Bluehelm, you tried to protect me."

He only blinked at me.

"Desmond, I *used you*, and—"

"Yes," he finally said. "You used me. As if everything we'd been together meant nothing to you, beyond its scientific potential." Pain and betrayal were etched into the lines of his forehead, echoing in the crinkles around his eyes. "A potential you didn't even fully understand. And the most wonderful—the most *horrible*—thing is that you were *right*. You did it, Amber."

The ardent gleam in his eye set a bell tolling in my soul—an alarm ringing from high in a tower.

"What did I do?"

"What even the scriveners haven't managed, in all this time. You completed your research. Your project. With the beyn you made from our . . . passion. I was angry. I was hurt, because I realized that nothing was sacred for you, outside of alchemy itself. Then you showed me what you'd done."

He looked simultaneously proud and wounded, and the incongruence set me *deeply* on edge.

"You'd found the formula, Amber. You'd come up with the very solution Lord Calyx described in the notes I'd stolen from the research library for you: a thick, gold-flecked silver suspension that glowed even when no light was present. You'd made *that very thing*, even though he never recorded his formula. You'd come up with your own. And all you had left to do was—"

"Square the circle." My voice sounded hollow. Distant. "That's the part he never figured out: how to combine spirit with mind and body."

"But you had. You *said* you'd figured it out, anyway, and squaring the circle was all you had left to do."

"How?" I found myself leaning forward, perched on my knees, though I had no memory of taking that position. "Did I do it?"

The disappointed look he gave me—as if my interest and enthusiasm had turned me into Past Amber all over again—broke my heart. "I don't know. I asked you not to do it, but I have no idea whether or not you did."

"You asked me *not* to complete the Philosopher's Stone? When hundreds of alchemists have tried and failed to do that very thing over the past century and a half?"

"Yes." His voice was soft, yet his tone was hard. Impermeable. He plucked at a loose thread on his trousers, then finally looked up again and met my gaze boldly, as the breeze stirred his dark hair. "I could see what it was doing to you. What it could turn you into. You were corruptible, Amber. Just like any of us would be, in your position. Even aside from the threat of the scriveners, this place had already changed you. And I knew that if you finished the stone, I would never get you back. You would never get *yourself* back."

"That's the point!" I snapped, anger flashing in a million fiery explosions all over my body. "That's what the Philosopher's Stone does! It changes everything it touches into something better! Transmutation, at its highest form."

"I didn't *want* something better!" He stood, a single eerily fast and smooth motion, and the boards creaked beneath his feet with a startling cacophony. "I wanted *you*! *You. As you were.* There is *nothing* alchemy could have done to improve you. It was only dragging you down, morally. Ethically. This place was making you into a monster, and if you'd finished the Stone, you would have *instantly* become the most powerful person here."

"And you were jealous!" The words exploded from some bitter font deep inside me, though I could not fathom its origin. I'd felt nothing of the sort since I'd woken up without . . . my memory.

Sudden understanding bruised me from the inside. It was *remembered* bitterness. The ghost of it, anyway. *This* was that inexplicable anger I'd felt at Desmond, over and over, though now it felt terribly . . . explicable.

I stood, facing him at the end of the dock, that same breeze ruffling my hair, and even the waves suddenly seemed fiercer, in concert with our discord.

"I was not jealous of your power, Amber." Disappointment echoed in his voice. "I am already a scrivener."

I blinked at him, shocked.

"I'm not above corruption either. I told you, it was *you* who pulled me back from that brink. Long before I joined their ranks—corruption does not begin or end with scrivening. You were a light in the dark, Amber. A flame lit beneath ice." He reached for my hand, and I let him pull me closer, across the dock. "You kept me human, and I'm embarrassed to admit this, but I *clung* to you because of that. Nothing seemed to have any depth or texture when you weren't around. The world had no color aside from the red of your lips and the gold in your eyes. You reminded me what the true goal of alchemy is, and I thought we would reach it together. But then—"

"I began to lose sight of it."

He nodded. "I wasn't jealous. I was terrified of losing you." He blinked, and it was like a veil had descended over his expression, blurring all of the detail. Shielding his thoughts from me. "But I lost you anyway. That night, you stormed out of the lab with your suspension, and the next time I saw you—when I came to your room to try *again* to make it right—I found you in bed with my brother."

He let go of my hand, and it fell to my side like a horrible dead weight.

"And you had no idea how he'd gotten there, and no memory at all of completing the formula. Of making the gold-flecked silver suspension. On one level, you were an entirely different person. You were a *good* person, who had no recollection of ever hurting me or any of your cohort. Who didn't seem capable of ever becoming that person again. Because you didn't remember what you'd done, or how you'd managed it. You'd lost skill, but you'd regained *yourself*. And I couldn't stand the thought of you becoming that other person again."

"And yet, I did." My eyes fell shut, and tears burned behind the closed lids. The ocean breeze felt suddenly frigid. "I got Wilder killed."

"No." Desmond pulled me close on the wooden planks, gripping my shoulders. Peering into my eyes. "No, you did not do that. As tragic as his death is—as excruciating as it is for me to even think about—Wilder did that to himself. Do you hear me?" He took my chin and stared straight into my eyes.

I could only nod, even though I did not believe a word of it.

"What happened to the solution?" I asked. To the gold-flecked silver fluid Lord Calyx had described and that I, evidently, had created.

Had I squared the circle? Or had I wound up with another beautiful, inert gem?

"I have no idea," Desmond said. "And I will admit that when I realized you'd lost your memory, I thought one of the scriveners had stolen your suspension, to complete it for themselves. That you'd lost your memory as a result of that theft or to cover it up. But you had no physical injuries, and no one ever claimed to have completed the Stone. So I have no idea what happened to your suspension, or whether you ever actually squared the circle."

Forty-Four

That night, I dreamed of my parents. Of a day during my childhood when my mother had packed a lunch and we'd picnicked at the side of a lake on the west edge of Innswood. In reality, my mother had collected herbs and various soils all afternoon while my father had sketched his latest commission in a notepad with a lead stylus. I'd skipped rocks, pouting, because I had not been allowed to bring Wilder Gregory on our family outing.

In my dream, however, my parents laughed while they nibbled their cheese and bread. They sipped wine and told me stories. My mother spoke to me in her native language—my dream recollection of it was flawless—and my father tutored me in Toolkeepers' notation. We swam together in the lake, and . . .

I woke up in a cold sweat, with a sudden epiphany firing through my brain like sparks from a flint stone struck in the dark. The dream was a message. A signal from Past Amber, who'd sometimes fought her way through during my subconscious hours and sent me confusing flashes of memory.

Toolkeepers' notation. And my mother's native language.

I slid quietly out of bed, careful not to disturb Desmond, and I settled onto the cold stone floor in front of the fireplace with my coded journal, pages angled so that they were illuminated by the fire.

And I realized, suddenly, that Past Amber hadn't merely given me a signal. Not just a message. She'd unlocked the vault of my memory and opened the door just a sliver. Just enough to restore recognition of the languages I used to know.

Only, Past Amber wasn't some stranger in control of my memories. She was me. *I'd* somehow loosened my own hold on the vault in my head. Almost certainly because of what Desmond had told me. *Knowing* had unlocked some small portion of *remembering*.

The writing in my journal was neither my father's Toolkeepers' notation nor my mother's native language but a strange and uneven combination of the two, so muddled that individual words were often formed of symbols from both tongues. No one who did not know both languages would ever have been able to decode the text.

It took me a while to parse out the first few pages, but the more I read, the clearer it became, and though I still could not remember writing it, I *understood* it.

I spent hours hunched in front of the fire, reading about Past Amber's theories and experimentation. About her triumphs and failures. About manipulations of her classmates, which she did not consider cruel, because of their potential to benefit all of mankind.

I remembered my odd impulse to keep my father's handkerchief. And Yoslyn's claim that I'd lent my handkerchief to Adria after *I'd* made her cry. I read about my development of a new "enhanced" beyn and my trials of it in every conceivable usage. And finally, as Desmond rolled over in the bed to face me, blinking sleep from his eyes, I turned the last page, my gaze racing over the cryptic text.

"Amber?" He sat up, feet flat on the cold stone floor, copper-flecked eyes swimming with unease. "What are you doing?"

I closed the journal and stared up at him, stunned. "I know what I did with the gold-flecked suspension."

"You *what*?" Desmond frowned, as if I'd spoken utter nonsense. And the truth was not far off.

"I drank it," I repeated as I hung his kettle over the fire. "Will you please portion out some leaves?" I waved one hand at the teacups lined up on a wall shelf mounted above his table.

"You *drank* the suspension?"

"Yes. I mean, I must have. I wrote in the journal that that was my intent, and as near as I can tell, I wrote that just as you were walking into the laboratory that night. The last sentence isn't even properly punctuated, as if you interrupted me right as I scratched out the final word."

He stalked to the end of the room, then spun and paced back, without going anywhere near the teacups. "But why would you—?"

"Because that was the only way I knew of to square the circle. My theory, at that point, was that there is no *one* Philosopher's Stone. There is no one formula. No one technique. I realized, as I was contemplating Lord Calyx's journals and my own path forward, once I'd made the silver-and-gold solution, that if the Philosopher's Stone is intended to elevate something—some*one*—to its highest form, the only way to square the circle would be to imbibe the solution. To let it simmer within the human crucible and form a *living* compound."

The look he gave me was part wonder and part horror. "But . . . that would mean that *you* are the Philosopher's Stone."

"Yes." I nodded. Then I shook my head. "And no. My theory—mine, not Past Amber's—is that I have turned myself into *a* Philosopher's Stone. I have accomplished a higher form of *my own* being. In theory. But that would likely look and feel—and function—differently for anyone else. I think that the Philosopher's Stone isn't one stone that can elevate everything it touches. It's the result of one person's grinding effort to do the best alchemy they can, and the result is as much about how much of your own heart and soul you put into that effort as about what the solution itself does. That's the spiritual part. The mind is the intellectual effort to create it. And the body . . ." I shrugged. "Well, you have to drink it—or maybe you could smear it all over yourself, like a full-body salve—to square the circle."

"Your blood," Desmond whispered. "It was flecked with . . . something reflective. That's what I saw that day, when you sat bleeding on my desktop. I couldn't tell whether it looked silver or gold, in the light of my lantern, but it was definitely metallic."

"That *has* to be because it's in my system."

"And your antidote from the Black Trial," Desmond mused.

"What about it?" I asked as I finally took the teacups down myself.

"You sprayed blood into it, when you coughed. That's why it worked better than it should have. Why no one could replicate it. You *are* the Philosopher's Stone, and you literally coughed tiny bits of yourself into the antidote. So it worked like it would have if you'd made it with your enhanced beyn."

"Yes!" I spun toward him, the cups clattering in my hand. "That *must* be what happened!"

"And the breathable water!" Desmond's eyes were wider than I'd ever seen them. "That's how you did it."

"What? No." I untied the cloth from atop his jar of dried tea leaves and poured a generous amount into each cup. "I didn't do that. The prevailing theory is that one of the professors or staff researchers—"

"No, it was you," Desmond said. "I knew it was you, almost immediately. But I couldn't figure out how you'd done it. You must have bled or sweated into your viable air catalyst, and when you'd emptied your first air bladder and let it go, it opened—"

"Exposing that catalyst to the water . . ." Stunned, I sank into the nearest chair. "You think that was enough to catalyze the entire arena full of water?"

"It must have been. And it's likely why you recovered from the toxic fumes, when Wilder did not." He grabbed my hand and squeezed so hard my bones ground together. "Amber, we have *no idea* what the limits of the Philosopher's Stone are."

"Well, we do know one limit," I said. "It seems that if you drink the metallic solution, you are at a high risk of wiping out your own memory."

"Of course . . ." he breathed. "You afflicted *yourself* with this amnesia."

"Unintentionally," I insisted.

"The Bluehelm did not drug you. Neither did the Toolkeepers." Finally, Desmond wrapped a cloth around his hand and lifted the kettle from the fire. He sounded both relieved and confused. "Then why . . . ?"

"Why what?"

"Amber." He carefully poured hot water into both cups, then he set the kettle on a cloth folded on the table and sat on the chair across from me. "Wilder . . . he was mired in something."

"What? Mired in what?"

"I don't know, precisely. But last year one of his typical misadventures landed him in significant trouble. The Bluehelm summoned him, and he would not disclose to me the result. All he would divulge was that he'd accepted an offer that would allow him to stay at the Alchemary. And afterward . . . he affixed himself to your side, at every opportunity."

I shrugged, denial sharp on my tongue. "We were best friends, Desmond. We had been for years."

"Yes, but you'd grown apart during your Fundamentals year. You were the darling of the academy, if not of your classmates, while Wilder struggled academically, despite an unerring talent. And he and Petyr quit their relationship about the time you and I became . . . physically intimate." Desmond sipped cautiously from his cup, seeming to consider his next words. "Wilder spun into a bit of a dark spiral for a while, retiring from the Dusty Beaker with a different student—or barmaid—every weekend. Breaking rules and curfews. Until the Bluehelm summoned him. Then, suddenly, he was reformed and was affixed to your side, despite his utter loathing of our relationship."

I shrugged and scooped a spoonful of sugar into my own teacup. "Sounds as if he were trying not to be expelled."

"Yes, but he said he'd accepted an *offer*, presumably from the Bluehelm. And I think it concerned you."

I frowned as I blew over the top of my cup. "Why would you—?"

"Because she'd already asked *me* for updates on your progress, and I'd politely refused."

"You think she was using Wilder to spy on me?"

"To observe you, certainly."

I shook my head, careful not to slosh my tea. "He would never—"

"He would, if his only choices were to inform on the progress of your research or be expelled, wherein he might never see you again. He loved you, Amber. Even if he didn't also love alchemy—and he *did*—he would have done anything to stay here with you."

The truth of that hit me like a blow to the gut, and I set my cup carefully on its saucer. "That's why I wrote in code. . . ." Past Amber had known. At least, she'd suspected. "I didn't trust you either. That's why I wrote all of my research notes in a language no one else could understand."

He nodded. "I think that's true. I thought you were being paranoid at the time. That it was another way this place was changing you. But maybe you knew the Bluehelm was trying to keep tabs on you."

I arched both brows at him. "Well, Past Amber was certainly no imbecile."

"Neither is *Current* Amber." His frown faded. "I don't think he stopped observing you after your memory loss. I thought it was odd, at the time, how the Bluehelm knew to appear at Dr. Winhoof's office during your examination. Wilder wanted to deliver you straight to her, but—"

"You insisted I go to the Panacea wing."

He nodded. "And yet the Bluehelm appeared there and observed most of your examination. I think Wilder alerted her."

"Seconds before he died, he looked relieved." I blew over the surface of my tea again, letting the fragrant mist wash over my face in an attempt to calm the pitching of my stomach.

I did not like thinking ill of the dead. Especially of Wilder.

"Relieved?"

"Yes. When the staircase opened in the Conservatory foyer. He looked distinctly relieved. I remember thinking that was odd, because I'd expected him to look as surprised as I was that the staircase even existed."

"He was going to tell the Bluehelm," Desmond concluded. "That's why he rushed in. You'd had no luck recovering your memory, and they didn't know you had completed the formula for the Philosopher's Stone. Wilder was running out of things to report, and your potential was looking . . ." He shrugged.

"Dubious. Which meant his time at the Alchemary was likely nearing an end. But he thought he could buy more if he brought her whatever we'd found in Lord Calyx's secret hiding place. And instead, it killed him."

"Do you think it's his formula for the Stone?" Desmond asked.

"I don't know what else it could be." I shrugged. "We know he finished the formula and that he used it. He described the gold-flecked silver solution. But he clearly never thought to drink it. Whatever method he tried to square the circle was a failure, and so his solution became inert. It took the form of that beautiful, clear stone, which he mounted in a ring. I cannot imagine what he would have hidden beneath the floor of the Conservatory, if not the formula for the Philosopher's Stone."

"She *cannot* get it," Desmond said quietly. "We cannot let the Bluehelm acquire that formula any more than we can let her find out what you are. What you've done. She is not the only rot at the Alchemary, but she *is* its wellspring, and—"

I sat straight, on the literal edge of my seat. "So, let's go get it."

Desmond frowned. "The noxious gas—"

"Has certainly dissipated quite a bit, with the passage of two days' time, yet the threat of it has likely kept everyone else away. If any of it *does* remain, it is unlikely to injure someone who has *become* the Philosopher's Stone."

"That's too much to risk—"

"Desmond." I reached across the table to seize his hand, which wrapped around mine with a warm strength, as if on instinct. "If the gas remains, I will not descend the stairs. You have my word. But I cannot remain here, simply *wondering*." I stood and sipped as much of the scalding tea as I could manage. "You may accompany me if you like." I divested my expression of any evidence of how badly I wanted that. "But I will go, regardless."

Despite his concerns about the danger, and to my great relief, Desmond would not let me sneak into the Conservatory alone. The front door had been barred, which we knew because he'd been forced to steal in the back way in order to make a postcoital elixir for me just hours before.

We snuck in that same way and were relieved to find that while the atrium was officially off-limits, there were no guards posted to bar our entry. No one else, it seemed, would dare disobey the

Bluehelm's orders. Especially when they might only be rewarded with death by a lingering noxious gas.

"It's gone," Desmond whispered as he peered into the dark stairwell, holding his candle as low as he dared without actually descending. "I think the fumes have dissipated. Though the official word is that that was expected to take several more days."

"That was said to keep people away," I whispered, and Desmond nodded. "I'll go first, just in case. If I start coughing, you turn around immediately," I ordered.

"Without hesitation," he said, his gaze locked onto mine. "But I shall be carrying you in my arms, upon my retreat."

I gave his hand a warm squeeze. Then I started slowly down the spiral staircase, holding my own candle.

Cobwebs stretched from the low ceiling of a narrow, stone-paved corridor, wafting gently under the influence of a breeze so slight I could not feel it. There were no branches or corners in the passage. No more traps or puzzles. At the end of the short path stood a plain wooden door with a decorative metal triangle set into it. A ring the size of my palm had been cut into the wood around the triangle, and inside it had been carved a square, and within that a smaller circle.

I knew the shapes, and I knew exactly what would fit into the empty lines, but as I reached into the left pocket of my frock for the metal ouroboros, the scrape of a shoe heel on stone made my head snap up. Desmond stiffened at my side as I peered into the darkness beyond our candlelight.

"Someone's here," he whispered, and suddenly I understood why no one had tried to stop us from descending the hidden staircase. "The Bluehelm was watching."

"Waiting for us," I agreed. Because she didn't have the pieces that would unlock this puzzle, and it would be easier to wait for me to bring them than for her to try to find them.

My pulse whooshed like ocean waves as shadows stirred at the base of the spiral staircase. A single right foot stepped into the light, bare and masculine, with a strong, high arch. It had an odd sheen in the flicker of my candle—an almost glowing golden cast.

An aurum. Yet even in the dim light, I could see that the tint of this poor man's skin was much deeper—much more golden—than the aurums I'd seen before.

My pulse spiked violently, and for an instant, the entire world seemed to swim around me. How was this possible? Had the mysterious illness taken hold of the Alchemary itself while Desmond and I were secluded in shared mourning?

A matching left foot stepped forward, along with the cuff of a simple pair of linen trousers, and as the man wearing them stepped farther into the light, a second figure appeared behind him. I couldn't even look at the second man, however, because my gaze had caught on the first pair of golden feet and the matching golden hands that swung at the sides of those linen trousers.

My heart thumped painfully. I knew those feet. I knew those hands. I knew that gait, for all its odd stiffness, and . . .

He took another step, and I gasped at an achingly familiar set of features as the light fell over them. They were cast in that same oddly golden tone, glimmering with a strangely metallic glow.

"Wilder," I whispered.

Desmond made a choking sound deep in his throat. "Aurums," he replied softly, and I shook my head, even though I'd had the same thought. Because that wasn't right. Aurums could not move. They were flesh made stone—yes, an oddly glowing, metallic stone, yet stone nonetheless, of a sort. Aurums were frozen in their own form.

And Wilder had died without ever getting sick, so he could not be an aurum, any more than an aurum could be marching toward me.

But how else could he be walking this way, living and breathing—presumably—after I'd *seen* him die? How could he and . . .

Petyr. The other strangely golden figure, who also stood shirtless and oddly solemn, was Petyr Lorena, who'd died during the Black Trial, five weeks before. But *had* he died? *Could* he have, if he was standing here in front of me?

"What is happening?" I whispered.

Desmond stood eerily still at my side, every muscle tensed. "I have not yet drawn a logical conclusion." Even without glancing his way, I could tell that his uneasy focus was glued to his brother's face. I could feel the grief and confusion—the *anger*—rolling off him like smoke from a bonfire, and I understood his shock.

Wilder's appearance was a knife plunged back into the still-gaping wound in my heart. In my soul.

"The facts do not support the conclusion stalking bodily toward us, substantial as the days they were born," Desmond whispered. "Petyr and Wilder *died*."

"Did you *see* their bodies?" I whispered.

He shook his head.

"I don't understand what is happening," I said as unanswered questions and unwelcome theories battled for space in my mind. "But I know that only one person has ever had any control over Wilder, and that same person is responsible for bringing aurums to the Alchemary under the Crown's seal in order to study the condition." She was also quite likely the most powerful alchemist in the world.

"The Bluehelm," Desmond whispered.

"Indeed," I said as the aurums stalked closer, golden skin shining in the light of our candles.

I did not understand what had happened to Wilder. I couldn't even be certain he was alive. But I *was* certain that if Lord Calyx's formula—or even a sample of his gold-flecked solution—was behind that door, it might be the only thing in existence that could help Wilder. That could cure him, if he was alive, or let him rest in peace, if he was not.

Unease crawling across my skin, I turned toward the door, but a horrific screech spun me around again as a golden blur suddenly raced down the corridor toward us. I screamed, and Desmond shoved me back as he lurched into the center of the passageway.

“Open the door!” he shouted. Then Petyr slammed into him. Desmond grunted from the impact, planting his feet on the stone floor, trying to stop the golden human battering ram from driving him bodily into me.

Wilder raced forward, oddly silent, and as I fumbled to fit the metal ouroboros into its circle on the door, I heard the repeated thunk of flesh against flesh, followed by Desmond’s grunts, both of pain and of effort.

Pulse racing, I glanced back as I dug the square from my pocket and saw Desmond swinging with one fist while he blocked a blow with his opposite arm, his knees bent, the toes of his boot dug firmly into the edge of a stone tile on the floor, to shore up his footing. Muscles stood out in his neck and through the material of his tunic, a bruise already forming on his chin.

“Hurry!” he gasped as he threw another blow, which thunked horrifically against golden flesh surely as hard as stone.

I whirled around and shoved the metal frame into the square etched into the door, then pulled Queen Avalona’s ring—Lord Calyx’s inert Philosopher’s Stone—from my other pocket. When I pressed it to the circle at the center of the symbol, a great grinding echoed from behind the door, rumbling up from the floor to thrum throughout my body.

Behind me, the grunts and blows echoed at a frantic pace, and I flinched with each one until a final, heavy clank rang from behind the door. It creaked open, just an inch.

Holding my breath in case of another toxic trap, I shoved the door open and rushed past it. Inside, my candlelight cast flickering shadows across a small chamber, entirely empty save what could only be described as a broad stone shrine at one end. An elaborate green gown lay draped across the long marble surface, layered with cobwebs and clearly brittle with age.

Tucked into the crook at the gown's elbow was a single dusty corked vial, its contents obscured by more than a century of grime.

Three portraits hung on the wall above the shrine. The one in the center depicted Queen Avalona wearing the inert circle ring and the green gown, though in this painting, she was not visibly pregnant. In the portrait on the right, she held her doomed infant son, in what was likely the only portrait of him ever painted.

In the portrait on the left, the queen stood side by side with Iris, Lord Calyx's assistant, whose hooded robe was fantastically detailed in black, gray, and honey gold. Unlike in the wedding sketch, in the painting, Iris's face was clear and detailed. As was her resemblance to the tragic queen.

I gasped as I stared at the stunningly familiar face of the woman who would go on to become the very first Bluehelm of the Alchemary—one hundred fifty years ago.

"Cressa," I whispered.

And in my shock, I finally noticed that the chaotic violence behind me had given way to absolute stillness and silence.

Forty-Five

"Beautiful, wasn't she? Avalona, I mean."

I spun, startled, and the light from my candle flickered over Cressa Baxter's face. My gaze raked over her features, assessing. Comparing. The same light brown skin and gray-ringed eyes. The same pouf of dark, red-tinged ringlets.

"My sister was renowned, in her day, as the most beautiful woman in the world. Few remember that she was also quite an intellect, and a very tender soul."

"Your sister?"

Her laughter held a bitter, sour note. "That bit, like so much else, has been lost to history. Still, sibling rivalry is an age-old story. One your Gregory brothers certainly understand," she said, tossing a glance through the open door into the dark, eerily quiet corridor.

"You're . . . Iris? The first Bluehelm?" I blinked at her, frowning as I struggled to draw a coherent conclusion. "How . . . ?"

"I am Iris, the *only* Bluehelm," she said, and though I knew that voice, its cadence—its odd gravitas—was entirely unfamiliar. "I have run the Alchemary under various names, wearing various faces, for a century and a half. But I always eventually come back to this one." She ran her fingers down her own smooth cheek in an eerily graceful motion. "When there's no one left to remember it."

"But you're a student." Clearly that wasn't true, but when comprehension would not come, my thoughts defaulted to what I knew. What I'd *thought* I knew, at least.

Cressa—*Iris*—looked coldly amused. "Every few decades I'm forced to operate by proxy while I rise through the ranks as a student, then as a researcher. Otherwise, people would notice that the Bluehelm never dies."

"You were never her assistant," I whispered.

This time she laughed, a sound like the ringing of a cold, hollow bell. "I am her . . . puppeteer. Though I *was* acting on my own behalf when I brought you to the Alchemary."

"*You?* I brought myself here," I insisted, though the truth was that I had no memory of the occasion. "After being recruited as a child."

"By a woman with pale skin and a single eyebrow, like a caterpillar crawling across her forehead?"

I sucked in a sharp breath.

She nodded at my recognition. "I came to your quaint mud puddle of a village a decade ago, wearing a different face, answering to a different name, and *I* set you on this path, Amber Fallbrook. It was I who recognized our Wilder's childhood instinct for alchemy, and I was thrilled to find you and our Desmond waiting in the wings, overshadowed by his zeal, yet harboring infinite potential."

She made a casual gesture over shoulder, and suddenly Desmond stumbled into the room, as if he'd been shoved.

He clutched one arm to his chest and his nose was bleeding, yet he stood straight, his jaw clenched, restrained power emanating from him with every tightly composed movement. I understood, then, that he'd fought to defend us both, rather than to injure his brother.

Wilder stepped into the stone chamber after him, golden flesh gleaming in the light of my candle, his gilded features utterly flawless, yet devastatingly expressionless.

Iris gave another wave of her hand, and he suddenly froze. I could not even be certain he was breathing.

"Amber." Relief swam in Desmond's voice as his gaze traveled my form.

"She's fine," Iris snapped. "But maintain your distance, or I shall reinstate the battle of the Gregory brothers, though I admit I have no more appetite for sibling rivalry."

I forced my attention back to her. "You're saying you brought us here? All three of us?"

"Not by force or coercion, if that's what you're implying. I simply presented you with an opportunity. I recognized what the three of you represented, even as children. Spirit . . ." She gestured at Wilder. "Matter." She shifted that open-handed motion toward Desmond. "And mind," she said, pointing directly at my chest. "A triangle resists pressure by equally distributing force from one corner into the other two, and I knew that if you learned to rely upon each other as alchemists, you could do *monumental* things here. Unfortunately," she added, her expression souring as her gaze shifted between us, "I underestimated the damage that sentiment—and unchecked lust—would play in this hot-blooded little triad."

"What have you done to Wilder?" Desmond demanded. "You've infected him, or—"

"There is no infection," I breathed. "There never was. She did this on purpose."

"There *is* a contagion, but it is not of my doing," Iris said, a brief twitch of her brow hinting at true irritation. "*My* aurums, as they have come to be called, are entirely within my control and intentionally created. I have not yet discovered the source of the others." Those who'd fallen ill suddenly, presumably, and with a less-saturated golden skin tone. "Or the manner of the contagion's spread."

"Every serum has an unintended effect," Desmond snapped. "What was the *intended* effect?"

"How are you *alive*?" I managed as the reality of it all finally crashed over me.

Iris ignored both questions as her gaze slid over my shoulder. Her eyes widened and she glided past me as if she were not the least bit concerned to have me at her back. She snatched the vial from the shrine, rumpling the dead queen's delicate gown, then held it up to the light of my candle. Iris scowled and wiped the dust from the vial onto the front of her skirt, and I could see through the clean glass that the solution inside . . .

"That is *not* the Philosopher's Stone," I said. It was an alchemical solution, certainly, but the coppery color was not right, and there was no metallic sheen.

"Of course it isn't." Iris tossed a disappointed look my way, as if I were a candle flickering at the end of its wick. "Calyx spent more than a decade trying to make such a thing before concluding that it is *utter* fantasy. Which I told him from the start. And what good would it do, even if it were real? If you could turn any base metal into gold, then gold would lose its rarity, and thus its worth. I said as much to you more than a year ago, and I made it clear that as a researcher, you will be expected to set aside childish indulgences"—her gaze flicked toward Desmond—"and stop wasting resources on—"

"That is *not* the point of the Philosopher's Stone," I snapped, ignoring the fierce lowering of her brows in my direction. "The Stone advances whatever it is applied to—not just base metal—toward its most perfect state. Whether that be—"

Desmond's brows rose. Pointedly, and in warning.

"Well, we don't really know what that would be," I finished.

"You have his look." Iris stalked closer to me, her gaze caught on my face. "So full of determination and wonder, just like Calyx.

So much potential, hampered by so much fancy. *I* had that look, once. He said I was interminable drive beholden to *endless* trivial emotion, and he said it all with a straight face, as if he did not fit that very definition. As if obsession with my sister—his *and* Eldon's—had not already broken an emperor, and crippled this institution, and sent the entire empire careening toward both war and financial ruin."

She tilted her head, looking oddly, honestly curious. "Have you yet noticed that when men feel something, it is lofty, noble, and important? It is worthy of dedicating statues and sonnets to. Of founding entire kingdoms upon. But when *women* feel it, it is a flighty and frivolous distraction from what really matters."

"I . . ." But Iris didn't seem truly interested in my answer.

Her teeth gnashed together. "We both finally understood, in the end, though. Whether it is noble or frivolous, *all* sentiment is a distraction."

"Lord Calyx hurt you," I whispered as the unspoken truth began to seep from between her disgruntled words.

Iris scowled. "He *ground* me, like ashes in a mortar. He boiled me, like a solution suspended over flame. He distilled from me what was useful and discarded the rest. Transformation does not come easily, child, and it requires an alchemist willing to destroy base matter in order to create something greater. *That* is your Philosopher's Stone," she spat, lips twisted into a bitter scowl. "It is not an alchemical solution, mixed from ingredients; it is an alchemical *process*, hard fought for."

She was not entirely wrong. But neither was she entirely right.

"In that sense, he succeeded," she continued, while Desmond wiped blood from his nose onto his sleeve. "But in every other sense—in any sense Eldon could monetize—the search for the Stone was an utter failure, and Calyx was humiliated by the time he gave it up and pursued—"

"The Elixir of Life." I hardly heard the words, even as I said them. Even as my gaze settled onto the vial still cradled in her palm. "He did it," I said, and suddenly I understood her wrath. "And that isn't what you want. Because *you've already taken it.*"

That was the only way a classmate of mine could possibly share a face with the first Bluehelm of this very institution. "Calyx gave you the Elixir of Life?"

"He *administered* it to me." The words sounded hollow and cold as she turned to stare up at the center portrait. "Yet he intended it for *her*. He wanted to be with Avalona forever. Long after Eldon, the sovereign fool, was rotting in his grave."

"But she died before he could complete the formula," Desmond concluded.

Iris huffed. "Yet he gave her many other things along the way. The ring." Her gaze dropped to Avalona's hand, then shifted toward the portrait of mother and infant son. "And the child."

Surprise drew my gaze to Desmond's. Emperor Eldon's doomed son was sired by Lord Calyx?

Iris aimed a toxic glance at Desmond. "Life is messy when two men love the same woman, would you not agree?"

Desmond only blinked at her, refusing to be baited. Or to look at Wilder, who still stood in eerily frozen golden perfection on the edge of the spill of my candlelight.

"It was certainly messy for Eldon. Naturally, he could not let the child live, and in the end, that was all it took to dull the shine of the golden queen. My *darling* sister."

I glanced at Desmond, who gestured subtly for me to step back, away from Iris.

"Eldon buried her with her bastard, not a week after that portrait was finished. He tried to have it burned, but I snuck it out of the palace, at Calyx's request."

"You?" I asked, and Iris nodded. "Because you loved her?"

She snorted. "Because I loved *him*. Because I was fool enough to believe that once he'd mourned her, he would *see me*."

"*You* told Eldon?" Desmond said, and though he phrased it as a question, his words carried the cold stone weight of utter fact. "About the baby. About Lord Calyx."

Iris nodded again. "I did not anticipate that he might kill them. I believed he would share my grief for an unrequited love and cast them out in shame. But I *should* have known. Eldon was a monster. He only let Calyx live because he needed a master alchemist. To make . . . *this*." Her hand suddenly clenched around the vial. "And I wanted that, too. I was a gifted alchemist in my own right, but I was not like Calyx. *No one* was like Calyx. So I made him an offer."

"You would run the Alchemary, while he made the Elixir," I guessed. A woman like Iris could not have been exiled to the Seminary or relegated to teaching. She had chosen her own path. And she'd set the father of alchemy down his.

Iris nodded. "I took on all of it. The entire institution. I freed up all of his time to build this. . . ." She extended her left hand to take in the entire Conservatory building. "And to make this." She lifted her right hand, still holding the vial. "Two doses. It took years, and by the end, we'd grown dear to each other. We were going to take the Elixir together. We would have eternity to perfect our craft. To lead the world into a new era of science and discovery."

"So then, where is he?" Desmond asked. And when Iris remained silent, I understood.

"He refused to drink," I said, my grip tightening on the candle holder. "Didn't he?"

"Oh, no. He drank from his vial, as I drank from mine," she spat. "But while my dose made my entire body tingle, restoring me to the very bloom and vitality of youth, his left him writhing on the floor in mortal anguish."

I exhaled, horrified by the truth. "He took his own life."

She nodded, gaze cold and hard with the memory. "He said, as he lay wracked with unfathomable pain, losing control of his failing body, that he would rather be with Avalona in death than with me in life."

I met Desmond's shocked gaze.

"He *condemned* me to eternity," Iris continued, gray eyes flashing with fury, brows drawn low with the memory. "Instead of perfecting alchemy with me, he sentenced me to do it on my own. To haul the world, kicking and screaming in protest, toward a progress it does not want and cannot understand. Toward a glorious future that no one is willing to pay for. A fragile advancement that must be secured and defended in brutal ways."

By the scriveners, certainly. But I knew better than to reveal my knowledge of that dangerous elite.

She sighed, her hand finally falling limp at her side. "I did not know this second vial existed until this very moment. I could not be sure he'd actually made a dose for himself. That he'd ever truly considered taking it."

"But this is not what you wanted," I said. "Not what you thought would be here."

"Of course not." Her hand clenched around the vial again. "This *cannot* be all there is." She ran her free hand over the marble top of the shrine, prying at the edges, examining every inch, as Desmond took advantage of her distraction to shuffle closer to me. "He must have left notes. . . ."

"What notes?" I asked. "What are you looking for?"

"For mercy!" She whirled on us, eyes flashing. "When I realized what you'd found, I hoped—for the first time in more than a century—that he might have had *some* compassion for me. That maybe all of this—the puzzles and whatever he'd buried beneath his precious Conservatory—was meant for *me*. That he hadn't sentenced me to eternity after all."

The truth washed over me like the glow of a lantern lit in a dark room. "You want a cure for immortality."

"What else?" she roared, swiping the ancient dress onto the stone floor in a paroxysm of rage. "And it is . . . not . . . here!" She whirled around, and her gaze landed on me. "But *you* are here." Something seemed to click behind her gaze, like a key turning in a lock. "And you." Her focus shifted to Desmond, then to Wilder. "And him . . ."

"What do you want with us?" I asked, chills rising as gooseflesh all over my arms.

"Only what you're already willing to give the Alchemary: your service."

A growl wound its way up Desmond's throat. "Why would we ever—"

"For him," Iris snapped, waving her empty hand through the shadows at Wilder. Then she turned to me. "As Desmond knows and you have likely already come to understand, one of the central pillars of the Alchemary is the idea that an alchemist's dedication to their craft—and to this institution—does not end in death. That matter—the body—can serve science, even after the mind and soul have passed on. We've always interpreted that edict as a dedication of the alchemist's corpse as components for the craft—an ashes-to-ashes sort of approach. But I've spent more than a century developing another way for alchemists to serve past death."

She stepped over the dress crumpled on the stone floor to gesture at Wilder. "Or rather, to suspend the animation of the human body, which is only possible on the very verge of expiry. And that was his state, when I saw him in the infirmary. I had no other choice. It was either this or death."

"This *is* death," I said through clenched teeth, my heart aching as my gaze lingered on Wilder's vacant expression. "This is the death of his *will*. Of his *autonomy*."

"Perhaps," she allowed. "And yet, he *is* living. Or, more accurately, he is dying very, very slowly." Iris slowly paced the floor in front of him, her shadow shifting across the stone walls of Calyx's . . . catacomb. "I've induced a state of biological dormancy, which allows me to take control of his physical function. I can tighten my grip. . . ."

She lifted her left hand, and when she clutched it into a fist, Wilder shuddered and collapsed to the dusty floor, his joints cracking and bending at odd angles.

"Stop!" I shrieked, lurching toward him, until Desmond pulled me back, one arm tucked firmly around my waist. "Let him up!"

"Or I can loosen it." Iris spread her fingers wide, and Wilder blinked, then he stood, more swiftly than should have been possible, and for one instant, I saw something in the fleeting clarity of his expression that I recognized.

He was still in there. Wilder was *alive,* inside the golden shell of his body.

"Let him go!" I demanded, and Desmond's grip on me tightened for a second.

"I cannot," Iris said. "If I release my control of him, that biological dormancy will end, and he will die. Unless . . ." She lifted the vial. "I am prepared to make you an offer. Both of you." She glanced at Wilder, just as his expression emptied into that disturbingly blank look. "All three of you, actually. The three brightest minds this institution has seen since Calyx died. Together, you might actually rival him."

"What are you offering?" Desmond demanded, finally releasing me.

"I will give your brother a drop from this vial," she said. "Just enough to bring him back from the brink of death, so I can loosen my hold on him."

"Give him all of it," I demanded. "Cure him. Let him go."

"No," she snapped. "Even if I could do that, it would be unfair to him. I would not sentence him to the very fate I'm trying to escape, and if you were thinking clearly, you would not ask me to. Do you think he wants to live to see both of you wither and die? To go on living after everyone he loves has passed on? Whether or not you spend that interval entangled in your own desire, in utter disregard for his affection."

I had no answer. In the moment, I didn't care what Wilder wanted, or what an infinite future might bring. I just wanted him back.

Iris paced across the uneven stones toward us, brushing aside a cobweb dangling from the low ceiling. "I will give him enough to reverse what the poisonous gas did to him, but you will need the rest of the Elixir in order to hold up your end of our deal. You will analyze what is left and use it to come up with the formula. And you will use *that* to find a way to reverse it."

"You want us to cure you," Desmond said. "Why would we do that? Why would we do anything you want?"

"We *will*!" I said, shooting a look at Desmond as I grabbed his hand to silence him. "You have *my* word." Then I nodded at Wilder. "Fix him. Now."

Iris cocked one brow in Desmond's direction, and when he nodded, somewhat hesitantly, she uncorked the vial and turned to stand in front of Wilder. He opened his mouth at some unspoken signal from her, and she dipped her finger into the serum. When she pulled it out, a single drop of a thick, viscous, coppery liquid clung to her fingertip, already forming a bulbous tip as it was pulled toward the ground.

She held her finger over Wilder's extended tongue just as that drop gave way.

The coppery drip flattened on his tongue, and his entire golden form seemed to shudder. He closed his mouth. He blinked, then he blinked again. Slowly, the golden sheen seemed to fade from his skin.

Wilder frowned. He blinked again, as if clearing his vision, and his confused gaze found me. "Amber?"

I burst into tears as I ripped my hand free from Desmond's. I raced past Iris to throw my arms around Wilder.

He returned my embrace, a little more slowly than I would have liked, and his arms were cold, though they seemed to grow warmer with every passing second.

"We have an accord, then," Iris said. "And in case you have any thoughts about abandoning your obligation therein..." She gestured again at Wilder, and he suddenly stiffened in my arms. He shoved me back, his eyes horrifically blank again, and seized my throat in his left hand, squeezing so that I could draw in only the thinnest of breaths, no matter how I clutched at his wrist and fought his grip.

"Wilder!" Desmond lunged forward. "Let her go!"

Wilder's right hand shot out and slammed into Desmond's chest, sending the larger man reeling backward into the shrine, gasping for breath, clutching his own sternum.

"You cannot break his hold," Iris said. "But I will let you have him, for now." She waved her hand again, curling her fingers, and Wilder's hand fell away from my throat. I stumbled backward, rubbing at my neck, while he blinked and awareness rushed back into his eyes like the morning tide.

"Amber!" He reached for me, but I shuffled farther away, until I felt Avalona's dress beneath my heel. "I'm so sorry. I don't know what—"

"He truly doesn't. He has no control over it," Iris said. "So understand that if you veer from the task in any way, I will take him back. I *will* set him to my bidding."

"What bidding?" Desmond demanded, still rubbing his chest.

She backed toward the door to the small chamber with Petyr behind her, and though I wanted to free him, too, I knew better than to ask, considering that we hadn't even truly managed to free Wilder.

"The wolves are at the gate, Desmond. They're coming from all angles. Some, in fact, have already dug their dens deep into our garden. And if you cannot do as you promised—or if you will not—then instead of working with you, Wilder will fight the wolves with me."

With that, she turned and marched into the dark corridor, leaving the three of us to stare at one another in utter shock.

Forty-Six

"He will never forgive me," Wilder whispered, hunched over the small table in Desmond's apartment, breathing deeply from a steaming cup of fragrant tea. Nearly a day after Iris had returned control of his body to him, he didn't seem to trust his own autonomy. He'd steadily refused to leave his brother's private apartment, for fear of what he might do, if she revoked it.

Or maybe he wasn't yet ready to be around other people. I certainly understood his reluctance.

"Desmond will forgive you," I insisted as I stoked the fire with an iron poker. "*I* have."

"You should not have. I surveilled you. I reported on your progress to the Bluehelm. To the woman I *thought* was the Bluehelm, anyway. I do not deserve—"

"Deserving is not the issue." I set the poker down and crossed the room to squeeze his shoulder. "We do not forgive people because they deserve it. We forgive people because we love them. Because we want them in our lives."

He blinked up at me as I poured hot water from the kettle into my own mug. "You want me?"

"In my life? Yes. Desperately." I laid one hand over his on the table. "As does Desmond."

"No. He—"

"He feels guilty for what happened to you, as do I. And beyond that, we *need* you. We need your mind, and your aptitude."

"You're really going to do it? You're going to cure Cre—I mean Iris?"

"*We're* going to do it." I squeezed his hand then sank into my own chair. "At least, we're going to try. But she need not know our *true* goal." I leaned closer and lowered my voice, as if there were anyone around to overhear. "We're going to cure you and Petyr, and all of the other aurums."

Wilder frowned. "What makes you think that's even possible? We have no understanding of how she made them, and we don't have access to her formula, or—"

"But we have you. We have *you,* and your blood, which will still have some trace in it of whatever she's done to you. And that can be distilled."

He nodded, slowly.

"Beyond that, we will have the Elixir of Life—at least the small portion she'll give us to work with."

"What has that to do with the aurums?"

"Everything, I suspect." I blew across my own teacup. "I believe Iris has been working on her aurum serum for more than a century, but I do *not* believe her original intent was to control people near death. You're the one who taught me that even when a new formula misses the mark, it often does something unexpected and sometimes miraculous. I think she made use of one of her mistakes, just like you often do. I think she was trying, all this time, to re-create the Elixir of Life, in order to come up with an antidote."

"But she couldn't do it."

"Precisely," I said. "If she could, she wouldn't need us. But I think that her error in creating the Elixir—maybe more than one of her errors—is what kept you alive long enough for the real Elixir to come to the rescue. And I think that as we deconstruct it and come up with a formula, we'll be able to undo everything she's done."

"So . . . you agreed to all of this for me."

I shrugged. "For you, and for the other aurums." And, in truth, because I *truly* wanted to work on the problem. Because I wasn't sure anyone else was capable of solving it.

"This is harder than it would be if you had your memory," Wilder said, his blue-eyed gaze burning into mine.

"Yet harder does not mean impossible."

We hadn't told him about the Philosopher's Stone. Not that I'd finished it or what I'd done with it. There was a limit, Desmond and I had decided, to what we could afford to tell Wilder, because Iris would almost certainly use him to spy on us again.

We had him back, but we did not have all of him. As the bruise around my throat could attest.

"Wilder." I took his hand again from across the table. "The time has come to tell me about that night. I need to know how we wound up in bed together, when . . . I was with Desmond."

Wilder paled. "He told you?"

I nodded. "He told me as much of the truth as he knows. And I need to know why I would betray him like that. Why *we* would betray him."

"We did not," he said. "As pleasing as it was to indulge the fantasy—the possibility that you might feel for me what I feel for you—you deserve the truth. You and I did *nothing* to betray Desmond."

My gaze narrowed on him. "But when I awoke, we were in bed, nearly naked."

"Yes, and that is how we fell asleep—because I could not get warm, despite the fire and the blankets. You found me that night, on your way to the Dormitory, in a state of profound physical distress. I had been taking the elixir I told you about. The one that gave me confidence and focus, but its unintended effects had become too great. I had decided to cease taking it. That morning, I had smashed my entire inventory, and that night, I'd left the student laboratory, after setting up my station, because I was suffering tremors I could not control. I had broken into a cold sweat, and when you found me, I'd just involuntarily purged my entire dinner. I could not get warm.

"You brought me up to your room to care for me. You made me tea and built a fire, yet still I shivered. I confided in you what I'd done—why I was sick—and you seemed so pleased by my decision, but you would not let me leave. You insisted on caring for me, even though you felt a bit sick yourself at that point. So we curled up in your bed, skin to skin, for warmth. That is how we fell asleep, and how we woke up the next morning. Only... you had no memory of it. You thought we'd acted upon some passion, and when I realized you could not remember your relationship with Desmond, I thought there would be no harm in letting you draw conclusions, just to vex my brother. To indulge my own fantasy. I did not think it would last more than an hour, because he would tell you about your affair. And I left that disclosure to him. Yet he never made it."

"Not until last night," I confirmed.

"No more secrets," Wilder said. "I think we should vow, all three of us, to share—"

The door flew open, and Desmond stood in the threshold, the darkened hallway behind him. His eyes were wide, his fists clenched around the doorframe. "Amber... I think the wolves truly are at the gate."

"What?" I stood, my pulse pounding, and Wilder's chair skidded against the stone floor at my back. "What's happened?"

"There is a mob of Toolkeepers on the bridge, demanding entry to Alchemary Island."

"And my father is leading the charge? Is this about my readmission? About Wilder's 'resurrection'?" The campus was abuzz about how inaccurate the rumor of his death had been, but there was no way for that good news to have proliferated beyond the island itself so fast.

"No," Desmond said. "Your father *is* with them, but . . . he's completely unresponsive. He's been infected. Amber, your father is an aurum."

To be continued in

The Alkahest

Coming Spring 2027

Acknowledgments

No book is ever only one person's effort, and that is doubly true for this one.

Thanks go first of all to Jennifer Lynn Barnes, who has kept me sane, not just over the course of writing this book, but for years. Her camaraderie and cheerleading—her generosity of spirit and of advice—have been both humbling and greatly appreciated.

Thanks to my agent, Ginger Clark, for making this happen.

Thanks to my students at Gaylord College for reminding me exactly why I love writing and for giving me the opportunity to pass on that love to so many bright young minds.

Thanks to my family for listening willingly to every bizarre question and logic check I've ever imposed upon them, and for dealing with my deadline brain. It's been a tough couple of years.

And thank you most of all to the team at Hyperion Avenue for stellar copy edits, beautiful cover art, and robust marketing efforts. It's great to know you have my back. Specifically, thank you to Adam Wilson, my editor, whose enthusiastic reaction to every idea I dumped on him, no matter how crazy it sounded coming out of my mouth at the pace of a mile a minute, kept me creatively engaged and fulfilled despite the pace of our deadlines.

This has all truly been my pleasure.